ALSO BY JACKIE ASHENDEN

Nine Circles series

Mine To Take
Make You Mine
You Are Mine

Kidnapped by the Billionaire

The Billionaire's Club E-Novella series

The Billion Dollar Bachelor
The Billion Dollar Bad Boy
The Billionaire Biker

IN BED WITH
THE BILLIONAIRE

JACKIE ASHENDEN

St. Martin's Paperbacks

This is a work of fiction. All of the characters, organizations, and events portrayed in this novel are either products of the author's imagination or are used fictitiously.

IN BED WITH THE BILLIONAIRE

Copyright © 2016 by Jackie Ashenden.

All rights reserved.

For information address St. Martin's Press, 175 Fifth Avenue, New York, NY 10010.

ISBN: 978-1-250-07786-8

Our books may be purchased in bulk for promotional, educational, or business use. Please contact your local bookseller or the Macmillan Corporate and Premium Sales Department at 1-800-221-7945, ext. 5442, or by e-mail at MacmillanSpecialMarkets@macmillan.com.

Printed in the United States of America

St. Martin's Paperbacks edition / November 2016

St. Martin's Paperbacks are published by St. Martin's Press, 175 Fifth Avenue, New York, NY 10010.

10 9 8 7 6 5 4 3 2 1

To my fabulous editor, Monique.
For liking things a little bit crazy.

ACKNOWLEDGMENTS

Once again I'd like to thank my agent, Helen Breitweiser, for all the good work she does. My family for all the work they do in supporting me. The usual suspects for supporting my neuroses. And my readers, for getting on board the Ashenden crazy train.

PROLOGUE

Zac stared at the woman sitting in the chair opposite his desk.

The woman stared back, her amber eyes giving absolutely nothing away.

Silence gathered in the room.

"I could have you taken care of for what you did to Eva," he said after a long moment, when he'd judged the silence to have done its job of making her uncomfortable.

Except she didn't look uncomfortable in the slightest. She was sitting back in the chair, one leg crossed over the other, totally at ease, almost as if she was sitting in her own lounge at home. Red curls he was more used to seeing tied up in a prim bun and tucked under a chauffeur's cap tumbled down over her shoulders, and the black uniform she'd worn while driving for Eva had been replaced by jeans, a T-shirt, and a black denim jacket.

It was all very nondescript for a notorious assassin.

She gave him a smile. "Except you haven't. Which means you won't."

Unfortunately, she did have a point.

He leaned back in his chair, steepled his hands.

It had taken him two weeks to track down Temple Cross, Eva's traitorous chauffeur, which was a good two weeks longer than he'd expected, a fact that was irritating in the extreme. It didn't usually take him that long to find someone, which said a lot for her skills. And perhaps if she hadn't delivered Eva to Evelyn Fitzgerald, the man who'd held her as a sex slave for two years, Zac might have been a hell of a lot friendlier.

Unfortunately, Temple had.

Equally unfortunately, once it had become clear that Temple was, in fact, a hit woman and not the soldier he'd believed her to be, she'd also become the perfect woman for a certain, highly specialized job.

Killing a man named Jericho.

"I suppose you want to know why you're here?" Zac said at last.

Temple tilted her head, giving him an almost flirtatious look from underneath coppery lashes. So very different from the upright, obedient woman he'd chosen to be Eva's driver. "Yeah, that would be great. Time is money after all, Mr. Rutherford."

Zac, immune to all female charms except those of one particular woman, pushed a manila folder across the desk toward her. "I have a job for you."

She didn't even glance at the folder. "What kind of job?"

"An exceptionally dangerous kind."

Her amber eyes gleamed. "Sounds promising. Who's the target?"

"It's in the folder."

"Tease. Come on, at least give me a name."

Zac studied her a moment. There was a feral kind of strength to her and an irreverence that reminded him oddly of Eva, his angel. He almost smiled. "His name is Jericho."

Temple went still, like a fox scenting prey. "Jericho," she echoed slowly, as if tasting the name.

"You've heard of him, I see."

She smiled, white and full of teeth. "Oh yes, I've heard of him."

"Then you'll understand how dangerous this mission is."

Temple leaned forward and picked up the folder. "The danger doesn't bother me. It's the money I'm worried about."

"The remuneration will be more than adequate, I think you'll find."

She still didn't look at the folder, though he noted that she was holding it very tightly. "What about a time frame?"

"You have two weeks."

"Not a lot of time to get close to a man like him."

"No, but I've heard you're a woman of many talents."

She spread her palm over the folder, an unconscious, possessive movement. "I'll need some up-front cash."

"Considering your previous record as an employee, you'll get nothing up front." He held her gaze. "In fact, you won't get a cent until you complete the job."

If that bothered her, she didn't show it. "Not a very attractive package, if you don't mind me saying."

Zac lifted a shoulder. "Then don't take the job." He could find someone else. There were always other options.

Another silence fell.

Temple looked down at the folder at last, but didn't open it, nor did she speak.

Zac let the silence sit there for a couple of minutes. "If you're not interested I can find—"

"I'm interested." Temple raised her gaze from the folder at last. "I'll kill Jericho for you. In fact, I'd be happy to."

CHAPTER ONE

Temple had expected a lot of things about the moment where she'd finally be in the same room as the man she'd been planning to kill ever since she was fifteen years old. Yet now the moment was here and nothing about it was as she'd expected.

For one thing she hadn't exactly imagined herself in one of the VIP rooms of the most exclusive and notorious strip club in Paris. Nor had she imagined that she'd be the stripper dressed only in a sparkly thong, a pair of silver star-shaped pasties, and silver eight-inch stilettos. She hadn't thought there'd be a pole, or a spotlight, or a black-velvet armchair facing that pole, the chair shrouded in darkness.

Hiding the man seated in it.

She couldn't see him because of the spotlight, but she knew he was there. Oh, yes, she knew.

The music began, filtering through hidden speakers.

Temple smiled in the direction of the armchair. The men who'd brought her in had been very clear: dance as if your life depended on it. Mainly because it did.

The choice was either dancing for the man they called Jericho or being sent straight away to the brothels of Eastern Europe the way they did with most of the other trafficked girls, where you'd be lucky to survive a month let alone a year.

Only the good ones, the pretty ones, were picked out to dance for Jericho and none of those chose the brothels. Everyone always chose the dancing. Because if you danced and you were good enough, you might get sent to one of the better establishments in Italy or Spain, where they looked after you, gave you nice clothes, made sure you looked good for their expensive clients.

But that wasn't why Temple was there. She was there because of the rumors. The ones that said that the notoriously secretive Jericho chose a girl from his latest "shipment" every Saturday night and kept her for the entire night. And if she pleased him, the rumors went, then she might get special treatment.

Temple wanted to be that girl. She wanted to be the one he chose for the entire night. Because she had some special treatment of her own to deliver.

She hooked her leg around the pole and arched her back, bowing her body in a graceful arc. Then she grabbed the cool metal with one hand and pulled herself up it. Keeping one leg curled tight, she leaned out and back again, her ribcage and breasts lifted, her copper red curls tumbling over her shoulders. The only thing keeping her on the pole was the strength of that one leg.

She wasn't a stripper. She hadn't had any practice. But before she'd gotten herself captured by the traffickers a week ago, she'd been to plenty of strip clubs and watched, replaying the moves over and over in her head. With her martial arts training helping her with the strength and balance aspect, it was almost easy.

Hanging there with her head back, she narrowed her gaze in the direction of the chair, trying to see past the glare of the spotlight to the man seated there. But she couldn't make anything out. Just his figure, long legs outstretched in front of him and crossed at the ankle.

He could be doing anything. He could even be fast asleep.

She knew he wasn't though. He was looking at her and she knew because she could feel the pressure of his gaze like a physical force. An intense, focused beam of light almost as powerful as that fucking spotlight.

It made her want to stare back. Stare him down.

But no, that was a bad idea. That would give her away. She hadn't worked this hard, for this long only to fuck it up now.

He was the most guarded, the most secretive, the most notorious crime lord in Europe and she had to be on her guard.

Gracefully she lifted herself back up, folding herself against the pole then sliding suggestively down it. As her feet touched the floor, she spun around so her back was to him and then she bent over, moving her hips in time with the music.

Some of the other girls she'd been brought here with had cried when their guards had tossed them the bag of stripper outfits and told them to get changed. Which was understandable given that they weren't strippers, just a bunch of lost girls who had the misfortune to be in the wrong place at the wrong time. Girls nobody would miss, nobody would search for.

Girls like Thalia.

Had this happened to Thalia? Had her sister performed for this man? Wearing this kind of outfit? Her beautiful, intelligent, protective older sister dancing for this . . . fucking prick?

Temple whirled gracefully around to face the chair again, keeping her gaze on the shadows and her righteous fury in check. She'd picked up a lot of skills over the years, and teaching herself to be able to sense people even in the dark had come in useful.

Except it wasn't so useful now with the spotlight shining directly at her. A deliberate tactic to prevent the girls from seeing his face.

Jericho's face.

She gripped the pole again, moving against it like a lover, doing a bump and grind, letting her breasts sway. She didn't much care about the fact that she was nearly naked and her body was on show. In fact, she'd long since ceased to see her body as anything more than a tool, a vehicle she needed in order to get herself to this point. A weapon that would help her bring down the man sitting in that chair.

She didn't need a gun in order to kill a man. She could do it unarmed, had done so before, and would do it again.

She'd kill him. She'd get the information she needed from him, and then she'd take his life as he'd taken Thalia's. And after that? Well, she didn't much care what happened after that. Her life wasn't exactly a valuable commodity to anyone let alone herself.

Temple faced him again, trying to penetrate the darkness as she moved. Fuck. It was next to impossible to see anything. If she wanted to see beyond that damn light she was going to have to get out from under it. Which was going to be tricky. They'd told her to stay near the pole, that she wasn't to approach him on pain of death.

They'd probably shoot her if she did. There was no one else in the small room, but she didn't make the mistake of thinking that meant the man in the chair was unguarded. She could defend herself against most attacks but not from bullets, and certainly not in her current outfit.

But then she wasn't aiming to kill him yet, and she wouldn't be able to here anyway. No, she needed information first. And the only way to get that was to get closer to him, literally and figuratively.

Perhaps she could fake a stumble? Fall off those stupid

heels? It might put at risk her chance of being chosen by him, but then at least she'd be able to see.

She was weighing up her options when very suddenly the music stopped. Caught in mid-grind, she blinked. Every instinct she had pulled tight, and she straightened, her body subtly tensing. Readying itself to launch into defensive mode.

There was a strange silence, full of the sound of her own heartbeat, already slowing in preparation for a fight.

"You're not afraid of me." A deep masculine voice rolled out of the shadows, rich and dark as the blackness around him. A beautiful voice, American, though she couldn't tell the region.

For some reason it hit her like a kick to the gut, and she felt herself tense even more. As if that voice was a threat, a ribbon of the deepest, softest black velvet wound around her throat.

She swallowed, an instinctive reflex. "I-I am," she murmured, injecting a shake into her voice and a small stammer for effect.

"No. You're not." He didn't sound annoyed, but there was a slightly harder edge to his tone now, the iron collar concealed beneath that soft, sensual velvet. "Most girls don't even look in my direction, but you haven't looked away. Not once."

Shit. That had been a rookie move. A thread of concern wound through her. She could *not* fuck this up. Not now.

Forcing herself to look away from him, she glanced down at the floor instead. The whole room had been carpeted in thick, expensive, dark-blue carpet, except for the area around the pole, which was wood. "I'm s-sorry," she said. "I didn't know."

Another silence. Then there came the sound of fabric rustling, the chair creaking as he shifted in it.

"Oh no, don't spoil it now." His voice was a low purr,

pure sensuality this time, the iron gone. "You were doing so well."

A strange shiver chased over her bared skin. That voice, that goddamned beautiful voice. It was like a spell he cast.

Anger stirred, because being actually affected by him was the very last thing in the world she wanted, and it was a struggle to fight it down. She had to though. Any sort of emotional reaction wouldn't help her here.

"I-I'm telling the truth." She hunched her shoulders, trying to make herself look frightened and small. Could she squeeze out a tear? Maybe she could. "Why am I here? W-what are you going to do to me? I don't know—"

"Let's dispense with the histrionics, sweetheart. We both know you're lying." And now there was the faintest hint of boredom in the words.

Fuck. Boredom certainly wasn't what she was after. Okay, so clearly her lack of fear had intrigued him. Perhaps that hadn't been such a dumb move after all.

Slowly Temple put her shoulders back and lifted her head, stared through the blinding light of the spotlight to the shadow in the chair. "Okay," she said in her normal voice. "You got me. No, I'm not afraid of you."

Another stretch of silence, longer this time.

He was watching her, she could feel it. Except his focus had shifted, had become sharper, more intense. She fought not to fidget, something she hadn't done since she'd been a little kid.

"Why not?" Curiosity in the words.

Because I can kill you with my bare hands. And I will.

"Because I'm not afraid of the dark." She didn't bother to hide the fact that she was trying to see him or mask the note of challenge in her tone.

"You should be." That voice curled around her, the velvet around her throat pulling tight. "The darkness isn't kind to little girls."

It made no sense at all to feel a small thrill shoot down her spine at the implied threat in those words. Then again, considering how dull the last three or so years had been, maybe it wasn't any wonder. Just contract after contract of easy pickings. Dirtbags and assholes who'd needed taking down. All in aid of perfecting her skills for this final showdown.

The meanest motherfucker of them all. Jericho.

She'd been working toward this for so long, and getting to this point had been surprisingly easy. Disappointingly so. She was hoping for more. She was hoping for a challenge.

Perhaps, now, here it was. A man worthy of her skills.

Temple lowered her eyelashes. "Oh, but I'm not a little girl. And maybe I'm not the one who's scared either." She paused and let one corner of her mouth curl up. "Considering you're the one who's hiding."

It was a calculated risk to be so blatant. To reveal her lack of fear when every girl who came in here must reek of it. It would prompt all kinds of questions. Questions she didn't want him to ask. But if she wanted to get close to him, then she was going to have to take those risks, throw the dice a few times. It had worked in her favor before. Maybe it would work again.

More silence. So complete it was as if her hearing had suddenly been taken away.

She lifted her hand to the pole in a casual pose, keeping her gaze on the shadows, knowing he was studying her. Feeling the intensity of it, as if he was memorizing every part of her.

Somewhere deep inside her, something she hadn't felt for a long, long time shivered awake. Fear.

Then came the sound of movement. Fabric sliding against fabric. The creak of the chair.

She stilled, internally every sense she had on high alert.

A man stepped suddenly into the light.

She'd studied that file Zac Rutherford had given her on him so she'd known who and what Jericho really was.

He was Theodore Fitzgerald, the son of Evelyn, a well-known New York high-society figure who'd been murdered a month ago, apparently by a business rival. Theodore, who'd faked his own death sixteen years earlier, had infiltrated the crime syndicate his father had secretly been hoping to take over.

And somehow she'd expected the stunningly handsome young man of the file photos to have changed over the years. For him to have become bloated through excess, aged and stained and jaded by the crimes he'd committed.

That wasn't what she got.

In fact, he was as far from any of those things as it was possible to get. He had to be in his late thirties, if she had to guess, and was tall. Way, way taller than she was, which wasn't difficult since she was only five foot two. He, on the other hand, looked to be six three or six four at the very least, with wide shoulders that stretched the cotton of his plain white business shirt, which he wore with no tie, the top buttons undone, the sleeves rolled up.

Yet that wasn't what made her stare. It was his face. Because that stunningly handsome young man in the photos she'd studied had somehow become even more beautiful. Genuinely drop-dead beautiful. His hair was longish, dark tawny at the roots, fading to light gold at the tips, his straight eyebrows the same deep, dark gold. He had high cheekbones, a straight nose, a long and sensual mouth. It was the kind of perfect, masculine beauty that graced magazines and movie screens around the world.

At least, it would have been perfect if not for his eyes. Because it was his eyes that gave him away. They were green with the faintest hint of gold, like a cat's, like sunlight on a deep, green ocean. A beautiful, haunting color, just like everything else about him. Except there was no warmth in those eyes, only shadows. Only darkness. The eyes of a man who'd done every evil thing under the sun and then some.

Yes, he was beautiful. But in the way a man-eating tiger was beautiful. Lovely to look at, but you wouldn't want to get close in case you saw the blood on his fangs. And you definitely wouldn't want to touch.

Very much like herself in too many ways.

Temple's fingers tightened on the stripper pole.

Jericho smiled, and that beautiful, beautiful voice flowed over her. "Coming, ready or not."

And the alien feeling, the one she'd thought she'd gotten rid of long ago, that fear, deepened.

It had been years since Jericho had been able to appreciate beauty in a woman simply because she was beautiful. Without automatically pricing her figure, her hair, her skin, or her general demeanor. And he didn't now, the habit was simply too ingrained.

Small and slender as a whip. High, firm breasts. Muscled like a dancer. An air of fragility. Curls red enough to start a fire with the color alone. A delicate, cat-like face. Large golden eyes . . . Yes, she would fetch a good price in any of his markets. Actually, probably more than good. She could fetch top dollar, especially with the dancing skills she'd just displayed.

Yet it wasn't her money-making potential that had propelled him off that chair, out of the protective darkness and into her spotlight. It was curiosity. Because it had been a long time since a woman hadn't been afraid of him, long enough that he couldn't remember what it was like to even have her meet his gaze. But she had met it. And she definitely wasn't afraid. He'd gotten to be exceptional at reading people, and this girl . . . well, she wasn't lying.

She *was* surprised to find him standing in her spotlight, however. At least, he'd caught a glimpse of it in her magnificent golden eyes, the barest flicker before she'd managed to hide it. She didn't bother to look away like the rest of them did, though. She didn't cower or weep. She didn't have that familiar, sour smell of terror about her that those girls always did, and she didn't beg either.

She only looked at him from underneath thick, coppery lashes, one small hand holding onto the metal of the stripper pole. It was very nearly flirtatious, that look. Different from the way she'd stared in his direction before, when she'd been dancing. Then it had been focused and sharp, determined. As if she'd been looking for him on purpose. And that alone was enough to spike his curiosity, because no one looked for him. No one who valued their life at least, still less a woman.

"I thought you had to stay in the dark so we couldn't see you," she said, her accent American, her voice light with a slightly husky edge he found inexplicably compelling.

He ignored what she'd said since it should have been obvious he could do whatever the fuck he wanted, studying her face instead, searching it for any signs of fear. There were none. "You really aren't afraid."

Her mouth, a small, perfect cupid's bow, turned up. "No."

"You were looking for me." He didn't phrase it as a question.

She gripped the pole and slowly swung around it, like a child on a jungle gym, the dim blue lights that gave the room an underwater glow shining over her pale skin. That small almost-smile curved her mouth, as if she knew a secret he didn't. "Maybe."

Nothing surprised him anymore. Nothing intrigued him. Those emotions had been wiped from him over the course of the past sixteen years, along with everything else. Love. Fear. Hate. They were all gone. Scoured away by what he'd done, by what he'd had to do in pursuit of his goal.

He didn't feel them anymore. So why he should be curious about this young woman simply because she wasn't afraid of him was anyone's guess. Maybe it was the paranoia kicking in. God knew, he'd always had to be careful and now, so close to achieving what he'd set out to do all those years ago, he had to be even more careful.

Nothing could get in the way of his mission. Nothing.

He watched her revolve around the pole for a moment, letting her keep that smile on her face for a few seconds longer. Then he said casually, "Tell me, little girl. I really don't want to have to kill you." Because he could. All it would take was a certain hand gesture and the room would be full of men with guns, shooting to kill. Either that or he could snap her neck. He'd done both before.

She came to a stop, eyeing him. Not a flicker of fear crossed her face, as if she had death threats every day. And shit, given how the girls usually appeared here, maybe that was true. Maybe she'd become so inured to living with death she didn't notice it any more.

But no, that wasn't the case with her, he was certain. Because again, he'd seen girls who'd long since ceased to care about their lives. They were dull with fear, the spark inside them extinguished. Yet not with her. As she stared up at him, he could see that spark still glowing in the depths of her eyes, so fucking bright.

"I guess you could." She tilted her head to the side, the brightness glinting through her lashes. "Or perhaps I'm here to kill you."

He nearly smiled at that. Plenty of people had tried; she wouldn't be the first or even the first woman to do so. But he was exceptionally hard to kill, as many had found out.

Jericho let his gaze travel down her undeniably lovely body, taking in the tiny pasties that were all that concealed her nipples and the even tinier thong that only just covered her pussy, leaving the taut curve of her rear bare. Then he lifted his attention back to her face again. "With what?"

If she found his scrutiny in any way embarrassing or affecting, she didn't show it. Instead she looked down at herself too. "Hmmm. True. Not exactly anywhere to hide anything." She glanced back up at him. "So maybe I'm not here to kill you. Maybe I'm here to seduce you instead."

Again, she wouldn't be the first, nor would she be the last. But he hadn't fucked a woman in years, least of all felt desire for one. Of course he had an image to maintain, and so he made sure it looked like he was discerning and perverse with his tastes, choosing one woman a week from his latest top-class shipment. Except he didn't sleep with them. He rescued them. It wasn't much to balance out all the shit he'd done—a drop in the ocean really—but it was the one direct, personal action he could take. The only one. Until the time came for him to pull his empire down.

Which he would. Very, very soon.

"Are you?" he murmured, holding her gaze. "And why would you want to do that?"

"Perhaps I've heard rumors. That the women you choose for a night get special treatment." She made another slow revolution around the pole, as if she wasn't standing next to the most dangerous man in Europe. A man who could have her killed in a matter of seconds if he chose. "And perhaps I want that kind of special treatment for myself."

Ah yes, the rumors. The ones he'd started. They thought he chose the girls on the basis of beauty, of lust. But he didn't. No, he chose them on the basis of fear. The ones who were terrified, but not too broken to recover or save themselves once he'd set them free.

This girl was not one of those.

"What makes you think I'll give it to you?" he asked lazily, watching her. Studying her. "Actually, what the fuck makes you think you can seduce me at all for that matter? I'm a man of singular tastes. And maybe I don't like cocky redheads who answer back."

Perhaps she heard the undercurrent of threat he'd put into his voice, because she stopped revolving around the pole, the look in her eyes shifting, changing. Reassessing.

Jesus. She might have told him the truth. She might very well be here to kill him. It was certainly an option he couldn't discount, and he hadn't survived this long by discounting options.

Ah, Christ. He should ignore this curiosity. It was dangerous. He should get rid of her, ship her off to the markets in Eastern Europe and hope she survived long enough to be freed when he put his empire to the torch. It would certainly be one less thing on his plate.

She frowned at him, her eyes narrowing. "I tell you what. Let's make a deal. I'll try and seduce you, and if I can't, I'll tell you the truth about why I'm not afraid of you."

Well, full marks to her for effort. But he wasn't a man who made deals with anyone, not these days. "Nice idea." He allowed himself a slight smile. "Except you're in no position to bargain for anything."

Her mouth pursed as if that answer didn't please her at all. Releasing the pole, she walked over to him, her breasts swaying, her hips swinging, perfectly balanced despite the height of her stripper shoes.

And at which point he should have signaled Dmitri, his Russian bodyguard, to get her out of here and end this . . . diversion.

Yet he didn't. Because he was still curious. Because it had been too long since he'd felt anything at all. And because he was the fucking boss. He could do whatever the fuck he liked.

So he stood there as she came closer, not taking his eyes off her. Intrigued by the way she held his gaze, since no one ever looked him in the eye. As if she didn't see the shadows that lay there or the demon that those shadows hid. As if all she saw was a man.

She stopped right in front of him, glancing up from underneath her lashes, gold glinting, flirtatious and confident of her appeal. Those sparkling star-shaped pasties were inches from his chest and he could smell the scent of her. Not fear. Not despair. Not hopelessness. But a subtle, feminine muskiness he found oddly disquieting.

She wasn't like the other girls, the ones that came to him distressed and terrified and broken. She was different.

Her small hand settled in the middle of his chest, and for some reason it hit him like a bullet to the brain that this was the first time a woman had come close to him in years. The first time a woman had even touched him voluntarily.

An echo of . . . something he couldn't immediately identify went through him. As if her touch was a stone thrown into a still pond, sending out ripples, vibrations.

She pressed her hand a little harder, her burnished gaze flickering up to his. "Am I in a position now?"

There was a confidence to her that bordered on arrogance that he wouldn't stand for in any other person, man or woman. And for some reason it made those ripples become currents, those vibrations a quake, adrenaline surging through him.

Fuck, he'd let her call the shots for long enough.

Now, it was his turn.

CHAPTER TWO

Temple wasn't sure if she'd overstepped the mark. The look on his beautiful face had hardened the moment she'd touched him, and yet there had been something glittering in his eyes. Something she was sure was interest.

She'd been careful not to let him see how satisfying that had been, and she was pretty sure she kept it hidden now.

Being so forward had been a gamble but from the looks of things it had paid off. She'd intrigued him, which was what she'd been hoping for all along. Lust was far too easy to inspire since most men were simple creatures. But curiosity? That was different. That was far harder to achieve. Especially with a man like this one, who'd seen everything, done everything.

His chest was firm beneath her hand, hard bands of muscle tensing under the cotton of his white business shirt. Okay, so that was good to know. His build suggested he didn't just sit around on his ass all day, fucking women and taking drugs, and by the feel of those muscles, that was definitely *not* the case.

Excellent. She didn't want this to be easy. She wanted to be tested. This had been a long hunt, and she wanted it to be worth the wait.

She glanced up at him again. His green eyes met hers, as sharp and as focused as she suspected they'd been since

she'd first been shoved into the room. And she became
conscious that his body was very warm, that he smelled a
bit like cinnamon and sandalwood, a spicy, expensive
scent. And that she . . . liked it.

His mouth curled in a lazy smile that didn't quite reach
his eyes. "You want to be careful, little girl. When you
make a deal with the devil, it doesn't tend to go well."

"Kick me out then."

"Oh no. I'm not going to do that." His hand covered
hers, sending a tiny, unexpected shock through her, and all
of a sudden he stepped back into the darkness, taking her
with him.

She had no choice but to stumble forward, the sudden
change in light blinding her as he drew her over to where
the chair stood. Then he sat, pulling her down onto his lap.

It happened so fast she didn't have a lot of time to
adjust to the fact that one minute she was standing underneath the glare of a spotlight, the next she was in the
darkness, sitting astride him in a black velvet armchair.

She almost let the mask slip, almost let him see her
shock. That she had to work hard not to show it was a real
fucking worry. She should be ready for anything, prepared
to handle any emergency. Especially after she'd played
with the truth a little bit earlier by telling him she was here
to kill him.

A stupid confession maybe, but then, a man like him
didn't get where he was today by being stupid. That suspicion would be in his mind already so naming it wouldn't
hurt. And if it got him even more intrigued then all the
better.

She just had to be in charge here and stay focused. Or
else she could kiss her mission goodbye.

His hands came up to rest on her thighs, large and long-
fingered and very, very warm. And she felt her breath

catch for some reason, an electric shock chasing over her skin. Shit. Men had touched her before and she'd never had a response like that. Normally she felt nothing, so what the hell was going on?

He'd leaned back in the chair, golden head resting against the black velvet, that smile playing around his beautifully sculpted mouth. He would have looked like a man extremely pleased with himself, if you didn't look into his eyes. If you didn't see the hard, cold edges gleaming like a sharpened blade in the emerald depths.

You could cut yourself to pieces on those.

Holy shit. Where had that thought come from?

"Now," he said in that low, purring voice. "Where were we? Oh yes, you were attempting to bargain with me."

God, the heat of his body between her thighs was insanely distracting. She could feel it even through the fine black wool of what looked to be expertly tailored business pants. His thighs were hard and muscular too, his hips narrow. Definitely a man who was physically fit and no doubt strong. But, that didn't matter. She'd taken down men bigger than he was.

She put her hands on the arms of the chair, forcing herself to relax on him. "Well?" she asked, only partly faking breathlessness. "Does this mean we have a deal?"

"Hmmm." His thumbs stroked along her thighs in a lazy, back-and-forth movement. "So, let me get this straight. You attempt to seduce me, and if you fail, you have to tell me why you're not afraid of me."

"Yes." She had to fight not to frown. His touch was doing something to disturb her concentration, and it was annoying.

He tilted his head, his eyes gleaming in the dim light of the room. "What if I don't want to be seduced? What if I just want the truth from you?"

She focused on him, tried to dismiss the feeling of his hands on her. "If that's all you wanted, then why am I sitting on your lap?"

"Good question." He moved his hands from her thighs, reaching for her wrists where they rested on the arms of the chair and gripping them. Then he sat forward and with gentle, inexorable strength, forced her hands behind her, crossing her wrists in the small of her back and holding them there.

Temple went very still.

He was close now, as close as he'd been under the spotlight, his chest inches from hers. Only this time, it was different. This time, he was the one who was very clearly in charge.

She didn't like it.

Right from the very beginning, when Thalia had been payment for their asshole father's drug debt, when she'd learned that men were the ones in charge, the ones who took what they wanted and to hell with who they hurt, she'd determined she'd never be a pawn. Never be used. Never be one of those women who let men have the power, the control.

Yet right now, she didn't have much choice.

The look on his face hadn't changed, the lazy smile still curving his mouth, his eyes still cold. Strange when he felt so hot and when he smelled . . . good.

What the fuck are you thinking? He's evil. He was the one responsible for taking Thalia. And you're going to kill him.

"There won't be any deals," he purred. "I take what I want when I want it. And the only reason I haven't taken you right now is that I don't want you."

Temple took a small, silent breath. She hated being restrained, hated being helpless, and his grip was very, very strong. It wasn't anything she couldn't break, though to do so now would be a mistake and would only cause him to be even more suspicious of her.

She eased the tension from her arms, looking up into his face. And sure enough, she couldn't see any of what she'd come to recognize as lust there, not even a flicker. She made a small movement with her hips, and yeah, despite the fact that she was nearly naked, there was no tell-tale hardness pressing against her there either.

Fuck.

His smile widened as if he'd read her mind. "Looking for something?"

Okay, so this was unusual. She wasn't vain, but again, men were simple. If a nearly naked chick got in their laps, they were usually pretty interested. But this man? Nothing. Why not? Did crime lords lose the ability to get it up after a certain length of time?

Temple raised an eyebrow. "Did you forget your little blue pill?"

He laughed, a soft, deeply sexy sound that had her almost shivering. "Or maybe you just don't have what it takes to be in my bed."

She let her lashes fall. "Hey, I can be whatever you want me to be."

"I'm sure you can." His grip tightened on her wrists, and he lifted his free hand to a lock of her hair, twisting it absently around his fingers, that scalpel-sharp gaze running over her. Dissecting her. "But if you don't know what I want, you can't be anything at all."

"Give me a hint, and I can try."

His gaze narrowed. "You don't like this. You don't like me holding you like this."

She had to fight not to show her shock. She'd perfected the art of hiding her feelings, of never letting anyone see what she didn't want them to see. And she couldn't imagine how this man had managed to spot what she herself was only barely aware of. How the hell had he managed that? She was sure she hadn't let anything slip.

Discomfort built inside her, but she ignored it, trying to think about how to respond instead. If he didn't want her, she had to figure out how to make him, because currently the only thing holding him here was the fact that she wasn't acting like all the rest.

She needed him to want her and badly enough to keep her, at least for a little while. Until she'd gotten the information she needed from him. Then she'd kill him as she'd promised Zac Rutherford and his friends. Kill him and collect the money she was owed.

Jericho was always going to be her last contract. And her most satisfying.

Temple looked at him from underneath her lashes. "I wouldn't have thought it would matter to you what I like."

He stared at her for a second, bright and sharp as a blade. "It doesn't," he said. Then he smiled again, like a tiger, lazy and hungry. And the finger in her hair pulled suddenly tight, a small shock of pain flashing over her scalp.

She couldn't stop the soft gasp that escaped her, nor did she miss the sudden flare in his eyes as she did so. "So," she said, and this time the breathlessness was completely unfeigned. "I guess you're into pain?"

He let the lock of red hair fall, his hand dropping to the side of her neck, his finger stroking lightly, gently down the side of it. And though she didn't want it to, the touch sent goose bumps rising all over her skin. "Not in particular. I was just proving a point."

"Let me go and I'll prove another."

"Really? What point would that be?"

"That I'm sitting here for a reason. And it's not because you don't want me." Her throat had gone weirdly dry, his finger stroking up and down the side of her neck. She could feel the touch acutely.

His finger moved again and this time didn't stop, brushing over her throat and down farther to the swell of her left breast. And in spite of all the years she'd spent expertly hiding and controlling her responses to just about everything, when he opened his hand and cupped her breast, for the second time that night all the air escaped her lungs in an audible rush.

And the bastard, the fucking bastard, saw it all with those cold, clear green eyes while that maddening smile lingered on his mouth. "Interesting," he murmured, studying her like a scientist. "You want me, little girl. Don't you?"

Her nipple had hardened beneath the pastie and he wasn't even doing anything, just cupping her breast gently in one hand. Fuck. How had that happened? She didn't want him. He was the very last man on earth she'd ever want. And this—*all* of this—was just pretend.

So just go with it and fucking pretend.

She fought to keep her breathing even, to keep her head clear. It seemed that he liked her wanting him, that her responses were fascinating to him, so why not? She had to hook him somehow, didn't she? And being different from all the rest seemed to be the way to do it. Which meant . . . perhaps she should just keep going.

"M-maybe I do." The stutter was a nice touch. Pity it was utterly unfeigned.

He examined her closely. "I think there's no maybe about it." With a flick of his finger, he got rid of the pastie covering her nipple, then brushed his thumb over it.

She trembled, a lightning strike of sensation arrowing through her. Shocking her. And a small knot of something she didn't recognize at first curled tightly in the pit of her stomach. Then she did recognize it. Panic.

His thumb made another pass over her nipple, a second jagged bolt of lightning flashing through her body. And before she could stop herself, she'd broken his hold on her wrists and had leaped from his lap like a scalded cat, coming to stand in front of the chair, her hands raised, ready to fight.

Jericho stared at her for a long moment, his expression utterly impenetrable. Then he leaned back in the chair, his elbows resting on the arms, long fingers loosely linked. "Something tells me you're not a stripper," he said mildly.

Her heart was thundering in her head in a way it had never done before, not even when she'd taken her first kill and she couldn't understand what had gone wrong. What the fuck did she think she was doing?

Focus.

She inhaled silently, forcing herself to get a grip, then she lowered her hands. "Actually. I was . . . studying dance in Berlin. As an exchange student. I was stripping for extra cash." The backstory she'd concocted. A poor American college student all alone in Europe, doing what she could to get by. "I didn't like being touched, so I took a few self-defense lessons."

The cold look in his eyes glittered. "And here I was believing you weren't scared."

"I wasn't." Dammit. She was going to have to give him the truth. It was either that or she lost the thing that had drawn him to her in the first place. "I'm just not used to . . . wanting a complete stranger."

He didn't reply, his intense green-gold gaze moving over her, right from the top of her head down to the soles of her stripper heels. Reassessing her. Again. "What's your name?" The sensuality had gone from his voice now, nothing but hard authority in each word.

Briefly she debated telling him it was whatever he wanted it to be, but she wasn't stupid. She knew the time for flirtation had passed. Shit, she'd fucked up majorly. "Kirsten," she said, going with the name she'd settled on for her current persona.

Jericho was up off the chair in a sudden, fluid movement,

coming toward her so fast she forgot she was wearing eight-inch stilettos, nearly stumbling as she shifted instinctively into a defensive posture. He caught her around the waist, hauling her up against him, one hand fisting in her hair and pulling her head back.

Every instinct she possessed told her to move, to bring her knee up to his groin then twist, pulling out of his grip. A hand on the back of his neck, jerking down then another knee to his face. That would take him out, easy. And it would all give her away completely, because those kinds of moves you didn't pick up via self-defense lessons.

So she had to ignore her instinct and stay where she was, letting him tug her head back, her hands pressing against the hard, hot wall of his chest.

"You're lying." His tone was casual, at odds with the ruthless way he held her. "You're lying through your fucking teeth." His smile was mirthless, cold, and if she hadn't been who she was, *now* she might have been afraid. "So let's try that one again. What's your name?"

She stared up at him. This was a test. He was pushing her, trying to frighten her, and she knew that because Jackson had done the same thing when she'd first started training with him.

Now's your chance to fix things. Do not *fuck this up.*

"Temple," she said, meeting his gaze. "My name is Temple."

He narrowed his eyes, not relaxing his hold on her one bit. "Temple? What the fuck kind of name is that?"

"The one my stupid mother gave to me." No lies this time. Only the absolute truth. "She wanted to call me Shirley Temple because of my curls. But my father didn't like Shirley, so they compromised with Temple."

The expression on his beautiful face was unreadable, but his gaze was like a laser beam, stripping her down layer by layer. Studying. Dissecting. Assessing.

Then all of a sudden he smiled. Fierce, bright and sharp. The tiger in all its fearsome glory, making her heart miss a beat at the savage beauty of it. His hand in her hair tightened, almost painfully so. "Pleased to meet you, Temple," he murmured.

And before she could move, he bent his head and kissed her. Hard.

At first Temple's mouth shut tight under his, her slender body going rigid. Then, as if she'd changed her mind, she relaxed, leaning against him, her mouth becoming soft, opening up, letting him in.

She tasted of peppermints from the breath mints his men gave all the girls before they danced for him, and yet there was another, subtler flavor there as well. Something sweet and dark. That took his curiosity and twisted it, deepened it.

But he hadn't kissed her because he'd wanted her. He'd kissed her to test her, see what she'd do.

The way she'd pulled away from him before had been unexpected and he hadn't missed the briefest flicker of shock in her eyes; she hadn't meant to do that. And he didn't think it was because she didn't like him touching her. No, he'd smelled the delicate scent of feminine arousal, felt the hard little bud of her nipple. Seen her fascinating amber eyes darken, the pupil widening.

She'd been turned on. Yet something about it had panicked her, and he didn't buy that it was because he was a stranger. If she'd been afraid and cowering before then, sure. But she hadn't been. So it was something else.

And then there was the way she'd broken his hold and sprang off his lap like a singed cat, landing on the balls of her feet despite the ridiculous shoes. Her hands had been up in a classic martial-arts pose, which meant her bullshit about self-defense lessons was exactly that. Bullshit.

There was something "off" about this girl, and he was going to find out what it was.

She was hot against him, her palms pressing against his chest, the softness of her breasts pressing there too. Her hair felt like skeins of silk in his hand, her skin like satin. He had his other hand on the curve of one buttock, and he stretched out his fingers, squeezing, feeling the taut muscle beneath. She shuddered in response, her body arching against his.

Years since you've kissed a woman.

Yeah, it had been. Though how long, he couldn't remember. But Christ, her mouth. So soft. Hot. That dark, sweet taste elusive, tantalizing . . . Another shift inside him, a crack running through the walls he'd placed carefully around his desires. Fuck. Who was this woman and where was all this curiosity coming from?

She definitely wasn't lying about wanting him, he already knew that. And she hadn't lied about her name either, at least not the second time. He'd used intimidation to try to scare her, but she'd told the truth when she'd said she wasn't scared of him. Which only left one other way to get under her guard. Sex.

Of course he could just send her away like he'd initially intended, find another girl to rescue. But his gut told him she was a threat, and his gut was usually right about these things.

You could just kill her.

Finally he lifted his mouth from hers, keeping his hand tight in her hair, looking down at her. She had high, slanted cheekbones and a determined little chin. A finely sculpted nose. Her features were elfin, catlike. There was a flush to her cheeks, her pupils dilated. Her mouth was full and pouty from the kiss.

A pretty thing.

But then, he'd killed pretty things before.

Once he would have found that thought horrifying, back when he'd been Theodore Fitzgerald, the privileged oldest son and heir to the fortunes of one of New York's oldest families. When he'd had a law degree to complete, a fiancée to marry, an illustrious career to start.

Until his father had introduced him to the Lucky Seven casino.

Until Theodore Fitzgerald had apparently committed suicide.

So he didn't find the thought horrifying. Because he was Jericho now, and Jericho had no problem with killing, pretty or otherwise.

Except then you'd lose the first thing you've found so intriguing in years.

Her eyelashes fluttered, gold gleaming from underneath copper. "Don't tell me," she murmured, her voice husky. "You don't know whether to fuck me or kill me."

Something shifted yet again, a heat that shouldn't be there. She was sharp, this woman. Perhaps too sharp. "Perhaps I'll do both." He flexed his fingers on the tight flesh of her buttock, testing himself. "I always like having my cake and eating it too."

She shivered at the touch, a faint, nearly imperceptible movement, and he caught a glimpse of it again, moving like quicksilver in the depths of her eyes, an expression like shock or trepidation. Ah, so it *was* his touch that did something to her. Made her want, definitely, but also made her wary. As if she wasn't used to it.

He squeezed her gently, watching as goose bumps rose all over her flesh in reaction. "Are you a virgin, Temple?"

"Why? You like virgins?"

Another squeeze, harder this time. A warning. "Answer the fucking question."

Her throat moved in a convulsive swallow, but there was

nothing but challenge in her response. "Do I look like a fucking virgin to you?"

He nearly smiled. "Appearances lie. I may look like a gentleman, but I'm as far from a gentleman as it's possible to get. So, let's try this again. Are you a virgin?"

A slight firming of her chin. "No."

Just as well. Jesus, why was he finding her so fascinating? He shouldn't be wasting time here. He had to check up on the mess that had been left in the wake of the collapse of his father's trafficking operation following his father's murder. Jericho's sources had told him that the whole thing was now being managed by Fitzgerald's former right-hand man, Elijah Hunt. Which, if it was true, would be a major blow to the delicate edifice of his take-down strategy.

And that was largely because he had it on good authority that his sister was now shacked up with the asshole.

A real fucking problem when taking down this empire involved the collapse of a global trafficking network that spanned continents and countries, all the alliances he'd spent so long building. And all so that when he went down, he took every other fucker down with him.

But taking down the operation in the States meant taking down Hunt too. And with him, Violet, his younger sister.

A sudden curl of unwanted emotion tugged at him at the thought of Violet, distracting him.

She saved you.

Yeah, she had. That asshole Hunt had been going to kill him, but Violet had stepped in front of the gun, saving his life.

Not that you deserve it.

Maybe not. But whether that was true or not, he had to think of a better way to manage the American alliance he'd been hoping to build. A way that didn't involve Violet.

You could always tell her your plans. She could help.

Ah, but he couldn't do that either. He'd thought about it on and off, but he always dismissed it in the end. The fewer people who knew what he was planning the better, and that included his sister.

Yes, it was definitely time to leave.

Yet he didn't.

"What do you want, kitten?" he murmured, tangling his fingers deeper in her red curls. "Because girls like you don't usually want me to fuck them. They're usually too afraid, and with good reason."

Her breathing had gotten faster, her lips parting slightly. She was soft in his hold, relaxing totally against him, her palms warm on his chest. "Why? Because you might kill them?"

Brave of her to say it out loud. Or stupid. "Of course."

"I'm not afraid to die." There was something defiant in her eyes. "And I'm not afraid of pain either."

There it was again, that lightning flash in his blood, that thrill deep in his gut.

He stilled. Holy shit, was that what he thought it was? It had better not be. He wasn't celibate only because he didn't feel desire anymore. He was also celibate because desire wasn't anything he wanted to inflict on the girls that were part of his empire. Any of the girls. There wasn't much of his soul left after so many years, but he did what he could to save the last few pieces of it. And keeping the seeds of violence his father had planted decades ago in check was part of that.

Like father, like son. Except in a few small ways. He was proud of those ways. They weren't much, but they were all he had. And he couldn't allow himself the temptation of ignoring them.

You should let her go then.

Except he didn't.

Warm, female flesh. The scent of musk. Silky hair against his skin. And no fear, no fear anywhere. She was starting to get to him, he could feel it.

"Only people with nothing to lose aren't afraid of death," he murmured.

Her pouty little mouth curved. "Considering where I am, perhaps I don't." Her hands slid up his chest to the buttons of his shirt. With a small movement, she flicked one open, then another, and another, the cotton parting. Then she bent her head and pressed that lovely mouth to his bare skin.

Heat, unfamiliar and completely unexpected, glowed suddenly, like an ember from a long banked fire igniting. And his breath caught. It had been a long time since anything had shocked him or surprised him. But fuck, he was both now.

He looked down. Even in her stripper heels, the top of her head only barely reached his chin, but somehow she'd undone another couple of buttons and her lips were against his skin. Then her tongue flicked in a delicate catlike lick.

His hands tightened on her reflexively, the little ember glowing hot, and when she glanced up at him, he saw the reflections of that heat in the gold of her eyes. A bright molten gleam.

Another thing he hadn't seen for years. Fire in someone's eyes. Desire and challenge and determination all rolled into one. Yeah, years, fucking years. The women he saw were all dull-eyed with fear, with hopelessness and despair, dead inside. They were broken. But this girl wasn't. She was whole, she was alive, and fuck . . . she *burned*.

"You think a few open buttons, a few kisses, is enough to seduce me?" he murmured. "You'll have to try harder than that."

"I was trying for subtlety." Temple's husky voice was soft, goading, and the look she gave him from beneath her lashes was a challenge all on its own. "But if you're not good at that, I can be more direct too." She moved one of her hands, sliding it down his chest and over the front of his pants, the tips of her fingers tracing the line of his cock through the wool.

A flash of heat spiked in his blood, jagged and raw and unexpected.

He didn't move, a part of him fascinated by his own re-action to her. Because what the fuck? There had been many women who'd tried this, desperate for his mercy, his pity, or because he was powerful, and they wanted a piece of that power. Yet he'd never had any reaction to any of them.

But he had one now, oh yes, he fucking did. Her fingers traced him lightly, up and down in the same way as he'd touched her nipple, and he felt it. Flickers of heat, flickers of desire. Electricity firing through long-dead circuits.

And he had no idea why. Because she wasn't afraid? Because she had some spark of life left in her? Because he hadn't had sex in a long, long time? Fuck if he knew, but her amber eyes were on his, watching him, gauging his reaction in much the same way as he'd watched her, and he was starting to get hard.

Jesus. He barely got a morning hard-on these days let alone responded to a woman's touch. What was she? Magic? She was no stripper, though. He had no idea what she was.

"Anyone can do direct," he murmured.

"Sure, but I think you like direct." Her hand didn't stop its lazy, almost hypnotic movement, fingers sliding up and down. One corner of that cupid's bow of a mouth turned up, the ember in her eyes gleaming with satisfaction. "In fact, maybe you don't need a blue pill after all."

Curiosity. It had always been his downfall. From the

day he'd first followed his beloved father into one of Manhattan's seedier neighborhoods to see where he went on his mysterious "trips," propelled by that same fucking curiosity. The thing that had led to him to this point, where he was head of the largest trafficking operation in Europe, if not the entire world.

He shouldn't listen to it. He should have learned his lesson.

"Are you going to kill me, kitten?" He stared down at her, keeping himself still, watching that fucking light in her eyes, that leaping flame. "Is that what you're after?"

She didn't look away from him, didn't stop touching him. "Maybe. Maybe I just want you to fuck me."

He smiled. "Ah, but you don't understand. I don't care what you want. And if I want to fuck you, I will, whether you want me to do it or not."

Perhaps the cold note he put in his voice gave her pause, because he recognized the flicker of expression on her face: She was reassessing her strategy.

He waited, his curiosity deepening even further despite the fact that he had shit to do and no time to be standing around letting a pretty girl get him hard. She really was very determined to be chosen by him tonight, wasn't she? Was it purely for the rumored special treatment? Or did she want something else? He'd been very careful with the women he helped escape. Very careful to make sure no one knew. The only other person who knew what he *really* did with those women was Dmitri, his bodyguard.

Maybe she did want to kill him.

The thought didn't bother him in the slightest.

"Well how about you stop talking about it and just fucking do it," Temple said softly, and there was no trace of fear in her voice, her gaze very direct and no longer flirtatious. "I'm strong. I can take anything you give me."

"That's not something you want to say to a man like

me." His voice had a slightly rougher edge to it than he'd intended.

"Oh really? I've heard you have . . . demanding tastes." She touched her tongue delicately to her upper lip, a deliberately sensual gesture. "Maybe I'd like to try them."

No, she really didn't.

And you shouldn't either.

But his conscience had been getting fainter and fainter over the years, and these days he barely heard it. He didn't listen to it now.

Yes, he had shit to do, and it was time to get out of here. Get back to his 7th Arrondissement apartment, go over all the intel he'd managed to collect about his father's U.S. operations. He needed that alliance to tap into information about the trafficking networks there. It was the last piece of the puzzle, the final hurdle before he could bring the whole fucking thing down.

He'd been a fool to leave it this long. A sentimental asshole. Negotiating with his father and getting the prick on his side should have been the first thing to do, but he hadn't done it. He'd concentrated on Europe and Eastern Europe first. A mistake. Because now his father was dead, and chaos had followed in his wake.

He couldn't allow that chaos to spread any further.

Catching her wrist, Jericho held it, pressing her palm against his inexplicably hardening cock. Fuck this curiosity. She was the closest threat to deal with, and perhaps he'd have her, perhaps he wouldn't, but one thing he was sure of: He was going to find out every fucking thing about her.

And maybe once he had, she'd wish she'd changed her mind about wanting to be his for the night.

Her eyes had widened, and he thought he saw triumph in them. Silly kitten. She didn't know whom she was playing with, not really. Time for her to find out.

"Is that a yes?" Her voice was slightly breathless.

He didn't answer. Instead he released her and stepped back, turning to the chair and bending to pick up the black cashmere overcoat that he'd thrown over the back of it. Straightening, he turned back to her and tossed her the coat.

She caught it, a crease between her brows. "Do I . . . put this on?"

Ah, how sweet. Did she think he was being gentlemanly? That he'd given it to her to keep her warm or so that she could cover up her nakedness? She would learn. "Of course not." He let a thread of lazy amusement wind through his voice. "I need a slave to carry it."

He caught another flicker of expression on her face, but it was gone before he could tell what it was, her features smoothing, lashes fluttering down. "I guess I'll carry it then."

"Like you have a choice." He lifted his hand in a small gesture that would call Dmitri in. "That's your first lesson for the night, Temple. You have no choices. Not anymore."

"Is that supposed to make me afraid?"

"I don't know, does it?"

That spark glittered beneath her copper lashes. Defiant. "Oh, you'll have to do better than that if you want to make me afraid."

And he felt it again, that raw, jagged flash, that heat deep inside. The predator stirring. The one he'd sealed in a metaphorical concrete box and dumped into the middle of a metaphorical ocean where it could never, ever escape.

A dark, possessive predator. That wanted to keep. To own.

He let his smile turn sharp. "Maybe I will, kitten. Maybe I will."

The door to the VIP room opened, and he turned as Dmitri came in, a tall, icy Russian wall of belligerence and barely suppressed violence.

"Boss?" Dmitri asked in Russian.

Temple was silent, her golden eyes watching him.

"Bring her," Jericho ordered his bodyguard curtly in the same language. "She's mine for the night."

CHAPTER THREE

It was cold as Temple stepped out onto the sidewalk dressed only in her pasties, thong, and heels. So much for spring in Paris. It was April, and yet the bite of winter was still in the air, making goose bumps erupt all over her skin.

The street was dark, the streetlights dim and so too were the stars. Ironic names the City of Light, the City of Love. Because there was no light and no love here, not where she was. This famous strip club for rich VIPs, Le Papillon Bleu, was a front for so much darkness, so much pain. If only those VIPs knew where the girls had come from . . .

But no, they probably wouldn't care even if they did. Men were like that.

She gripped Jericho's overcoat tightly as he spoke to a couple of men just outside the club's entrance. He'd made her stand behind him, warned her not to speak on pain of death, but that was fine. She didn't want to say anything anyway, hoping to be able to listen instead to what they were talking about. Sadly they were speaking in French, and she didn't understand a word.

Fuck. Perhaps she should have taken up French in addition to all that martial-arts training.

A cold wind whipped around her bare legs, but she was practiced at ignoring physical discomfort, so she barely felt it. People walked past her on the sidewalk, their gazes lingering on her, noting her mostly nakedness, yet she ignored them as well, too busy watching the interaction going on in front of her. Too busy watching Jericho.

The neon from the club illuminated the beautiful planes and angles of his face in a wash of silver, turning his hair gilt and bleaching the gold from his eyes, making them seem silver-green, unearthly.

He was so very beautiful, and that got to her. It didn't seem fair that he should look like that, not when she knew the rottenness deep at the core of him. A man who bought and traded women. Who sold them into slavery, into death, and made money out of it.

She shifted on her feet, staring at him, the softness of his cashmere coat against her skin. Luxury and wealth. Did he do it all for that? Or was it the power? Men loved power, loved being in control, so maybe it was that. Not that she was curious about his motives, not in the slightest. He'd taken Thalia, he'd created this evil. And he would pay. Simple as that.

Jericho said something, and the men around him laughed. Smug, arrogant male laughter.

Temple schooled her features, keeping the instinctive rush of anger locked away. Rage made a good fuel, but Jackson had taught her well: never let it burn out of control or else it would end up being less of a fuel and more of a liability.

A flash of silver and emerald as Jericho's attention shifted to her, his gaze catching hers. He said something else in a low, purring voice, and the men around him suddenly looked at her too. There was more laughter.

The prick. This was a power play, wasn't it? Or a test of some sort. Her standing there in the cold, holding his coat while half naked.

She looked away, directing her gaze to the pavement, giving them back nothing. If she didn't present them with anything to interest them, they'd soon forget about her. Besides, it wasn't the rest of these men she wanted. Only him.

There was more talk, the rise and fall of voices, the beautiful cadence of French conversation washing over her.

Jesus, she wished she could speak it. She'd be extremely interested to know what they were talking about.

She shifted again, her heels scraping on the pavement. Her mouth felt tender, reminding her uncomfortably of that kiss, the burn of it lingering on her skin. Which was annoying. And no, for fuck's sake, she wasn't going to think about that. Not the feel of his lips on hers or the way she'd opened her mouth to let him in or how her body had relaxed against his.

That was just simple reaction, nothing more. A kiss was meaningless. Sex was meaningless except for how it could be used as a weapon, and she'd used that particular weapon before.

Men weren't difficult to handle—show them a pair of tits and they were anyone's. Except with her, they were more often dead.

Yeah, there were bonuses to being female, and in her humble opinion it only made her a better assassin.

Jericho turned from the men he'd been talking to, the group breaking up, some going back into the club, a few others setting off down the sidewalk and disappearing into the darkness. He didn't look at her, heading straight toward the long black limo that waited at the curb.

The big Russian guy who looked like a bodyguard was waiting by the limo door, pulling it open for him.

Without turning, Jericho lifted a hand and she knew that he was gesturing for her to follow, so she moved over to the limo, waiting until he'd gotten inside before getting in too.

The interior was warm and smelled of expensive leather, and it made her shiver in spite of herself as the bodyguard shut the door after them, closing out the cold night air.

Jericho paid no attention to her, taking a call on his cell, settling back in his seat as he did so. He was speaking in German now, switching languages without any apparent effort.

The car pulled away from the curb, out into the narrow street, and Temple resisted the urge to spread the soft cashmere coat in her hands over her cold legs, keeping hold of it in her lap instead.

The warmth of the car was insidious, stealing through her and making her want to relax, but she didn't. There could be no dropping her guard, not now, not here, and definitely not with him.

Streetlights moved across the black leather of the seats, shining on Jericho's face. He was sitting back with one ankle up on one knee, his arm lying along the back of the seat. Even speaking the harsh German consonants, his voice sounded like molten caramel. Holy shit, that was a weapon all on its own.

Temple took a breath, allowing herself a small moment of triumph. Okay, so this was all going according to plan. She'd managed to get him to choose her for the night and regardless of what would happen once they'd gotten there, it was a start. She'd get him to talk, get him to reveal his secrets and then, once she'd found out what happened to Thalia, she'd deliver her punishment.

Simple.

She just needed to figure out the best way to get him to talk, although that really wasn't too difficult to figure out.

Especially given his response to the way she'd touched him earlier.

Her fingers tingled at the remembered heat she'd felt all the way through the wool of his suit pants. At the feel of him slowly hardening, long and thick under her hands.

"Are you going to kill me, kitten?"

Her feeling of satisfaction abruptly drained away and she looked down at the expensive coat in her lap, smoothing it in a reflexive gesture. He was too perceptive, that was the problem and her usual defenses weren't working so great tonight. He'd seen past her scared stripper act almost instantly, which left her with only one option. Being herself. A dangerous prospect.

Against her better judgment, she glanced at him, expecting him to be deep in conversation and not paying any attention to her whatsoever.

But he wasn't. He was still talking to whoever was on the phone, but his green-gold eyes were looking straight at her.

Something kicked deep in her gut, and she couldn't tell whether it was that long-forgotten emotion fear, or whether it was something else. Something even more alien. Desire.

Jesus, that was disturbing. A part of her wanted to look away from him, but she'd be damned if she showed him that kind of vulnerability, so she didn't, holding his gaze instead.

Come at me, prick. I'm fucking untouchable. But you're not.

His mouth turned up in a faint smile, but he kept looking at her as he spoke, watching her as if she was fascinating to him in some way, as if he was waiting for her to do something and didn't want to miss it.

Well, hell. If he was waiting for her to do something, perhaps she shouldn't disappoint him. Slowly she lifted the coat across her lap, shook it out a little. Then with a certain amount of deliberation, she slid her arms into it and drew it around herself, keeping her gaze on his as she did so.

Yeah, asshole. I'm not going to carry your fucking coat anymore. I'm going to wear it like it was mine.

His expression didn't change, but his gaze followed her every movement.

She smiled at him, settling back against the seat and kicking her feet up onto the cushions of the seat opposite her, the shiny silver stilettos gleaming in the light. The expensive fabric felt good against her chilled skin, warming her up nicely, and it smelled good too, of cinnamon and sandalwood . . .

Him.

Jericho murmured an "auf wiedersehen" into his phone then punched one of the buttons. Carelessly he threw the phone onto the seat cushions near where she'd put her feet and turned, angling his body around so he nearly faced her. His wide shoulders pressed up against the window of the limo, his head tilted against the glass, one arm on the back of the seat.

"I told you to carry my coat, not wear it." His voice was mild, a certain kind of cold amusement glimmering in his eyes.

She lifted a shoulder. "I got a little chilly. Standing around in a thong and pasties while a group of assholes talk about nothing can do that to a girl." She shot him a glance from underneath her lashes. "Anyway, you're not wearing it."

His gaze traveled over her, all the way to where her feet rested on the leather seat opposite then back again. "You're pushing, kitten. And I can't figure out whether you think that's a smart move or whether you're merely too stupid to understand what you're doing." Those cold, sharp green eyes rested on hers. "You're not a stripper. You're not a whore. And something tells me you're not a poor exchange student studying dance either. Because if you were, you'd be sitting there with your mouth closed, not wrapping my coat around yourself and putting your feet on my new leather seats while talking about assholes."

She could feel it as he spoke, the menace slowly deepening around him. The sense of threat gathering close. His voice was like a drug, a balm to lull her into thinking nothing was wrong, that she wasn't in any danger, and only once he'd come to the end of what he was saying would she realize that she was on the edge of a precipice. And that she was about to walk over it.

Hell, maybe she would walk over it. But she wouldn't smash herself to pieces on the ground. She'd fucking fly.

She tilted her head, folding the coat more comfortably around her. "So what do you think I am then?"

He gave a low laugh, the sound rolling over her skin like rough velvet. "This isn't a game, Temple. We haven't just met in a bar and are indulging in a bit of light flirting and getting to know one another before a one-night stand." His smile was very white, a shark's. "You're my fucking prisoner. You're my slave. And I will do whatever the hell I want with you. So if that means giving me the truth exactly when I want it, that's exactly what you'll give me."

Something surged inside her, and it wasn't fear. Not yet. It was something else, a hotter, more intense emotion. Almost like . . . excitement. Because again, here was the challenge she'd been seeking. The chance to pit herself against someone worthy of her skills.

Her ultimate enemy.

And maybe he too felt something similar, because she

thought she saw the same excitement gleam in that mesmerizing green and gold gaze. A spark of heat that hadn't
been there before. Perhaps subconsciously he knew what
he was facing and wanted the same challenge she did.

No, fuck perhaps. He did want it.

She smiled. "You know what? I have a theory. You don't
want easy, Jericho. And you don't want me to give you the
truth just like that. I think you want me to make you work
for it."

He shifted in his seat, a lazy, languid movement. "Interesting theory. And why would I have any interest in
working for it?"

"Because you're a man who can have anything he wants
when he wants it. Because everything is easy for you.
Because everyone does exactly what you say." She crossed
her feet at the ankles, the city lights glinting off the silver
straps of her stilettos. "You want a challenge. And threatening me with death if I don't tell you the truth makes
everything far too simple."

"It would if you were afraid of me."

"But I'm not."

A silence fell, heavy, dense. Full of the same kind of
pressure found at the bottom of a deep ocean.

He was still, the sharp intensity of his gaze locked with
hers. And her heartbeat sounded loud in her head all of a
sudden, her mouth dry, a hot, tense feeling coiling tightly
in her gut.

She couldn't work out what it was, why she wanted to
keep staring at him and yet look away at the same time.
Why she felt oddly vulnerable, as if he could see everything about her. The feeling was similar to the one she'd
experienced as she'd sat in his lap, as he'd toyed with her
nipple, making her feel . . . things. Unexpected things.

Jericho moved slowly, lazily, like a great cat unfolding
from sleep. He leaned forward, a faint smile playing around

his beautiful mouth. "Yes, kitten," he said softly. "Yes, you most certainly are."

She didn't like that, not at all. Her amber gaze widened and, beneath the veneer of confidence she drew about herself the way she'd drawn on his coat, he caught another glimpse of it. The flicker of fear. The same fear that had made her leap out of his lap back in the VIP room.

Yet now she covered it as she had the last time, fussing a little with the lapels of his coat, sighing as if the conversation bored her. "Haven't we talked about this? You seemed to think I wasn't afraid of you."

"You're speaking as if all fear is exactly the same. And it isn't. There are many types of fear, Temple."

"And you would know, I suppose?"

She said it as if she didn't know who she was talking to. As if he hadn't seen fear in every form there was, hadn't felt it himself every single fucking day. Or at least he used to, until he'd gotten rid of that, along with every other emotion that got in the way of what he was trying to achieve.

"I do know." He watched her small, delicate face. The currents that moved in the gold of her eyes. The threat of physical harm had only made the fire inside her climb higher, as if danger made her burn more intensely, so no, it wasn't that she was afraid of him. It was something else.

Casually, he reached for the edge of his coat that she'd wrapped herself in and flipped it aside. She blinked yet didn't move, letting the coat hang open. But he could sense the tension in her.

He put his hand on her bare thigh, letting it rest there, her skin chilled from her wait outside while he'd talked to some of the club's clients. He'd let her wait longer than strictly necessary, but he'd wanted to see what she'd do, what she'd give away.

Nothing as it turned out. Like she gave away nothing now.

She smiled. "Are we getting to that now then? I thought you were going to make me wait." There was no break in her voice, no shake. Not like there had been back in the VIP room. When he'd touched her, when she'd sprung away from him in what had looked like an involuntary movement.

She'd been scared then, oh yes, she had. This little kitten may not be afraid to die, but she *was* afraid of something. And he thought he knew what that was.

Maybe it was time to test a theory of his own.

Haven't you got more important shit to do than play with this little girl?

Sure, he did. But there was something about this woman, something that niggled away in his gut. She was a threat to him in some way, and if there was one thing that had helped him stay at the top of this cesspit of an empire of his, it was the fact that he never let a threat go un-guarded.

Slowly, he slid his palm higher up her thigh, feeling her skin begin to warm beneath his hand. "And what is it that you think we're getting to?"

"I wouldn't have thought I'd need to spell it out."

He moved his hand higher, letting the tips of his fingers push up beneath the thin elastic waistband that was all that was keeping the sparkly g-string on, settling his thumb in the warm, sensitive crease between the top of her thigh and her groin. Feeling the muscles of her stomach tense in instinctive response. "Maybe you do need to spell it out," he said softly, watching her face. "I want to know what it is you think you're going to get."

Her gaze flicked down to where his hand rested on her skin, then came back to his face again. The pulse at the base of her throat beat fast. Faster than it should have.

This was what she was afraid of. His touch. And not because she didn't want it. As he'd already established, she *did* want it. Which meant that what she was afraid of was her own desire. For him.

Interesting. No, not interesting. Downright fucking fascinating.

"Well sex, I assume." She paused, tilting her head, red curls falling over the shoulder of his coat. "I mean, isn't that what you do with the women you take home?" Another pause, those quick, golden eyes searching his. "Or maybe you don't. Maybe you tuck them into bed with a cup of hot cocoa instead."

Perceptive little bitch, wasn't she? She was guessing, of course. She would have no idea how close to the truth that was.

He moved his thumb, stroking her gently, feeling a shiver ripple through her in response, slight and barely imperceptible but there nonetheless. "That sounds like wishful thinking." He kept his voice soft, watching the ember in her eyes begin to glow.

She gave a short laugh that sounded forced. "It's not. Personally I'd be disappointed. All the rumors, all the build-up, and then hot cocoa? Yeah, I'd be *very* disappointed."

Her confidence was slipping just a bit. There was a sense of fragility to it now, as if all it would take was a sharp blow to make it shatter. And he could do that. He *should* do that. No woman talked to him like she did, no one period. They shut their fucking mouths and did what they were fucking told, and they certainly didn't tell him about how disappointed they'd be if the rumors *weren't* true.

Dangerous. She was dangerous. Who the *hell* was she? Christ, she was right about one thing though: He was going to find out *everything* about her and no, he didn't want her to make it easy for him. He wanted the test. Yeah, so his whole life up until this point had been a giant test, and being Jericho had pushed him to his limits and beyond them, but he had to admit that lately he'd gotten comfortable. Too comfortable.

Maybe she was just the threat he needed to keep him on his toes.

He didn't say anything, stroking her again, the softness of her skin beneath his thumb. So warm. He missed warmth. In her amber eyes there was another glimmer of tension, though her body remained relaxed. Strange she should feel discomfort now when she'd had no problem handling him or touching him back at the club. But of course, that had been when she'd made the first move.

"You don't like it when you're not the one in charge, do you?" he asked, keeping his thumb moving on her.

She remained ostensibly relaxed, one arm along the back of the seat, the other resting on the thigh still covered by the coat. "What makes you say that?"

"Because you tensed the moment I touched you here. Yet you had no problems touching my cock back in the club."

A smile played around her mouth. "Who's to say I'm not the one in charge now?"

He paused the movement of his thumb, letting it sit there, studying her. She gave nothing away, delicate features full of amusement, hiding all trace of that tension, of the discomfort he'd seen before. She had herself well under control.

Whoever she was, she was very, very good.

Sadly for her, he was better.

He gave a soft laugh. "You're not the one in charge, kitten. I am."

"Really? Interesting since I wasn't the one with the hard-on back there."

"True. And yet you were the one who leapt off my lap when I touched you."

"Like I said, that was because—"

"You don't like wanting a stranger," he finished for her. "You also don't like being restrained, and you don't like being told what to do either."

An emotion chased across her face, so fast he couldn't tell what it was before it was gone. "Well, sure." She rolled her eyes as if he'd pointed out the obvious. "Who does like being told what to do?"

"Some people do." He stared into her golden eyes. "But I think you're a woman who knows what she wants and who takes it regardless. A woman who likes to have control."

She lifted a shoulder. "Or maybe I'm as submissive as they come."

"Oh no, kitten, I don't think you're submissive." He paused, looking at her, reflecting. "Or maybe you are? Maybe that's secretly what you long for."

And there it was again, a shadow deep in the amber depths of her gaze. A current of discomfort or doubt. *Fear* . . . She didn't look away from him, and he knew that was because she was trying to hide it. But he saw anyway.

She gave a derisive snort. "Sure I do. Hey, I can be whoever you want me to be. Isn't that what all the girls say? If you want submissive, I'll be submissive." A hint of amusement glittered beneath her lashes. "Or if you want my boot on the back of your neck, I can do that too."

She was playing with him, the little bitch. But that was

okay, he was letting her. Sometimes lulling a person into a false sense of security was necessary to make them drop their guard. You made them think they were dealing with a pussycat and then you turned around and bit their heads off.

"Let's make another deal," he said lazily. "If I win, you answer one of my questions as honestly and completely as you can. If you win, the same goes for me."

Something in her posture changed, though she didn't actually move. And he had the impression that her focus had narrowed suddenly and completely on him.

So, she liked the idea of asking him questions, did she? Well, since he'd ruled out her being a stripper, maybe she was a spy sent by one of his competitors to get information from him. Or, shit, she might even be an undercover cop. That could be . . . fun.

He studied her. "You like that idea?"

"What? Of asking you questions?" Another of those secret smiles. "I like the idea of beating you better."

Little liar. He'd let that pass for now. "But you don't know what the terms of the deal are yet."

She rolled her eyes. "Come on then. The suspense is killing me."

Yeah, this was going to be fun. She was too fucking confident, too fucking sure of herself. He was going to break her wide open.

"The terms are as follows." Keeping one hand on her thigh, he reached for the other edge of his coat, pulling that aside too so she was fully exposed. "I'll touch you where I like, however I like, and with whatever I like." Gently, he peeled off the other pastie from her breast. "If you manage to go the whole night without telling me to stop, you win."

Again that quality of stillness to her, as if she was a cat suddenly conscious of a bird within reach of her paw. "That sounds potentially painful."

"I'm not talking pain. I'm talking absolute and total control."

"What?" Her brow creased. "You mean I have to stay in control?"

He smiled, because she wasn't going to like this. Not one bit. "Oh no, kitten. Where's the fun in that? No, I'm talking of me having absolute and total control of you."

CHAPTER FOUR

That maddening, smug smile played around his beautiful mouth like a song, the kind that stuck in your head, that was impossible to get rid of.

Absolute and total control . . .

He knew. Somehow, he knew exactly what made her uncomfortable. What she didn't like. What . . . disturbed her.

The fucking asshole.

She thought she'd been totally in command of herself, letting nothing slip, not even when he'd put his hand on her thigh, when his thumb had started stroking over her skin, making everything inside her pull together in a hard, tight knot of sensation. Somehow he'd picked up that she found the touch disquieting, though how, she had no idea. And now he was going to use that against her.

Dammit.

Come on, this is nothing. You've had pain, you've had torture, you've had all kinds of different shit. A night of kinky sex isn't going to break you.

No, it goddamned wouldn't. Hell, if worse came to the worst, she could just kill him and questions be damned. Then again, if she did that, she'd never find out what had happened to Thalia. And she wanted to know. She *had* to know.

So, she was just going to have to suck it up, wasn't she? No point getting all worked up over it anyway. It was just sex and yeah, she'd had that many times before.

Going to be slightly different this time around though.

Temple looked into his cold, sharp green eyes, making no attempt to cover herself because that too would give away more than she was willing to reveal. "Do I have a choice about this?" she asked bluntly. "I mean, given that I'm your prisoner and all."

"No," he replied, just as blunt. "I'll do it anyway since you're mine for the night. But at least this way you have a chance at getting something from it."

"Why? I thought you didn't give a shit about what I wanted?"

"I don't. But maybe you're right. Maybe I don't want this to be easy." His gaze followed down the length of her exposed body, studying her in a curiously detached fashion, as if she was a canvas he was going to paint on and hadn't quite decided where to start. "Maybe I want the challenge like you said. I don't think threatening you with torture or death would work anyway." His gaze flicked back to hers. "Pleasure is certainly a different approach."

As if being under someone else's total control would be pleasurable. She'd been her own woman ever since she'd been sixteen years old and she liked it like that. The thought of him—especially him—being in charge of her was . . .

Frightening?

Firmly she pushed that thought away. Sex, it was just sex. A weapon, a tool. Meaningless. That's all she had to keep thinking of it as.

"Fine," she said, keeping her voice steady and level. "You have a deal."

"Perfect." He didn't smile, just held her gaze for a second. Then he shifted, reaching over to the seat for his phone and, picking it up, looking down at the screen and punching in some numbers. Turning away from her, he began another conversation with someone in French, ignoring her as if she wasn't lying stretched out beside him, the coat open to reveal her bare breasts.

For some reason that annoyed her even more than his stupid deal had. So she made herself stay where she was with the coat open, lying there as if she didn't care that he wasn't looking at her, that she wasn't bare to the waist, watching the lights of Paris shine through the windows of the limo and listening to the rise and fall of his beautiful voice.

Maybe she slept or dozed, or fell into a kind of half-daze, because it seemed quite suddenly that the limo stopped and the door was pulled open, a rush of cold air over her bare skin making her nearly gasp.

"Out," Jericho murmured in her ear. "We're here."

Pulling herself together, Temple gathered the coat around her and managed to get out of the limo without falling over her stilettos.

Ahead of her was a beautiful old building of weathered gray stone, with huge windows covered by shutters, small wrought iron balconies, and steep, sloping roofs of dark gray slate.

She knew nothing of Parisian architecture, nothing of Paris at all really, but this building seemed to encapsulate everything she'd dimly heard about the city. About its beauty, its elegance, and its age, not to mention the fact that it looked like a place someone with millions, if not billions, of dollars would live in.

Perfect beauty for a perfectly beautiful crime lord. Perhaps this building was rotten to the core too.

The Russian bodyguard shut the limo door behind Jericho then strode up to the arched front door of the building. Punching in a code on some buttons on a control panel set into one of the stone pillars that stood on either side of the door, he then pushed the door open. His attention flicked down the street and back again, clearly on the alert for any threats.

Jericho—supremely unworried—strolled up the stairs without waiting for her and stepped through the front door, leaving her standing there on the sidewalk by herself for a moment.

What the hell? Wasn't she supposed to be his prisoner? Didn't he care that were she any other girl, she might have tried to run?

From the top step, the Russian watched her, no expression at all on his face. Perhaps he was hoping she would run. Perhaps he wanted something to do.

Temple gave him a smile and pulled the coat more firmly around her, walking up the stairs and deliberately swinging her hips as she did, the stilettos making soft crunching noises as the soles scraped against the ancient, uneven stone of the steps.

He remained expressionless as she drew level to him. Then, as she passed, he said, in a low, rough voice, "I know what you are. You do not fool me."

A shot of adrenaline surged inside her, but she didn't let any of it show, didn't bother to even look at him. He didn't know what she was. No one knew. And sure, he might have sensed that she wasn't one of the usual trafficked girls he normally dealt with, but he wouldn't know anything beyond that. For all he knew she was a working girl looking for a way to make things better for herself.

Ignoring him, she stepped through the front door, coming to stand in the middle of a high-ceilinged foyer. An ornate and extraordinarily beautiful chandelier glittered above her head, illuminating a flagged stone floor and a grand staircase that spiraled up into the darkness of the next story. There was art on the walls, a sculpture in one corner, and the whole area was full of the kind of thick, heavy quiet that only a lot of money can buy.

For a moment, she stood there, staring around, a weird and completely alien feeling of being out of her depth filling her.

This wasn't her world. She hadn't come from this. She came from a shitty, rundown, blue-collar town in Michigan, where meth was the local industry, and good girls didn't go to college—they went to the street. She'd left not long after Thalia had been taken, sure, and yes, she'd been in places like this before. Her latest contracts had tended to be rich assholes with more money than sense, who'd pissed off the wrong people.

So, really, it was strange for her to feel her poor-girl roots strongly now. Especially given she'd spent so many years putting them behind her.

"You like my house?" Jericho's low, velvet voice came from her left, and she turned to find him leaning back against a set of double doors, his arms folded, watching her.

Jesus. He'd better not have seen her staring around like a fucking hayseed.

She shrugged. "It's very nice."

"You're still wearing my coat."

"It's cold."

"Not in here it isn't." His gaze was heavy-lidded, emerald gleaming from underneath thick, dark lashes. "Take it off."

There was no mistaking the order, and it made a part of her bristle in response. Because he was right. She didn't like being told what to do. At all.

Crushing the automatic response, she gave him a look. "So it starts now? Our deal?"

He only smiled. "Take off my coat, kitten."

"And if I don't?"

"Try it and find out."

Asshole.

Come on. Do it. What's one night? You can take it out on him in pain later.

Silently, she let out a breath. Then, in a fluid, sinuous movement, she shrugged out of his coat and let it fall carelessly to the ground, kicking it behind her and grinding it a little with her toe for good measure.

If that annoyed him, he didn't show it. His gaze swept over her, glittering like the chandelier above her head, and again she felt that kick deep inside, like when he'd touched her in the limo. It made everything in her stiffen in denial, in rejection.

She did *not* want to be attracted to him. She did *not* want to want him.

His gaze rose to hers and stayed there. "The G-string too."

Okay. Fine. She'd been virtually naked the whole evening. Being actually naked wasn't going to make too much of a difference. And shit, if she won this stupid deal of his, it would make everything worth it.

Just think of killing him. That makes everything better.

Fuck, yes. It really did.

She didn't look away, putting her hands on her hips and pushing down the waistband of the G-string, wriggling a little to get it down her thighs and then off. Stepping out of it, she straightened, the scrap of fabric dangling from one finger, then sauntered over to him, her heels making tapping sounds on the stone as she walked.

He remained where he was, his expression unreadable as she approached. He didn't look down either, his gaze locked with hers. Which gave her another little flick of inexplicable irritation. What was the point of being naked if he wasn't going to look?

She stopped right in front of him and extended her hand, the G-string dangling from it. "I assume you want this?"

For a moment, he didn't move, staring at her, the look in his green-gold eyes enigmatic. Then he took the G-string from her finger, examined it a second before ripping it to pieces in a series of short, sharp, calm movements.

Another kick inside her, though surely it wasn't fear. Because there wasn't anything very threatening about the cold way he tore up the glittering fabric. It was just something a man like him would do. Destroy something pretty just to prove a point, to prove his power.

Jericho opened his long fingers, the remains of the silver material fluttering down between them, swirling like snow onto the stone floor. He didn't watch it. He watched her, and there was such menace in those mesmerizing eyes of his. A threat she didn't quite understand, but somehow, her body did. Because it made a part of her clench right down low in her gut.

"You've forgotten already, haven't you?" he said, his mild tone totally at odds with the look in his eyes. "I'm the one who's supposed to be in control. Not you."

She tensed, the assassin in her gauging the threat.

Chill the hell out. He doesn't want to kill you. He just wants to fuck you.

Yeah, and before he did that, he wanted to feel like he had power over her first. Which must mean he felt threatened by her in some way.

Good.

"Hey, I'm just doing what you said." She glanced down at the floor then back up again, watching him from beneath her lashes. "So do you want me to get down on my knees now?"

He gazed at her a long moment then, unexpectedly, he reached out, one long finger catching her under the chin, tilting her head up. And the breath froze in her throat for reasons she couldn't have explained. The tip of his finger burned against her skin like a lit match, sending little forest fires of sensation chasing all over her bare skin, making her nipples tighten and a strange pulse of heat clench hard between her thighs.

"No," he murmured, "I don't want you to get on your knees. I have some business to do with some colleagues before we get to that."

"That sounds . . . boring." Her voice sounded unsteady, which was annoying.

"Perhaps it will be for you." His thumb stroked along her jaw, sending more shock waves through her, making her have to work hard to keep still. "They're important men, and they're used to looking at something pretty. I think they'll like looking at you."

She blinked. So did that mean he was going to . . . display her? "You want me to sleep with them too?" Might as well ask. Because if that was the case then they'd be dead long before they ever got a chance to touch her. And so would he.

And risk never finding out what happened to Thalia? Didn't you promise her you'd do anything to find her? Anything at all?

A sharp thread of feeling that didn't have anything to do with Jericho curled inside her.

The night her sister had disappeared, so long ago now, she'd promised herself she'd do anything to find her. That she'd lie, cheat, or steal. That she'd kill. That she'd do things that would strip away the last parts of her soul. And she had. She'd done all of those things and more. What was sleeping with a couple of assholes compared to that?

Jericho's tawny brows came down, and for the second time that night, she thought she saw something hot and fierce and golden burn through the cold green of his eyes. "You're mine, Temple. Mine for the night. And what's mine stays mine, understand? They can look, but they can't touch." His beautiful features were hard. "And if they do, I'll cut off whichever body part is doing the touching."

She shouldn't have felt the small thread of reassurance that twisted through her. Shouldn't even have been aware of it. Because what the actual fuck? He was the head of a human trafficking network who'd just made her strip in front of him, who was going to make her stand naked in a room with his supposed "colleagues." So why she should feel reassured by the fact that he wasn't going to let them touch her was simply insane.

Not that she needed anyone's reassurance, not when she could cut off any offending body part herself. "Well, that's something, I guess," she murmured. "Lucky me."

The hard look on his face faded. He ran his thumb along her lower lip, following the line of it as if it was an indulgence he was allowing himself. "Ah, kitten," he said softly. "There's no such thing as luck. If there was, you wouldn't be here."

She frowned at that, at the strange note in his voice, the one that sounded almost like regret. But before she could say anything, he dropped his hand from her and stepped back, pulling open the door. "Inside," he ordered. "Time to prove yourself."

"So, what is Jericho planning to do about the American situation?" Vassily Lychenko, head of the Russian mafia family who controlled much of the human trafficking in the Baltic region and as cruel an old bastard as Jericho had ever met, knocked back his third vodka of the night and slapped the crystal shot glass back on the table in front of him with a bang. "And I presume he *does* have a plan?"

The Lychenkos were Jericho's least-favorite people to deal with—if he could be said to have favorites out of any of the connections he had with various European and Asian crime networks. The Russian family had been his most recent alliance, and he was still having issues with them. Mostly because they didn't like the fact that he'd insisted on full control over the American market negotiations.

The tricky thing was managing them while preserving the secret of Jericho's identity. He preferred to keep his negotiations through third parties whenever possible so Jericho remained a shadowy figure, but keeping tabs on people through personal meetings was also necessary. Especially with these Russians and most especially when he had to keep them happy.

So he often pretended he was a nameless lieutenant of Jericho's, one authorized to give out information and to receive it, but not to act. No one he met face-to-face in any of these kinds of meetings knew he was Jericho and he wanted to keep it that way.

Anyway, he couldn't let any of the alliances he'd painstakingly built over the years break apart, couldn't let any of those people escape, not if he wanted to take them down with him when the time came. And he most certainly wanted to take them down. The Lychenkos in particular.

They were needlessly cruel and insufferably arrogant, and he would quite happily have crushed them under his boot years ago if he hadn't needed them to pull in the Russian trafficking networks.

No stone left unturned, etcetera.

Beside Vassily sat his nephew, Anatoly, an unpleasant little prick who clearly wasn't listening to the conversation, his gaze glued to Temple instead.

Jericho had gotten her to serve the vodka when the two men had arrived, and though Vassily had ignored her as if she was merely just another piece of furniture, Anatoly had been giving her openly lascivious glances for the past hour.

It made a little prickle of annoyance sit in Jericho's gut for no reason he could see.

Having a naked woman present at a business discussion wasn't usual for him—unlike some of his supposed business partners who considered it nothing more than advertising. But on occasion he sometimes got one of the prostitutes or strippers from the club to serve drinks and generally be there as some pretty eye-candy, having them there to either intimidate or attract, depending on what kind of discussion he was having or what point he wanted to prove. They were paid well for their efforts.

It had never bothered him when his business partners wanted to do more than look, so he couldn't understand why Anatoly was pissing him off quite so much now. But he was.

Temple was doing exactly as instructed, waiting silently beside the sofa where the two Russians sat, holding a silver tray with a bottle of horrendously expensive vodka sitting on it. He'd told her not to speak, her only task to fill up the glasses when they were empty, and she'd only nodded her head, ostensibly obeying him.

In fact for the whole past hour she hadn't done anything to draw attention to herself except stand there naked, holding her tray, obeying him like she'd promised. So there shouldn't have been any reason for his gaze to be drawn to her as inexorably as iron filings to a magnet. To the curve of her slender shoulders and the way her red hair cascaded over them. To her pale, milky skin dusted with little freckles like golden sand sprinkled over a fresh fall of snow. To her supple, lithe body, muscled and toned like a dancer's. To her pussy, shaved bare as most strippers' were.

He'd never been so distracted by a woman before. It was fucking annoying, because what he should be doing was paying attention to the discussion he was having with the Lychenkos and ignoring her the way he usually ignored any naked woman. The way he'd had no difficulty doing for the past decade.

Yet he found he couldn't. And it wasn't only due to her unconventional beauty. She was so slender and pale that she should have looked fragile and yet she didn't. There was a power to her. And he didn't know what that power was, but it burned bright, glowing underneath the surface of her beautiful, pale skin. It was there in the way she held herself, in the toned shape of her thighs and calves, in her flat stomach, in the proud jut of her chin.

It had been a long, long time since he'd seen a woman who burned like she did. A woman who wasn't one of the lost, broken trafficked girls. Who wasn't from one of his crime connections and who didn't have money or her own personal army to back her up.

A woman who was powerful all on her own.

"Well?" Vassily demanded. "Am I wasting my fucking time here?"

Irritated with himself, Jericho dragged his attention from Temple and sat back in his armchair, unhurried.

What the hell were they talking about again? Ah, yes. They were talking about Fitzgerald and what the plan was now the bastard was dead. The Lychenkos were concerned about seeing a potentially lucrative deal go down the drain and were getting impatient.

Jericho met Vassily's belligerent light blue gaze, swirling the vodka he was drinking around in his glass. "I'll be taking at trip to the States in the next week or so to see to the situation personally. There won't be any problems, I assure you."

Vassily glared, clearly unconvinced. "And what about these rumors? About this so-called Elijah Hunt bastard taking over? You told us the negotiations with Fitzgerald were—"

"Fitzgerald's death could be useful to us," he interrupted, letting the edge of iron tinge his voice. "Whatever hold Hunt has on the operations over there is bound to be tenuous at best. After all, he's only had a month or so to cement his authority, which won't be nearly enough. Should be relatively easy to take it from him."

Beside his uncle, Anatoly was lounging back on the sofa. He'd drained his glass and now held it up. "More," he demanded in thickly accented English, looking in Temple's direction.

Instantly she moved to obey, keeping her head down as she rounded the side of the sofa with lithe grace. Stopping in front of Anatoly, she lifted the vodka bottle and poured more liquid into it.

The younger man's gaze was all over her, and as Temple handed him back the freshly refilled shot glass, he reached out and put one hand on the back of her thigh, sliding it up to cup her ass.

Jericho tensed, the annoyance in his gut gathering instantly into anger. Who the fuck did that uppity little prick think he was? She wasn't Anatoly's tonight, she was his.

Temple herself had gone very still, but it didn't seem like she was afraid. The tension in her posture spoke of readiness, wariness. Like an animal prepared to stand and fight rather than run.

Interesting, don't you think?

Yeah, it was. And maybe on a different night, with a different woman, he might have wanted to explore that further, push her, test her. But again, for yet another inexplicable reason, he'd made her a promise that they wouldn't touch her. That he'd cut off any offending body part if they did, and he didn't know why, but he found himself wanting to keep that promise.

"Since when did I give you permission to touch my property?" he asked, keeping the question casual yet letting an undertone of steel color it. Pissing off the Lychenkos was a bad move, but the sight of Anatoly's hand on Temple's ass made him want to break it off.

Proving his complete stupidity, Anatoly ignored the warning, digging his fingers into Temple's flesh, squeezing. "Ten thousand," he said thickly. "For the night."

Jericho shifted his attention to Vassily, meeting the other man's icy blue stare. "Your nephew is in danger of losing his hand," he said coldly. 'I suggest he removes it."

Temple remained still, holding her tray, the bottle on top of it not even quivering. She had her back to him and all he could see was her straight spine, her wealth of red hair, and Anatoly Lychenko's hand on her ass.

Vassily's gaze flickered. "Why?" he grunted. "It is just a woman."

Fuck. It looked like the old man was gearing up for another of his pissing contests, which meant continuing to argue would only make him look weak, and he couldn't ever afford to look weak, not even when he was pretending to be a mere lieutenant of Jericho's. Not with these bastards breathing down his neck.

"What do you want, sir?" Temple's husky voice, soft and full of respect filled the room suddenly. "I'm at your service."

Jericho tensed even further. What the hell did she think she was doing?

"Down," Anatoly said in his thick English, spreading his knees. "On the floor."

Temple turned, bending to put the tray back down on the table, and as she did so, her bright golden gaze caught Jericho's. Again, there was no fear there anywhere. If anything, she looked impatient, as if she wanted to get this over and done with so she could get on with more important things. And there was also just the slightest hint of a defiance there too, as if she was pushing him again.

Little bitch. Was this to test his word? To see if he'd do what he promised? Or was this to see how far he'd let this go?

Well, he could let this go as far as he fucking liked. And if that involved her having to suck Anatoly Lychenko's dick in front of everyone then maybe he should let her.

You don't want her to do that, though.

No. Christ, he really didn't. She was his tonight. The only dick she'd be sucking was his.

He sat back in his armchair and raised his hand. Instantly the doors of the lounge crashed opened and Dmitri strode in.

"This little shit is touching what isn't his," Jericho said without inflection. "Show him what we do to thieves."

Dmitri didn't even break stride. He moved to where Temple stood and pulled her out of Anatoloy's grip. Then he took the younger man's wrist in one powerful hand and jerked him bodily out of the sofa, forcing the hand down onto the glass of the coffee table.

Vassily was on his feet, shouting something, while Anatoly cursed and struggled.

Dmitri, ignoring everyone, drew a long knife from its holster strapped around his thigh and raised it over Anatoly's wrist.

Jericho could not afford for these men to ignore him. He could not afford to show weakness. And since the only language they were familiar with was violence, that's the language he would speak. Luckily he was well versed in it.

He let Dmitri start to bring the blade down, Anatoly already screaming in anticipation of the pain, then he said sharply and coldly, "Stop."

Dmitri's blade froze, inches from Anatoly's pallid wrist.

There was a moment's silence, full of the echoes of Anatoly's scream and Vassily's loud curses.

But Jericho didn't look at either of them. He looked at Temple. She was standing to the side, watching Dmitri with an expression that he thought seemed almost . . .

professional. Then, when the blade didn't continue its downward fall, she glanced at him, and he saw it, the slight curl of her mouth in a smile that could only be called wicked. As if this was what she'd been wanting all along.

Christ, had she been playing him? Had she been playing *all* of them?

It moved through him then, something like respect and something else, deeper, darker. Hotter.

This woman, whoever she was, *whatever* she was, he wanted her. He wanted that spark inside her, that wicked smile, that defiance. He wanted to take it, explore it. Own it.

Somehow she'd taken a situation where she had no power at all and had turned it on its head, completely disrupted it. She'd forced his hand and all because of a promise he'd made to her.

Fuck, since when had *anyone* forced him to do *anything*?

He was going to crack her open and take whatever was inside. He was going to take it all.

Vassily was shouting again, spouting nonsense about how Jericho was going to pay for this, about how he was going to suffer and how there would be no alliances. The usual bullshit.

"*Silence.*" Jericho shaped his voice like a blade, as sharp as Dmitri's knife, cutting the older man off. "Stop posturing, Lychenko. We both know Anatoly is a little prick who needs to learn to respect his betters, especially his betters' property."

The Russian's face was beet red. But since his bodyguards were all outside, he could do nothing. "This alliance is dead," he snarled pointlessly.

Jericho slowly put down his own vodka glass. "No, it isn't. You need it, and we both know it. Now, Jericho is a generous man and a forgiving one. Anatoly made a mistake, but he can keep his hand this time." Holding the old man's gaze, he went on. "Dmitri? See that the Lychen-kos have unrestricted access to the club, and I do mean unrestricted. Everything is on the house."

That should keep things sweet for a while at least. The Russians were a pain in his ass, but in the end they were simple, and at least his point would have been made.

Now he had to make another one.

"Come here, kitten," he ordered Temple.

She hesitated only a second, coming over to his chair, her head down, not meeting his gaze. Her manner was subservient, and yet the way she moved was as far from subservient as it was possible to get, a swing in her hips, her shoulders back and proud.

Oh, he was going to enjoy taking her down, yeah, he really would.

"We were having an interesting business discussion, and now you've ruined it." He kept his voice mild, knowing it sounded all the more threatening for it. "On your knees."

She blinked at him, meeting his gaze for a second, and he could see first the surprise then the fleeting look of annoyance in her eyes.

"Are you questioning me?" he asked, making sure she heard the edge of menace in the words.

The annoyance in her eyes flickered. "No."

"Good. Now turn around and get down on your knees."

There was no hesitation this time as she obediently turned to face the rest of the room, dropping gracefully to her knees in front of his chair as if she was sitting down at a table ready to dine.

He reached forward and buried one hand in the softness of her hair, closing his fingers tight on her curls and jerking her head back hard. Her intake of breath was barely audible, but he heard it, the darkest part of him savagely pleased at the sound.

You shouldn't be doing this. Let someone else find out who she is.

No. She was his now and so were her secrets. He would be the one who discovered them, no one else.

He tightened his grip in her hair, drawing her head back even farther, exposing her throat and arching her back. "Apologize to my guests, kitten."

"I'm . . . sorry." Her voice sounded strained, her body quivering with tension, but he didn't let go or loosen his grip.

Anatoly was shaking his hand and cursing, his narrow face pale as he got up from the sofa. "Fucking not worth it anyway," he muttered furiously in Russian. "Redheaded slut. I'll fucking kill you."

But his uncle laid a heavy hand on his shoulder and pushed him hard toward the doors.

Jericho kept Temple exactly where she was as the two men left the room, her hair soft and warm against his skin. He didn't want to let it go. He wanted to wind it around his wrist like a leash, holding onto her as he did whatever the hell he wanted with her.

He looked down at her as the doors closed behind the Russians, her head bent back so her gaze was directed to the ceiling, her body arched. The pulse at the base of her throat beat fast, and there was a slight flush to her lovely, milky skin.

"A crime lord who keeps his promises," she murmured a little breathlessly, her subservience melting away as if he wasn't pulling her hair so hard that it had to have been hurting. "Who knew? Except you told me you'd cut off any body part that touched me and that bastard still has his hand."

"Perhaps you shouldn't have manipulated me then." He adjusted his hold, drawing her head farther back so she was staring directly up at him. "I don't like being played."

Her eyes glinted. "Bullshit. I think you love it. Anyway, I didn't disobey you, did I?"

Oh, she was skirting the line, beautiful little bitch that she was. He studied her face, trying to see behind those amber eyes, figure out where all this confidence, this power, came from. "You were encouraging Anatoly, don't think I didn't notice. Why? What were you trying to do?"

She shifted and that had to be because she was uncomfortable, bent back the way she was, but no sign of it showed in her face. And he was conscious once more of the subtle scent of her body, something musky and sweet, filling his senses and making him hard. Of the feel of her hair around his fist, silky curls spilling over his thighs. Of her mouth, that perfect little cupid's bow, curving in a secret smile as if even now, even like this, it was she who had the upper hand.

Of the brilliant gold of her eyes, staring up at him, swallowing him whole.

"If you want to know that, you'll have to win this deal then, won't you?" Her voice was soft, taunting.

He smiled down at her, tightening his grip on her hair. "I'm not sure you want to keep throwing down challenges like that." He raised his other hand, placing one finger on the pulse at her throat, feeling it race beneath his touch. "Not when you have no idea what I really am." And she really didn't. No one did. Who he was inside was a secret he kept all to himself.

"So why don't you show me?" There was a hard glitter in her eyes. "I can take it. I'm stronger than I look."

Oh yes, she definitely was, no doubt about that. "This isn't about pain, Temple, I told you that in the car." He moved the finger at her throat, slowly sliding it over smooth, silky skin, down to the curve of one breast, gently circling one proud nipple. "This is about pleasure."

A flush tinged her skin, her pupils dilating, her body

tensing. A flash of anger moved in the golden depths of her gaze. No, she didn't like wanting him. Didn't like the way she responded to him. Maybe this deal would be easier to win than he thought.

Christ, he hoped not.

"I can take that too." Her voice was thicker now, but her jaw had hardened, as if she was bracing herself for something.

"Can you?" Gently he took one little nipple between his thumb and forefinger. "Prove it then."

And he pinched her.

Hard.

CHAPTER FIVE

Sensation arrowed from her nipple straight down between her thighs like a flaming sword, and it was all she could do to hold in the sudden gasp it drew from her.

Instinctive anger rose, but she fought it down. Whatever she felt didn't matter. Just like those stupid Russian assholes hadn't mattered. Just like standing there serving them vodka hadn't mattered. Just like that prick's hand on her ass hadn't mattered.

Just like the way Jericho protected you didn't matter?

God no. Especially not that. She didn't need any man's protection, not these days.

No, none of it mattered. The only thing that did was getting the information out of him. The man with his fist buried in her hair, who was holding her at his feet with her head bent back. So she had no choice but to look up into his sharp, green-gold eyes. Into his beautiful face.

Oh, she could have gotten away. A twist here, an elbow there, and she'd have loosened his hold on her. But she couldn't. No matter how much she didn't like being this willingly helpless in front of a man, she had to ignore her own feelings.

She was going to win this deal, she just fucking would.

"This is hard for you," he murmured, the soft velvet of his voice rolling over her. "You don't want to feel anything when I touch you." Another pinch, just as hard, the same white-hot bolt of feeling piercing her.

She gritted her teeth silently, staring up at him. He was right, but she wasn't going to tell him that, wasn't going to give him any more ammunition. She just had to keep telling herself that pleasure didn't matter. That it meant nothing. "What makes you say that?"

"Your jaw is tight and I can see you resisting."

"Maybe I just don't like having my head jerked back like this."

"I know you don't. That's why I'm doing it." The pressure on her nipple released, and she could feel his palm against the underside of her breast, cupping her. "You don't like me touching you like this either." This time a gentle stroke of his thumb over her achingly hard nipple, making her want to shiver. "In fact, I bet even now you're trying to think of some way to get back the control."

"No." Her voice sounded hoarse and thick. Dammit. "You want to win this and so do I. Which means I do what you say, and you have the control."

"It also means I'm going to push you until you say stop."

She made herself smile at him, a "fuck you" straight in his face. "I'm not going to say stop. I told you, I can take anything."

Gold flared deep in his eyes. "We'll see about that."

Pressure released all of a sudden, her head freed, and she found herself kneeling facing the beautifully appointed lounge with its expensively upholstered white couches and antique furniture. It looked like something out of a magazine, from a movie star's house, from the art on the walls to the bowl of exquisite white roses on the coffee table. A place where people came to sit and enjoy the surroundings or talk about intellectual subjects.

Not a place where a woman stood naked merely to add to the decor. Where a man could grab her, only to have that hand nearly cut off. Not that she cared—she would have done it herself if all this hadn't been so very important. But the beauty of the room was just another reminder of where she was. Of who was sitting in the chair behind her, as classically beautiful as the room ahead of her.

A man with poison in his veins. A monster.

A monster who nearly cut off that asshole's hand just because he touched you. A monster who makes you wet.

A breath shuddered out of her, the pressure between her thighs acute. She didn't want to look down at herself, didn't want to see the evidence of what he was doing to her. She just had to keep thinking of the end result. Of Thalia.

"Come here," he said quietly, an unmistakable order.

She turned, looking over her shoulder at him.

He was sitting back in the white armchair, his long, lean body stretched out. The white cotton of his shirt was open at the throat, the strong column of his neck exposed, revealing smooth tanned skin. He looked ostensibly relaxed, safe in his power, but she didn't make the mistake of thinking he wasn't dangerous, not for a second. This was a predator merely waiting for its prey.

Good thing she had no intention of being prey.

She rose to her feet, making the movement lithe and graceful, then turned to face him. Raised a brow. "Anywhere in particular?"

His head tilted and he stared at her for one long second. Then he smiled, hard-edged and bright as a sword. Slowly, he pushed himself out of the chair, unfolding himself to his full height right in front of her. A broad-shouldered wall of hard muscle and warm skin, towering over her, no doubt trying to intimidate her.

But she wasn't intimidated.

She looked up at him, meeting his gaze head-on.

"You're not very biddable are you?" His hand lifted, and strangely, he touched her cheek lightly in an almost-caress.

She blinked, put momentarily off balance by the touch. "Hey, I did what you told me to."

His hand dropped, and he hooked an arm around her waist, pulling her suddenly and hard against him. The heat of him stole her breath, her palms coming up instinctively to press against the firm, hot wall of his chest, trying to keep some distance between them.

But there was no distance to be had. He bent his head, his mouth covering hers before she even realized what he was going to do. The kiss was as raw and demanding as the one back in the club had been and another deep, hidden instinct had her stiffening in preparation for pulling away.

Except his hand was at the back of her head, holding her there, keeping her exactly where he wanted her. And then he slid his tongue deep into her mouth, taking what he wanted whether she wanted to give it to him or not.

Her heart seized, an electric thrill moving through her. He tasted hot, the bite of the vodka he'd been drinking giving the kiss an alcoholic kick that made her dizzy. A wave of uncontrollable heat prickled, her skin tightening, making her acutely aware that she was naked. That the cotton of his shirt was rubbing against her sensitive nipples, the wool of his pants against her bare pussy . . .

Temple tried to breathe, tried to shift in his arms, anything to relieve the pressure that coiled tightly inside her, to take some of the control back. But she couldn't move.

And then she felt his hand slide between them, his fingers pushing down between her thighs without any hesitation, spreading the folds of her pussy and finding her clit, brushing a fingertip over it. She stiffened, the intensity of the sensation catching her by surprise.

Oh, shit, this was . . . *good. It feels so good. And you want it.*

His finger circled again, his mouth hot, demanding, the kiss becoming deep and wet and carnal. Unlike any other kiss she'd ever had. But no, she couldn't think that, couldn't make this different in any way. This was a means to an end, that's all.

And yet she shuddered under the touch of his stroking finger, the pleasure so acute it was almost pain. A dim panic began to twist inside her, but she tried to ignore it. So what if he made her feel good? It was only physical. It didn't touch her in any real way.

It's a betrayal. And you like betrayals.

No . . . No, the past had nothing to do with this. Nothing.

His finger circled her clit then pressed down on it, and this time there was no stopping the sharp gasp that escaped her or the sharpening of the panic that followed it.

She wasn't used to physical pleasure. No one had ever given her any. The only time she'd ever taken some for herself was when she was alone, when she was tired and needed to sleep, to relax.

It wasn't like this, being held in a man's arms. Where she wasn't the one directing how fast or how slow. How hard. When to stop and when to keep going. Where she was completely at his mercy.

At the mercy of her enemy.

His hand moved again, ruthless, inexorable, his finger pushing inside her, sliding in deep, and there was no resistance, none whatsoever. She was wet for him.

She groaned, unable to help herself, the sound taken from her as he explored her mouth, tasting every part of her. Oh, God, so good. Her body clenching hard around his finger, wanting movement and friction and more, the pressure inside her intensifying. And along with it, the inexplicable panic.

Temple twisted in his arms, a deep animal instinct making her seek escape. But he only tightened his grip, immobilizing her.

Making her take whatever he wanted to give.

His finger moved, sliding in and out of her, a second joining the first, and her hips began to flex against him, following the movement. Her body arched, restless and hot. Desperate.

Then he bit her lower lip, the pain a sharp, bright shock.

He's going to make you come. He's going to make you scream. He's going to make you feel something other than rage. And you know you don't fucking deserve it.

No. Shit no. She couldn't let him do that. Couldn't cede him that much control over her and her feelings. Couldn't let herself be so fucking helpless. Because she needed that rage. It was her only fuel.

Because it's better than shame, right?

She twisted again before she could stop herself, bringing her hands up in a hard, jerking movement, breaking his hold on her, sidestepping as she did so and pushing so that he stumbled back against the armchair and nearly fell back into it.

For a moment there was silence, broken only by the sound of their shared, frantic breathing.

Jericho stared at her, his eyes gone almost as gold as her own. They were full of flames, full of heat, the sharp edge of his aristocratic cheekbones stained with red. He was as hungry as she was, that was obvious, and it should have made her feel some kind of triumph at how she'd affected him.

But she didn't. She was too busy preparing to defend herself against the explosion of anger because there was always an explosion of anger when a man was denied something he wanted.

Yet Jericho made no move toward her and didn't speak.

Instead, he straightened up, his beautiful mouth curving into one of those dangerous, hungry smiles. As if he'd won.

Fuck. *Fuck*. What had she done?

"I didn't say stop," she said shakily, before he could speak.

"Didn't you?" His voice was hoarse, the velvet frayed and ragged, which somehow only made it even more compelling. "Pushing me away is the same thing."

"No." Her heartbeat thundered in her ears. She had to fix this somehow because there was no way she was going to lose this. "I have to say the word, that was the deal."

He remained where he was, his gaze on hers, green and gold like sunlight glittering on the deep ocean. "If you keep betraying yourself like this, kitten, I won't have to ask you any questions at all."

The panic hadn't gone away, somehow migrating to her throat instead, strangling her, and she had to swallow hard to get rid of it. Jesus, he wasn't wrong. "I didn't give you anything."

"Sure you did." He tilted his head, desire still stamped across his beautiful face, and he made no effort to hide it. "I can see your fear, Temple. I know what you're afraid of."

You don't deserve it, little slut. After all the lives you've taken, all the things you've done . . .

She crushed the voice in her head, the one that sounded like her father, because seriously, the past had no place here. She'd exorcised it from her life. Mustering up a smile to match his from somewhere, she raised a brow. "Oh? And what am I afraid of then?" She was pleased at the sarcasm in her voice. "Do tell, since you appear to know."

"Pleasure." His frayed velvet voice dragged over her skin like a caress. "You're afraid of wanting it."

Her laugh was forced, but it was there. "Afraid of pleasure? Seriously?" Somehow she knew she didn't sound as convincing as she wanted to. "Why the hell would I be afraid of that?"

"I don't know, you tell me." His gaze burned into hers. "But that's the second time you've pulled away tonight."

Her heartbeat echoed like a drum, the pressure between her thighs insistent.

She'd never thought this man would be different from all the rest. She'd never thought his focus would be her. Because why should it? When every single other man she'd been with had been completely selfish about their own pleasure. They weren't curious about her, they didn't care whether she got off or not. They weren't interested.

But he was.

It had never bothered her before since with all those other men, sex had only been a means to an end. Yet . . . it bothered her now.

Which left her with only one option. If she wanted to take control of this and still win, she had to turn his focus. Make him selfish. Make him desperate. Make him intent on nothing but his own pleasure. Difficult when she didn't know much about him. Then again, she'd picked up a few things during the past couple of hours. She had an inkling about what would get him panting for her.

He liked control, but even more than that, she suspected he liked a challenge.

Time to be that challenge.

"I think you like it," she murmured. "I think you like me pulling away. It gets you hot, makes you want to come after me. In fact, I bet that's what you're waiting for now. Why you're holding back."

His gaze roved over her. "What makes you think I'm holding back?"

"You're a man who takes what he wants and you haven't taken me yet." She gathered herself, shifting her weight onto the balls of her feet, ready to move, stripper shoes be damned. "Because you're waiting for me to run."

And sure enough, something ignited in his expression, a flare of intensity that had her already fast heartbeat accelerating.

"Ah." The word was soft, quiet. A mere exhalation of breath. "So what are you waiting for then?" There was something savage in his smile now. "Run, kitten. *Run.*"

She moved almost as soon as the words were out of his mouth. Fast. And he reached for her because she wasn't wrong, that's exactly what he'd been waiting for. Except he hadn't known it himself until she'd said it. Until he'd seen the muscles in her slender, supple body tense and felt his own raw, primal response.

He didn't know how she knew that about him, but she did. And maybe it should have concerned him that she was able to read him so easily. Yet concern was the last thing on his mind.

He wanted her. Holy fuck, he wanted her.

And when his fingers closed on empty air, he wanted her even more.

Christ, she was fast.

She was off to his left, her golden eyes glowing, her beautiful body all flushed and pink. He could still taste her on his tongue, sweet and hot, and his fingers were still wet from where they'd been buried in the liquid heat of her pussy.

Yeah, she wanted him. Despite how she pulled away from him, she wanted him. Her body didn't lie. Yet something was holding her back.

Well, he'd find out. He'd find out everything.

He made another grab for her, moving fast. And again she dodged out of the way, her body bending and shifting, supple as a stalk of grain bent by the wind.

"You're slow," she said, a taunting smile curving her mouth.

Bitch. Time to stop fucking around.

He lunged forward, lightning fast, a move she shouldn't have managed to escape from and yet somehow, his fingers once more closed on nothing.

She laughed, and he whirled around to find her standing behind him, near his armchair, grinning. "You'll have to do better than that. I'm not even running yet."

Excitement twined with desire, a low pulse deep inside him. So, she wasn't going to make this easy. Good. He'd been hoping she wouldn't. That she'd be something special, something that would test him.

He drew in a slow, silent breath, loosening his muscles. "You're not a stripper. You're not a dancer. What are you, kitten? An agent? CIA?" Because she had to be. She'd broken his hold on her earlier so easily and the way she moved now . . . Even dancers didn't move that fast.

"If you want to know that, you'll have to catch me." Gold glittered bright in her eyes, her muscles shifting and tensing beneath smooth, pale skin.

Again, there was no fear anywhere in her. Only . . . excitement. As if she was enjoying this as much as he was.

He smiled and moved, coming at her fast, watching her, trying to predict which way she'd go. She started to move right so he changed direction mid stride, his reflexes honed by long years of practice at the dirty street fighting he'd had to learn in order to claw his way to the top.

Yet, as he swept an arm out to hook around her waist, she dropped to her knees and rolled away, coming to her feet and dodging back quicker than he'd thought possible. Jesus Christ, this woman . . .

He didn't pause, coming straight for her, and she laughed again, leaping back and spinning, matching him move for move. It was like trying to catch air or grasp a handful of water. She kept shifting, staying just out of reach, and he had the impression that she was playing with him, as if he was a cat trying to catch the end of a piece of string she kept dangling in front of him.

No wonder she hadn't been afraid back in the club. No wonder she wore power and confidence like a cloak. If no one could catch her, no one could touch her. No one could hurt her.

Except he didn't want to hurt her. He wanted to make her scream.

He swept a foot out, hoping to trip her, but she only leaped like a dancer, spinning around and putting the coffee table between them. She grinned again, her skin bare and flushed and glowing with a light sheen of sweat. Her nipples were pink and hard, and there were coils of fire-red hair sticking to her shoulders. "Come on, Jericho. Who knew you'd be *that* slow?"

He was hard now, and it was almost painful. It was starting to make him lose patience.

You shouldn't be doing this. You shouldn't be enjoying this.

The voice was faint in his head, echoes of a past long gone. A past that would choke him in guilt if he thought too much about it. This wasn't the same though. This was different.

She wanted him. And she liked this just as much as he did.

"Am I slow?" He held her bright gaze. "Maybe I'm just trying to tire you out."

"Or maybe I'm just too fast for you." She lifted one hand, raking red curls away from her face. "Maybe you'd better start ordering me to do as you say, because I have to obey, right?"

Well, he could do that. But they both knew that would

cede her the victory and there was no fucking way he was going to do that. No, he was going to catch her fair and square.

He gave her no warning, leaping straight over the coffee table toward her, and he saw the flare of surprise in her eyes. But then she was turning, springing toward the sofa, one foot on the cushions, launching herself up and over the back of it like a gymnast.

Stopping would mean giving her time to plan, so he didn't stop, flinging himself forward, aiming for that slender ankle balanced on the couch cushions. And this time his fingers closed around warm, damp skin.

Satisfaction surged through him like a hit of cocaine, and he held on tight. She gave a cry, kicking back at him, but he dodged, jerking her foot out from under her at the same time. She turned as she fell, twisting onto her back, pulling her feet up to her chest. Her shoes had long gone and when he made another lunge for her, it was the soles of her feet that caught him, kicking him with such power that he flew back, crashing into the coffee table. The roses went flying, and the glass top of the table shattered as he fell heavily onto it, the unexpected strength of her kick winding him.

She didn't wait for him to recover, already leaping off the couch and dodging to one side to avoid the coffee table, aiming for the doors that lay behind him.

Adrenaline pumped hard inside him, wild and hot. He had no idea if she'd broken a rib with that kick of hers or whether his back was full of glass from the shattered coffee tabletop, but he didn't care. Only one thing burned in his brain—he had to catch her. He had to win.

He swept out a foot, heedless of the glass around him, tripping her as she moved past him and she went down, her body once again tucking into a ball and rolling as she hit the floor. He leaped to his feet, excitement burning alongside the adrenaline in his blood, moving fast to where she'd landed, behind one of the white armchairs.

Without pausing, he gripped the chair guarding her and hurled it out of his way. It crashed into the wall, knocking an expensive piece of art onto the floor. He didn't even notice, too intent on getting to the woman crouching behind it.

Her head came up, her golden eyes like flames, and she exploded out of her crouch, launching herself right at him.

The balls of her. Holy fuck.

She leaped, but his reflexes had always been fast, and this time he knew what to expect. She was going to climb him like a tree, using her own momentum and speed to launch herself over the top of him. As her foot connected with his thigh, her hand grabbing for his shoulder, he angled himself away at the last moment, knocking at her ankle with his forearm. As he'd hoped, her foot slipped, but he wasn't the only one with super-fast reflexes.

Again, she changed direction, letting herself fall heavily against him and pulling hard on his shoulder so he was bent over. At the same time, her knee came up, aiming straight for his groin.

Her scent hit him as he tried to grab her, warm and musky and sweet, her skin slippery with sweat. Desire rushed in like the tide, dizzying him, so that he almost let her knee him in the balls. But he managed to twist so her knee hit him in the gut instead, knocking the wind out of him.

God, she was strong.

He closed his arms around her, but he couldn't get a proper grip and was unable to dodge as she launched her fist to the underside of his jaw. It was like getting hit with a jackhammer. His head snapped back, stars exploding, pain radiating out. At the same time, she pulled herself out of his arms, dancing back, her hands up, ready to defend herself from retaliation.

His head rang and he blinked, staring at her. Fuck. The delicious little bitch had hit him. Had actually landed a punch on him. And it fucking *hurt*. Since when had anyone been able to touch him, let alone land a hit that actually hurt him? Not for years. Not for goddamn years.

Something spiked inside him, something raw and hot, and it wasn't anger. Christ, he felt . . . alive. More alive than he had in a long time. Almost as if he'd been awoken from a long, dark sleep by this woman. This burning, beautiful flame of a woman.

He was panting, his jaw aching, blood in his mouth. And his shirt was torn almost open, several of the buttons ripped away. He smiled, never taking his gaze off her. "You'll pay for that."

"Will I?" That same hot glitter was there in her eyes, the same thrill. The excitement of having met your match for what felt like the first time. "Only one problem with that. You still haven't caught me."

She hadn't even finished speaking, and yet she was moving, throwing herself toward him. But he'd seen the glance she'd flicked behind him. She was aiming for the doorway again.

This time he didn't bother trying to grab her. Instead he turned, heading for the doors at the same time she did, hurling himself in front of them as she tried to dodge him and grab for the door handle. He crashed against the wood, knocking away her hand as she aimed a hard punch to his face and avoiding her second fist, her knuckles landing hard on the door with a crunching sound.

He reached for her wrist, but she'd already snapped her hand away, dancing back from him.

Outside the door someone said, "Boss? Are you okay?"

Shit, that would be his guards. They must be wondering what the hell was going on.

Jericho leaned against the dented wood, panting, grinning savagely at the woman in front of him. "Anyone opens that door and I'll kill them," he ordered.

In the muted light of the room, Temple's naked body gleamed with sweat, red curls sticking to her forehead. Her eyes were on fire, great golden flames lighting up the night.

He'd never wanted a woman so badly in all his life.

After he'd killed off Theodore Fitzgerald, the man he'd once been, he'd spent a lot of time just trying to survive, going from town to town, earning cash under the table, making and breaking plans to take down his father over and over again. One thing he'd always been clear on though—if he was going to take down the biggest and baddest motherfucker on the planet, he needed to be bigger and badder.

So he'd found someone to teach him how to be dangerous, how to take his college boxing and turn it into something more lethal. How to kill. And even now, even when he had bodyguards and guns and a hundred mean and violent thugs at his beck and call, he never let himself become complacent. His skills were still as sharp and as honed as they had been the day he'd first heard about the man they called Jericho. The man he'd killed and then taken his place. The man he'd become.

No one had beaten him, not since that day, but this woman . . . Christ, she was good enough and just as lethal as he was.

He was going to enjoy taking her down.

Pushing himself away from the door, he advanced slowly. There wasn't anywhere for her to retreat to since there was broken glass at her back and she was barefoot. Which left her only two options. Head right or head left. She was right-handed, which would give her a natural inclination to head right, and yet, given her already obvious fighting skills, she was probably an expert in strategy too. Which meant she was likely to try a feint right then head left to catch him by surprise.

Sure enough, as he advanced, she feinted right.

He flicked out his left arm, catching her around the waist as she changed direction. She cursed, trying to duck under and slide away, but he twisted with her movement, pulling her into him. They fell and he twisted again so he was on his back and she was held to his front, protecting her pretty skin from the broken glass of the tabletop in the carpet. Full of adrenaline and desire and the wild thrill of the hunt, he felt nothing as he landed, glass crunching beneath him. There was only the heat of her body and the supple strength of it as she lifted her arm and drove an elbow into his gut.

He grunted in pain, unable to avoid the blow, tightening his hold on her. But she wasn't done. Her hips moved, grinding the softness of her bare ass against his by now painfully hard cock. Then the little bitch lifted her head and brought the back of it down hard on the bridge of his nose.

More stars, more pain exploding. And she'd managed to get free of him, rising to her feet, heading straight for the doors.

Jesus Christ. She'd beaten him to a pulp, and now she was going to escape.

No. Fucking. Way.

Ignoring the pain, he surged to his feet, the hunger for his prey driving him forward, and he lunged for her, grabbing her around the waist. She cursed and struggled, but this time he didn't make the mistake of holding onto her. Instead he turned and threw her bodily over the mess of glass on the white carpet and onto the couch. She landed on her hands and knees like a cat, muscles tightening in preparation for hurling herself away from him.

But as he'd tossed her, he'd followed, throwing himself on top of her on the couch, pinning her with his own body weight as he landed.

She was facedown, struggling beneath him, her lithe body all slippery and hot, every movement she made, every shift of her hips an agony as she pressed against his groin.

Adrenaline had him panting, had him desperate, and he put a firm hand on the back of her neck, holding her down as he leaned over her, his mouth near her ear. "I caught you, kitten. Which means now it's time to pay. So keep fucking still."

But she didn't. Her elbow came up, narrowly missing his nose, her back arching as she tried to throw him off.

Christ, she was lethal. He was going to have to do something about that.

Straddling her and keeping her pinned, he tore off the remains of his shirt, buttons popping off and bouncing away. Once it was off, he reached for her arms and jerked them behind her, into the small of her back. She gave a small cry of anger and pulled hard, trying to loosen his hold, but he wrapped the white cotton around her wrists, tying them expertly so no matter how fucking lethal she was, she couldn't get free.

Still, she tried, swearing viciously, the muscles of her arms straining as she tried to escape. It was no use, though. He knew how to tie a person up so that no amount of struggling would help.

"I told you you'd pay," he murmured as she bucked beneath him, trying to shake him off. "I warned you."

"Fuck you." Her voice was hoarse, muffled. "Prick."

"And you're a sore loser." He flexed his hips, pressing his aching dick against the softness of her ass, glorying in the feel of her heat, in the anticipation of what he was going to do.

She shivered, and for a second he thought it was over, that she was going to be quiet and still. That he'd won. He was almost disappointed.

And then she bucked hard, kicking with her legs, nearly shaking him off.

He laughed, unable to help it, the thrill of the chase, of the hunt, electric inside him. Quelling her was going to take more than bound wrists clearly and thank fucking God, because he was ready for this to be over. He didn't want quiescence. He wanted the fight.

Reaching for one of the stupid little cushions whoever had decorated this mansion of his decided was a good idea, he ripped the white silk apart with his bare hands. Then, discarding the cushion filling, he tore the cushion cover into strips. Shifting his posture, he turned around, keeping his weight planted firmly on the small of her back to keep her still, running his hands down the length of her toned, muscled thighs, wrapping white silk around her knees, pulling it tight and knotting it. Then doing the same for her ankles.

A shudder went through her, a gasping, panting breath. "What the hell are you doing? You don't need to tie me." There was a hoarse edge to her voice, one that sounded like desperation.

He shifted again, straddling her once more so her butt was pressed hard to his groin, his knees pressing into the couch cushions on either side of her thighs. Something warm slid over his top lip and there was more blood in his mouth.

"Are you fucking kidding me? You nearly broke my nose." He reached for what was left of the white silk cushion cover and wiped his mouth with it. The fabric came away stained red.

This woman . . . She'd nearly broken a rib, his jaw, and

his nose. And catching her had almost destroyed this room. He was bleeding, he'd probably have a black eye later, it hurt to breathe, and he was sure his back was full of broken glass.

And he was so hard he could barely think. The thrill inside him deep, primal, savage.

The pain and the desire was a bright blade of sensation, cutting away the nothingness that had surrounded him for so long, hacking it apart like an ax hacking at the dead wood of a tree. Leaving behind living growth. Leaving behind life.

He looked down at the woman beneath him, the long, elegant curve of her spine, the graceful sweep of her shoulders, the bonfire of her hair cascading everywhere. Even now she was fighting, moving against him, trying to loosen the fabric he'd tied around her.

"Serves you right, asshole," she panted. "Untie me."

"Fuck, no." He ran a hand over her ass, her skin slippery and hot beneath his palm, and she shuddered again, her hips shifting, pressing back against his dick. "I think I'm going to keep you all tied up and at my mercy."

Jesus, it was getting difficult to think. Difficult to even breathe. Because he could smell her musk and a soft, sweet scent that he couldn't place. Could feel the heat of her beneath him like the promise of a fire on a cold winter's day. And it had been so long, so *fucking long*.

"Bastard." Her voice sounded raw. "Is that what you like? Helpless women? I knew it. Of course you do."

He laughed and leaned forward, discarding the bloodstained silk, putting one hand near her head and bending over her, bracing himself. "No, Temple," he murmured near her ear. "I don't want a helpless woman. I want a woman who can fight me. Who can match me." He pushed the hard ridge of his cock against her ass, making sure she felt it. "I'm not hard because you're helpless. I'm hard because you fought. Because I had to work to bring you down."

Her head was turned to the side, the curve of her cheek deeply flushed with exertion and he could see the golden gleam of rage in her eyes.

"I'll untie you," he went on softly. "But only if you stop fighting." Another pause, watching her. "Are you going to stop?"

You don't want her to. You want her to keep struggling. You sick fuck.

Something caught inside him, something skipped a beat.

But then she drew a ragged, harsh breath, her body tensing beneath his, and the thought disappeared. "No," she gasped out. "No, I'm not going to stop."

He grinned as her muscles gathered and tightened, as her back bowed and she bucked like a horse trying to get rid of its rider. She was tenacious, determined as he was, and fuck, this was better than alcohol. Better than drugs. This was better than anything that could be bought or sold or mixed together in a chemist's lab.

This was what he'd been craving and didn't even know it.

"In that case . . ." He drew back one hand and slapped her on one ass cheek, the hard crack of his hand on her flesh resounding in the room. "An eye for an eye, kitten."

She cursed, savagely, and tried even harder to dislodge him. So he hit her again, her skin flushing red under his palm. "Bastard," she gasped. "Fucking bastard!"

But he only laughed, sliding his hand down the curve of her ass, his fingers finding the heat between her thighs, finding the truth. Christ, she was so wet, so slippery and hot. "Protest all you want, little girl," he growled, sliding a finger inside her pussy. "You want this as much as I do."

Temple groaned, her hips jerking, trying to pull away, but he only leaned harder on her, using his weight to hold her in place. Her bound wrists lifted, so he took those with his free hand and pinned them too, keeping her immobilized as he sunk another finger deep.

He hadn't touched a woman like this in years, and he'd forgotten how erotic it was. How tight and slick a woman's sex was when she was aroused, how it clenched around his fingers, and how she gasped as he drew his hand back, fingers sliding almost out of her before pushing back in. Again. And again.

"Oh . . . F-F-Fuck . . ." Her voice was anguished, like she was in pain. But there was no mistaking the wetness of her against his skin, no mistaking the heat.

He tortured her with his fingers, sliding them in and out, punishing her for the punches she'd dealt him, for the bloody nose, for the glass in his back. And her hips flexed, matching the movement of his hand, her breathing harsh.

His mouth curled in a savage smile as he watched her. Hell yes. He wanted to keep going, making her scream with his hand alone, watch her come apart completely. But his body had waited too long. And so had he.

Keeping her wrists pressed into the small of her back, he slid his fingers out of her and leaned over to the remains of the coffee table. There was a drawer beneath it, with a small stash of condoms inside that he kept mainly for his clients' use in case they got caught short. The drawer was now full of glass from the shattered tabletop, but luckily the condom packets were still intact.

Grabbing one, he tore apart the packet with his teeth and took out the condom. Then he jerked the zipper of his pants down, pulling his boxers down too, getting out his cock and rolling the latex down.

Temple was still moving, down but clearly not out. She was trying to draw her knees under her, maybe so she could shove herself up and perhaps shake him off. God, he couldn't help but admire the way she refused to give up.

An incredibly dangerous woman and yet here she was, bound for his pleasure.

Desire was like a vice, squeezing him, nearly choking him. Wrapping around the pain of his jaw and his nose and his back, twining with it to create something so inescapable, so erotic, he was helpless to resist it.

Looping an arm around her waist, he hauled her ass back against his groin, then he positioned himself, the tip of his cock pressing lightly against the entrance of her body. She stiffened then tried to get her knees under her again, exactly as he'd expected her to do. So he leaned over her, putting one hand on the back of her neck, pressing down, holding her still.

Then he thrust hard. Deep. Slamming himself into her.

She jerked, a hoarse cry escaping her.

And fucking finally the wet heat of her pussy was around him, clamping down hard on his cock. Almost too much.

He stopped, dizzy with sensation, his lungs working hard just to get some goddamn air, the beat of his own heart raging in his head. Had it been like this the last time? Had it *ever* been like this?

No, he knew the answer to that. It hadn't.

She bucked against him, still fighting, prompting another erotic surge, and he almost groaned. Jesus, this woman was going to kill him.

She could kill you with her bare hands, you realize.

Yeah, well, that was obvious now. But he'd deal with that later. Right at the moment, he just wanted to fuck her senseless.

He withdrew then pushed back in, another hard, deep thrust. What he could see of her face was deeply flushed, coppery gold lashes lying on her cheeks. Her mouth was open, her lips full and soft, and as he thrust again, her expression twisted in agonized pleasure, another cry coming from her.

Beautiful. Goddamn beautiful.

Pleasure was a live electric current winding through his body, shocking his deadened senses awake, bringing them back to life. The air in his lungs felt brand new, the musky scent of aroused woman, of sex, of his own blood the sweetest thing he'd ever smelled.

He moved again, harder, deeper, driving himself into her, feeling her muscles tense as she tried to push back against him. But he didn't let her. He kept her immobile with the weight of his body and the hand on the back of her neck, holding her down, making her take everything.

"N-no . . ." She sounded ragged, raw. "Oh God . . . no . . . I . . . please . . ."

"You want me to stop, kitten?" He bent his head so his lips were near her ear, taunting her as he thrust, not pausing, not letting up. "Is that what you're trying to say? Have you had enough already?"

She shook her head violently. "N-no . . ." Another harsh, panting breath. "I didn't say it. D-don't stop . . . Oh God . . . don't fucking stop."

He laughed, a twisted, savage sound. That was a surrender, and they both knew it.

Running a hand over her hip, he slid it around and under her, so his palm was against her stomach, feeling toned and powerful abdominal muscles tense as he did so. Then he eased down farther, his fingers finding the soft heat and wetness of her pussy, the hard bud of her clit.

She gave a hoarse little sob, her body shaking as he began to circle and tease it, stroking her ruthlessly, pushing his cock into her as he did so, deep, savage thrusts that pressed her down into the cushions. And she fought him, right to the end she fought him.

But he only gripped the back of her neck, kept up the pressure on her clit, stroking her roughly as he continued to drive himself inside her.

"Tell me to stop," he murmured hoarsely in her ear. "That's all you need to do. Just one word and I'll let you go."

But she turned her head away, burying her face in the cushions of the couch, and he felt it as her pussy clenched hard around his cock, as she shook like a tree in a hurricane. Her scream of release audible even through she was trying to muffle it. And even though it wasn't the word he was hoping to hear, savage satisfaction turned over inside him nevertheless.

He leaned his weight into her, thrusting faster, pinning her body, making her take him.

It was so good, so fucking good. He felt like a god, he felt like himself. He felt free after too many years buried alive.

You're a fucking monster.

Yeah, well, that was what he was. And maybe he'd been a fool to deny it all these years, to pretend there was something left of the man he'd once been.

Maybe it was time to embrace the darkness.

She bucked against him, her sex squeezing him tight, but he didn't let her go. He fucked her hard and without mercy, and when the climax hit him he thrust his fist into her hair, jerked her head back, and bit her throat like the animal he was.

She screamed again and it wasn't with pain, not when he could feel her body convulsing around his a second time, another orgasm shaking her.

And he was aware of only one thing.

One night wouldn't be enough.

CHAPTER SIX

Temple pressed her face into the couch cushions, not caring that she couldn't breathe or that doing so made the grip Jericho had on her hair even more painful. It was either that or she burst into tears, and there was no fucking way she was going to do that.

She didn't even know why she felt that way, not when it was only sex. Only an orgasm.

Two orgasms. You came when he bit you, when he held you so you couldn't move. You wanted him to do it, you wanted him to take control . . .

She screwed her eyes shut tight, focusing on the hot darkness behind her closed lids because that was better than feeling the hard length of his cock still deep inside her, or the furnace heat of his body against the bare backs of her thighs. Or the weird release of emotion that flooded through her chest.

She hadn't cried for years, not since the day her father had told her what he'd done with Thalia, the day she finally understood what her older sister had been protecting her from. So she wasn't going to cry now, not after a stupid orgasm.

The main thing was that she hadn't broken. She hadn't told him to stop. It was a victory, wasn't it?

Behind her, she felt him shift at last, the pressure easing

as he released her hair, withdrawing from her. Now would be the time to roll over and make some snarky, sarcastic comment, but she couldn't seem to bring herself to move. The darkness was easier.

The couch dipped, the heat behind her disappearing, cool air against her skin, and she was trembling with some kind of belated reaction.

Get yourself the fuck together.

She slowed her breathing, trying to get a handle on her out-of-control emotions and failing. Anger surged inside her, the frustrated rage of a warrior who'd been bested. Because no one had managed to beat her, not since she'd managed to take down Jackson, her old mentor and the man who'd taught her to fight, himself. No one had been good enough.

Apparently Jericho is. And now you've given yourself away completely. Well done.

Something else twined through the rage, that unfamiliar sense of panic she'd felt back at the strip club. She *had* given herself away. She should never have fought him like that and yet . . . she just hadn't been able to stop herself.

It had been a long time since she'd been tested, since she'd met someone who was a match for her. And it had been exciting, thrilling.

A turn on.

She scrunched her eyes up tighter, trying to ignore the tingling electric shocks left over from those orgasms and the deep clench inside of her at the memory of his powerful hand on the back of her neck. At the hard thrust of him inside her. At the way she was held immobile, leaving her with no choice but take what he gave her. The pleasure so bright and blinding it felt like it was going to rip her apart. Making her want to beg him to stop—

No. No. She wouldn't think of that. She wouldn't think of how close she'd come to breaking. She'd only meant to taunt him into taking her selfishly, for himself. So he wouldn't turn that relentless focus on her. And she'd thought when he'd finally brought her down on the couch, that's exactly what she'd done. Except . . .

You didn't expect to enjoy the way he matched you. You didn't expect to be angry that he beat you. And you certainly didn't expect to love the way he fucked you.

Temple groaned and turned her head to the side, sucking in some air, trying not to think about it.

The room was silent.

She blinked away the moisture in her eyes and carefully rolled herself over.

There was nobody there, the room empty. She was alone.

Thank God.

She sat up, straining to get rid of the fabric he'd wrapped around her wrists, but there was no give in it and attempting to slide her wrists free only seemed to draw the knot tighter. The evil prick. What the hell kind of knot was it?

After a futile minute or two, she had to admit defeat and just sat there on the couch, panting, surveying the rest of the room that they'd apparently destroyed during their fight.

The coffee table was shattered, glass glittering on the carpet. The roses were scattered and crushed, the vase they'd been sitting in also broken. One of the armchairs lay upside down against a wall, a fallen painting lying on top of it, the glass cracked. A cushion filling lay on the carpet amid the broken glass and water from the roses, threads of white silk everywhere. Dots of red stained the carpet. Blood.

Jesus. It didn't look like a perfectly decorated, tasteful French drawing room anymore. It looked like a bomb had exploded in it.

At that moment, the door opened, and Jericho came

back in from wherever he'd gone, carrying what looked like a shirt in one hand.

Temple stared at him. There were bloodstains under his nose, a cut on his lip, a darkening bruise on his jaw and around one eye. Her marks on him.

He paused in the doorway, meeting her gaze. And he smiled, a wicked, dark, savage smile that had something inside her shivering with excitement and anticipation.

No. God, no. Not again.

"See what you did to me?" he said in that low, purring voice. "You gave as good as you got." There was no anger in his expression, and the look in his eyes . . . Shit. They weren't cold any longer. Embers of gold smoldered there, as if all it would take was one breath to make them catch alight.

Yes, you want to catch alight too. You want to burn.

She gritted her teeth, forced the thought from her head. "Well, you deserved it. How about you untie me now that you got what you wanted?"

His smile deepened, and he moved over to her, avoiding all the broken glass and crushed flowers, coming to stand in front of the couch.

And despite herself, her breath caught. Because he was bare to the waist, all smooth tanned golden skin and the kind of broad chest and sculpted abs that spoke of long hours spent in the gym. Except, given the fact he'd actually managed to catch her and hold her down in submission, she didn't think he'd spent hours lifting weights. No, she'd bet anything he practiced some form of martial arts.

His pants sat low on his lean hips, only partially zipped, giving her a tantalizing glimpse of the crisp golden hair arrowing down his flat abdomen and disappearing beneath the black wool. The definite outline of his cock pressing against his zipper showed that he was still semi-hard.

Her mouth dried. He was so fucking beautiful it hurt.

And that was wrong. There should be nothing beautiful about a man like him. Nothing that she should want.

"Hmmm. No, I don't think I will." He sank down on his haunches in front of her, the shirt he was carrying still held tight in one fist, all coiled power and tightly leashed strength. "I caught you, Temple, which means you have to give me the truth."

"That wasn't the deal. I had to tell you to stop."

"I don't believe we agreed on the details." He reached out, sliding his free hand up her thigh, making everything inside her clench hard with desire. "Something tells me you're not just a dancer trying to make ends meet, hmmm?"

She made herself smile back at him, not giving anything away, though part of her whispered that was pointless when she'd revealed so much already. "Untie me and I'll tell you everything."

He laughed and the desire inside her twisted at the dark eroticism of the sound. "Always with the bargains, kitten. No, I think we've come to the end of bargains. I want to know who you are and you know I can make you talk. I don't need to use pain to do it." His fingers moved higher, brushing the inside of her thigh, sending shivers of helpless pleasure through her. Proving his point.

Asshole.

She stared into his eyes. The glowing embers of heat were still there, but behind them burned something else, an implacable will, a determination like a force of nature. Nothing would stop this man from his goal, nothing would keep him from it.

He was like her.

Who am I? I'm the woman who's here to kill you.

No, she couldn't tell him that. He probably already suspected, given the fight she'd put up, but even so, she wasn't going to give him a heads-up on what she intended. Then again she had to give him something. Because that look in his eyes was clear: He wasn't going to give up, not until he'd taken her apart even more thoroughly than he already had.

She was silent a moment, turning it over in her head. Then she said, "I'm here for information."

His gaze narrowed. "What information?"

"I'm looking for someone. And apparently you're the man to ask when it comes to finding people who've gone missing."

She couldn't tell what was going on behind those fascinating eyes of his, the expression on his face completely enigmatic. "Who?" The dark sexiness had faded from his voice, the question hard, curt. An order.

Before she could answer, a cell phone started to ring.

Jericho stared at her silently, something intense in his gaze. Then he cursed and let her go. Straightening, he reached into his pocket and pulled out his phone, glancing down at the screen before hitting a button. He answered in Russian, turning away, his beautiful voice cold as he asked a question.

She let out a breath she didn't know she'd been holding, keeping half an ear on his conversation despite the fact she couldn't understand it. Shit, she should have learned a few languages. That would have come in handy right about now.

Telling him about Thalia though . . . She really didn't want to give out her sister's name. Didn't want to reveal her own relationship to her either, because there was no telling how he'd use that information. Keeping it impersonal and distant was the only way.

Like he's seriously going to tell you?

She looked up at him. He was turned away from her, giving her his broad back. A full-color Chinese tattoo had been inked into his golden skin, covering most of his back. It was of a tiger climbing a rock, its head turned, its mouth open, snarling at the world. It was strong and so achingly beautiful, just like the rest of him.

Then her gaze narrowed. Hidden in the colors of the tattoo were a lot of dark spots that looked like . . . blood. In fact, now that she looked closer, she saw that there were many small cuts all over his back, some of them long and ragged. And then she remembered how he'd caught her as she'd leaped at him, holding on tight and turning them both over as they fell so that she'd landed on top of him.

The glass in the carpet. He must have fallen on it.

She blinked as another thought slowly made its way into her consciousness. He'd turned so he was the one who'd taken the brunt of the fall, who'd taken the cuts from the glass. He'd protected her from it.

Just like he protected you from that Russian asshole and his wandering hands.

A feeling she didn't want to name or even acknowledge shifted in her chest.

Only one person in her life had ever protected her and that was Thalia. And after Thalia had gone, she'd had no one. Only herself. And that had been enough, more than enough. She didn't need anyone else.

But you like it all the same.

No. No, she didn't. Anyway, he wasn't a man who protected women. He was a man who hurt them.

Jericho finished his conversation with a curt word, turning back as he returned his phone to his pocket. "The Lychenkos are causing issues at the club. I need to deal with them." He came over to her and tossing the shirt he was holding onto the couch beside her, he bent, pulling at the white cotton around her wrists before moving on to where she was tied around her thighs and ankles, undoing the knots quickly. "You will stay here."

She lifted a shoulder, rubbing at her wrists absently. "I'm not planning on going anywhere yet."

He eyed her a moment. "Get up."

"Back to the control part of the evening, I see." Nevertheless, she did what she was told, getting slowly to her feet.

"Arms out."

She stared at him. "What?"

Letting out an impatient breath, he picked up the shirt he'd dropped onto the couch then, without any fuss at all, began to dress her in it.

Temple opened her mouth to protest, but by the time she'd gotten over the shock, he was already doing the buttons up. She blinked, not quite sure how to take this. It seemed . . . odd. He hadn't covered her up as they'd left the club and that was in public, so why now?

His head was bent, his movements deft and focused, and the scent of him, warm and spicy, made her momentarily dizzy. Enough that she just stood there and let him finish doing the buttons up, dressing her like she was a child.

As he finished the last button, he stepped back then strode over to the door where there was an electronic panel on the wall. He pressed a button, issued some kind of order in French, then turned back to her, the look on his face unreadable.

Almost instantly, the door of the lounge opened and three guards came in, all with semi-automatics slung over their shoulders. Jericho said something to them, again in French, then he glanced at her. "The guards will escort you to my room," he said in English. "And they'll make sure you stay there."

So. She was to be a prisoner. Unsurprising. "I told you I have no plans for going anywhere else. Isn't three guards a little over the top?"

"I'm not stupid, kitten, don't treat me as such." A green

spark glinted deep in his eyes. "Especially after you nearly broke my nose. One guard won't be nearly enough."

Okay, so no, he wasn't stupid.

"Guess that cat's pretty much out of the bag then."

Jericho murmured something, and the guards all swung their semis around, pointing them directly at her.

She folded her arms, not giving the guns the slightest bit of notice, staring at him instead. "I thought I was going to be escorted to your room? Or have you decided that killing me is easier?"

"I don't want to kill you, Temple. You're mine for the night, remember? Besides, I don't have any of the answers I want from you yet."

"Then you don't need the guns or any of this heavy shit. I told you, I'm here for information. And I'm not going anywhere until I get it." She paused a moment, sweeping her gaze over him, making sure he knew that she wasn't in any way cowed. "I'm not going to kill you if that's what you're afraid of." May as well name it, say it out loud.

One corner of his mouth curled, as if he was in on the joke. "Oh, I'm not afraid. Trust, though, is a different story and I don't trust anyone. Least of all you." He glanced at the guards and said something sharp, then he turned and before she could say anything more, strode from the room, leaving her staring down the muzzles of three guns.

One of the guards jerked his head toward the door, his meaning clear. Time to move.

She went, because although she could probably have taken all three out, they were armed and that weighed the odds in their favor. And she wasn't into odds like that, not quite yet, not when she hadn't figured out what had happened to Thalia.

They took her upstairs and pushed her unceremoniously into a large room, locking the heavy wooden door behind her. She didn't bother trying to see if she could unlock the door, turning instead to give the room a quick scan.

It was massive and decorated with the kind of low-key opulence that was only within the reach of the super-rich. The floor was dark, old parquet covered with silk rugs from the Middle East, and on the ivory walls, paintings were hung. She didn't know who the painters were, but given the heavy gilt frames, she thought they were probably very important.

Across the room, tall windows faced the street, an arrangement of white armchairs with a dark wood coffee table gathered beneath them. And in the center of the room, pushed up against the wall, beneath a huge painting of a man on horseback wielding a sword, was a massive dark oak bed, piled high with white pillows and a thick white quilt.

Temple narrowed her gaze, scanning the room again. Yes, it was luxurious, no question, but it was also completely impersonal. There were no clothes over the backs of the chairs, none on the bed either. No shoes lying on the floor. No photos on the antique oak nightstand by the bed and none on the matching oak dresser.

It was like a hotel room. There was no personality to it at all. It even smelled of . . . absence.

If this was Jericho's room then he hardly ever slept in it, if he even did at all.

She paced over to the windows, checking the catches. There were locks on them, electronic and heavy-duty, and not ones she could get open. She was betting the glass was bulletproof, as well.

Putting her hands on the sill, she peered out into the night beyond. A dark garden lay beneath, surrounded by high stone walls, and every now and then she caught the movement of a shadow around the perimeter. Guards.

Escape would be difficult. Not impossible certainly, but difficult.

She turned around and began another check on the room, going through the drawers in the dresser and finding nothing but neatly folded masculine clothes. Jericho's? But then who knew? There was nothing in the nightstand drawer at all.

Interesting. He didn't sleep here, hell, he barely even lived here.

A sliding door on one wall revealed a huge walk-in closet, but again, despite an in-depth search, she found nothing but more clothes. Suits and business shirts mainly. If these were Jericho's then he had boring taste in clothes, that was for sure.

Another door led into a huge, ornate bathroom with a big, white marble tub and a shower big enough for four or more people at least.

Temple stood for a moment in the bathroom doorway, debating what to do, not that she could do much given that she was locked in this room. But a plan for what she was going to do when he got back would be good.

She couldn't let herself slip again, be broken open again, not the way he had downstairs. She couldn't afford to give away any more secrets. Already she'd revealed far more than she'd initially intended.

You didn't know what he'd be like. You didn't know you'd want him.

Her jaw tightened. Fighting him had been exhilarating and she'd let herself get carried away—too carried away. And going down like that on the sofa, letting him screw her the way he had . . . Jesus. Sure, she'd expected she'd have to fuck him at some point, but not like that. Not screaming into the cushions as he'd made her come.

Letting out a breath, she attempted to calm herself. Okay, so none of this had gone the way she'd planned, but that was okay. She'd adjust her approach, no biggie.

Anyway, nothing had changed. Find out what had

happened to Thalia. Kill the evil crime lord asshole who'd taken her. Get back to Zac Rutherford and his friends, and claim the money. That's all.

She was exactly where she'd meant to be. In his house. Close to him. And he clearly was intending to keep her for the night. It was all good.

The only thing she needed to figure out was how to play their next round.

He'd want to know who she was, especially now that he'd realized she wasn't exactly defenseless. Which meant the pressure was on in terms of getting the information she needed out of him. She had to get it and get it fast, then do what she'd come here to do: kill the son of bitch.

But how to get it out of him?

He's curious. He likes to be challenged and he likes a fight. And he wants you . . .

Sex was the obvious answer. That had always been her plan, after all, even before she'd come face-to-face with him. Seduce him, get him to tell her everything she wanted to know, then kill him. Easy.

Not so easy. Not given what he did to you downstairs.

No, he'd done *nothing* to her downstairs, only given her an orgasm. It didn't mean shit. But she wasn't going to slip up again. Next time he touched her, she'd be ostensibly welcoming, lulling him into a false sense of security, getting him to drop his guard.

Then she'd either lay an arm across his throat or close her fist around his balls and get him to spill his guts. Her own secrets would stay safe, but this time, *he'd* be the one broken open. *He'd* be the one with his head buried in the couch cushions fighting tears.

She'd make sure of it.

"The woman is dangerous." Dmitri delivered the observation in his customary flat tone.

Jericho raised an eyebrow at him. "You think I don't know that? Do you not see what she did to my face?" He shifted then winced. "Not to mention my back."

They were driving back to Jericho's house from the club, dawn breaking clean and crisp over the city. A pink and gold sunrise gilded old buildings and ancient spires, distracting from the dirt and decay of the streets, highlighting the beauty of the city.

Jericho loved Paris, always had. Which was why he'd made it the center of his operations. The home of artists and dissidents, poets and politicians, it had always seemed like a city where a person could do anything, be anyone. Where ideas and greatness could be born.

Or a place for a monster to hide.

Yeah, well, pity it had turned out that way for him. The only idea that had been born to him was the plan he'd formulated the day he'd come here, the one that had involved taking out the man who'd been Jericho before him. The only greatness, the end to that plan. The fall of the trafficking network that spanned countries and continents.

Nothing else mattered. Nothing else even came close to mattering.

Least of all one woman who'd given him the fight of his life and the bruises to prove it.

"She's a threat." Dmitri glowered at him. "She looks like an assassin."

Jericho had known Dmitri ten years, ever since the Russian had appeared as one of the former Jericho's new recruits. Recognizing something of himself in Dmitri, that drive for revenge, Jericho had befriended him and eventually, after the Russian had ended up saving his life after a job gone wrong, he'd revealed his plans to the other man. It had been a risk, but he knew he couldn't do it on his own, that he needed help.

The risk had paid off and Dmitri had become the only

other person he trusted in the entirety of the empire he'd claimed for himself. Yet even so he kept his real identity as Theodore Fitzgerald hidden. No one knew that and no one would. If only to keep Violet safe.

Jericho turned his attention to the city outside the windows of the limo. "Don't think it hasn't crossed my mind." He'd in fact been thinking about it all night.

From the moment he'd left his house to the moment he'd left the club, his head had been completely full of her. Of Temple and the mystery she represented.

A woman who'd fought him, had managed to get not only one but several hits on him. Who'd then let him tie her up and screw her on the couch—and she'd definitely *let* him. If she hadn't wanted him to do that to her, he had a feeling one or the other of them would be dead now, he had no doubt. Yeah, she was definitely lethal. But if she'd been there to kill him, she'd had ample opportunity and yet hadn't made a move.

Yet. There's still time.

"She wants information," he said, keeping his gaze on the city as the car maneuvered through the narrow streets. "Which makes me think she's not going to do anything until she gets it."

"What kind of information?"

"Well, if the Lychenkos hadn't been such pains in my fucking ass, I would have found out."

He'd had to spend all night in the club reassuring and soothing Vassily's ruffled feathers. The older man had started to make a big deal of the fact that he'd threatened to cut off Vassily's nephew's hand purely for the sake of a woman, that Jericho himself needed to know who his bastard lieutenant was threatening. Jericho didn't reveal that the bastard lieutenant wasn't actually a lieutenant at all, but Jericho himself—his real identity had to stay secret. But when Vassily had started threatening to pull his family's support from the American venture, he'd had to do something.

It was trouble he didn't need, not now, not when he'd worked so hard to get the Russians on board in the first place, and as much as he needed to figure out the mysterious Temple, he couldn't afford for the Lychenkos to pull out. Luckily, pouring as much vodka down the older man's throat as he could, while making sure his nephew forgot about the threat to his hand with his pick of the club girls, had seemed to do the trick.

"Give her to me," Dmitri said. "I'll find out what she's up to."

"No." The answer was automatic. "She's mine."

"She's dangerous."

Jericho finally lifted his gaze from the city and met his bodyguard's disapproving dark stare. "So you keep saying. But like *I* keep saying, the answer is no." He didn't want to examine why he felt so possessive of her, but nevertheless, he felt it. As if she was a secret he'd discovered, a wonderful, terrible, exhilarating secret he wanted to keep to himself, if only for a little while.

A deep thrill twisted in his gut, the excitement of the earlier fight with her and the explosive sex afterward lingering like a smoldering fire in his bloodstream. Ready to catch alight again at the slightest touch.

Dmitri snorted. "You should have put her under guard if she was a threat, not choose her for the night. There were other girls who could have used rescuing."

Yes, that was true. He could have. But he hadn't and there were no good, altruistic reasons for why he hadn't done so. He'd chosen her because she was different. Because he was intrigued. Because he wanted her.

You can't afford to think of yourself. You know this. You've always known this.

He did. But this was only one night. And he hadn't

taken anything for himself for a long time. Besides, she was a threat and he needed to find out the extent of that threat, especially if his bodyguard was right and she was aiming for him.

He had no problem with dying. He just didn't want to do it before he'd managed to do what he'd been preparing for these past sixteen years.

"Those other girls will be rescued eventually," he said, eyeing the other man. "What exactly is your problem with her, Dmitri? Do you want her? Is that it?"

Dmitri's frown became ferocious. "No."

"Good, because you can't have her."

"I'm your bodyguard. My job is to protect you. And she is—"

"Yes, yes. She's dangerous. I get it. But you forget I've managed to survive for years in a job that hasn't exactly got a high survival rate. I think I can outlast one small red-head."

Dmitri's frown didn't lift. "You want her," he said flatly.

Well, Jericho supposed it was obvious. "So?"

"You haven't wanted a woman in years."

Goddammit. Dmitri was too fucking observant. "Again, so?"

"She'll distract you, get under your guard."

Dmitri meant well, Jericho knew that, but still. The man was crossing the line. "Noted, Dmitri." He held the Russian's gaze. "But the subject is now closed. Understood?"

The bodyguard grunted in response, his expression even more disapproving.

Too fucking bad. It had been years since Jericho had felt challenged. Christ, years since he'd been able to get it up for any woman at all, and now he'd found one he could get it up for, he wasn't letting her go so easily.

Besides, if she was here to kill him, as Dmitri seemed to imply, then the best way to keep an eye on her was to keep her close. Friends close, enemies closer and all that bullshit.

First, he'd find out who she was. Second, he'd find out what this information she wanted was. Third . . . well, then he'd cross that bridge when he came to it. But he had an idea it would involve more of her beneath him, more of him inside that sweet, tight little pussy of hers . . .

His cell rang.

Dmitri continued to glower, while Jericho pulled out the phone and looked down at the screen. Fuck, it was Roth, one of his lieutenants. And if he was calling directly, it meant this was not going to be good.

Hitting the accept button, he answered the call. "What?"

"It's Elijah Hunt," Roth said without preamble. "He's started taking down some of the Southern network."

Anger flared, unexpected and hot. Fuck. *Fuck*. Hunt had been Evelyn Fitzgerald's right-hand man until Fitzgerald had been murdered and Jericho should have had the asshole killed weeks ago, but he'd left him alone for one reason and one reason only: Violet. Jericho's sister, whom he'd tried to save and who, as it turned out, had preferred to ally herself with Hunt instead of him.

A stupid move not to kill Hunt, as it turned out. What the hell was the guy doing? He'd gotten word that Hunt was taking over, filling the power vacuum left by Fitzgerald's death, and Jericho been gearing himself up for the fact that he was going to have to open negotiations with the prick.

But clearly the man wasn't there to take over Jericho's asshole of a father's empire for the sake of power. He was there to end it.

This shouldn't come as a surprise. Violet wouldn't be with him otherwise.

Jericho ended the call without another word, throwing the phone down on the seat beside them, then looking out the window again. The sun was stretching over the Seine, turning the water into a sheet of silvered glass.

"What is it?" Dmitri asked, picking up on his anger.

"It's Hunt," he replied shortly. "Looks like he's started dismantling the American network."

There was a silence. Then Dmitri said, "We have to stop him."

"Yes." He didn't say anything more because there wasn't anything more to be said.

They *did* have to stop him. Because if any of Jericho's painstakingly built alliances heard that the American trafficking networks were under threat, they'd pull out. The Russians especially wouldn't hesitate, not when they were already looking for an excuse to leave, and if they went, then so would the others.

He'd lose them all. Everything he'd been working toward for so long.

Ah, fuck, this was the worst news possible. If they pulled out, if the network of alliances he'd slowly built over the past sixteen years started disintegrating, he was screwed and so was his plan.

"Organize my jet," he said after a moment. "I'll want to leave for the States as soon as possible."

"A personal visit?" Dmitri's gaze narrowed. "Again? Are you sure that's wise?"

No, it wasn't. Not so soon after the last visit. He didn't like revealing himself to too many people because the more people who knew who he was, the greater the chance of one of them taking him out. The man who'd been Jericho before him had built up quite a smokescreen of rumor and misinformation, all designed to hide his real identity, to make killing him as hard as possible, and when Theo had taken over, he'd carried on the tradition.

But he didn't have much of a choice now. There was the option of sending someone to take Hunt out, yet that would involve hurting Violet, who was in love with the guy. And he didn't think he could do that.

Good to know there's still some of your conscience left.

Maybe that was a bad thing, though. Maybe this would have all been a lot easier if he'd gotten rid of his conscience the way he'd gotten rid of so many other aspects of himself.

It's not too late. You can still order a hit.

"No," Jericho murmured, watching an early-morning jogger keep pace with the limo for a little while. "It's not wise. But sometimes the personal touch is needed."

"I can take him out for you," Dmitri offered. "That would solve things."

It would. So many things. Then he could move in, put one of his men in Hunt's place, take control finally of his father's empire, put the last piece of the jigsaw puzzle in place.

And you would hurt Violet more deeply than anything else would. How does that make you different from him?

The jogger was a woman, with short, spiky blond hair. If he squinted, he could almost pretend it was Violet the last time he'd seen her, with her hair cut short and despair in her blue eyes.

Violet, who'd flung herself between him and the gun Hunt had pointed at him.

Violet, who'd tried to save him, despite the fact she'd known who he was and what he'd become.

He couldn't tell her the truth about what he was doing, because that would put her in the firing line if the shit hit the fan, and there was no way he'd do that. Even if she thought he was a monster.

So? You are.

Yeah, he was. But not today.

"No," he said, as the jogger fell behind the limo. "I'll handle it myself."

Dmitri was silent, but Jericho could feel his disapproval. Too goddamn bad. His way was the only way and it remained so while he was in charge.

What about Temple?

Thoughts of his sister vanished as the fire in his blood woke to aching life.

Shit, yes, that was a situation that needed seeing to before he left and quickly. Which meant he and Temple were going to have a little chat. And she was going to tell him everything. Who she was, where she came from, and what she wanted. And if she wasn't going to give him the information willingly, then he'd make her.

Excitement, desire, and a wild exhilaration he hadn't felt for years clenched into a tight, aching knot.

He wouldn't use force this time. Oh no, he had a far more effective weapon in his arsenal. She wanted him, that much had been obvious, which meant he could use it against her. Could use her desire and pleasure to get what he wanted from her.

And he would.

Because if she had indeed come here to kill him, then all bets were off.

CHAPTER SEVEN

Temple came awake almost instantly, every sense on high alert. Her training had drilled the response into her so often and so hard that by now it was reflex, her subconscious sending her signals to wake whenever it registered a threat. The threat could be as subtle as a change in temperature or the slightest noise, even the whisper of a breath on her skin.

She didn't move, not wanting to give away the fact that she was awake, trying to figure out where the threat was coming from.

She was in the big bed in Jericho's room, having decided that sleep was more important than pacing the floor, waiting until he got back from the club, because who knew what he would do when he returned? Whatever it was, she'd need all her energy and concentration, and she wanted to make sure she was ready for any eventuality.

Keeping her eyes closed and her breathing regular, she extended her awareness into the room, trying to figure out what had woken her.

And there it was, the warm scent of cinnamon and sandalwood, exotic spices and heat.

Jericho.

He was back.

Something tightened inside her, a deep pulse between her thighs.

She ignored the sensation, concentrating instead on trying to pinpoint where he was, listening for the faint sound of his breathing.

"I know you're awake, Sleeping Beauty." The rough sensuality of his voice wrapped around her, the mere sound of it making goose bumps rise all over her skin. "So stop trying to pretend." And then she felt long, strong fingers wrap around her ankle beneath the quilt.

It took every ounce of her control not to kick and twist, to just lie there and let him hold her. But she wasn't fighting this time. Or at least, not yet.

Instead she rolled over slowly and opened her eyes.

He was standing near the end of the bed, that dangerous, almost savage smile turning his bruised mouth. Obviously he must have dressed after leaving her earlier because he wore a black business shirt unbuttoned at the throat and rolled up to his elbows, a casual look for a man who was anything but.

The bruises on his face were darkening, and it hit her weirdly, almost like a punch to the gut. She'd put them there. She'd marked him. And she didn't know why that felt so satisfying, but it did.

His green eyes glinted with the gold of molten coins, the heat in them connecting with that deep pulse between her thighs, making it clench. Making it twist. Stealing her breath and setting her heartbeat racing.

Jesus. You want another round.

She swallowed. No, she wasn't going to do that, not this time. She was aiming for something different and less . . . intense. Less explosive.

Gazing sleepily at him, she stretched like a cat, watching his gaze drop to the movement of her body beneath the quilt. "Hmmmm. Have you been dealing with the Russians all night? Poor you."

There was a dangerous edge to his smile. "They weren't very happy with my treatment of poor Anatoly." He reached out and took a corner of the quilt in his free hand. "But don't worry." With one hard movement, he jerked the quilt entirely off her. "They'll live."

She'd kept his shirt on as she'd crept beneath the covers earlier, and now it was all she could do not to grip the edges of the cotton and pull them closer around her. Which was ridiculous. Since when had nakedness bothered her? It hadn't the night before, or at least not much.

Yet now, strangely, she felt exposed.

Irritated with herself, she didn't move, forcing herself to remain still as that hungry green gaze roved over her. "I'm not worrying. I'm just annoyed that you woke me up at the crack of dawn then took away the quilt."

He laughed. "You're my prisoner, kitten. I can do whatever the fuck I want with you." His grip on her ankle tightened as he began to draw her slowly down the bed, pulling her toward him. "Besides, we have some unfinished business."

She went lax, not fighting him as he tugged her down to the end of the bed then loosened his hold on her ankle. Excellent. This put her in a good position to try a little something on him. A little something that should make him lose his mind while giving her all the power.

Temple sat up, leaning back on her hands, letting the fabric of the shirt part so he got a glimpse of her pussy. That should distract him for a moment. "Oh?" she murmured. "You mean the information I want?"

Sure enough, his gaze dipped between her thighs. "I mean, the answers you're going to give me."

Slowly she eased herself upright. He stood right in front

of her and she didn't hesitate, lifting her fingers to trace the heavy, hard outline of his cock beneath the black wool of his pants. And she heard the almost soundless intake of his breath. Saw the almost imperceptible tightening of his muscles as she touched him.

She tipped her head back, looking up into his beautiful, bruised face, meeting the heat in his eyes, feeling the flames of it lick her too. "Just answer one question and I'll give you everything you want."

One corner of his mouth curled. "Everything I want," he echoed softly. "If everything I want is a blow job, right?"

Temple let her fingers move over the sensitive head of his cock, pressing down harder against the material. She didn't take her gaze from his, trying to concentrate on what she was supposed to be doing and not on the fact that he was so very, very hot. And very, very hard. She smiled back. "Isn't that what every man wants?" She lifted her other hand, reaching for the fastening of his pants. "Just answer the question and—"

His hand closed hard around her wrist, his grip nearly painful. She stilled. The curl to his mouth was gone, a muscle ticking in his jaw. His expression was intent, deadly, and for some reason it made the excitement, the deep thrill of desire, twist even tighter inside her.

"There will be no questions." The rough heat in his voice had her catching her breath. "Not for you at least."

She stared up at him, trying to gauge him. He wanted answers himself, that much was obvious and understandable. Especially given the bruises on his face. Unfortunately though, it looked like he wasn't going to let her distract him the way she'd planned.

Then again, she wasn't a woman who gave up easily.

Gently she spread out her fingers on the front of his pants, pressing down with her palm, feeling the already hard length of him get even harder. And she made herself smile. "No questions then." She lowered her voice, making it throaty, sultry. "I'll give you one anyway."

His grip on her other hand didn't relent and the look in his eyes turned glass-sharp. "Don't think I don't know what you're doing, kitten. I've had a hundred women try and seduce me to get something they want, and not one of them managed to do it. What makes you think you're so special?"

"You really have to ask me that question?" She pressed harder, holding his gaze. "I'm special because you want me."

And then that savage, feral smile was back, and she felt it deep in her gut, in her bones, in her sex. Making her breath catch and excitement rise. She wasn't wrong, and they both knew it.

He shifted, gripping her other wrist and pulling her hand away from him. Then, in a slow, inexorable show of strength, he forced her hands down on the bed, propelling her onto her back along with them. Then he held her wrists down on either side of her head, bending over her, his mesmerizing gaze inches from hers.

"Yes," he said softly. "That's right. I do. But I want answers from you more." He moved again, pushing one knee between her thighs, the material of his pants brushing against the sensitive skin of her inner thighs and pussy. A couple of inches higher and he'd be pressing right against her. All she'd need to do would be to tilt her hips and her clit would come into contact and—

What the fuck are you thinking? You're *supposed to be the one seducing* him.

She gritted her teeth, trying to bring her awareness back to the goal she was aiming for, the information about Thalia, because God, that was more important. More important than anything. And way, way more fucking important than this inexplicable, hateful attraction to the man who'd bought and sold her sister.

Who'd maybe even murdered her.

"You're trained to kill, Temple." His voice was soft, hypnotic. "In fact, you were only barely holding yourself back before. Don't think I hadn't noticed. So the only real question remaining is this: Why are you here to kill me, kitten?" His knee shifted as he spoke, closing those mere couple of inches, lifting to press gently against her sex, sending a shockwave of pure, electric sensation ripping through every nerve ending she had. Drawing from her a gasp she didn't want to let out and yet was powerless to stop.

No. No, she wasn't going to do this again. She wasn't going to be at his mercy again. This had to end and end now.

"I'm not here to kill you," she forced out. "I just want information. That's why I'm here."

His knee pressed a little harder, that gaze of his searching her face, and she tried not to give him any reaction. Tried to stay still.

"You're lying," he murmured. "I can see it in your eyes."

The pressure between her thighs intensified, his knee pressing harder still, making her want to rock against it, relieve the ache that was becoming more and more insistent by the second.

Why was it so difficult to ignore? What the hell had he done to her?

The broad, muscled length of his body stretched out over hers and the scent of him filled her senses, making it difficult to think. All she could see were those green-gold eyes and the fire in them that made her feel as if the blood was burning in her veins.

No one had ever looked at her that way in all her life. No one had ever looked at her as if they wanted to eat her alive. And she didn't know why some part of her responded to it.

Christ, none of this made any sense at all.

Think of Thalia. Think of what you have to do.

Yes, that's right. Think of her sister. Think of what this man had done to her. Get angry, get fucking furious because wasn't that her fuel? Wasn't that the thing that got her up in the mornings? The thing that made her pick up her gun and pull the trigger, because every death brought her closer to her actual goal. And now that goal was here within reach. Lying on top of her and holding her hands down.

Making you wet. Making you want.

Fuck. No. Not again.

Temple relaxed beneath him, letting all the tension bleed out of her, letting him think she'd surrendered. His knee moved, the delicious friction of it against her pussy making her shudder, but she didn't hold back this time or try to hide it. She even arched her back, lifting her hips, steeling herself against the intense rush of pleasure.

"Tell me the truth, Temple." His voice was a whisper, that velvet cord around her neck, pulling tight. "You're here to kill me, aren't you?"

She didn't wait. Time to end this.

With a quick, hard movement, she twisted her hands from his grip and jerked them away, rising up to slide her arms around his waist. Then, pressing down with the heels of her feet, she jerked her hips up hard, pulling him down in the same motion, twisting underneath him and pushing him over to the side, using her body's momentum and element of surprise to roll him so that he was the one lying on his back while she was on top of him.

Then she rammed her forearm hard across his throat before he could move.

"Okay, asshole," she said savagely, staring down into the fire blazing in his eyes. "Give me the information I want and maybe I won't crush your windpipe."

Jericho lay there, barely able to breathe, the pressure across his throat like an iron bar.

Fucking hell she was fast.

She'd positioned her body over his, straddling him, her thighs squeezing him tight. Dislodging her was going to be tricky, especially with her forearm over his windpipe. He had a feeling she'd crush his trachea without a second's hesitation.

Her golden eyes were full of anger and heat, the desire she thought she could hide blazing there just as surely as her rage.

Dmitri was right. She is here to kill you.

Maybe that should have concerned him more than it did. Hell, the way she'd flipped him onto his back and was holding him pinned should at least have made him angry.

Yet he didn't feel angry.

He felt . . . exhilarated. Excited. And so fucking hard. As if he hadn't already had her not a few hours earlier.

She could kill him right here, right now, and for some fucked-up reason that excited him intensely.

Christ, she was incredible. Naked but for his shirt, and this was the second time in twelve hours that she'd managed to be a serious threat to him. And there was no doubting she was serious. He could see her intent burning in her eyes along with her anger and her desire.

The information she wanted . . . It was personal to her, he'd bet his life on it.

Curiosity was electric inside him, an intense current moving through his bloodstream. He wanted to know more, but of course, if he didn't get out of this, he wasn't going to find out anything.

He moved experimentally and was rewarded by the pressure on his throat suddenly becoming excruciating.

"Try it, prick," she whispered, leaning down near his ear. "I'll kill you before you can take another breath."

He couldn't speak, not with her pressing down like that, so he stilled, forcing himself to relax under her.

Her gaze searched his face for a long moment, then she eased off, if only slightly.

"I'm not going to be able to tell you anything if you keep your arm there," he managed to get out, his voice sounding so hoarse it was like he'd swallowed a handful of gravel.

In contrast to the press of her arm, the rest of her body was a slight, hot weight against him. Her pussy was against his cock, he could feel the heat of it like a fire seen through a window on a cold winter's day, almost there and yet just out of reach. It was maddening.

A fleeting look of frustration rippled over her features, then it was gone. She eased back a little more, not enough, unfortunately, to let him flip her, at least not before she crushed the breath out of him.

"Talk," she said flatly. "And fast."

He smiled. "Why? You're going to kill me anyway, aren't you?"

"Why?" she echoed. "Because I know how to cause pain. You'll be begging to tell me before I'm through with you." There was no doubt in her eyes. She'd do it, that was clear.

Yeah, this was personal to her. Deeply personal. And it looked like he was the object of her anger. And so much anger. She hated him, though she was trying her best to hide it.

"What did I do to you?" he murmured, watching the ebb and flow of the emotions she thought she kept secret in her eyes. "What did I do to make you hate me so very much?"

Her full red lips drew back in a fair resemblance of a snarl. "That's not the right answer." The pressure was back, crushing. "I want information, asshole. I want to know what happened to a girl called Thalia Cross."

Pain burst through his head, and he nearly laughed because when had anyone been able to dish out this kind of hurt to him? Never. And it was such a fucking thrill. That feeling of being so vividly alive had never been stronger. He could hear the blood pumping in his veins, feel the hard ache of his dick. Pain was a beautiful flower, slowly opening its petals, revealing itself in all its glory, reminding him that he was mortal.

That you're going to hell when all of this is over.

Yeah, he would. But he'd come to terms with that long ago. It would be worth it in the end. The lives he'd hurt in pursuit of his goal would be worth all the lives he'd actually save. All the people currently caught in the web would be free, and all the people who were in danger of being caught would have that threat removed. The perpetrators would be brought to justice. His father's handiwork and that of all the men like him would be destroyed.

That was worth the price of his soul. Fuck, he had to believe that. It was the only thing he had to hold onto that got him through.

He stared up at Temple, part of him wanting to just let go. Because it would be a fucking amazing way to die. Looking up into the golden eyes of a woman like this one, who was fire all the way through. A Valkyrie come to take his soul to Valhalla.

Like you're going to Valhalla. Hell, remember?

Right. And he couldn't let go yet, no matter how tired he was. The job was unfinished.

Temple eased back, allowing him a fraction of breathing room again. "Speak."

He swallowed, his throat aching, watching as her gaze dipped to the movement, making him want to smile. Instead he shifted his hips fractionally, rubbing the hard length of his cock against the slick heat between her thighs. The look in her eyes flared in response, the catch in her breath infinitesimal, but he heard it all the same.

"Thalia Cross," he murmured thickly, letting the sound of it roll into the air like honey. "Pretty name."

The look on her face tightened for an instant, before it smoothed again. "Just tell me what you know about her."

The name had vague familiarity to him, like a half heard song lyric, but he couldn't immediately place it. "I'm not sure I know anything about her." He shifted his hips again, a small movement and once more, that flare of heat in her eyes. "Tell me more."

Her mouth had firmed, becoming hard and tight. "Stop."

"Stop what?" Another gentle rock against her.

"That." There was a breathless edge to her voice now, her gaze dropping to his mouth then back up again, her cheeks flushing. "Do it again and I'll kill you."

"Why? Because you like it?" He shifted again, subtle yet insistent, the heat of her soaking through the fabric of his pants. "I don't think you want to kill me, Temple. I think you want to do something else with me first."

The pink flush to her cheeks deepened, and the color should have clashed with her hair yet it didn't. She was a woman composed of different tones of flame, red and gold and pink. He was going to burn himself holding onto her, and he didn't give a shit. He just didn't care. It would be worth it.

"No." The breathless edge in her voice had gotten more pronounced. "I don't. So stop it, asshole. Unless you want to die."

He didn't want to die, not yet. But he didn't want to stop either. So he ignored the threat, moving his hips in a circle, pressing against her sensitive clit, watching as she shivered in response. "But you don't want me to stop," he murmured. "You want me to keep going."

Temple shifted her weight, clearly trying to pull away from him, and the pressure on his throat eased as her angle changed. She muttered a curse, shifting yet again, but he didn't let her find a more comfortable position, moving with her, making sure the hard line of his cock ground against her sex.

"Tell me what you know about Thalia, asshole," she panted, the movement of her hips restless and searching. As if she wasn't trying to pull away but seeking more friction. "And tell me now because I *will* kill you."

God, she was passionate. And sensual. More than she herself realized, which was probably the only reason he was still breathing.

He gave her a feral smile. "Do it then, kitten." Taunting her. Tempting her. Not stopping the grinding movement of his hips. "Kill me if you can. Because I'm not going to give you another chance."

She gave another snarl and the forearm across his throat pressed down hard. The flame in her eyes glowed bright and hot, full anger and heat and frustration. She wanted to kill him, that much was obvious and yet . . . there was no real weight behind her arm. As if something was holding her back.

He rocked against her, gentle and slow, watching the golden glow in her eyes glaze over. "Fuck," she whispered, barely audible. "Fuck . . . stop . . ."

But he wasn't going to, not now. Because he had her, he fucking well had her. If she hadn't killed him now, she wouldn't.

"Come on, sweetheart," he murmured, for some reason unable to stop pushing her. "You want to kill me, I can tell. Here, I'll even make it easier for you." He put his head back, arching his neck, exposing his throat. And at the same time, he reached lower, finding the warm, smooth length of the back of her thigh, running his hand up the back of it and cupping the rounded curve of her ass.

She shuddered, her gaze on his throat, the snarl still twisting her pretty, pouty mouth. It would have been easy for her to lean forward and crush his trachea. So very easy for a woman like her. Yet she didn't. Instead she kept staring at his throat as if in a daze.

He squeezed her gently, allowing his fingers to slide between her thighs and brush against the soft, slick folds between them.

A sharp exhalation of breath sighed out of her, copper lashes fluttering. She didn't move.

Satisfaction surged inside him. Yeah, she didn't want his death, she wanted his touch. Wanted him to give her pleasure. Why else hadn't she dealt her killing blow?

Turning her over and putting her beneath him would have been the logical thing, the way to neutralize the threat. And yet, he found he didn't want to just yet.

There was something dizzyingly erotic about lying this close to his own death. About feeling the strength slowly bleed out from her as he touched her. And part of him wanted to prove to her how helpless she was against the desire that flared between them, and how utterly she was at its mercy. That she would let him live, put her own safety at risk, purely because she couldn't bring herself to make him stop touching her.

He liked that, yeah he did. Because Christ, he wasn't going to be the only one caught in the grip of this lust. He wanted to make sure she was caught too.

Keeping his gaze steadily on her flushed face, he found the entrance to her body and began to circle her slippery, wet flesh with one finger. Her jaw went tight and hard, but he didn't hesitate, sliding his finger deep inside her.

She inhaled sharply, her eyes meeting his.

"Do it," he whispered, pressing his finger deeper, feeling the astonishing heat of her body close around it. "Kill me."

She panted, and he felt the arm across his throat tremble, her gaze burning into his. She wanted to, she really wanted to.

He slid his finger out then pushed it back in again, her pussy slick and hot, ready for him whether she liked it or not. "Last chance, kitten."

"Bastard." The curse ended on a low moan, her lashes sweeping down, her mouth relaxing, becoming all full and soft and pouty. Her back flexed, arching as if to invite a deeper touch, her hips moving against his hand.

The pressure against his throat vanished.

Looked like he wasn't going to die tonight.

Halle-fucking-lujah.

But it wasn't relief that coursed through his veins. It was triumph. The raw, primitive pleasure of defeating a worthy opponent. Because she had been worthy. She'd nearly done what no other asshole had managed over the course of sixteen years. She'd nearly killed him.

He shifted, removing his finger from her, flipping her over onto her back and reversing their positions so she was the one beneath him. She didn't even protest, lying there with her hands flung above her head, watching him with big golden eyes.

And he felt savage with the satisfaction of it. Because if there was one thing that really got him off it was a victory, and he did like to win. He always had.

"Remember this," he murmured, staring down at her. "Remember that I gave you a chance, and you didn't take it." He eased apart her thighs with his knees, leaning forward and putting one hand beside her head, trailing the other down her body before sliding over the slick flesh between her thighs. "Remember that you should have killed me, and you didn't." His finger found the stiff jut of her clit, teasing, circling. "Remember that you wanted my touch, my cock, more than you wanted my death."

Something intense crossed her face. Whether it was rage or desire or despair, he couldn't tell. Then she turned her head to the side, and closed her eyes, her lashes lying still on her cheek. Tuning him out.

Oh, hell no. She wasn't checking out like that, just because he'd defeated her. He wanted her participation. Her active, enthusiastic participation.

He leaned farther down, gently brushing her mouth with his, at the same time as he toyed with her pussy, sliding his fingers along her folds, pressing inside her. "You're doing it again, Temple. You're being a sore loser."

She didn't move, but her body trembled, her hips shifting against his hand. "And you're being a gloating prick." Her voice was low and husky, and it felt like a caress against bare skin.

He smiled, pushing another finger inside her, stretching her delicately, watching as helpless pleasure unfurled over her face. "I notice you didn't deny it."

Her throat moved. "Deny what? That I'm a sore loser?"

"Well that." He sunk his fingers deeper, pulling them out before sliding them back in. "And the fact that you're here to kill me."

She arched her back restlessly beneath him, lifting her hips. "That's not a question."

"No, it isn't. That's a fact. Isn't it?" He brushed his thumb over her clit.

The breath rushed out of her in a hoarse exhalation, her hands clenching suddenly into fists at her sides. "If it's a fact, then surely you don't need me to confirm it."

"I don't, it's true. But it would be nice if you would all the same." He brushed his thumb over her again, more insistent this time. "Are you a cop, Temple? An assassin? Is this a paid hit?" Part of him actually didn't give a shit what she was. The most important thing was that she was wet and hot and willing under him. But he knew which part of him that was. The part with no brain. And it wasn't that part that had enabled him to survive all these years.

"Does it matter?" Her voice was even huskier, even more ragged.

He brushed his mouth over hers again, her lips so incredibly soft, he couldn't help but nip the lower one, just to test it. "Yes, it matters." He nipped her again, a punishment for the ridiculousness of the question, even though he was now beginning to wonder that himself. "Tell me."

Her sex clenched around his fingers, her hips flexing in time with the movements of his hand. Her lips parted beneath his, shuddering in reaction as he nipped her a third time. "N-no," she whispered. "I'm not telling you anything."

"That's a shame." He pressed on her clit with his thumb, a hard pressure. "Because you're not going to come until you do."

Her breath hissed between her clenched teeth. "Fine. Then I won't come."

Jericho laughed. She was so goddamn impressive. Even now, even having failed to kill him, even wanting him and the pleasure he'd give her, she still wasn't giving up. She was still holding out.

The satisfaction and the triumph burned inside him, twining with his desire until there was only a bright, pulsing thread of sensation, white hot and electric, drawing tighter and tighter.

He slowed his movements, the air around him thick with the scent of feminine arousal, with the heat of her body and the soft rush of air in time with her quickened breathing.

It wasn't only her he was testing, it was himself too.

Lowering his head, he bit the delicate cords of her neck, applying a slight pressure, allowing his thumb to circle agonizingly slowly around her clit. "Come on, kitten. If I can make you give up the perfect chance to kill me, I can make you tell me who you are."

Her jaw was tight, her body trembling. She must be so close to the edge now. "No-n-no," she whispered, a desperate edge to her voice. "No, you can't make me do anything."

"Yes, I can." He sped up, sliding his fingers in and out, at the same time pressing down with his thumb, giving her the friction and the pressure he knew she was desperate for. "Tell me, Temple."

She groaned, her breathing coming harsh and hard, moving against him helplessly. "N-no."

"Tell me, and I'll make this stop. I'll make it all go away."

She was shaking, her eyes shut tight, her knuckles white as she clenched her fists. There was such determination in her, he'd seen it burn there in her golden eyes. She'd hold out against physical pain, that was clear, but something told him she couldn't hold out against this. Pain was one thing, pleasure was quite another, and she didn't understand that.

But she would. Oh yes, she would.

He slowed his hand on her, made his touch light, tantalizing.

"D—d-don't," she said raggedly. "Please . . . stop . . ."

"Just tell me," he whispered. "That's all you have to do."

Something slid down her cheek from the corner of her eye. A tear. A surrender. A good man would have stopped right then. But he wasn't a good man.

"No." The word was a hoarse scrape of sound. "I'm not a cop. I'm . . . an . . . assassin."

It wasn't a surprise. Given what she'd managed to do to him, it was even obvious.

"Good girl," he murmured, giving her another light brush of his mouth. "Such a very good girl."

Putting his thumb on her clit, he pressed down hard.

And watched her as she shattered.

CHAPTER EIGHT

Temple didn't know what had happened. One minute she'd had the bastard under her with her arm across his throat. At her mercy. The next . . . She was lying on her back, shaking with the aftereffects of the orgasm that was still ricocheting around the interior of her body.

All while Jericho leaned over her, his hands working their terrible magic on her. Stealing her strength and her determination. Robbing her of her rage. Taking it and turning it into something else, into desire, inexorable and unstoppable as the tide.

And she still didn't know how he'd done it.

She'd wanted to kill him so badly, had been prepared for it. This mission needed to be over, and she'd decided to make her move. Shit, she'd nearly succeeded. She'd had him at her mercy, his life could have been measured in minutes, in seconds. All it would have taken was one hard push on his windpipe and this would be over. This whole mission accomplished.

But that hadn't been what had happened.

He'd moved against her, so subtly, so gently, she hadn't even realized he was doing it until it was too late. Until her body had begun to demand things of her. Demand that she stop what she was doing and concentrate on what he was doing to her instead.

She didn't understand why she'd listened to it. Why she hadn't made that final move and ended him while she'd had the chance, while he'd refused to stop that movement of his hips, while her body had clenched hard and tight, and everything had begun to get lost in a haze of lust.

How had he done it? How was she now on her back, trembling so badly she didn't think she'd ever stop? How had he thwarted her from the one goal that had been driving her for the past seven years?

And not only that. You told him what you were.

Shame filled her, bitter and hot, and she turned her head to the side again, unable to bear it. There was something wet on her cheek, and the shame broadened, deepened. Jesus Christ, she was crying.

Strong fingers gripped her chin, turning her head back, but she didn't want to look at him. She couldn't seem to remember how to move to get away from him either, as if her body, still humming and sated with pleasure, had lost the ability she'd trained into it.

Something warm touched her cheek, the brush of soft skin. And again on her closed lids. A third time on her lips then staying there. His mouth.

She'd told him she was an assassin. He knew she was there to kill him. And he was kissing her, coaxing her mouth open, then the slick glide of his tongue inside. A deep, intense, hungry kiss.

Temple tried to pull away, but he wouldn't let her, his grip on her chin tightening.

Now. Kill him now. You can do it.

Except she couldn't remember how. He was exploring her mouth, so slow and delicious and hot, and her brain didn't seem to be working. Nothing seemed to be working. She was lying on her back on the bed, and she wasn't fighting. She wasn't even protesting.

She was letting him do whatever he wanted to her.

You fucking loser. What would Thalia think of you now?

Tugging on the shirt she wore as he undid the buttons, spreading apart the fabric, his mouth was moving down her throat, over the curve of one breast. Then there came the hot touch of his tongue on her nipple, licking, teasing.

Temple put her fists over her eyes, pressing hard until light burst behind her closed lids.

This was what Thalia had protected her from for years, standing between Temple and the sleazy bastard who was supposed to be her father. The sleazy bastard who had used his eldest daughter when he was high.

Jericho's teeth tugged on her nipple, a gentle bite before drawing it deep into his mouth and sucking hard. A sound ripped from her throat, a low moan she couldn't stop.

You need to think. You need to plan your next move.

But thinking was impossible. The inexorable pull of his mouth on her nipple was causing everything inside her to tighten, the ache between her thighs that had only just been satisfied beginning to build again.

No. No, she had to stop this somehow. She had to move. She had to fight.

His hands slid down her sides, stroking down over her hips to her thighs. Then moving inward, pushing her thighs apart.

Stop him. Why aren't you stopping him?

She didn't know. There was a hunger in her she hadn't understood was there until now. Until he'd started moving his hips, pushing his hard-on against her pussy, making her tremble and burn. Seeing into her with those sharp, impossible green-gold eyes.

He'd known who she was already. He hadn't needed her confession. But he'd dragged it from her anyway. It was a humiliation, a demonstration of his power over her, and she shouldn't have given in. She should have held out the way she would have with any physical torture.

But this was . . . different from pain, and she didn't know how to resist it. She had no experience of it.

His body shifted on her, the press of his broad shoulders between her thighs, his thumbs parting the folds of her sex, opening her up as delicately as a flower. She trembled again, like she was a fucking virgin. This was insane. What the hell was she doing just lying here?

Thalia didn't fight. Thalia just lay there and kept quiet because if she'd protested he would have come for you.

"S-stop." The word broke from her shakily and she dug her fists into his shoulders, pushing him hard. "Don't."

But he only bent his head and gave her one long lick, straight up the center of her pussy, his tongue lingering on her clit, sending a lightning strike of pleasure right through her.

She groaned, her body tightening.

Fight, damn you. Fight.

But his tongue licked her again, and this time it pushed deep, dragging a small, hoarse scream from her. She arched back on the mattress and her hands were no longer in fists over her eyes but twisted in the heavy, dark gold silk of his hair. Holding onto him.

It had been so long since she'd felt anything but anger. Anything but the despair and pain that lurked underneath that anger. And something inside her was desperate to feel something different. It wanted the pleasure he was giving her, it wanted the thrill and the excitement, the adrenaline rush. It was starving for it.

Even if the man who's giving it to you is the man who probably had Thalia murdered? The man you've just failed to kill?

"You hate me, I know." His breath was warm against her skin, his beautiful voice winding its coils around her, velvet and smoke. "And you hate yourself for taking this from me."

She shivered as his hands moved on her thighs, his finger moving to her clit again, circling as she felt his tongue explore her again. Her heartbeat pounded in her head, the pleasure drawing impossibly tight once more.

How did he know? How had she given herself away? God, what had he done to her? She shouldn't have this, not from him. Not after she'd failed to take the chance he'd offered her. That one moment where she could have ended this, ended seven years of hell.

Of course you shouldn't have this. What makes you think you deserve it?

"But you'll take it anyway, because you want it. You're desperate for it."

That sensual, hypnotic voice. The terrible skill of his finger, moving so insistently. And then the subtle glide of his tongue in her pussy making her arch her back, making her scream. Making another climax crash over her whether she deserved it or not, whether she wanted it or not, leaving her shaking so hard she wasn't sure she'd ever stop.

Even as the aftershocks rocked her, she couldn't look at him. Couldn't move.

The bed dipped, and she felt him get off it. Then there came the sounds of fabric rustling and foil tearing. The bed dipped again, and this time she felt the heat of his bare skin on hers, so hot she nearly gasped.

His weight settled on her, heavy and sure as an anchor, pinning her to the mattress.

"Look at me."

There was something in his voice, an implacable authority that had her responding instinctively even though she didn't want to. She so didn't want to.

But her eyes opened nevertheless and met the gold flames in his.

And her breath caught in her throat. Because there was something else there, behind the desire and the heat. A cold, clear intent. Unlike her, he wasn't distracted by physical pleasure. No, as he'd warned her, he was going to use it. As a weapon to break her open.

"Am I your contract, kitten?" The question was soft and rough and dark. "Were you paid to take me out?" His hips shifted, and she could feel the head of his cock pressing against her, a tease. "Or is this more personal than that?"

Of course he knows this is personal for you. If he knows you hate him, then he must know that.

The realization hit at the same time as she felt him begin to push inside her, as she felt the exquisite stretch of her pussy around his cock. Not all the way in, just enough to make her shake, to make her burn.

The sharp edges of his determination glittered in his eyes, emerald tinged with gold, half molten heat, half cold shattered glass. As if he was holding himself apart from the flame igniting her.

And it wasn't fair, it just wasn't fair. How could he keep himself untouched by it, while she felt as if she'd lost a part of herself? The part that made her the assassin she was?

She felt stripped. Exposed and vulnerable. Like he'd scraped off a layer of her skin leaving all her nerve-endings raw. And she hated it. Hated feeling so helpless. Hated him for revealing her weakness so very thoroughly.

No, she didn't know pleasure. Didn't know how to respond or how to handle it. But she was learning. And if he could use it as a weapon, then shit, so could she.

She hadn't killed him when she'd had the chance, but she wasn't going to just lie there and burn while he remained cold as ice. He was damn well going to burn with her.

Without waiting, Temple reached up, shoved her fingers into his blonde hair and dragged his mouth down onto hers. Then she lifted her hips, driving his cock deep inside her, closing her legs around his waist and holding on tight.

And she opened her mouth, kissing him hungrily, exploring him the way he'd explored her, all slick heat and desperation. The smoky taste of whiskey hit her, along with a musky sweetness that must have been herself, and instinct had her wanting to rear back and let go.

But she didn't. She kept her mouth right where it was, moved her hips against his in a slow, undulating movement, until he growled, right down low in his throat.

Then there were no more questions and no more distance.

There were only the flames and the burning heat, the hard thrust of his cock as he took charge, sliding his hands beneath her butt and lifting her, holding her steady as he slammed himself into her. Hard and fast and deep.

And then the starburst of pleasure, a white shock of sensation that had her turning her face into his throat, inhaling musk and cinnamon and sandalwood. Opening her mouth to scream against his skin. Biting down to the powerful muscle of his shoulder to stop herself from sobbing.

But even then she failed.

As the orgasm smashed her into pieces, his fingers sank into her hair and twisted, his grip so tight it was almost pain. "This isn't over," he whispered, soft and hot and dark. "I will have all your secrets, kitten. Every last one."

And as if to prove it, he made her sob aloud before he finally claimed his own pleasure.

She was shaking in his arms, her sobs echoing in the air around him, her truth laid bare before him, and yet all he could seem to think about wasn't the fact that she was indeed, as Dmitri had suspected, an assassin. Or that it was starting to look like she *was* here to kill him.

No, the thing he couldn't stop thinking about was that tear. That single fucking tear that had slipped down her cheek as she'd given him her confession.

A beautiful, deadly red-haired assassin who cried.

His fingers were still buried in all the red silk that was her hair and he was still deep inside her hot, tight little pussy. But that goddamn tear was still stuck in his memory like a barbed fishhook.

He looked down at her. She had her head turned away from him, her cheeks flushed, coppery lashes hiding her gaze. But there was a small tear stain on her skin, faint and barely noticeable but there all the same.

He knew tears. He'd seen plenty of people cry over the years. The women that had turned up in his club, the poor, lost girls that the men in his network had taken, purely because no one would know they were gone. That didn't stop them from crying harsh, desperate sobs.

The first few times he didn't think he'd be able to bear the sound of such despair, but he'd made himself listen. Imprinting the sound on his memory so he'd never forget why he was doing this. And who he was doing it for. Adding to the cold, hard certainty that this was what he had to do if he was going to free every last person from the net his father had woven.

He'd been a betrayed boy back then, a fresh-faced college kid burning with the fire of his own self-righteousness and sense of justice. His own guilt too. But over the years, that kid had steadily been eroded away, the sounds of despair corroding him like acid. Until tears were just another part of the backdrop. Just another misery he had to tune out to keep himself sane.

But Temple's single diamond of a tear . . . That wasn't despair. That was rage.

Initially he'd thought it was because she'd hated to lose, and he very definitely had scored a victory over her. Yet he'd caught a glimpse of the look in her amber eyes, and he'd known immediately that it wasn't so simple as merely anger at being beaten.

If he knew despair, he also knew shame. Because he'd felt it himself every single day for the past sixteen years. A shame he kept locked and hidden away and unacknowledged, because to do so would mean he couldn't travel the path he needed to. It would lead to doubt, and he couldn't afford doubt. He had to keep walking it, had to go on. Had to believe in his heart that this was the right way to do what he had to do.

So he knew it when he saw it. And he saw it in Temple.

She was ashamed. Though for what he couldn't tell. Maybe for letting herself be beaten by him, or for giving in to the chemistry that surged between them. For admitting the truth to him.

Whatever it was, for some completely inexplicable reason, it hit him like a crossbow bolt straight to the gut.

He didn't want her to be ashamed. She was so strong, so powerful. A lethal, beautiful animal. The thought that she should feel any kind of shame about herself was . . . painful.

Maybe this is new to her. Maybe you're the one who should be ashamed, using pleasure against her like that.

Fuck no. She'd been going to kill him. That arm across his throat had been like an iron bar, and he'd had no doubt at all she would have done it. Yet the justification rang hollow in his head the moment it crossed his mind. He didn't want her . . . humiliated. It felt wrong.

He released her hair, sliding free of her body and shifting his weight off her. She kept her head turned away from him, motionless. But he had the sense that she was curling up inside, rolling up like a hedgehog to protect herself.

"Temple," he said and reached out, gripping her chin and turning her to face him.

Her lashes swept up, her gaze guarded and enigmatic. "What?"

Whatever vulnerability had made her cry, it was gone now, but he still felt the need to give her something, fuck knew why. "There's no shame in losing. You understand that, right?"

Her expression didn't change. "What the hell makes you think I'm ashamed?"

"I know shame, kitten. I've seen every form it takes. And I saw it in you."

"Stop calling me that." Sparks of anger glowed in her eyes. "That's a load of bullshit anyway. Besides, why would you imagine I lost?"

Gently he touched one finger to the tear track on her cheek. "This."

Instantly the look on her face became shuttered, and she jerked her head out of his grip.

So she was going to bluff it out. Understandable given she was a fighter through and through. He probably would too. Letting her pull away, he said merely, "All I'm saying is that no one loses when pleasure is involved."

She didn't reply, somehow managing to extract herself out from under him, her lithe body sliding off the bed. He stayed where he was, watching her because she was beautiful, her movements liquid and graceful.

Idly he wondered whether she would come for him now and whether he should do something to protect himself. But she didn't even look at him, pulling together the edges of his white shirt she still wore that had come undone while they'd been in bed. Then she turned and without a word headed toward the door that led to the *en suite* bathroom, slamming it shut behind her.

He stared at the shut door, fighting the urge to go to her, peel back those guards of hers, hunt out all her secrets. Why she'd cried and why she'd given in and told him who she was. Why she hadn't killed him when she'd had the chance. Why she'd felt the shame she insisted she didn't feel. And maybe, most especially of all, find out who exactly was Thalia Cross.

Maybe whoever she was would give him the answers he needed about Temple.

The name lingered in his brain, annoyingly familiar. Goddammit.

Making a mental note to go back through his files and do a search on it to see what came up, he slipped out of the bed, getting rid of the condom in a nearby waste-basket.

It was strange to have such a reaction to a woman, especially what seemed to be an emotional reaction. He'd trained those responses out of himself a long time ago, simply because he'd had to. Emotions of any kind would derail him, make it impossible for him to finish his task, so he'd deadened himself to them. Which made it odd that this one woman should have woken them back up again.

She's dangerous in more ways than one.

Yeah, but only if he let her get to him. He just wouldn't let her get to him.

His phone buzzed, so he went over to where he'd left his pants on the floor and extracted it, glancing down at the screen. A simple text from Dmitri: *Everything has been organized.*

Excellent. Goddamn, Dmitri was efficient.

Quickly he pulled on his pants then sent back a reply: *Get me a car in an hour.*

He wouldn't need much longer than that to get ready.

Aren't you forgetting something?

On cue, the door to the bathroom opened again and Temple came out. All signs of tear tracks were gone, her face clean. She'd been wearing makeup and without it she looked so much younger than she had before. Jesus, she looked like she was in her early twenties, if that. So fucking young.

But not innocent.

No, she wasn't. One glimpse into those big golden eyes of hers could confirm that. And besides, no one who killed people for money could be termed innocent.

Right now though, she looked as far from an assassin as it was possible to get with her scrubbed face and cascade of red curls falling down all over her shoulders. The white shirt—his white shirt—came down to mid-thigh, leaving bare her beautifully toned legs, but sadly she'd done it back up again, concealing the rounded curves of her breasts. No, she didn't look like an assassin. She looked like a fresh-faced college kid he'd picked up in a bar.

And yet, fifteen minutes ago she had her arm on your throat and death was staring you in the face.

Temple folded her arms. "So what now?"

Good question. He couldn't leave her here, no matter how many guards he put on her because she was simply too dangerous to leave alone. Which left him little option but to take her with him.

Oh sure. You just don't want to let her out of your sight. Or your bed.

Yeah, that too, he'd freely admit to that. He hadn't had a woman in his bed in years and since this trip to the States was going to be a bitch, he could use some distraction. It was even necessary. But first, he had to neutralize the threat she represented.

The obvious solution would be to keep her in handcuffs or some other kind of binding until he wanted her, and yet he found he really didn't like that idea. Another stupid, emotional reaction of course, but that didn't change the fact that he didn't like it. Again, it felt . . . wrong. Like caging a tiger felt wrong.

"Now," he said calmly, zipping up his pants, "we have a truce."

Her eyes widened. "A truce?"

So he'd surprised her. He liked that. He liked that a lot. "Yes. You know what that is presumably?"

She narrowed her gaze at him. "Why?"

"Why the truce? Because I have to fly to the States, leaving in an hour." He smiled. "And you're coming with me."

"But I—"

"You don't have a choice. You're my prisoner, and you're too dangerous to leave on your own. Besides . . ." He paused, letting his gaze sweep over her, making sure she could see the heat in his eyes. "I haven't finished with you yet."

Her lashes came down, and she was silent a moment. Then one corner of her mouth curved in the sexy, flirtatious smile he remembered from the club, where she'd tried to seduce him. "Any man in their right mind would be afraid of me. Why aren't you?"

It was an act, he could see that. Yet that smile, that glitter of gold from beneath her lashes, that spark of danger, was like an electric shock delivered straight to his cock. "You think I'm afraid of you because you want to kill me? I'm *always* around people who want to kill me, kitten. I'm sorry but you're nothing special."

A lie, of course. She *was* special. She'd managed to make him want for the first time in years, but there was no way he'd let her know that. She didn't need another weapon to use against him.

Something flickered in her gaze, the flirtatious front dropping. "So you're bringing me with you as your . . . what? Mistress? Whore?"

He lifted a shoulder. "Nothing wrong with being a whore. Or a mistress. Both honorable professions."

"And you expect me to keep sleeping with you?"

"I expect," he said gently, "that you will do whatever I tell you."

Her mouth tightened. "I could kill you right now, right here, exactly where you stand."

"You could. But you won't. Just like you didn't before when you had the chance." He held her gaze. "Because I'm not the only one who's hungry."

Color stained her cheeks, but she didn't look away. "This isn't about sex."

"Isn't it?" He wasn't quite sure why he wanted an admission from her, but he would have it all the same. "You were going to kill me. But you didn't."

"Sure I didn't. Because I wanted that information."

Ah, so that's how she was going to play it. He smiled, because that was a bullshit excuse, and they both knew it. "So it had nothing to do with you rubbing yourself against me and panting in my ear? Letting me flip you onto your back and getting the truth from you in exchange for orgasms?" *Crying in rage because your body wanted something you didn't want it to have?*

Again that flash of gold in her eyes, sparks of pure anger. "What? You think winning one fight wins you the entire battle?"

"I think you won't win any battle while you want information only I can give you."

Her mouth hardened. She was trying her best to hide her frustration, but he could see it in her eyes all the same. She probably wasn't often rendered helpless, wasn't often caught on the back foot. Well, neither was he. But that was life, wasn't it? There was always something around the corner you weren't going to like. "This truce then," she said after a moment, her voice flat. "What did you mean?"

He studied her. She didn't like this, and she was pissed

about having to concede, that was obvious. Which meant that this information must be very important to her, especially if she was willing to give up a fight for it. So who was Thalia Cross? And who was she to Temple? Because she had to be someone. This was personal for Temple, he could feel it.

"I mean," he said slowly, "that I'll investigate this woman for you. And in return, you promise to play the part of my meek, biddable lover. Which means, of course, no attempts on my life and your presence in my bed at all times."

She blinked. "So all you want is sex in return for anything you have on Thalia?"

Casually, he closed the distance between them, coming to a stop right in front of her. Her head tipped back as she looked up at him, the expression on her face set and hard. Not giving him a thing.

But those beautiful eyes of hers betrayed her. He could see the currents of her emotions there, the ebb and flow of her rage, the sudden surge of heat as he got into her personal space, the eddies of frustration. She was so warm and vital and alive. So expressive.

"No," he said softly. "That's not all I want. I told you I wanted your secrets. And I will have them. Sex will just be the method I use to get them out of you."

Her jaw tightened. "I'll act however you want. But I'm not sleeping with you again. And if you try to force me, I'll castrate you."

He nearly laughed at that, because he had no doubt at all that she would. And that far from putting the fear of God into him, it only excited him.

You sick fuck.

Yeah, he was sick. Sick for liking the chase, for liking the fight. For wanting the resistance and the sweetness of eventual surrender. But he'd always known that. And it turned out embracing that sickness was easier than fighting it.

Maybe that's why your father was the way he was. Maybe one day he just got tired of fighting.

A sliver of ice slipped beneath his skin at the thought. No, he wasn't the same. He hadn't given up, not where it mattered. He had his plan, and every step he took was another step forward, another step to taking down this terrible empire he'd helped create. What did it matter if he took a little something for himself? With a woman who was certainly not helpless in any way, shape, or form?

"Perhaps you'll like me forcing you, Temple," he said, reaching out to cup her jaw, brushing a finger over her cheekbone because he just couldn't seem to stop himself from touching her. "Perhaps the surrender is exactly what you want."

She jerked her head back, the golden sparks in her eyes turning to ice. "If you don't have a cock, you can't force anyone."

This time he did laugh, the thrill of her challenge reaching somewhere deep inside of him. "Try to take it then. You know how I like a fight. You know you like one too."

"Get me the information about Thalia, and I might think about it."

Jesus, she never stopped pushing, did she? "Didn't I say no more bargains? No, only one thing is going to be happening. You will be coming to the States, and you will be sleeping in my bed. No argument." He gave her a feral smile. "Resistance is futile. In fact, resistance is preferred."

The gold in her eyes froze even further. "How will I know you'll even get me the information I want?"

"You don't." He turned on his heel and started heading toward the door since he had shit to do before they left. "You'll just have to trust me."

"Seriously?" she called after him. "Over my dead body."

He didn't bother to turn. "If it comes to that, kitten. If it comes to that."

CHAPTER NINE

Temple gazed out the window of the gracious Upper East Side brownstone for the fiftieth time that morning, and tried not to grind her teeth with frustration.

She'd been here two days and already she felt like an animal in too small a cage.

She was used to being in control, and being so utterly at the mercy of someone else sucked. Especially when that person was the biggest crime lord in Europe.

The man you failed to kill.

Like she needed that reminder.

Temple turned away from the view of the Manhattan street, trying not to remember the last time she'd been in New York, where, after a very uncomfortable half an hour with Zac Rutherford, she'd accepted a chance to take down what had proved to be their mutual enemy. Jericho.

Two weeks Zac had given her, and, God, it had already taken her a week and a half to get to the club in Berlin and get herself taken, another few days of kicking her heels with the other trafficked girls until Jericho had finally chosen her for the night. And now another three days had passed and she was still no closer to finding out about Thalia. And Jericho was no closer to being dead. And if she didn't find some way of contacting Zac soon, he might hire someone else to finish the job.

Cold slid through her. No, that couldn't happen. Jericho wasn't going to die until she'd found out where her sister was.

Which meant she had to get out of this elegant brownstone she was locked into, unable to go out on pain of a bullet in the head, or steal a phone from someone. If she played her cards right, she might have been able to steal Jericho's, but unfortunately, she didn't know where he was. She hadn't seen him since he'd left her standing in his bedroom in Paris.

Not five minutes after he had, a woman had entered and dumped a pile of clothes on the bed then left. The clothes, including underwear, had all fitted her perfectly. Jeans and a close-fitting long-sleeved T-shirt, a biker jacket of soft black leather to wear over the top. There were even heavy black boots to go with them.

She'd tried not to notice the softness of the fabric or the cut of the clothing as she'd dressed, since clothes were a guilty pleasure she seldom indulged in. But she couldn't control the shiver of delight as she'd pulled on the jacket, relishing the feel of butter-soft leather beneath her fingers.

She hated to admit it, but despite his boring taste in business clothes, Jericho had good taste in everything else.

After that, she was taken to a car by the sullen Russian bodyguard and then whisked straight to Charles de Gaulle airport. Somehow a passport—which had to have been fake—was presented and she was processed through customs and placed in a room on Jericho's luxurious private jet. The door to the room was locked and remained so throughout the flight.

She didn't bother to break it down since doing so would be pointless. Instead she spent the time allowing herself some sleep in the surprisingly comfortable bed, though half of her kept expecting Jericho to join her at any moment.

He didn't.

And she didn't see him after they'd arrived in the States either. She'd been taken to the brownstone and left there with Dmitri, the sullen Russian bodyguard. Again.

It was infuriating. She didn't even know why they were here, what Jericho had come here to do, though she assumed it had something to do with the American trafficking networks.

God, she hated not knowing.

She'd attempted to leave, if only to check Jericho's security measures, and found that not only were the windows bulletproof, but they were also alarmed, any interference bringing approximately ten guards down on her all armed to the teeth.

Escape wasn't going to be easy.

She stared around the room, an elegant lounge area with a sofa and armchairs beautifully upholstered in rose-colored velvet. Apart from the chairs, everything else in the room was white, the furniture sleek and modern, the white walls hung with various abstract art canvases.

It was an irritating room, mainly because it should have felt cold and uncomfortable with all that white, but it didn't. The velvet of the chairs and the rose color gave the room warmth and a sensual feel that it otherwise wouldn't have had.

Temple moved slowly over to the couch, letting her fingers trail along the soft fabric. Like the biker jacket she was still wearing, it was an indulgence to let herself enjoy the feel of it, but what the hell, no one was watching. And it wasn't like she had anything else to do.

She frowned as she stroked over the back of the couch, turning some ideas over in her head. Getting to a phone was imperative, except she didn't quite know how she was going to accomplish it. There were no landlines in the house, and the only cell phones she'd seen were the ones that the guards—

A smile curved her mouth. Ah, yes. The guards.

Glancing around the room, her gaze settled on a side table near the couch. On it was a delicate glass lamp. The floor was carpeted like the house in Paris, with plush white carpet, but that wasn't a problem. She could smash that glass nicely.

Temple walked over to the table and picked up the lamp, putting it on the floor. Then she brought one booted foot down hard on it. The glass shattered beautifully, but she didn't waste any time admiring her handiwork. Tipping the table over with one hand so it fell heavily among the smashed glass, she then followed it down onto the floor, allowing herself to fall bonelessly as if in a faint.

Sure enough, she only had to lie there a minute before the door to the lounge door bounced open and she felt the vibration of heavy footsteps approaching. She gave a little groan for effect, fluttering her eyelashes like she was coming to.

"What the fuck is wrong with you?" A deep voice demanded. Yes, definitely one of the guards.

Temple raised a hand to her forehead, murmuring an answer he wouldn't be able to hear, cracking open one eye to check on where he was.

A tall figure was standing there, his head bent, eyes narrowed as he stared down at her. She murmured again, and he cursed, finally crouching down beside her.

"What's the matter?" he asked again, belligerence lacing his tone.

"I'm . . . not sure. I just . . ." She let the words trail off into inaudibility again, closing her eyes and turning her head to one side, giving him another glance from underneath her lashes. He was wearing jeans, his cell phone in his back pocket. Excellent.

The guard muttered another curse, beginning to rise to his feet again. She gave a subtle twist, shifting one leg and tangling it between his, putting him off balance. Then she moaned and thrashed, her leg knocking his ankle out from under him, and he went down, giving a surprised shout as he did so.

She could hear more footsteps coming down the hallway, no doubt wanting to investigate what was going on, which meant she'd have to move fast.

The guard had landed on his front, as she'd hoped, his back to her, but was already twisting to get his legs underneath him again. Still he was an easy target. She'd pickpocketed people for years after she'd escaped from her father's house, before she'd found Jackson, using the money to buy herself food and clothes. And luckily the skills she'd learned hadn't deserted her.

Quickly she lifted the phone from his back pocket, tucking it into the waistband of her jeans and under the long-sleeved T-shirt she wore before he'd even managed to get back on his feet again.

Ten seconds later, the room was full of guards, and she was feigning coming back to consciousness, muttering and opening her eyes, staring around her in surprise. Only to meet Dmitri's dark eyes scowling back at her in suspicion.

Great, that was the last thing she needed.

She blinked at him, pretending to be a little dazed. "What happened?"

"Apparently you passed out." His voice made it clear he did not think that had actually happened.

"Oh." Levering herself up, she paused a moment as if she was a bit dizzy still. "Yeah, I have low blood pressure. That can happen sometimes."

"Can it?" The suspicious look on his face didn't waver.

Temple drew in a deep breath, climbing slowly to her

feet then leaning not-so-surreptitiously against the couch. "Yeah, it can. Get a doctor if you're so worried about it."

He didn't respond, his dark gaze moving down her body, looking at her without heat or any trace of desire. As if she wasn't a woman at all, but a building he was examining for structural defects. But obviously he didn't find any because his brows lowered, his glower becoming even more intense. "Jericho shall hear of this," he said flatly.

"I'm sure he'll be interested." She passed a hand over her forehead. "You got any Advil? I've got a headache."

He stared at her for one long moment more, then he snorted and turned away, ordering the other men to follow with a sharp gesture of his hand.

A minute later, she was alone again, the door firmly locked behind them.

She grinned, allowing herself a small measure of triumph, and reached down into the waistband of her jeans, pulling out the phone. It was pass-coded, but she'd learned a few hacks to get around that. In fact, before she'd found Jackson, selling hacked cell phones she'd stolen had earned her some good money.

Gaining access to the phone, she stalked over to the windows, as far away from the door as she could get, then punched in the number Zac Rutherford had made her memorize over two weeks earlier.

He answered almost instantly. "You're late."

Temple steeled herself. "There have been difficulties."

"I don't want to hear about your difficulties. I only want to hear that you've done what you were contracted to do."

Jesus. Why was the world full of asshole men? Okay, so Zac had reason to doubt her, especially since she was the one who'd delivered his friend and lover, Eva King, into the hands of their enemy just over a month earlier. But that had just been a job she'd done for Elijah Hunt. It hadn't been personal.

Zac didn't see it that way naturally enough, and he wasn't impressed that she'd worked for Elijah. Temple didn't care what he thought. She'd met Elijah when she'd been scouting out a strip club down in Atlanta, one she'd heard rumors about as being a potential trafficking hotspot. Elijah had tried to warn her away, and she'd realized then that she wasn't the only one interested in helping trafficked women.

Jackson, with all his undercover crime contacts, had known who Elijah was too, and when he'd told Temple that the guy worked for the biggest and baddest names in the U.S. trafficking business, Temple had known she had to contact him in some way.

She'd only been seventeen back then, too young and too untried. But a few years later, she'd tracked Elijah down and asked him to help her find Thalia. In return she'd do anything he wanted her to do. She'd been expecting him to ask for sex since that had been what most men had wanted from her, but he'd refused. He had told her to get close to a woman named Eva King instead, the head of one of the largest tech companies in the States. So she had. And had ended up delivering Eva into the hands of Evelyn Fitzgerald, her enemy.

Elijah had promised her that Eva wouldn't be harmed, and the information Elijah had given her in return had led her to Jericho, so as far as she was concerned, it was all good. Zac, however, was a man who didn't forgive easily.

"I'm with Jericho," she said tersely. "In New York."

There was a silence. "And he's still alive?"

"Yes. But not for much longer."

"I'm disappointed to hear that, Miss Cross."

"You won't be disappointed long. I'm only calling so you won't hire anyone else. I'll finish this mission, but you have to give me a little more time."

"Why should I give you anything of the sort? Two weeks is what we agreed."

"I realize that." She paused, listening for any footsteps coming to investigate why she might be speaking out loud to herself. There was nothing. "But do you realize that I'm in a prime position to get information about his networks? About his business? About his intentions?" She paused again, to let that sink in. "I'm here as his lover." The words sounded raw in the silence, but she made no attempt to pretty them up or make them into something they weren't. "I can find things out that might be useful to you."

There was a silence down the other end of the phone.

Finally, Zac said, with some reluctance, "Any information we could pass on to the authorities would, indeed, be useful."

Something inside her eased a little. She could have told him about Thalia, could have told him why she wanted to keep Jericho alive a while longer, but that information she'd never told anyone. They were her secrets to keep. She was the one who'd caused Thalia to be taken. She would be the one to rescue her.

If there's anything left to rescue.

Firmly, Temple pushed that thought out of her mind.

"Do you have anything else I could use?" she asked. "Any other information that might come in handy in the meantime?"

Another silence echoed.

The folder Zac had given her when he'd hired her hadn't contained much in the way of information. Only a few clues as to where she could find Jericho's networks, that Berlin club being the main lead. She'd gone there straight away, acting the part of the poor American exchange student who'd run out of money and who'd had to take on a stripping job to make ends meet. Soon enough, after she'd put it around that she had no family or much in the way of friends, she'd been picked up by the traffickers.

Investigating Jericho himself hadn't amounted to much, which was frustrating, especially when she'd drawn blanks at every turn. Then again, she did have one thing she was beginning to suspect no one else did: his real name.

The sound of faint cursing could be heard from outside the door. Dammit. Had they discovered the guard's missing phone?

"What about his identity?" she asked. "We know who he is. Isn't that valuable?"

"I don't like your tone, Miss Cross."

"And I don't like you holding out on me with information."

Yet another pause while more curses and raised voices could be heard in the hallway.

"Zac. Fucking tell me."

He let out an audible breath. "Jericho's identity is a closely-guarded secret. No one knows who he is."

"No one at all?"

"No. No one except us."

Temple went still as implications she hadn't really considered before sunk in. "Which means we could use that."

Footsteps sounded in the hallway outside the lounge. Christ, she had no time.

"You could," Zac said. "There's a reason he kept his identity hidden. He doesn't want anyone to know he's Evelyn Fitzgerald's son."

Holy shit. Of course not. His real name and details had all been in the file Zac had given her initially, and she'd been planning on using the info when she'd finally gotten close to him. Except in the whirlwind of sex and adrenaline in the days after meeting him, it had slipped her mind.

So here was her leverage, and she *really* needed leverage.

At that moment, the door banged open for the second time that day, and Dmitri was coming through the doorway, murder in his eyes.

Temple wasted no time with good-byes. She threw the phone onto the floor and stepped on it hard, shattering the screen and crushing the delicate technology inside. Now there was no way anyone could track the call.

"Bitch," Dmitri growled. "Tell me what the fuck you were doing with that phone."

And he drew his handgun from the holster under his arm and pointed it straight at her.

Jericho stopped dead in the doorway of the lounge. In front of him was Dmitri, a gun in his hand and pointing it directly at Temple, who was standing by the windows, the crushed remains of a cell phone on the carpet near her feet. She'd put her hands up, her stance tense, as if she was preparing to launch herself at the bodyguard.

He hadn't seen her dressed before, not in actual clothes. But now she wore close-fitting jeans and a turquoise long-sleeved T-shirt, a black leather jacket over the top, the clothes he'd had brought for her. And she looked . . . normal. Like one of the hundreds of fashionable, lovely young women who walked the streets of Manhattan or Paris or London every day.

And a peculiar feeling went through him, an unfamiliar feeling. The need to go and put himself between her and Dmitri's gun. To protect her somehow. Which was the most patently stupid urge in the history of the world considering what Temple was capable of.

She was a fucking assassin for God's sake. She could protect herself.

"What the fuck is going on?" he demanded instead. "Dmitri? Put that goddamn gun down."

His bodyguard didn't move. "She stole a cellphone, and she called someone with it. I heard her talking."

Temple had relaxed for some reason, her tense stance easing. She flicked him a look, her mouth curving into that sexy little smile he found so erotic and yet so maddening at the same time. "Hello, Jericho," she said. "I was wondering where you'd gotten to."

There was something different about her, and that smile said it all. Whatever she'd been doing with that phone had pleased her very much.

He cursed under his breath.

Relax. She doesn't know where in Manhattan she is. There's no way she could have called for back-up or for help.

Still, there were ways and means. People could track cellphone signals, and no security system was perfect. There was always a way out or a back door somewhere.

He shouldn't have absented himself for the past two days, but he'd had little choice.

As he'd left Paris, word had come through that shit was currently hitting the fan with the American market. Elijah Hunt beginning to dismantle the networks Evelyn Fitzgerald had built was starting to have repercussions in the form of competition, and Jericho had spent the past two days in New York making sure that competition was taken out.

It had been messy trying to keep it all hidden and make sure Hunt himself didn't catch a whiff of it since Jericho didn't want to spook the guy until he was ready to confront him himself.

He'd even just been to Hunt's apartment in the West Village to check on him, though he'd tried to tell himself that had nothing to do with wanting to see if Violet was okay and everything to do with wanting to check out Hunt's routines.

As it turned out, he'd managed to spot Violet coming out of the building, all dressed in black leather with her short golden hair in artfully styled spikes. She looked determined, tough, very different from the shocked, desperate woman he'd kidnapped a month earlier in order to get her out of the country and away from the chaos left by their father's death.

As he'd watched her, he'd been almost tempted to step out from the shadows of a nearby doorway, just to say hello. To see her smile at him the way she'd used to, back when she'd been his adoring little sister. But he'd held back, because of course she'd never smile at him that way again. Not when all she knew of him was that he was a trafficker, a pimp, a drug dealer, and murderer just like their father.

He could never tell her the truth, not if he wanted to keep her safe. Besides, all of those accusations were true. So he stayed where he was, watching as she went by, a grief he shouldn't have felt twisting sharply inside him.

Then someone had called her name, and she'd turned around, and he'd seen her smile like the sun coming up, a joy crossing her face that made the grief even sharper.

A man had joined her, tall and dark and scarred. A familiar man. Hunt.

Violet had reached out a hand to him and he'd taken it, the smile on his face an exact mirror of hers. They'd walked together past Jericho, each of them so caught up in the other that they hadn't noticed him standing there. They probably wouldn't have noticed a bomb going off either.

So he'd stayed there and watched them walk to the apartment, his insides twisting with emotions he'd thought long dead as Hunt paused by the open door and kissed her before they both went inside. Jealousy. Anger. Envy.

He'd made a mistake to come, he'd known that straight away. And he'd made a mistake to stay and watch her. Seeing her like that brought back too many memories and too many feelings he couldn't afford.

It wouldn't happen again.

"Get the fuck out of here, Dmitri," he ordered flatly, his mood already shitty. "I'll deal with this myself."

There was a moment when Dmitri didn't move and Jericho wondered if the Russian was actually going to obey him. And what the hell he would do if Dmitri didn't. Then the bodyguard abruptly lowered his gun and put it away. He turned, giving Jericho a dark look loaded with recriminations, before moving past him and out of the room.

Jericho ignored Dmitri and kicked the door shut behind him, his attention on the small, slender woman by the windows.

She'd pulled her hair back in a ponytail, the black leather jacket giving her a tough edge. But the blue-green of the T-shirt made her skin glow and set her red curls blazing, and all he could think about was how it had been two days since he'd had her. Two days since he'd been inside her.

Two days too many.

Slowly, he walked toward her, watching as her chin came up and she folded her arms, that irritating smile still playing around her mouth. Yeah, she looked confident and pleased with herself. As if she'd discovered a big and very satisfying secret.

He stopped in front of her, looking down into her eyes, close enough to catch the scent of what smelled like roses. It was sweet, yet underlying it was a definite edge of feminine musk that grabbed onto his cock and refused to let go. Soap or body wash probably, mixed with Temple's intoxicating personal scent. God, he was so hungry for it.

"I suppose there's no point asking who you were talking to," he murmured. "Especially when you're not going to tell me, are you?"

She lifted a shoulder, supremely unconcerned. "I wouldn't worry your pretty little head about it. You know why I'm still here and what I want. If I was going to get away I would have by now."

Beautiful, smug little bitch.

He put his hands in the pockets of his jeans, watching her as she tracked the movement, her gaze lingering on his groin. Looked like two days had been a long time for her too.

"So, no pleas for rescue?" he asked. "No demands for backup?"

She glanced up at him, her expression guileless. "Nope. After all, it's not like I even know where we are, right?"

"You've gotten very cocky for a prisoner." He took a couple of steps toward her, but she held her ground. "Are you sure you don't want to tell me exactly who you were calling and why?"

She lifted one coppery brow. "Or what?"

Definitely he shouldn't have absented himself. He needed to keep the pressure on her, keep her off balance. Not to mention the fact that he could have used the fucking distraction too since everything else was going to hell in a handcart.

And it wasn't just what was happening with Hunt. The ache of seeing Violet felt like a raw wound, and he hadn't fully realized how painful it would be until now.

Wanting something warm beneath his hands, he reached out, gripping Temple by the hips and lifting her up onto the broad windowsill. Then he pushed her thighs apart with his body and stepped between them, keeping his hands on her waist.

She didn't move or protest, merely putting her palms flat on the sill beneath her and looking up at him from underneath her lashes. "Well, I guess being sat on a windowsill is very threatening. Should I be scared?"

He liked the scent of her. He liked her warmth. They were exactly the kinds of distractions he was looking for. And her challenging him was just an added bonus. "Yes, you should." He firmed his grip. "Feel free to fight me. You know how much I like that."

"I'm not sure I need to fight actually, Jericho." Her amber eyes gleamed. "Or should I say . . . Theodore."

He froze, a sharp blade sliding down the length of his spine, cutting through skin and bone and sinew, opening him up, exposing the heart of him.

She couldn't know who he was. *Nobody* knew who he was.

He struggled with the shock, trying not to let it show. "That's a fucking terrible name." His voice, luckily and only through years of long practice, was level, not a shred of emotion in it. "Where did you hear that?"

"Oh, around." Her gaze was scalpel-sharp, searching his. "I also heard another name. Fitzgerald. Theodore Fitzgerald. They go together rather nicely, don't you think?"

His thumbs were digging into her soft flesh hard and he knew he was giving himself away, but he couldn't seem to loosen his grip. The only person to say that name in sixteen years had been Violet. The name of a dead man.

He smiled, probably with too much teeth. "I wouldn't know. I've never heard of him."

Temple cocked her head like a bird. "Haven't you? That's not what I was told."

"And what exactly were you told?"

"That you had another name. A name you're clearly

trying to hide." Although she hadn't moved yet, it felt like she'd kicked him in the gut, taking the wind out of him. "Why is that, *Theo*? Did you not want your father to know you were in the same business?"

How did she know? Who had told her? There was only one person who knew, and that was Violet.

Not the only person. Hunt knew.

Ah, fuck, he did.

"Is that who you were talking to?" He didn't bother trying to deny it. There was no point, not with that name out there. "Was it Elijah Hunt?"

Her smile promised a wealth of secrets. "Wouldn't you like to know?"

He moved before he was even aware of doing so, one hand gripping her ponytail and jerking her head back hard, leaning all his weight forward, pressing her up against the glass of the window at her back. With his other hand, he held her chin, pinning her where she was with the weight of his body. "Tell me where you got that information," he demanded, cold and flat. "And I won't hurt you."

She'd gone very still. Her breathing was absolutely steady, and there was no fear at all in her eyes, only a savage kind of satisfaction. "You won't hurt me, Jericho. And I'm not fucking telling you anything until you give me the information I want." The determination in those golden eyes of hers was hard, certain, and sure, as if she was the one holding the upper hand.

Clever little bitch.

"You can't do anything with that." He held her tightly, keeping her right where she was. "No one gives a shit what my real name is, not as long as I deliver them the power and the money they want. And as far as the rest of the world is concerned, Theodore Fitzgerald died jumping off a bridge sixteen years ago. So you have nothing. And making demands of me right now is a seriously bad fucking idea."

"Maybe. But there's a reason you don't want anyone to know who you are." Her voice was level, her gaze like a laser beam, cutting into him. "What is it, Jericho? Or maybe . . . *who* is it?"

There were so many reasons why he'd assumed the name of the man he'd killed in order to take his place. Why he'd made sure Theodore Fitzgerald stayed dead.

It was a repudiation of his father. A way to protect his sister. A kind of vengeance. And a vow.

A promise he'd made to himself that he'd do whatever it took in order to bring down the empire he'd built. Become something he despised.

Become Jericho. Murderer. Drug dealer. Pimp. Trafficker. Scum of the earth.

He couldn't do that as Theodore. So Theodore had to die. And that was a good thing, because poor, craven Theodore would never have had the balls to do it.

You should kill her. End this madness now.

He should. That's exactly what he should do. Get rid of her and the threat she presented. And not only because of what she'd just found out, but because of what she made him feel. He already had Violet buried like a thorn in his heart. He didn't need to start having feelings about another woman. Even if those feelings were more to do with his cock and years of celibacy than anything else.

Yes, do it. How can you do what you need to do with distractions like Temple around anyway?

Good fucking point.

Perhaps she sensed the change in him, because without warning she twisted, her knees jerking up, the soles of her booted feet planting themselves right in the center of his gut, and she shoved hard.

Taken by surprise, he lost his grip on her hair and stumbled back, knocking over an armchair. She'd slipped from the windowsill, her arms loose at her sides. She looked relaxed, but he knew she wasn't. She was ready to kill if necessary.

Well, maybe they should both try it. Let the strongest and the best survive.

He straightened. Smiled.

Then he came for her.

CHAPTER TEN

She didn't know what had changed for him, but something had, and it wasn't just the mention of his real name. There was a darkness behind his green eyes, a shadow she hadn't seen before. It was bleak, cold, and she recognized it. It was the darkness she'd seen in the eyes of her victims just before they died.

And she knew because she'd made herself watch every death.

Why the hell it should be in the eyes of this man she had no idea, but the last thing it should have done was matter to her. Yet for some reason she didn't understand, it did. Which was just fucking unacceptable.

She didn't want to be curious about him. She didn't want to know anything about him.

Especially when he was crossing the room with the express intention of killing her.

Like moonlight shining on the sharpened blade of an ax, he was all cold, brutal power, and she couldn't look away. Because somehow that power was made even more mesmerizing by that bleak darkness lurking behind the blazing emerald of his eyes.

She shouldn't be looking at him in the way she was, shouldn't be letting the sheer physical beauty of him distract her. Even coming toward her, all deadly lethal intent, he was beautiful.

He wasn't in suit pants and business shirt today. Instead he wore worn jeans that sat low on his hips and a plain black hoodie, nondescript clothes that should have masked the charisma of the man who wore them. But they didn't, not even a bit.

Yet there was no time to stare at him, no time to even think, not when his fist was coming fast toward her face. Fuck, he wasn't holding back.

She barely managed to dodge it, the brush of air against her cheek giving her a taste of the power he'd put behind it and yeah, he really *wasn't* holding back. Dropping to the ground, she swept out a foot, but he avoided her, stepping in close and reaching for her shoulder, probably to pull her down so he could deliver a knee to her gut.

She didn't oblige him, bending and twisting so his hands closed on empty air, ducking then rising to deliver a kick of her own inside his guard, in the center of his chest. Her foot connected, but it wasn't until his fingers wrapped around her ankle that she realized he'd let her do it. Dammit. She should have been paying closer attention.

He jerked her ankle, pulling her off balance, so she went with the movement, twisting her foot out of his grip before she ducked and rolled away from him. He went straight after her, aiming a kick to her abdomen, but this time it was her turn to snatch a grip at his boot and twist hard, using her strength and the movement of her body to jerk him off his feet.

He cursed as he went down, somehow folding his long body and reaching for her as he did so, and she'd thought she'd managed to avoid him, her forearms coming out to knock his hands away. Yet his reflexes were incredibly fast because she found herself hitting empty air, his hands settling on her hips and crashing her down to the floor with him.

She hit hard, her head banging against the carpet, but there was no time to recover. His grip was so strong and she knew if she hesitated she'd be toast. Dazed, she rolled onto her back so he was above her, then brought up her knee, aiming it at his groin. At the same time, she shot up the heel of her hand to the underside of his jaw, putting all the power she could behind it.

He avoided her knee with a twist of his hips, his own coming down hard on her inner thigh, making her gasp in pain. But he didn't quite avoid her hand, his teeth snapping together as she hit his jaw, blood trickling down the side of his mouth. She didn't wait to see if she'd dazed him, giving another violent twist of her body, flipping over onto her stomach, trying to loosen his hold and get out from under him.

Jericho cursed and suddenly the whole weight of him was lying on her, crushing her to the carpet, pressing her face into the white wool and forcing all the air from her lungs. She fought for breath, trying to buck him off, but it was like moving a mountain. Trying a different tactic, she attempted getting her knees underneath her so she could use her quads to push up with more force, yet he shifted his legs, trapping hers beneath them. Then his arm came around her throat, heavy as an iron collar, and he jerked her head back.

She tensed her neck muscles, bending her head forward to relieve the pressure on her throat, but he only shifted, pulling even harder. She moved her arms, trying to turn her body enough to elbow him, yet again he shifted out of the way, the iron collar of his arm around her throat closing, pulling tighter, squeezing.

Her vision began to darken around the edges, warm breath brushing by her ear.

"I'm sorry, kitten." His voice was so soft, so unbearably gentle. "I don't want to have to do this, but you're getting in the way. And I can't have *anything* getting in the way, now that I'm so close."

It was strange, but even with her lungs screaming and her vision darkening, all she could think about was what was she getting in the way of? And what was he so close to?

You'll never find out if you don't get out of this.

No, she wouldn't. But he was too strong, too fast. And she'd let herself get in this position. If she hadn't been so distracted by him, if he hadn't been as good as he was . . .

There is one option you're forgetting.

Temple blinked. Christ, of course. This fascination, this chemistry, it went both ways. And maybe, if she was lucky, she wouldn't be the only one to miss her chance to kill.

You will *be lucky. You know he likes a fight.*

Yeah, and hadn't he told her that himself? She closed her eyes and gave a minute shift of her hips. And sure enough she felt the heat pressing against her butt and the hard line of his cock. Excellent.

A surge of adrenaline went through her, clearing her vision a little, giving her the strength to move again, an undulating movement of her hips, rubbing the curve of her butt against his groin.

More breath at her ear, ragged and harsh. "What are you doing, little bitch?"

She didn't waste precious air in answering him, just kept up that slow, undulating movement, feeling the press of him against her get more insistent.

The arm around her throat loosened fractionally, the pressure easing. "Oh, kitten." The rough velvet of his voice was fraying around the edges. "Don't make this harder than it already is."

She licked her dry lips, forcing herself to speak. "Actually

I don't think it's hard enough. Not nearly hard enough." And she circled her hips in a long, slow grind.

"This won't stop me." His breathing was even harsher. "All it'll do is put off the inevitable."

Temple swallowed, her throat sore, staring down at the white carpet beneath her. She'd never begged for anything, never wanted to make herself so vulnerable to anyone, but here, right now, she knew he meant what he said. He would kill her. And she couldn't let him. If there was a chance that Thalia was still alive and that Temple could have rescued her, but let herself get killed instead . . .

"I don't want to die," she said hoarsely. "Please. I can't. Not yet."

There was a silence behind her, the hot, heavy weight of him pinning her to the ground, the iron collar of his arm around her throat. "Why not yet?"

She closed her eyes. "Because I have to find my sister first."

More silence and it seemed to echo strangely in her ears, though that could have been her heartbeat, wild and loud in her head.

Then he moved, the arm around her disappearing as he flipped her onto her back. The look on his face was intense, fierce, his eyes gleaming in the light coming from the lounge windows. Emerald green yet lit with golden flames. The light also touched the gilt tips of his hair and the dark gold stubble that lined his strong jaw.

He looked like a fallen angel. An angel with a demon's soul.

"What sister?" he demanded.

Perhaps it had been a mistake to tell him, to give him that secret. And certainly if he hadn't been holding her down with the intention of strangling her, then she wouldn't have told him. But it was done now, it was out. She'd given him something of herself, and she couldn't take it back.

So she stared up at him, not looking away. "The name I gave you. Thalia Cross. She's my sister. And I'm trying to find her."

A strange expression crossed his face, one she couldn't immediately identify. "And what makes you think I know anything about your sister?"

She didn't want to tell him, didn't want him to confront her with it. Because this wasn't going how she'd thought it would. She'd wanted to have him at her mercy, perhaps begging for his life while she told him all the reasons he couldn't have it. Told him why it was so important that she find Thalia, what her sister had saved her from. Told him all the things she'd done and all the lives she'd taken, each one stripping little pieces of her soul away from her until all she had left was the determination to go on. And the rage she had for the man who'd put her in this position.

The man who'd turned out to be him.

No, she didn't want to tell him that while she lay beneath him, defeated on the floor, her life in his hands. It wasn't supposed to be that way.

But then life never happened the way you wanted it to.

"Because you were the man who took her," Temple said harshly. "You were the man who trafficked her. And if she's dead, that makes you the man who murdered her."

For a moment he could only stare down at the woman on her back, her red hair spread all over the white carpet like spilled blood. Like she had been in Paris, only this time it was different. Very, very different.

He should have finished the job, he knew he should have. And he still couldn't think why he hadn't. Sex shouldn't have been able to distract him and certainly one fucking hard-on shouldn't. How curious to have his own tactics turned back on him. How curious for them to actually work.

Yet it wasn't only his dick that had stopped him. There was something else too, the last bit of his conscience, the one he'd tried very hard to protect and preserve over the past sixteen years. The bit that whispered to him that killing her was wrong. That if he did, he'd fall the rest of the way into the darkness, and there would be no coming back. Pretty fucking curious thing too since he hadn't planned on coming back anyway.

His conscience. And the shake in her voice as she'd told him she didn't want to die. Because she had a sister she wanted to find.

A sister she was now accusing him of having murdered.

There are so many sisters you murdered. Can you even remember one of them?

Molten anger moved in her gaze, the rage he'd seen there before. No wonder he'd thought this was personal. It was.

"What happened to her?" He shifted his hands to rest on the carpet on either side of her head, keeping his weight on her, pinning her.

Her throat moved, pale and graceful. "I don't know what happened to her. That's why I'm fucking here. To find out where she is, what you did to her."

"What makes you think I had anything to do with it?"

"I'll give you one guess." Her eyes blazed. "Because you're a fucking human trafficker! That's what you do. You take women, and you sell them. And my goddamn sister was sold. Like a fucking animal!"

He couldn't say why her words hit him the way they did, when he'd had so many other people hurl those same accusations at him before. With as much hate and as much despair. But something in the way Temple said it hooked into that last, remaining shred of his conscience and wrenched it apart.

She had a sister like he had a sister. A sister she'd clearly loved. Who'd disappeared.

What if someone had taken Violet?

Ice congealed in his gut, and he shoved himself abruptly off her, getting to his feet and turning away, moving restlessly over to the windows.

No one would take Violet. No one would fucking touch her.

Perhaps he'd been wrong to let her slip away from him the way she had a month ago. Perhaps he should have gone after her, made sure to keep her safe. Now she was with Hunt and things were going to go down with him that would put her at risk.

"What? You don't like me telling you the truth?" Temple's voice was sharp behind him.

He stared out the window, at the people passing by on the sidewalk outside. "I have no problem with the truth. And yes, buying and selling people is what I do." He'd trained himself to hear the words without flinching, to say them too because he wasn't going to dress it up, pretend what he did was anything but what it was.

Yet still, he didn't like the words in Temple's mouth.

"So you did take her then." It wasn't a question.

It could have happened. So many girls had been taken. "When did she disappear?" He kept his gaze on the street.

"Seven years ago."

Seven years . . . He'd been the previous Jericho's right-hand man then, the cruel old bastard's most trusted lieutenant. And then Theo had killed him and assumed the Jericho mantle himself, just as he'd planned. But . . . his father had controlled the American trafficking networks, which meant that he was the one who'd taken Temple's sister.

That doesn't abrogate you of responsibility.

Hell no. If his fucking old man had taken her, he'd likely have passed her on through his own channels, such as the Lucky Seven or Conrad's casino in Monte Carlo. But that name . . . it was still familiar to him and he didn't know why.

"I'll look into it," he said flatly.

"Oh yes, you'll look into it." She was right behind him now, and there was nothing but intent in the words. "Because I'm the only one who knows who you really are. And if you think I won't use that, you're mistaken."

He turned.

Temple stood there, her expression fierce. Her hands were in fists at her sides as if she was only just holding herself back from launching herself at him. Rage glowed in those beautiful eyes of hers, and it connected with something similar inside of him too. A rage that had been there a long, long time.

"I'll kill you before you do that," he said before he could stop himself, the rage leaking out whether he wanted it to or not.

"Oh, like you killed me just now?" Sarcasm laced her tone. "Yeah, of course you will. Because nothing's more important than your own fucking hide."

"I don't give a shit about my own hide." He stared at her, held her gaze. "But you're not the only one with people to protect."

"What? You mean you?" There was nothing but disbelief in the words. "Like you'd protect anyone."

She had no idea what his eventual goal was, and he couldn't tell her, couldn't take that risk. But it had been years since he'd met anyone who knew his real name, who knew where he'd come from. Not even Dmitri, with whom he'd shared his actual mission, knew he was Theodore Fitzgerald, and part of him just wanted to be able to say Violet's name aloud, to acknowledge her existence.

So the words came out of him before he had a chance to stop them. "I have a sister too." His voice was thick, much thicker than it should be. "Her name is Violet."

She blinked, shock crossing her features. "You . . . what?"

"She's younger than I am." He couldn't seem to stop talking. "She's vulnerable. And if people know my name, they will use her to get to me."

"So? My sister was vulnerable too." The anger in Temple's gaze glowed hot, and she took a few more steps toward him. "She was supposed to go to college, get a degree. But my father decided he needed more fucking heroin and didn't have any money. So he paid for it with the only currency he had." She took another step, virtually spitting the words at him, and they landed like blows. "He sold her to his goddamn dealer, and I didn't even know until it was too late."

That's when Jericho heard it, the pain in her voice, an edge of vulnerability to her that she probably hadn't meant to reveal and yet was so obvious now.

It made his chest feel tight in a way it hadn't in at least a decade.

"I didn't even notice she was gone until that night." Temple took another step, until she was right in front of him, fury radiating from her like heat from the sun. "Until I tried to ask Dad where she was, but he was so fucking out of it he couldn't even speak. It wasn't till the next day he told me what he'd done. And I couldn't do a thing. I couldn't do a fucking thing about it. Not when I was only fifteen."

Fifteen. Christ. So goddamn young. Seven years her sister had been gone, which must mean she was only twenty-two. So what the hell had she been doing for seven years that had turned her into this . . . weapon?

You know what she's been doing. It's obvious. She's on a mission, just like you.

The realization hit him like one of her kicks, powerful and hard, driving all the air from his lungs.

"But you're doing something now, aren't you?" He couldn't stop his hand from lifting, from cupping her proud jaw, wanting to touch her since he always seemed to be wanting to touch her. "That's why you found me. That's why you're here. You want revenge."

And maybe you should let her take it.

Maybe he should. Not now, not before he finished what he'd started, but afterward, when it was all over. Death at her hands would be something he might even enjoy.

She didn't try to pull away from his touch, not even given the fact he'd been trying to choke the life out of her not five minutes earlier. She only stared up at him, tough and angry and burning like a flame. "I want to find my goddamn sister, that's all that matters to me. And yeah, getting the chance to kill you is an unexpected bonus."

"I'll find out what happened to your sister." He let his thumb trace the line of her cheekbone, her skin soft and warm. "But only if you keep my identity to yourself. If you put Violet at risk, you get nothing. And if Violet dies . . . so do you."

Temple had paled, but she didn't look away. "Does she know what you are?"

The question caught him by surprise, the answer unexpectedly painful. "Yes. She knows."

"Then why doesn't she get the hell away from you?"

"She has. She did. But . . ." He stopped. These were Violet's secrets, not his. He shouldn't be giving them out like this.

"But what?"

He stared down into Temple's amber eyes. "I don't owe you answers, kitten. Stop demanding them."

"Then stop touching me."

Yet he couldn't. Her warmth felt like it was burning his skin, and he welcomed the pain. Craved it. The very sweetest kind of punishment.

He swept his thumb down across her cheek to the curve of her mouth, tracing the line of her upper lip, watching her face. "No."

"Then give me an answer."

She was learning. Back there on the ground, she'd moved her hips, giving him a little taste of the torture he'd put her through back in Paris, grinding against him. And he was semi-hard even now.

He shouldn't keep talking to her. He shouldn't keep touching her. He should prove his strength by pulling away and leaving her here. And he most definitely shouldn't give her any answers about himself or about Violet.

"I wanted to get Violet out of New York," he found himself saying. "I wanted to get her away, but she refused to go. Because she wanted to stay with someone. A man she shouldn't be with."

Temple's mouth was so unimaginably soft beneath this thumb, her lower lip as sensual as a courtesan's. He stroked his thumb back and forth over it, the heat of her skin sinking deep inside, a third-degree burn that was going to leave a scar. "No wonder she didn't want to go with you," Temple said, her voice hoarse, her gaze drifting down to his mouth as if she was imagining doing to him what he was doing to her. "She must hate you."

That hurt. And it shouldn't. Because plenty of people hated him, and he'd come to terms with that fact. But not Violet. Never Violet.

"She thought I was dead." He pressed his thumb gently against that soft, pillowy lip, wanting the pain, wanting the scar. "And I let her believe it for years because I thought that was safer for her. But . . . things changed, and she wasn't safe anymore, so I had to do something about it."

"So what did you do?" Temple was standing very still, her breathing a little faster, a little harder.

"I kidnapped her. And unfortunately, that involved revealing who I was to her." He stopped, because anything he admitted now could reveal himself and he couldn't. Because ultimately how he felt about Violet, how he felt about anything at all, didn't matter. Nothing mattered but taking down what he'd built.

Yet Temple wasn't looking at his mouth now, she was looking straight into his eyes. Looking straight at the demon inside him. "She didn't know then, did she? She didn't know that not only was her brother alive, he was also a human slave trader."

A memory came back to him, of a run-down lounge in Alphabet City. Of Violet standing in front of him, protecting him from the scarred man who'd pointed a gun at him, hate in his tar-black eyes. And the words that man had said to him . . . *"Two years she was in that fucking Russian brothel . . . That's what your cocksucker of a father told me. He also told me that you were the one who sold her there. You made the deal. And you were the one who let her die after a client slit her throat."*

Violet had heard, and he hadn't denied it. Because he couldn't. Hunt's wife was another woman his predecessor had bought and sold just before he himself had taken over. Yet he was still complicit. He hadn't gone to find her, hadn't gotten her out.

Individual women didn't matter, couldn't be allowed to matter.

Only the end could justify the means. It had to.

"No," he said, a bleak edge creeping into his voice that he couldn't quite seem to tune out. "She didn't know. But she does now."

An odd expression flickered over Temple's face. Puzzlement. "You didn't want her to know, did you?"

He pushed on her lower lip harder, because it felt like part of him was changing, a part that should never be altered and yet was changing all the same. "No," he repeated. "If I'd had my way, I would have stayed dead."

"Why?" she demanded, suddenly fierce again for some reason. "Why the hell should you care?"

He allowed himself a smile that didn't quite reach his eyes. "You think human traffickers don't have feelings too?"

She lifted a hand, moving so fast he didn't see the hit coming until her fist slammed into his cheekbone, snapping his head back. Pain radiated out like cracks in a windowpane, shattering something hard and cold inside him, and he had to heave in a breath, fighting for air.

Temple hadn't moved, not even to raise her hands to defend herself against retaliation. She was only looking at him, absolute fury in her gaze. "Don't you dare make fun of this. Don't you fucking make this into a joke. You *destroy* people. You *hurt* people. So yeah, I'm asking why you care so deeply about your fucking sister, when it's clear you don't give a shit about anyone else." She was breathing fast and hard too, her T-shirt pulling tight across her high, round breasts.

And it filled him suddenly. The pain and the desire, feelings he hadn't let himself have for a long, long time. Feelings he shouldn't be letting himself have now, and yet they were there all the same, sharp and raw, cutting through the heart of him.

Because of her. Because of the way she burned, bright and terrible as a star.

He reached for her, jerking her hard against him, bringing all that heat and fire right up close, and he thought she might hit him again, and God knew, he fucking deserved it. But she didn't.

Instead she just looked at him, as if she could see everything he was, everything he'd once been. His judge, jury, and executioner all rolled up into one sexy package.

"Oh God, you do care," she said, the words so hard they were almost an accusation. "Jesus Christ, you do and *that's* the problem, isn't it? You care, and you don't want to."

CHAPTER ELEVEN

Temple was nearly vibrating with rage. He'd looked so bleak when he'd told her about his sister, his beautiful voice hoarse as he'd spoken her name. And then he'd smiled that horrible, cold smile and made a joke about it, and really, it was good she hadn't been holding a knife because she would have put it through his black heart right then and there. Which wouldn't have helped Thalia in the slightest.

Luckily all she'd had was her fist, but punching him didn't make her feel any better. Especially not when a fleeting weariness had crossed his face. A weariness she knew had nothing to do with physical exhaustion and everything to do with bearing a heavy emotional burden. She should know, after all, she'd been carrying her own for years.

Infuriating when she didn't want to feel the same things he did. Didn't want to understand him. But almost against her will, she was starting to see the man beneath the crime lord, a man who was far more complicated than she'd ever thought possible.

He obviously cared about his sister, and that weariness . . . A man who bought and sold people the way he did shouldn't feel emotionally weary. A man like that shouldn't have had any emotions at all. Yet . . . Jericho did, and it was there in that bleakness in his eyes, in the hoarseness of his voice, in the weariness, the terrible,

terrible weariness that had crossed his face after she'd hit him.

And there was only one reason for all of those things, and it wasn't because he didn't care. It was because he cared too much and didn't want anyone to know.

She could see it now as the doors behind his eyes slammed shut, his expression closing up, hardening. The gold in his eyes faded until there was nothing but those cold, hard, emerald edges that cut like knives.

"That's enough." His voice was like ice, all the velvet heat stripped right out of it.

But she ignored him, ignored the pressure of his fingers on her hips, staring right up into his face, trying to see beyond all those walls and closed doors. "Bullshit it's enough. What are you doing, Theo? And who the hell are you really?"

She hadn't said his name deliberately, it had just slipped out, yet she saw the effect it had on him, the flare of some expression she didn't understand deep in his eyes.

He pushed at her suddenly, trying to put her from him, but instead she shoved at him, hard enough that he went back into the windowsill. He tensed, anger leaping in his gaze, and for a moment she thrilled to it, because that was better than that horrible cold look.

What do you mean "better"? Why the hell should you care?

She didn't know, didn't really understand what the fuck was wrong with her since he'd as good as admitted he'd been the one who'd bought Thalia. And that should have meant his death. Instead she was standing there looking at him, desperate to know what was going on.

Knowing his motivations won't make any difference to what he's done.

Shit, she knew that intellectually. And yet . . . A part of her wanted to know more anyway. Such as why he was doing this. Why he was the head of an empire that bought and sold people. How could he justify it? How could he live with it?

You're a fine one to talk. How do you justify murder?

As if he'd had a direct line into her brain, he said, "No, you don't get to ask me about why I'm doing this. About caring or otherwise. Not when you kill people for money."

She could feel it then, the hot wash of shame, welling up from a deep place inside, and every part of her wanted to fight it, to deny it. "My targets are all assholes," she shot back. "They're all criminals who deserve what's coming to them. I don't take contracts that hurt innocent people."

He laughed at that, but there was no amusement in it, only anger. "Innocent? Who the fuck determines that? No one is innocent, Temple. We all have our sins, we're all guilty of something."

"So what are you saying?" She tried to hold onto her anger, ignore the shame that was curling around her heart. A shame that went deeper than what she'd had to do as an assassin. A shame that led all the way back to her parents' run-down apartment and a sister who'd done more for her than any sister should. "That all those girls deserved what was coming to them?"

"No. What I'm saying is that you're not in any position to throw stones."

"And what I'm saying is that nothing can justify what you're doing to all those women!"

He stared down at her, his body tense and hot. And she realized she had her hands on his lean hips, holding him like he'd been holding her. Keeping him in place as if this was vitally important. As if she wanted him to understand and that was weird too because she didn't want to have this conversation with him. .

"I'm not trying to justify it," he said fiercely, his hands coming down over hers. "Nothing can excuse what I've done. Nothing can absolve me of blame. And I don't want anything to either. I take full responsibility for all my actions. All I'm trying to point out is that things are more complicated than they seem and nothing is black and white."

His palms were warm, the gold glitter of his temper heating the cold emerald of his eyes. Yeah, complicated all right. She should have killed him when she had the chance, because she had a feeling that no matter how many chances he gave her, actually doing the deed was only going to get harder. Especially when the more she saw of the man behind the crime lord, the more fascinated she became.

For years, everything *had* been black and white. Everything had been simple. Find Thalia. Kill the man who'd taken her. Yet the closer she'd gotten to the truth about what had happened to her sister, the less clear everything else had become.

She'd thought it was the man who'd bought Thalia that she was going to kill. And then she had, with a stolen handgun and only the rudiments of firearms skills. But it hadn't been enough because Thalia had been shipped on, sold to someone else, and on down a chain of people that had led to Fitzgerald. And then from Fitzgerald to the man standing in front of her now.

And nothing was clear anymore, nothing was simple. Fitzgerald was dead, and this man, his son, wasn't the smug prick she'd been expecting. He was beautiful, and there was something in him she recognized because the same thing burned in her.

A cause and a deep loyalty to it. A determination to carry on no matter the consequences.

For her that cause was Thalia. For him it was . . . Violet? No, it was more than that, she was sure of it.

"How complicated?" she demanded.

His mouth twisted, his fingers curling around hers. "Why the fuck would I explain myself to you?"

"Because I asked. Because you owe me."

"I don't owe you anything, kitten. Not a single fucking thing."

A wise woman would have stopped pushing. But she'd stopped being wise a long time ago. "Yes, you do." She turned her hands against his palms, lacing her fingers through his and holding on. "You took Thalia, which means you fucking owe me everything."

The sun coming through the window backlit him, drawing deep golden tones from his hair and from his skin, casting his face into shadow. He pulled his hands back, tugging her toward him and she went because she couldn't seem to stop herself, couldn't seem to drag herself away. Getting closer until she was standing right up against him, her whole body pressed along the hard, muscular length of his.

She shivered. Two days since he'd touched her, and she couldn't tell herself she didn't feel the deep pulse between her thighs. Or the way her skin felt tight and sensitive. And she couldn't tell herself she wasn't still buzzing from the fight they'd just had or the death that had hovered so close.

Maybe she was sick getting off on it. How he'd fought her and matched her. How he'd pushed her down onto the ground, pinning her there so she was unable to move.

God, she hated giving up control. Why had she liked him taking it from her?

"All I owe you is your sister," he said softly. "So that's all I'm going to give you. Understand?"

That's not all you want.

Stupid. It *was* all she wanted. The rest was just . . . curiosity.

"What about your sister?" she asked, her voice slightly roughened because the feel of him against her was making her breathless. "What about your identity?"

"You'll tell no one."

"Why not?"

"Because you don't want to hurt Violet any more than I do."

He was right. She didn't. Her own sister meant too much to her to willingly put anyone else's at risk. Even Theo's. And apart from anything else, poor Violet sounded like a victim of the usual kind of male threats. Which unfortunately left her without her newfound leverage.

Fuck him.

"I'm still going to kill you," she said. "I'm still going to make sure you pay for what you've done."

A ghost of a smile turned his mouth, and this time it almost reached his eyes, making her wonder what it was that he found so damn funny about his own death. "Sure. I'll even load the gun for you when the time comes. But not yet, kitten." He tugged her even closer, putting his hands behind his back, drawing hers with them so her arms came around his waist. Then he unlaced his fingers from hers and curled them around her hands instead, keeping them there at the small of his back. "I have things to do."

He was so hot. So strong. And there was a darkening bruise on his jaw from where she'd hit him, blending in with the other ones already there from their fight two days ago.

"What things?" she demanded, trying to pay attention to the conversation and not to the press of his hardening cock against the zipper of her jeans.

But he didn't answer. He bent his head instead and his mouth covered hers.

Kissing her was the most logical way to shut her up, make her stop asking questions, stop pushing him for answers he couldn't give her. But really, he kissed her because he wanted to. Because now she was against him, her soft warmth along the entire length of his body, and he just couldn't stop himself.

Because if you don't do something to occupy your mouth, you'll tell her everything.

But he couldn't think of that, couldn't focus on the sudden intense need to tell someone about his plans, to share the burden. It had been so long keeping everything to himself, making sure no one ever found out. Only Dmitri knew, but he couldn't tell Dmitri everything. Couldn't tell him the doubts that came in the darkest part of the night, the fear that all the terrible things he'd done, all the filth he'd covered himself with, would all be for nothing.

No, he couldn't think about telling anyone, least of all the woman who'd tried to kill him twice now.

So he kept his mouth on hers and it wasn't demanding this time because he wanted to take his time. Slowly exploring her, parting her lips with his tongue and sweeping inside for a deeper taste. She let him, angling her head to kiss him back, just as slow and just as sweet.

It was strange to kiss someone like this, to take it gently and slowly. The last time had been with the woman he'd one day thought he'd marry, Lily. The lovely daughter of one of his father's friends. He'd thought he was in love with her, thought his future was set. And then his father had brought him the trafficked girl that night in the Lucky Seven. The girl who'd wept and begged him not to hurt her, begged him to rescue her.

Who you ran away from and left there.

A deep, intense anger turned over in his gut. An anger at himself, at Theodore Fitzgerald, pathetic little shit, who'd fucking run like the coward he was, leaving that girl there to his father's mercy. Who'd done so much more than that too.

Who doesn't deserve deep, slow kisses from women like this one?

Ah, yes, but he wasn't Theodore Fitzgerald anymore, was he? He'd put that asshole in the ground. Now he was harder, stronger, more powerful than anything Theodore Fitzgerald could have imagined. He was fucking Jericho. And he could have whatever he fucking well wanted.

You care. You care too much . . .

He gave her lower lip a sudden, hard nip, feeling her body tense, hearing the sharp rush of her indrawn breath. A punishment for what she'd seen.

Christ, she was too perceptive, and he had no idea how she'd managed to see through him like that. People couldn't know. None of this could be seen to matter to him, because it was a weakness he couldn't afford.

But she wasn't wrong. He did care. He cared about his mission and that's all.

Unexpectedly, Temple pulled away from him, tugging her hands from around his waist and taking a few steps back. Her breathing was fast, her color high, amber eyes glowing in her flushed face.

He wanted to reach for her and drag her to him again, yet he remained where he was, meeting her gaze. His own heartbeat was loud in his head, desire for her pumping hard and fast in his veins.

"What things?" she repeated. "What things do you have to do?"

Fuck, he should never have said anything, never have tried to explain himself. He couldn't even figure out why he had in the first place. Because what did it matter what she thought of him? He *was* everything she'd accused him of being anyway, so it wasn't like he could deny it. Nevertheless, something deep inside him wanted her to know the truth.

"Oh you know, people to traffic," he said, leaning back against the sill and putting the heels of his hands on the edge of it, gripping the edge with his fingers. "Assholes to kill." A flippant response that would probably earn him another punch to the jaw, but what the hell. It was no less than he deserved, so she could fucking bring it.

But this time there was no flash of anger across her features. Instead her brow furrowed, and those lovely golden eyes narrowed as they searched his face.

"No," she said, slowly. "I know you're lying. There's something more, isn't there? There's something big."

"You think I would tell you? After you've just told me you're going to kill me?"

Again she just looked at him and it felt like she was turning him inside out.

He pushed away from the windowsill sharply, coming toward her, suddenly sick of feeling as if all his defenses were being slowly and systematically stripped away. No one did that to him, especially not one deadly little redhead he'd only met a couple of days previously.

"I think you want to tell someone." Temple's voice was quiet. "I think you have to."

He stopped dead, cold creeping over his skin. She saw too much, this woman. She saw far, far too much. "Don't be silly, little girl. You know nothing about me whatsoever."

Her chin lifted. "I know you like a challenge. That you like a fight. That you were once Theodore Fitzgerald and that something happened to you to make you into . . . *this*. I know you like rough sex, and I know you love your sister. I know you care deeply about the fact that what you do destroys people." She stopped. "How am I doing so far?"

More anger twisted inside him, thick and hot. Defensive. *You want her to know you.*

He shook his head to get rid of that particular thought, because no, no, he fucking didn't. And she was the very last person in the world he'd want to know him anyway.

Instead of answering, he closed the distance between them, reaching for her and jerking her back into his arms, crushing her mouth beneath his. Trying to bury the mad urge to do exactly what some fucking idiot part of him— probably his goddamn dick—was telling him to do and reveal all his secrets to her.

And maybe she knew exactly what he was doing, because her hands came up, her fingers pushing into his hair, gripping him and trying to pull him away.

"No," he said against her mouth, unable to stop himself, half desperate and knowing she would know that too. "Don't. Let me have this, kitten. Please."

He could feel shock go through her, tension making her body stiffen against him, as if that was the last thing she was expecting him to say. Fuck, it was the last thing he'd expected to come out of his mouth too. He didn't plead, and he didn't beg, not ever.

And then she softened in his arms, her grip on his hair loosening. "Let you have what?" The words were soft, her breath warm against his lips.

"You."

"You mean sex."

Of course he meant sex. Of course. He kissed her again, covering her mouth so he didn't have to say it, because he was very much afraid that what would come out wouldn't be that but something different. Something far more revealing.

Her. You want her.

No. He didn't. He couldn't. He couldn't afford to want anything, because what he wanted didn't matter, and it never had. That would negate everything he'd done. Every. Single. Thing.

So he kissed her harder, burying the words he wanted to say in the sweetness of her mouth, in her taste, in the feel of her body against his. Running his hands over the curve of her ass and bringing her more firmly against him.

Her fingers curled in his hair, her nails scraping over his scalp, sending prickles of delicious pain through him. And her lips parted under his, the taste of her hunger rich in his mouth. There was something different in the kiss now, a demand she hadn't given him before. Almost as if she'd granted herself permission to not only have it, but to take it for herself too.

He felt his own desire rise to meet hers, wanting to give her the same challenge she'd given him, wanting her demanding, wanting her desperate. Just like he was. So he raised a hand to the back of her head and gripped her, holding her in place, deepening the kiss, turning it hot and open-mouthed and carnal.

She made a sound in the back of her throat, her nails digging in hard on his scalp, biting his lower lip the way he'd bitten her. The small pain shot through him, heading straight to his cock, making him so hard he ached.

And then she let go of his hair, her hands pushing down between their bodies to unfasten the button of his jeans, going for his zipper and tugging it down. She was panting, her movements sharp and hard as if she couldn't wait.

Her desperation was infectious, and suddenly he was breathless and panting too, his own hands shaking as he pushed the jacket from her shoulders then jerked up her T-shirt. She cursed, her hands fumbling with his boxers while he tore apart the cups of her bra, baring her breasts.

"Oh . . ." A soft gasp escaped her as he slid one hand up the delicate arch of her spine, bringing one breast to his mouth, taking her nipple between his lips and sucking hard.

Then she groaned. "No, damn you." And pulled away,

breathing hard, her hands finding their way beneath the cotton of his boxers, her fingers circling his cock.

He shuddered. Ah, fuck, that felt so good. But he didn't want her having the control, she already got under his skin enough as it was, so he took her wrists in his hands and pulled her fingers away. She fought him, because that's what she always seemed to do, fight to the bitter end, trying to twist her wrists out of his grip.

And perhaps a couple of hours ago, that's exactly what he would have wanted too. But not now. Somehow things had changed. She'd gotten under his skin, seen things in him, made him reveal things he didn't want to reveal, and he'd had enough.

He wanted her and he wanted to be in control. That's all.

So he held on tight to her slender wrists and pulled her hard against him. Then he turned his head so his mouth was right next to her ear. "No fighting, kitten. Not now." And because he wanted to give her something in return, he added, "Please."

She was panting, the heat of her bare skin soaking through the cotton of his T-shirt. "What . . . do you want then?"

He brushed his mouth over the sensitive skin beneath her ear, relishing the shiver that went through her in response. "That's easy. I want your surrender." He hadn't understood fully how important that was to him, not until now.

"I've already given you that."

"No, you haven't." He nuzzled her again, inhaling her scent, intense desire gathering hot and heavy inside him. He wanted this. He *needed* it. "I want you to surrender willingly."

She made a soft, ragged sound. "Why?"

He couldn't have said. It was just a gut deep instinct.

You know why. You want her trust.

He shut his eyes, letting the scent and the feel of her seep into him. He could lose himself in her. He could let go of everything. Which made her dangerous since letting go of everything was exactly what he *shouldn't* be doing. But . . . God, why couldn't he have this? Why couldn't he have just one person he could turn to? One person to talk to?

One person to trust. The woman who wants you dead.

A low, bitter laugh escaped him. "Why? Because if you want me to tell you anything at all, I'm going to need it."

It was crazy. Shit, maybe *she* was crazy. But standing there, held against him, her bare breasts pressed to the hard wall of his chest, his breath on the sensitive skin on the side of her neck making her tremble, she couldn't seem to think of a single reason to refuse him.

She wanted to know everything. What deep, dark secret lay behind his sharp, green gaze. Where the bleakness and the weariness came from. Why he'd told her he'd give her the gun she could use to kill him and put the bullets in there himself. Why he wanted her to surrender to him . . .

So many questions. And she couldn't understand why she was still curious—no, not curious, but desperate. Yes, she was desperate to know.

It would be dangerous to give up control to this man, to *truly* give it up. To put up no fight whatsoever and let him do whatever he wanted. It went against every survival instinct she'd learned over the past seven years. Mainly because it would mean trusting him, and trust never came easy for her, if at all. Because why would it? Especially with him. He'd done those things to Thalia, he hadn't denied it.

And yet you could learn everything if you just gave him this.

He brushed his mouth over her skin once again, and she trembled. Because the truth was, she didn't want to only surrender so she could gain his trust and get under his guard. Find out all his secrets. She wanted to surrender because she wanted him. Because it would feel so good.

Because you haven't let anyone in for such a very long time.

Unable to help herself, she angled her head away from him, exposing the side of her neck, inviting the brush of his mouth. And he took the invitation instantly, soft, burning kisses trailing off her skin, small nips against the base of her throat. "Well?" His voice was a rough murmur. "Last chance, Temple."

She closed her eyes as a cold feeling twisted in the pit of her stomach. A familiar feeling. "I . . . I'm afraid," she heard herself say.

For a second, he went still, his mouth lifting from her skin. "Afraid of what?"

"I . . . don't know. I just . . . You're the very last person on earth I should be surrendering to, and I . . ." She swallowed. "I should be fighting you."

"You have fought me."

"Yeah, and I lost."

"You didn't lose." He kissed her again, his tongue tasting her skin, and she couldn't stop the soft sigh that escaped her. "There are all kinds of different victories."

She didn't quite understand that, not with the way he was sensitizing every one of her nerve-endings with that beautiful mouth of his, making her skin feel tight. Making her nipples hard and her pussy wet and aching. "I c-can't." She couldn't seem to stop herself from shaking. "Not after what you did to Thalia."

"I know. So pretend that the world doesn't exist for a moment. That the past and the future are meaningless.

That I'm not Jericho. That you're not Temple. We're just a man and a woman who want each other."

She wanted to do that. Wanted to do it desperately. "It's wrong."

"Yes. It is." He bit the side of her neck gently, making the breath hiss between her teeth. "But wouldn't you like, just this once, not to have to fight?"

Her soul ached at the words, and she didn't know why. Fighting was all she'd been doing her whole life. She didn't even know what it would mean to stop. "N-No." But even to herself the word sounded weak. "I . . . have to keep fighting. I have to."

He was holding her hands in an iron grip, but now she felt his thumbs stroke the soft skin on the inside of her wrists, sending a cascade of shivers through her. "You care too, don't you? You care too much too."

Tears pricked at the insides of her lids, though she had no idea why she'd teared up. Why her throat felt thick.

He's just like you.

She swallowed, a great wave of inexplicable emotion coming from God knew where. "Yes," she said quickly, as if she was afraid someone would stop her. "Yes, okay. I surrender."

It was stupid. Insane. And she'd probably made the biggest mistake of her life, but it was too late. The words were out, she'd revealed herself. And she couldn't take it back.

Jericho pulled slowly back from her, staring down into her eyes. She couldn't meet that look, it was too intense, too exposing, so she turned her head away, blinking furiously and hoping like hell the tears weren't still there.

But he took her chin in his hand, forced her gaze back to his.

"Don't." She couldn't stop the word from coming out.

He stroked his thumb across her lower lip, gentle and soft. "I wanted surrender, Temple. Not reflex."

She took a shuddering breath. His touch felt like a scrape over raw skin, painful. And yet there was a part of her that yearned for it, that wanted to lose herself in it. Jesus, she didn't even know why she was doing this, why she'd said she'd give him this.

"It doesn't mean loss." The velvet of his voice, all soft, rough heat, felt like the lick of flame. "It doesn't mean defeat. Sometimes surrendering is the most powerful action you can take."

"How would you know?" Even now, she couldn't bring herself to look into his eyes. "Like you've ever surrendered to anyone."

There was a long silence. He didn't stop touching her, his fingers sliding along her jaw, his thumb brushing over her cheekbone. There was something so unbearably gentle about the way he did it that it made her throat ache.

She hadn't ever been touched with gentleness before.

"I have surrendered," he murmured at last, and she heard the darkness in his voice, the shadow he wouldn't tell her about. "That's all I've been doing for the past sixteen years."

This time she did look at him, and this time the bleak expression in his gaze wasn't hidden, but laid bare for her to see. Despair and weariness and determination all mixed together. The look of a man walking into hell, who knew he had no chance of redemption, yet kept walking anyway.

"Theo." His name was a murmur and she didn't even know why she said it.

"I'm not Theo." There was something unutterably sad in his expression. "Theo died a long time ago."

Her chest felt tight, pain in her heart. And she couldn't tell herself any longer that she didn't know why she cared about that look on his face. She couldn't tell herself it was inexplicable, a mystery. She knew.

She knew what it was like to keep going, to keep pushing. To cross lines and boundaries normal people wouldn't even consider going near. And she knew what it was like to accept that there would be no forgiveness for what she'd done, not ever.

She knew what it was like to pursue something even though it meant losing pieces of yourself, because in the end, it wasn't you who mattered. Only the goal. Only achieving the end you were striving for.

He had done all those things, crossed all those boundaries and lost pieces of his soul in the process.

He was like her. They were the same.

She moved, even though she wasn't conscious of doing so, rising up on her toes, pressing her mouth to his, a kiss of comfort and forgiveness, even though there could be no forgiveness, not for either of them.

He remained motionless as she kissed him, still as a statue. And then suddenly he wasn't a statue anymore, his mouth open and hot, his arms tight around her, holding her as if he was afraid she'd get away. He took control of the kiss, and she let him, closing her eyes, melting against him. And this time it wasn't gentle or sweet. It was feverish and savage and raw, and he took everything. There was no time for breath, no time to even think. She just put her head back and gave him everything he wanted.

His hand swept down her body, cupping her breast, stroking her already hard, aching nipple, making her shiver. The he stroked down over her stomach, reaching for the fastenings of her jeans and pulling them open, pushing his fingers under the lace of her panties, finding the slick, hot heart of her.

She wanted to reach for him in return, touch him the

way he was touching her, but she'd promised him a surrender, and so she would give it. And as his finger moved on her clit in a slow, aching circle, she couldn't even remember why this was a bad idea. Why she shouldn't be doing this.

There was only him. Only his touch. Only his kiss. Only the beat of her pulse and the deep clench of irresistible desire.

He took his hands away after a moment, sinking down in front of her to get rid of her boots and to pull her jeans and panties down. Then when she was naked, he picked her up, carried her over to the windowsill and put her down on it. The wood was cool beneath the bare skin of her butt, the glass cold at her back.

Oh God, people would see them, wouldn't they? The sidewalk was right there.

"Wouldn't the couch be more comfortable?" she asked hoarsely, goose bumps rising all over her skin as he pushed her thighs apart.

His jeans were already open from where she'd pulled at his zipper earlier, and she could see the press of his hard-on through his boxers. His stomach was flat and ridged with muscle, crisp golden hair leading down beneath the cotton. "I don't want comfortable." His voice was as hoarse as hers. "I want to see you burn."

"But I—"

He put a finger on her mouth, stopping her words dead. "Surrender, kitten. You promised."

She had. So she didn't speak as he reached into his back pocket and drew out his wallet, getting a condom from it. Biting hard on her lip instead as he ripped the packet open and shoved his boxers down, rolling the latex over his cock. Her fingers itched to do that for him instead, but yeah, she'd promised.

He pushed her back against the glass, sliding one hand

beneath her thigh and hooking it up around his waist. Then he pushed the other wide, opening her up as he positioned himself. The sunlight was full on his face, turning his hair and his skin a deep, dark gold, drawing sparks from the molten look in his eyes. There was desire there as he stared at her, and possession, and a complicated mix of other emotions she couldn't untangle.

"You're mine," he whispered fiercely, intensity blazing from him. "From now on, you're nobody's but mine."

She should have hated that, but she didn't, something way down deep inside her, thrilling to the words. And when he pushed into her, hard and sure, joining his heat to hers, she felt herself tremble. She didn't want to feel like his, yet she did, the cold glass at her back, him hot as a furnace at her front, deep inside her. Marking her.

His hips flexed again, and the pleasure began to spiral outward, tearing a gasp from her throat. On the pavement outside, she heard people walking by, the sounds of laughter drifting on the air, but suddenly it didn't matter. Nothing mattered.

And it came to her that this was what he'd been trying to tell her. That there was only this moment. Only each other.

Only the pleasure building higher and higher.

She leaned back and put her hands on the glass behind her, bracing herself so she could push against him, increase the friction. She didn't look away this time either, holding his gaze, letting him see what he did to her. And he was right. Surrendering didn't feel like a defeat or a loss. As she watched the flames climb high in his green-gold eyes, listened to his breathing come fast and harsh, felt his hold on her tighten, the evidence of his desire for her clear on his face, it felt like one of the most powerful things she'd ever done.

Then, as the pleasure became almost overwhelming, he

leaned in close, resting his forehead against hers. And she didn't think about Thalia or claiming revenge. Didn't think about the death she was going to have to take.

She just looked into his eyes and let herself have the moment.

Let herself have him.

CHAPTER TWELVE

Jericho opened his eyes just as dawn was stretching itself over the city. And it wasn't the earliness of the hour that surprised him as he turned to check the clock on the night-stand. It was the fact that he'd even been to sleep at all.

He didn't sleep much these days and wouldn't have thought he had now, but there was nothing else to account for the blank passage of time in between holding Temple's warm body close and opening his eyes just now.

She was still asleep, twined around him like ivy, breathing deep and slow, and he lay there for a couple of minutes just watching her.

He very deliberately didn't think of what had occurred between them downstairs the day before. All the things he'd said to her, the secrets he'd revealed about himself, because even though he hadn't said anything aloud, she'd been able to read him like a fucking open book.

No, he couldn't think of that. So he thought about what had happened after that instead. Of fucking her up against that window, watching the sun fall across her naked body, turning her hair into a bonfire of brilliant red and gold. The freckles on her milky skin had been like gold dust and the look in her eyes molten.

She hadn't held back this time. She'd given him every-thing. He'd seen the aching vulnerability of her beneath that dangerous edge, the little girl who'd never stopped being scared. Because why else did she protect herself so fiercely? Both physically and emotionally?

Her father had sold his oldest child for drugs. Jesus. What kind of childhood had she had?

You know what kind.

Yeah, he did. The kind he saw evidence of every day, in the lives of the girls who got trapped in his network. In the lives of the drug dealers and users he came into contact with all the time. His world . . .

A world she should never have been a part of, and yet by an accident of birth or a cruel twist of fate or just fucking life, she was.

No wonder she was protecting herself.

She had her head on his chest, strands of red hair falling over her face so he pushed them back, hooking the silken red curls behind her ear.

Her relationship with her sister was obviously important to her, or at least had been, and it made him wonder what exactly Thalia had done for her little sister. Maybe like he had with Violet, Thalia had protected Temple. Maybe she'd kept her safe. And when she'd disappeared . . .

Cold moved inside him, though what a fucking hypocrite he was to worry about this one small woman, to hope nothing bad had happened to her and yet, knowing what he knew, to realize that something bad probably had. Because something had to have set her on the path toward finding her sister. Toward vengeance.

She's not the only one. What about all the others?

So many other women who'd had it worse than Temple. So many trapped in the trafficking web who still did. He couldn't make one woman more special than all the rest, no matter how much his body wanted to. They all mattered. They all needed saving.

Suddenly restless, he eased her off him, untangling her gently so he could slide out of bed. Since going back to sleep wasn't going to be happening, he really should go do something productive.

His usual schedule was to spend the early hours of the morning in the gym, so he went over to the dresser. The drawers of his Manhattan house were always kept stocked with fresh clothes so he managed to find himself some work-out gear and pulled it on.

Then he went to the door and pulled it open only to find Dmitri leaning against the wall opposite. His bodyguard pushed himself upright the moment he saw him, his expression grim.

Fuck, there was always something wasn't there? "What?" he demanded.

Dmitri got straight to the point. "It's Hunt. Someone else made a move on him."

His gut clenched hard, but he made himself close the bedroom door behind him so as not to wake Temple, a slow measured movement that would give him a chance to get his fucking emotions in order and not let a hint of anything show.

Because all he could think about was the look he'd seen on Violet's face the day before as he'd stood in the shadows watching her. As she'd turned to see Hunt come toward her, joy brightening her features, happiness sparking in her blue eyes . . .

Jesus, if Hunt had been taken out, what would that mean for Violet?

"Is Hunt dead?" Another demand, but he didn't give a shit. He had to know.

"No. But it's looking like he's lost control of his Southern operations."

Jericho folded his arms, keeping his face blank as

relief flooded through him. Strange to feel relieved that the prick was still alive when he'd been thinking of taking him out himself.

Dmitri's gaze narrowed. "This is bad, boss. We can't be losing operations like this."

Christ, he had to get himself under control. Dmitri asking questions could lead to suspicions about Violet, and that in turn might lead to the discovery of Jericho's own identity. It probably wouldn't mean anything to Dmitri, but he didn't want the guy knowing all the same. The fewer people who knew who he'd once been the better.

"I know it's bad," he said curtly. "We're going to have to take control before we lose the whole fucking thing."

"Do you want me to take him out?" Despite the early hour, Dmitri looked like he was ready to kill at a moment's notice. Then again, he always looked like that. "Should be relatively easy to do since we know where he lives. The place is a fucking fortress, but we have the weaponry to deal with it, I'm pretty sure."

It was clear from the look on Dmitri's face and the way he was already looking down the hallway toward the stairs, that he expected Jericho to tell him to go do exactly that.

He'd be waiting a long time.

Taking Hunt out wasn't going to work, Jericho knew that as surely as he knew the man he'd once been was dead. It was the most logical thing to do, the easiest, and the surest way to take control of the American trafficking networks.

It was what he should do in order to make absolutely sure he took down every single sonofabitch when the time came.

Yet he couldn't seem to give the word. Because of Violet. Because her heart was involved. And like Temple, he cared. She'd lost a lot, his sister. She'd lost her father, then discovered he'd been a murderer and a human trafficker.

She'd lost him too, her brother, and then found out that he was just as stained as their father had been.

She'd lost too much, and he didn't want to be the reason she lost any more.

So instead he turned and walked down the hall without a word, making for the office at the end of it. Behind him, he heard Dmitri curse then come after him.

Slamming open the office door, Jericho strode in and went over to the heavy oak desk where a sleek silver computer stood. He pressed a button, and the machine woke up, the screen flickering on. There was a map of Manhattan glowing there, a blue dot in the center. Violet's location. He'd had one of his staff get a lock on her phone and had been keeping tabs on her for the past month, just making sure she was okay.

So far it looked like she was in Hunt's apartment, so that was good. It would actually be for the best if she stayed there.

"What the fuck is going on?" Dmitri growled.

Jericho didn't answer him, pulling his phone out of the pocket of his work-out shorts, and texting an order to one of the team who dealt with IT. A minute or so later, they came back with the cell phone number he'd requested. Hunt's number.

Ignoring Dmitri, Jericho walked over to the windows, looking out over the leafy Upper East Side street. Already people were up and making their way to work as the sun rose, the traffic getting heavier.

He called the number and waited, and eventually someone answered.

"Who the fuck is this?" The voice was deep and gravelly and familiar.

"I think you know who it is," Jericho said flatly.

There was a silence.

"What do you want?" Just as flat.

"There's a café near Bryant Park. Meet me there at nine. We need to talk."

"Why the fuck would I want to talk to you? The only reason I didn't kill you is because of Violet."

Jericho stared out into the dawn. "It's because of Violet we need to talk."

"I'm not—"

But he didn't wait to hear what the other man wasn't, hitting the disconnect button and ending the call. Hunt would be there, he was sure of it. If he cared for Violet, he would.

"Who's Violet?" Dmitri's voice was suspicious.

"Hunt's woman." Jericho put his phone back in his pocket. "He'll be very careful with her."

"Is she a threat or leverage?"

He glanced at the Russian, who was standing near the door, his arms folded. "I mentioned her name as a reminder of what's at stake." It was the closest he could get to the truth without making Dmitri suspicious.

The other man scowled. "Why the hell are you setting up a meeting with him? Don't we want to take him out?"

"No." He turned and met the other man's gaze head on. "We don't."

Dmitri blinked. "What the hell?"

He ignored the question. "We need to get his operations on lockdown. Take out any asshole who's gunning for more power. Do we have any more intel on who else might want to take potshots at Hunt's little empire?"

Dmitri's scowl deepened. "Not yet."

"Get someone on it. I need to know, and I need to know now."

"What's going on, boss?"

Jericho came slowly back over to his desk, glancing down at the computer screen and the little blue dot. Violet. "We can't have the U.S. networks look like they're going down, not given the situation with the Russians. They need to look strong, and taking out Hunt would weaken them."

There was silence from his bodyguard and just as well. He wasn't in the mood to argue.

Stopping Hunt from taking down any more of the network was vital. How exactly he was going to convince him of that without actually revealing the truth was . . . uncertain.

Why not tell him? He might be more amenable if he knew what you were actually doing. Especially since you both have a common goal.

Well, they did. But he couldn't tell Hunt what was really going on, he really couldn't. Not when Violet could be put at risk. Not when the more people who knew, the less safe a secret was. No hint of what he planned could get out, not the merest breath.

Because if the various crime syndicates caught even a whiff of it, he was a dead man. Not that that bothered him overly. What bothered him was that they'd pull out of the agreements, start protecting themselves. And once they started doing that, all the information he'd spent years collecting would be worthless.

He had to catch them unaware. It was the only way his plan would work.

"Hunt will never work with you," Dmitri said at last. "You know that."

Jericho looked over at the other man. "I'll convince him."

"How?"

"Incentive."

The bodyguard's expression became even grimmer. "His woman?"

It was the only way. The truth simply wasn't an option, which left him with only one choice. If he couldn't kill

Hunt, he'd have to get him on board somehow. And the only way to do that was to make him think Violet's safety was at risk. The man didn't need to know that, of course, Violet would never be harmed. He only needed to believe she might be.

Which meant Violet had to believe it too.

She already believes the worst of you. It won't be too difficult.

He looked away, back down to the screen with the blue dot. His chest had started to ache, the pain reaching deep inside of him.

It didn't matter what she thought of him. It didn't matter if she hated him. His feelings weren't important.

All that mattered was that Hunt lived. That Violet was safe. And he took control of his father's empire.

The rest was just dust in the wind.

"Yes," he said flatly. "I want her in our custody by nine."

The big man nodded, his expression clearing at being given something to do.

"Oh and Dmitri?"

"Yes, boss?"

"If she is harmed in any way and I do mean in *any* way, I'll feed your balls to the dogs. Am I clear?"

Temple stepped back quickly as footsteps started heading toward the doorway of the room Jericho and Dmitri had gone into. There was no time to return to Jericho's bedroom but luckily there was a door to another room behind her, so she pulled it open and slipped through it, shutting it after her as quietly as she could. Then she pressed her ear to the wood, listening as the heavy footsteps passed by the room she was hiding in.

She waited there a minute until the footsteps faded, then she let out a breath and turned around, leaning against the door.

The room looked to be some kind of bedroom, not that she really cared, not after hearing what had gone on with Jericho and Dmitri. They'd been speaking in Russian so she didn't understand what they'd said, but she'd heard Hunt's name. And Violet's. And Jericho's voice when he'd issued that last order had been hard, cold.

She didn't know what the hell was going on, but she had a horrible feeling Violet was going to get caught in the middle.

Fear began to form in her gut, an icy lump of it, and that didn't make any sense, because she didn't even know Violet. It shouldn't matter to her what happened to the woman. Yet it did.

Because of him.

Temple closed her eyes and swallowed, her mouth dry, her throat aching.

Yeah, she couldn't deny it. She was worried for him. Afraid that whatever he was doing, whatever goal he was aiming for, it was more important to him than the safety of his own sister. That he would sacrifice her if it came down to it. And she couldn't let that happen. She just . . . couldn't.

It would kill him, she knew it in her bones. Maybe not physically, but it would kill *something* in him. He was a man who'd lost a good part of his soul already, and she knew, she just fucking well *knew*, that if anything happened to Violet, it would destroy whatever was left.

Why should you care? You want him dead yourself.

Yeah and that's why it didn't make any sense.

But yesterday had . . . changed things. She hadn't been able to get the look on his face when he'd told her he'd surrendered out of her head. She wanted to know what it was he'd surrendered to. Was it the pull of money? Was his greed greater than his capacity to care? He felt very strongly about things, that was for sure, so maybe that was it. And yet . . .

That thought felt wrong. He'd told her it was complicated, and in her experience greed wasn't complicated. People always wanted more than what they had, and so they took it, and they didn't give a shit about the consequences.

Okay, so he'd been greedy with her. After he'd fucked her up against that window the day before, he'd picked her up and carried her up to his bedroom, and kept her there all night. Making her scream. Making her burn. Taking her control from her and giving her pleasure in its place.

Yeah, he'd been greedy all right. But men who wanted power or money or even just sex didn't get that bleak look in their eyes. They didn't look as if the gates of hell had already closed behind them.

No, it wasn't greed that motivated Jericho. It was something else. And that something had changed things. She didn't want to examine exactly what it had changed yet—if fucking ever. But one thing she did know. She couldn't let him hurt his sister. She couldn't let him destroy himself.

Because after all, it was she who had that honor. He'd promised.

Temple opened her eyes and turned around, pulled open the door and slipped out.

The hallway was empty.

She walked silently over to the door she'd seen Jericho and Dmitri vanish through, and put her hand on the door handle. Then she took a breath and pushed it open.

The room beyond was an office, a heavy oak desk near the windows, bookshelves full of books lining the walls. The walls and floors were white, the same as in other rooms, and it was elegantly and expensively furnished. Yet still, it had the sterile, unlived-in look of a hotel room. Just like all the other rooms in this house. Just like all the other rooms in the house in Paris too.

Clearly nowhere was home for Jericho.

He was sitting behind the desk, his gaze on the computer in front of him, a faint crease between his dark golden brows, and something inside her clenched tight. A weird feeling that was hunger, need, and aching sadness all tangled together.

He looked up as the door swung open and she saw the glitter of gold in his eyes as his gaze met hers.

A stillness fell over the room, the space between them almost oppressively thick with tension.

"I thought you were asleep," he said after a moment, leaning back slowly in his chair.

Since her clothes had been left downstairs, she'd had to go through his drawers to find something to cover herself with, eventually finding a plain black T-shirt. She was naked underneath it, and clearly he knew that too because his gaze swept over her, avid and hungry.

Her nipples hardened, and she had to fold her arms to cover them. "I was."

"Did I wake you?"

Might as well go straight to the point. "I heard you and Dmitri talking."

A faint smile turned the corner of his mouth. "I'm sorry. I should have been quieter."

"You were talking about Elijah Hunt and Violet."

His smile faded. "You listened?"

Temple moved into the room, crossing over to the desk and standing in front of it. "Yeah, I listened."

The distance separating them wasn't far now, but the tension hadn't dissipated. If anything it grew thicker, heavy with menace. He didn't like her eavesdropping, that was for sure.

He linked his fingers, put his hands behind his head, biceps flexing with the movement, making her mouth go dry again as desire turned over inside her. "You won't have gotten much," he said, his voice mild. "Unless you know Russian."

He looked lazy and relaxed, but she knew he wasn't, not with that gleam of sharp emerald in his eyes.

"I don't know Russian, but I heard you mention Violet and Elijah."

"They don't concern you."

She ignored him. "What order did you give Dmitri? It had something to do with Violet, didn't it?"

His expression became even colder. "You should go back to bed. This has got nothing to do with you."

She ignored that too. Instead, she placed her hands flat on the desk and leaned forward, holding his gaze. "Are you going to hurt her, Jericho?"

A bright spark of anger flared briefly in his eyes, before the dark gold of his lashes covered it. "Go back to bed, Temple," he ordered, the heavy authority in his voice landing on her like a lead weight.

"No." She stayed exactly where she was, staring at him. "If you hurt her, I'll use any means necessary to stop you."

"Try it. You couldn't the last time as I recall."

There was nothing of the man she'd seen the night before in his face now. No hint of that darkness, that despair. This was the crime lord. This wasn't Theo.

Theo died a long time ago.

No, he was wrong. Theo was still alive, she'd bet anything on it.

"Don't hurt her, Theo," she said softly, deliberately. "It'll kill you if you do."

He remained ostensibly relaxed. But she could see the tension in his jaw, in his shoulders, in the green of his eyes. "Why the fuck should you care?"

She hadn't thought she'd ever tell anyone, but for some reason it came out anyway. "Because I know what it's like to be the reason someone else got hurt. It steals something from you." She paused. "And I get the feeling you don't have a lot left."

He got up suddenly, pushing himself out of his chair and coming around the desk. And she braced herself, waiting for the hard touch of his hands, wanting it, craving it. But he stopped as he drew level with her, making no move toward her. He was dressed in a tank and shorts, as if he was about to hit the gym, and all she could do was stare at him, hungry and wanting despite everything.

"I'm not going to hurt her," he said quietly. "But that's all you'll get."

She moved quickly, coming to stand in front of him, blocking his way, prepared to push, prepared to fight because that's all she knew how to do. "You promised me last night," she said fiercely, because this felt vital all of a sudden. "You promised that if I surrendered to you, you'd tell me what was going on."

He looked down at her, his expression shuttered. "I can't."

But she wasn't finished. "I gave you everything last night. I gave you my surrender. What more do you want? The truth about me? Okay, I'll tell you then. Dad sold Thalia for his fucking drug habit, but that's not the only reason." She said it flatly because that was the only way to say it. Deliver the facts like orders, like a shopping list that didn't mean anything. "He sold her because she wouldn't give him what he wanted anymore, because she was too old. And because she was protecting me."

His gaze had sharpened, the edges like a scalpel cutting her skin, the blade so keen that at first there was no pain. And then there was. And it hurt, it hurt like fuck. But the words had taken on a momentum all their own, and now they couldn't be stopped.

"He'd been abusing her for years as it turned out," she went on, her tone becoming husky even though she tried to keep it clear. "He tried to turn his attention on me, but she stopped him. She let him have her so he wouldn't touch me. But then he lost his taste for her, and wanted her out of the way. So he sold her. And then that night he told me all about it." She held her jaw tight against the pain, held everything tight against it, and her voice shook, but she went on all the same. "So that's why I have to find Thalia. For years she protected me, and now it's my turn. Now it's my turn to protect her."

Jericho stared at the half-fierce, half-desperate expression on her face and for a moment there was nothing but silence.

He should say something, but rage was starting to get in the way. For what she'd told him. For what had happened to her. For what had been done to her.

You can't let it matter. You have a goal remember?

One hand had unconsciously closed into a fist and he had to make himself relax it. "Why are you telling me this?" he demanded, forcing the anger down.

She didn't look away, and he could see the pain in the depths of her golden eyes. Along with a certainty, that determination that was always there. "Not being able to do anything for Thalia, not even knowing what was going on, and then finding out I was the reason she had to put up with that fucking asshole . . . It hurt."

It more than hurt, he could see that. It was goddamn ripping her apart.

"Temple—"

"I can't let you be the reason she's hurt. I won't." She stared at him, all stubborn will and ferocity. "You have to draw the line somewhere, Jericho."

Draw the line.

The words were like a sword, sliding slowly and painfully through him.

When he'd started all of this, getting himself deeper and deeper into the criminal underworld, he'd had many lines and yet, over the years, one by one, they'd disappeared. There were a few left but they were getting fainter and fainter. Like they'd been drawn in wet sand and the tide was coming in.

And now, close to the end point, those lines were so indistinct they almost weren't there at all. But hell, that was a good thing, wasn't it? He couldn't afford scruples or reservations or regrets. He had to keep pushing all the way through. Didn't he?

"And where is your line?" he asked, because right in that moment, he didn't have an answer for her. "Does an assassin even have one?"

She blinked, an odd look passing over her face. Then her copper lashes swept down, veiling her gaze. "I don't . . . know." There was a husky note in her voice. "I mean . . . when I started out trying to find Thalia, training and perfecting my skills, I thought I didn't. I never left a contract unfulfilled. Never missed my shot, never hesitated. I couldn't second-guess myself . . ." She trailed off.

"Because if you second-guessed yourself, you'd never go through with it," he finished.

Her lashes came up at that, her amber gaze finding his. "Yes. That's exactly it. I couldn't think because if I did, I'd remember why doing this was wrong. And it couldn't be wrong. Without it I wouldn't find Thalia. I wouldn't be able to get revenge for her. I . . . couldn't afford to have a line. Not if I wanted to do what I needed to do." She looked away, down at the ground. "So what does that make me?" The question was soft, almost inaudible, and he knew she wasn't asking him. "What kind of person doesn't have a line?"

There was something lost in her voice, something bewildered, and it somehow got inside him, twisted his insides all around. She stood there dressed only in his T-shirt, her long red hair falling over her shoulders, her legs bare. The vulnerable young girl, not the hardened assassin.

And he moved, acting entirely on instinct, reaching for her and drawing her into his arms. Her hands came against his chest, holding herself away from him. But he didn't let her go. "You have a line, Temple," he said quietly. "You're not a monster, you're not a psychopath, if that's what you're worried about. You're just angry, and you love your sister."

Her gaze was aimed at his chest, her hands a gentle warm pressure on the cotton of his tank. "She told me I was a good person. That I was brave and loyal. That I could be anything I wanted to be." There was no need to ask who she was talking about. He knew. "But I'm not any of those things. I kill people for money. And when it comes to finding her . . ." Slowly, she tipped her head back and looked up at him. "I have no line."

She believed it, he could see that. Just like he could see her pain and her vulnerability. And her fear. Because yeah, she was scared too and he knew why. She was afraid of what she'd become.

Just like you are.

Ah, no there was a small difference. He knew what he'd become. There was still hope for her.

He cupped her face between his hands, allowing the warmth of her skin to seep into him, letting himself fall into her golden eyes.

And he realized with a jolt that this was her true surrender to him. Not what they'd done last night. Oh, physically she'd given him everything, but here, right now, she was giving him everything emotionally. He didn't really understand why because she had no reason to trust him, no reason at all. Yet she'd told him about herself all the same, revealed things he suspected she hadn't told anyone. And to the man she was doing to kill.

Her sister was right, she *was* brave.

Beneath his fingertips he could feel the fast beat of her pulse on the underside of her jaw, could almost feel her fear vibrating through her body. But she didn't pull away or take her gaze from his.

The logical thing to do would be to kiss her, take her back to bed and ignore what she'd told him. Let none of it touch him. Because her past and her pain had nothing to do with him, and they certainly had nothing to do with his plans.

He certainly shouldn't tell her the truth.

But maybe one of those faint lines in the wet sand was deeper than he thought, because he found he just couldn't do either of those things.

"I'm going to destroy it," he said hoarsely. "That's what I'm doing. That's what I've been doing for the past sixteen years. I built it up so I could pull it down. Every last bit of it."

She blinked, a crease deepening between her brows. "Destroy it? Destroy what?"

He shouldn't tell her. He really shouldn't. It would put everything he'd worked for under threat. And yet he couldn't let what she'd told him, the vulnerability she'd revealed, mean nothing.

"Jericho's empire." The words were surprisingly easy to say, as if they'd been waiting in his mouth all this time. "I'm going to destroy Jericho's empire."

CHAPTER THIRTEEN

As the black sedan drew up to the curb, Temple glanced out of the window at the packed Manhattan sidewalk, people rushing to and fro. The street a mass of parked cars and vans, taxis, and other traffic sounding their horns. People were shouting, and across the street, on the steps of the entrance to Bryant Park, a guy was holding up a sign and ranting about the end of the world.

Typical New York in other words.

She felt like it had been years since she'd been here, instead of only a couple of weeks. But then a lot had changed.

Including you?

She ignored that thought, the seat dipping as the man beside her leaned forward to speak to the driver. "Just park here. Do we have confirmation he's inside?"

"Gimme a minute, boss."

No, she hadn't changed. Why would she? She was just the same.

You're not. Not after what he told you.

Her throat tightened.

She'd suspected something big was going on with him, she just hadn't suspected the extent of it. The explanation he'd given her was bare bones, basically that he'd faked his own death then infiltrated one of the trafficking rings. Had risen up through the ranks to become Jericho, the spider at the center of the web. And all with the express intention of destroying that web.

He hadn't told her what was driving him, hadn't told her how he was going to do it, but right at the moment, the fact that this was what he'd been doing all this time, the facade he'd been building for himself, was a little much to take in.

She hadn't been wrong when she'd suspected he was like her. That he had a mission he was on, a vitally important mission, and he wasn't going to let anyone stop him. She just hadn't guessed at how big, how wide, and how deep that mission went.

He wanted to take down the whole fucking thing, not just a network here and there, not the odd crime organization being brought to justice, but everything and everyone. He wanted to obliterate the whole thing.

It either made him mad or it made him a fucking genius.

A tortured genius.

He hadn't mentioned what he'd had to do in order to infiltrate the network to the extent that he had. But she could guess. It made her wonder what kind of man he'd been when he'd first made the decision to walk the path he had, and how different he was now.

Theo died a long time ago.

The tight feeling in her throat tightened even more.

Jesus. She had the feeling that the man who sat beside her now bore no resemblance to the man he once must have been, and no wonder. He must have had to sacrifice everything he was in order to become who he was now. How had he managed to even survive it?

You know how.

Anger. Pain. Those were the things that drove people to do things they'd never imagine they'd ever do. That pushed people beyond their own boundaries. At least those were the things that pushed her. Was it the same for him too? Was it anger and pain or something else?

Unable to help herself, she flicked a glance at him.

He was sitting back on the black leather of the seat, talking to someone on his phone. He hadn't wanted to bring her, but she'd told him she was coming whether he wanted her to or not. She still didn't know why.

The look on his beautiful face was impenetrable, the black of his tailored business shirt and suit pants only highlighting the brilliant gold of his hair. He looked like some dark angel come back from hell.

Something had motivated him to do this. Something had forced him hard along the path. And it *had* to have been pretty fucking powerful given everything he'd sacrificed to do it.

An odd mix of emotions churned in her gut, so tangled she couldn't even begin to figure them all out, just like she couldn't figure out what she thought about his confession.

One thing was clear though. He wasn't who he said he was. He wasn't the enemy.

"I've told Dmitri to leave Violet alone," he said as he ended his call, putting his phone into the pocket of his black suit jacket. "But to keep a watch on her."

A thread of relief wound through Temple's gut. "What were you going to do to her anyway?" He'd never explained back in the house.

"I was going to use her to ensure Hunt's cooperation. At least, that was the plan."

"Are you going to tell me why you're here then? What this meeting is all about?"

He glanced at her, wariness flickering in his eyes, and hell, she got it. He'd been keeping this secret a long time and old habits died hard. If she got it in pieces, she got it in pieces.

After a moment, he met the driver's gaze in the rear-view mirror, and, without a word, the man got out.

"Hunt is losing control of the various operations here," Jericho said as the driver shut the door behind him. "And I can't let that happen. It's taken me years just to get the Europeans on board and if they find out that the markets here are at risk, they're going to get cold feet. They'll pull out of the alliances I've managed to build, and I can't let them."

"Why not? Why do you need them?"

"Because when I take down the whole operation, I want them all to go with it. And for that to happen, the end needs to be sudden and unexpected, leaving them with no time to protect themselves." He ran a restless hand through his hair. "But if Hunt can't stay in control of the networks here, they'll lose confidence, maybe pull out altogether. And I can't let that happen, not quite yet. I need to take charge before he fucks the whole thing up completely."

"So is that why you're here? In the States? To take control of—" She stopped suddenly, as if she remembered something. "This is your father's empire isn't it?"

The restlessness in him stilled, the look on his face hardening. But all he said was "Yes."

She studied him. She was getting closer, wasn't she? Getting more personal, and he didn't like it. Like her, he was used to protecting himself, keeping people out, not letting them in.

It still terrified her in a way she wasn't completely ready to admit that she'd told him all about her father. He hadn't spoken of it since, and she was glad. She didn't want to talk anymore about it. Didn't want to disturb the tight little knot of shame that lurked deep inside her.

God . . . did he have something similar inside him too? Was that why he kept her at a distance?

"That's why you're doing it, isn't it?" She let her gaze

rove over his face, noting the tension in his muscles. He hadn't moved his position, as if frozen into place. "It's because of your father. Because of who he was."

"It doesn't matter why." There was a hard edge to his voice. A warning. "The only important thing is that at the end, the whole fucking thing is destroyed."

Maybe the whys didn't matter. Maybe it was only the action that counted. But she wanted to know anyway. It made her feel less . . .

Alone?

Yeah, and what was wrong with that? They were so similar in so many ways, and that gave her comfort. She'd been alone a long time, so why shouldn't she feel kinship with another person?

With the man you were sent to kill? Who hurt Thalia? Sure, he's not who you thought he was, but he still let something happen to her. She still disappeared into the network he created.

Temple shoved the thought away. "No," she said instead. "I suppose it doesn't matter why in the greater scheme of things. But . . . right now, it matters to me."

He stared back at her, sun in his hair, shadows in his eyes. All black and gold, darkness and light, a visual representation of the man himself. There was nothing easy about him, nothing simple. Nothing black and white.

If he'd been a villain through and through, it would have been so much easier. But he wasn't a villain. He was a hero. A stained and blackened hero.

At least his goal is a selfless one. Unlike yours.

Her chest tightened. Another fucking thought that wouldn't shut up. What the hell was wrong with her head?

"It shouldn't matter to you." The hard edge in his tone had melted away, leaving only the black velvet of his voice. Soft and rough and gentle. "Don't forget what I am, kitten. Don't ever forget that."

"What you are? You're a man on a mission, just like I am."

"I've done things—"

"I've done things too. You know that."

He let out a long breath. "Why do you want to know? What possible difference could it make?"

She had nothing to offer him but the truth. "Because it makes me feel less alone. Like I'm not the only one who has a journey to make."

Something crossed his face, a flash of that infinite weariness. "Temple . . ." He reached out a hand, gently brushed her cheek. "I'm not a man you want to get close to."

"I don't want to get close to you. Maybe all I want is to understand."

His finger lingered on her cheekbone, his gaze moving over her as if he was memorizing her. "My father was a monster. And I . . . just want to make it right."

It was something. But it wasn't the whole story, she was sure of it. "It's more than that, though, isn't it? He did something to you, didn't he?"

Jericho's hand dropped from her cheek, though the warmth of his touch lingered. "Yeah, he did something. He made me into a monster too." His mouth curved into that sad smile, the one that made her ache deep inside. "That's why I have to follow this all the way to the end, that's why I have to succeed. Because if I don't, everything I've done will have all been for nothing."

The ache in her chest deepened. She'd taken lives. She'd killed people. Using the only skills she'd developed so she could earn money, so she could find Thalia. Take her revenge. But if she failed . . .

You'd be a murderer for nothing, just like him.

She couldn't bear the look in his eyes, couldn't deal with the sharp sadness that pierced her, so she glanced down at her folded hands instead. "So that's it? You're going to take control of this operation and then shut it down with all the rest? What's Hunt going to think of that?"

There was a brief silence.

"Hunt will resist," he said at last. "He doesn't know what I'm planning, obviously."

"You should tell him."

Jericho gave a short laugh. "You really think that's a good idea? He hates my guts."

She glanced at him. "Logically, you should have killed him and taken control yourself."

"Yeah, I should have." This time there was no sadness in his smile, but something else. Warmth. "But someone made me believe that wasn't the right thing to do."

She frowned. "What? Who?"

"You." For a second, the smile even touched his eyes, making the gold in them glow. "Violet is in love with this prick. Which means I can't touch him, at least not without hurting her. And leaves me with only one option. I'm going to need to work with him to secure the networks so we can end it."

She was conscious of something shifting inside her, a subtle tremor like a small earthquake. She didn't know quite what it meant, so she ignored it. "But . . . if Hunt hates your guts, how are you going to get him to do that?"

His smile faded, and for some reason it felt as if the sunlight in the car had lost its warmth. "Well, that was where using Violet was going to come in. She's important to him, so I was going to take her, make him think she was in danger, ensure his cooperation that way."

"And if you're not going to do that now?"

"Then we'll have to think of something else."

She didn't quite understand why she reached out, put her hand over his where it sat loosely on his thigh. Maybe it was only to feel the deep warmth of his skin against hers. Maybe it was something more. "Perhaps I can help."

He glanced down where their hands rested, his brow furrowing. But he didn't pull away. "How?"

An idea had begun to take shape. It was probably stupid and maybe it wouldn't work, but if it could help him, then she had to try.

What? You're fucking helping him now?

He wanted to take down the trafficking networks that had destroyed so many lives. Why wouldn't she want to help? Of course, he could be lying just to lull her into a false sense of security, but she didn't think so. He was telling the truth. The look in his eyes when he'd told her had been so raw there hadn't been any room for doubt.

What about Thalia? You have your own mission to accomplish.

A filament of ice wound through her, pulling tight. She'd gotten so caught up in his confession and what that meant, she'd nearly forgotten the main reason she was here in the first place. Yes, those other women mattered, of course they did, and taking down the network was obviously important. But Thalia . . . If her sister was lost then everything, all the money she'd stolen, all the lives she'd taken, all the lines she'd crossed, would have been for nothing.

Temple kept her hand on his. "I could be your collateral."

His dark gold brows drew together. "What are you talking about?"

"Give me to him as surety for your good behavior. A gesture of trust."

A fleeting expression crossed his face, so fast she couldn't decipher it. But she thought it looked like anger. "And why would he accept that?" His voice was level, betraying nothing.

She held his gaze. "He would if he thought I meant something to you. If he loves Violet, he'll understand what kind of gesture you're making."

Jericho's gaze lowered once more to her hand where it rested on his. There was no expression at all on his face now. "You're mine, kitten. And I don't give up what's mine."

A thrill shot down her spine, hot and raw, and she had to take a silent breath to get her heartbeat back under control again. Those words . . . Why did she like them so much? Why did she like feeling as if she was his?

"I'll be safe." Slowly she interlaced her fingers with his. "You know I can look after myself."

Still he didn't look at her, keeping his gaze on their linked fingers. "And what do you want in return?"

The question hurt for some obscure reason. Almost as if she wanted him to believe that she'd offered to help because she cared. Because she wanted to do something for him, without strings, without wanting anything in return.

But of course she couldn't.

Finding her sister was more important than anything.

"I want you to tell me what happened to Thalia. I want to know where my sister is."

He didn't blame her for pushing. In her place he would have done the same. After all, if there was one thing he'd learned in the past sixteen years, it was that nothing was ever given for free in this world.

So why do you want her to give you this now?

No, it was better that she didn't give him anything. She'd given too much away already.

He pulled his hand away from hers. "If I give you that information now, there's nothing stopping you from killing me right here."

Her gaze flickered. "I'll . . . at least wait until after this is all over. How's that?"

"Is that a promise? Perhaps you'll take this opportunity to escape."

"I could have escaped days ago. But I didn't."

"Because you wanted the information. If I give it to you, there's nothing to hold you here."

Again, that flicker in her eyes as if she was uncertain. Strange when determination had always radiated so strongly from her. "What about if I gave you my word?"

"Maybe I should give you a contract instead. Isn't that what assassins usually respect?" It was an asshole thing to say and he wasn't quite sure why he'd said it. But he knew he'd hurt her in some way when color rose in her cheeks.

"Theo—"

"No. What did I tell you about that fucking name?" He pulled out his phone. Fuck, it was after nine already. Hunt would be there waiting. Which meant he had to deal with this fast.

He was going to have to give her the information. There simply wasn't another option that didn't involve some kind of coercion. Hunt felt something for Violet, of that he was certain, and the guy would take Temple if he knew she was important to him. He couldn't think of another way to get the man's trust.

Scrolling through some icons on the screen, Jericho called up the document he'd downloaded into his online storage account before Temple had found him in his office that morning. Taken from information stored around seven years earlier.

Records of a "shipment" of "choice stock," taken from New York and shipped to Germany. There were no names, because their names weren't important, but there were pictures. And one of those pictures was of a freckled, red-haired girl with hazel eyes. There was no mistaking the resemblance. It was Temple's sister.

He'd never forgotten that girl. He'd just taken over as Jericho and not wanting to make too many changes too quickly, he'd had to keep up that old bastard's Saturday habit of choosing a girl for the night from the best of the "shipment." She'd been among the girls paraded in front of him, and he'd found he couldn't look away from her.

She'd been terrified, but she'd kept her chin up, a certain strength to her that was so very different from all the rest. So he'd chosen her, because he had to choose, planning on keeping her in his room to keep up appearances but in actuality leaving her alone.

Yet once she was there, looking so scared and so vulnerable, he knew he had to help her. He had his goal and his plan, but it wasn't going to happen fast, which meant he had to stand by and watch, let the most terrible things happen to these girls. Yet he had to do something in some small way, otherwise he'd go mad.

So he'd decided that night that at least she would get out. He would make it happen. And it had been easy in the end, especially given his contacts. A forged passport and a private jet to take her back to the States. Dmitri doing the transport.

She'd told him her name, and though he'd forgotten it, he'd never forgotten her. Because she was the first. The first girl he'd managed to save.

He hadn't known how to deal with the relief that Thalia had been saved rather than lost in the brothels of Eastern Europe or Asia, mainly because there had been so many other girls who hadn't been saved. The fact that she was Temple's sister shouldn't have made any difference.

So he kept it locked down as he handed her the phone with Thalia's picture on it, kept his voice flat as he said, "Your sister was one who got out. I helped her escape."

Temple stared at him, shock on her face. Then she glanced down at the phone. The shock fled, her features crumpling, and she turned away from him, her head bent over the phone's screen.

Every part of him wanted to pull her into his arms and hold her, but he stayed exactly where he was. Allowing her a moment of privacy.

Her shoulders shook, yet she didn't make a sound.

"That's what I do with the girls I choose for the night," he said into the silence, "I help them escape. She was the first one."

There was a long silence.

"She's alive?" Temple's voice was thick.

"As far as I know."

Another silence.

She handed him back his phone, keeping her face averted. She'd been so vulnerable to him before, had let him see everything, but not now. Now, she remained silent.

Jericho put the phone back in his pocket. "I've held up my end of the bargain." He knew he sounded cold and impersonal, but he couldn't seem to alter his tone. "It's now time to hold up yours. Are you ready?"

Temple didn't speak, only gave a short nod.

He didn't push it, opening the door of the sedan and getting out. She followed him, wrapping the black overcoat she wore more securely around her. Nevertheless he still got a flash of the dress she was wearing. It was gold lace, completely see-through and completely inappropriate to both the weather and the place they were going to. However, as his ostensible lover, she had to be seen as the stripper she'd been posing as when dealing with the opposition, and jeans and a T-shirt weren't going to cut it like they had on the flight over.

She looked so fucking sexy he felt himself get hard, which was completely inappropriate as well, certainly when they were going into a life-or-death kind of meeting. The fact that her eyes were red-rimmed didn't make it any better either.

Controlling himself, he went into the café, Temple following behind him.

The place was packed, which was why he'd chosen it in the first place. A crowd would help muffle their own conversation, plus it would also put a limit on the kinds of stunts a man like Elijah Hunt might pull.

Then again, the guy had managed to kill an employee of Jericho's in the middle of Battery Park the month before, so it wouldn't pay to underestimate him, crowd or otherwise.

Hunt was sitting by himself at the back of the café, but he clearly wasn't alone. The tables around him were full of people, yet Jericho spotted at least five guys hanging around who were clearly there as protection.

Jericho gave a quick, surreptitious scan of the crowds, spotting his own guards already sitting at various tables around the café. He'd sent them in fifteen minutes earlier, but he was pretty sure Hunt knew who they were in much the same way as he'd already spotted Hunt's.

He smiled, threading his way through the tables to where Hunt sat, pulling out a chair and sitting down, Temple beside him.

"What the fuck is this?" Hunt's belligerent black gaze settled on Temple and scowled.

"This?" Jericho slid an arm around her, pulling her in close, putting on a show. "This is Ginger. She's here for a reason."

"Ginger?" Hunt virtually spat the word.

There was fear in Temple's eyes. She was pretending obviously, setting up the impression of a woman completely out of her depth. "It's my stage name," she said, her voice quiet.

An odd expression crossed Hunt's face, but before Jericho could puzzle it out, he turned his black gaze on him. "What do you want?" Hunt demanded. "You said this was about Violet. If you've touched a hair on her head, I'll—"

"Relax Mr. Hunt," Jericho interrupted lazily. "Violet's safe. I wouldn't hurt her."

"Then what the fuck is this about?"

Excellent, straight to the point. "You've been having problems, I hear."

The other man's eyes narrowed. "I'm not having any problems whatsoever."

"Bullshit you are. You were nearly taken out a couple of days ago by a traitor in your own ranks." He sat back in his seat, giving the illusion of complete relaxation. "I know all about it, Mr. Hunt, believe me. You're having difficulty hanging on to your empire, aren't you?"

Hunt was silent, staring at him. But Jericho didn't make the mistake of thinking he had the guy on his back foot. Those black eyes were assessing, calculating.

Jesus Christ, what kind of man had Violet gotten herself involved with? When he'd gone after her the month before, he should have shipped her straight to Paris whether she wanted to or not.

Since Hunt didn't look like he was going to break the silence any time soon, Jericho went on, "You're not denying it. Good. Now, of course this is a problem for you, but you should know it's also a problem for me. It's putting Violet at risk, and I can't have that."

Violence entered Hunt's dark eyes. "Stay the fuck away from her," he growled, his voice thick with menace. "I can protect her, and I will."

"I don't doubt that. But this is still a problem." He paused, holding the other man's gaze. "I'm in the States to do a deal with you. If I help you secure your empire, you give me access to the American markets."

Something black and cold glittered in Hunt's gaze. "What the hell makes you think I'll do anything for you? I let you live for Violet's sake, but I'll be fucked if I accept your help. And as for the markets—"

"I'm trying to take them down." Jericho said the words flatly, quietly. It was a risk, a huge risk to reveal himself to this man. But he didn't have any other option. The guy wouldn't accept any kind of bargain or any kind of help, so it was either that or he take control forcibly and that wouldn't end without blood being shed. Probably Hunt's blood.

The other man had gone completely still. "What?"

Beside him, Temple was motionless too. Waiting.

Another person who knew his secret, another person who could potentially destroy the last sixteen years. What the fuck was he doing? Yet he couldn't take it back now, it was too late for that. He'd told Temple, and now he'd told Hunt. He could only keep going.

He stared into Hunt's black eyes. "You knew my father. You knew what he was. Imagine being his son. Imagine having to live with the knowledge that your father was a murderer. A rapist. A slaver. And then try to imagine being slowly turned into that very same monster by the person who was supposed to protect you. Love you."

Temple had stiffened. He could feel the warmth of her body against him, the scent of her in his nostrils. And for some reason he found that comforting. So he kept his arm around her and made himself go on. "No one got away from him. No one left his little empire unless it was in a box. So I chose the box. And for the past sixteen years, I've been turning myself into the monster he wanted me to be . . ." He paused, tightening his arm around the woman next to him. "So I could take it all down."

Hunt didn't say anything, just stared at him.

This was the moment of truth.

Jericho didn't look away. "I'm not going to say this again, so listen carefully. We need to secure the U.S. networks, make it look as if everything's fine, and that I've formed an alliance with you. Once that's in place, I will release the information I've gathered over the years to the authorities. There should be enough intel there to incriminate just about everyone I've involved in the trafficking networks, and if I do it quickly, they won't have any time to prepare to protect themselves."

Hunt's eyes glittered. "That's what you've been doing all this fucking time?"

"Yes. Incorporating all the smaller networks into mine, making sure no one was left out, was a long process. As was getting the proof I need to put them all away. But you must understand, the alliances I've formed are shaky ones and if they see trouble here, they're going to get cold feet. I can't have them pulling out. I want them *all* to go down, Mr. Hunt. Every single last one of them."

Finally the other man shifted in his chair, yet the intensity of his gaze didn't waver one iota. "Were you responsible for her death?" The question was hard and flat, and he didn't elaborate. But Jericho knew what he meant anyway.

"Seven years ago, right?"

"Yes."

"The man who controlled the European networks was called Jericho. My father did business with him. So I killed him. And I took his place." A quiver ran through Temple, though why he had no idea. He wanted to look at her but kept his gaze on Hunt instead. Because this was important. "That was seven years ago. Your wife was taken before I took over. So no, I was not responsible for her death."

There was no expression on Hunt's face, nothing to betray what he felt except the black glitter of his eyes. "You killed him?" An innocuous sounding question, but there was an undercurrent in the other man's voice that Jericho recognized.

He smiled, and it wasn't pleasant. "I cut his throat."

Hunt's scarred mouth twisted and Jericho thought he saw the briefest glimpse of satisfaction move in the other man's eyes. Yet all he said was "I still don't trust you."

"I know you don't. Which is where Ginger here comes in." He eased his arm from around Temple, even though some deeply possessive part of him insisted that giving her to Hunt was the last thing he should be doing. "She means something to me. So as a demonstration of trust, she'll go with you as surety for my good behavior."

Hunt glanced at Temple for a second, his expression unreadable. Then he looked back at Jericho, gaze narrowing as if he was searching for something. Tension gathered in the air between them.

"She knows everything, doesn't she?" Hunt asked curtly.

"Yes."

"So any information she has could be used against you."

Ah, of course. Hunt wouldn't hurt Temple. Which meant he had to find some other way of using her against him. "She knows everything you do. So yes, it could."

Hunt let out a breath. "Why should I do any of what you said?"

"Because if you want the biggest human trafficking network in the world taken down and all the fucking perpetrators brought to justice then that's what you're going to have to do."

The other man looked down at his hands, clasped together on the table. "Violet will want to know."

Something painful twisted inside him, a kind of yearning. Could it finally be possible for her to know the truth? He'd never thought he could tell her, purely because of the danger it presented to her. Plus there was also the fact that

Violet would probably want to involve herself and maybe risk herself getting hurt too.

"I don't want her put at risk," he said carefully. "The truth could hurt her."

Hunt looked up from his hands. "Not more than the lie already has."

Like he didn't know that. "There were reasons I couldn't tell her and you can probably guess what they are."

"I can. And if you're lucky she might even understand that."

The painful thing inside him twisted harder. "I'm not lucky, Hunt. I've never been fucking lucky." Christ, it was time to end this. He had shit to do.

He almost reached for Temple again, to bring her with him, and then he remembered what he'd promised. He had to leave her here. Fuck.

The painful thing grew edges, cutting him, every instinct he had telling him that she belonged with him. And it didn't matter that he knew she could take care of herself, that she was probably as deadly as he was. He didn't want to let her out of his sight.

Locking the feeling down, he reached for her again. He needed to touch her before he went, and if that cemented the belief that she meant something to him for Hunt then, shit, he was good with that.

Taking her chin in his hand, he turned her face toward him. She met his gaze, no trace of the redness of before around her eyes. They were wide, a clear, bright gold, and he couldn't read the expression glowing in the depths of them. The things he'd told Hunt, he hadn't told her, because sometimes it was easier to give the facts to someone you hated than to someone you . . . didn't.

Had it changed things between them? Did knowing he'd saved her sister change things too? And if they had, how? And what did it mean for them?

It won't mean anything. You know how this is going to end. How it was always supposed to end.

Yeah. He did.

Jericho gripped her chin and kissed her, and he'd meant it to be soft and gentle, but it wasn't. It was as if he wanted to impress himself on her, mark her indelibly in some way. He kissed her hard, sweeping his tongue into her mouth, exploring deep, giving no quarter. Yet she didn't protest, her head going back, allowing him access, letting him take whatever he wanted.

So he did. He sank one hand into her red hair, holding her there as he took the taste of her, took the feel of her lips beneath his and the scent of her deep inside. Imprinting her into his memory so he wouldn't forget and leaving her with something of himself too, a hard nip on her bottom lip.

Then he released her without looking at her because he knew if he looked into her face again, he wouldn't let her go. Instead he looked at Hunt, right into the other man's black eyes. "If she gets hurt, I'll kill you." He didn't even have to pretend the vehemence in his voice.

The other man didn't flinch. "If what you've just told me is true, she won't."

It shouldn't have been so hard to get up from his chair then, to turn around and leave.

It shouldn't have been so hard to resist the urge to look back.

But it was both those things.

CHAPTER FOURTEEN

"This is bullshit." Eva King's silver-gray eyes were hostile. "You can't possibly believe him. I mean, where's the proof? How do we even know if any of what he said is true?"

Temple sat on the black leather sofa of Elijah's West Village warehouse apartment, watching the four people in front of her argue.

She knew them all, of course—all except the woman with the short, spiky blond hair sitting on the arm of the sofa. The woman was wearing black leather leggings and a black button-down shirt, the sleeves rolled up. She looked tough, like she took no shit from anyone. She also looked so much like Jericho that Temple kept glancing in her direction, unable to help herself.

This must be Violet.

The other three people were Zac Rutherford, the ex-mercenary who'd hired her to take out Jericho. Eva King, head of the Void Angel tech company and whom she'd once chauffeured for. And Elijah Hunt, who'd hired her to deliver Eva into Evelyn Fitzgerald's hands. And they were all arguing about what Jericho had told Elijah that morning in the café.

It seemed they were mightily pissed. As was Violet herself. From the way her arms were tightly folded and her shoulders stiff with tension, it looked like she was only just holding herself back from attacking someone. Which was understandable since Zac and Eva had only just revealed the fact that they'd hired Temple to take out her brother.

Interestingly, Violet hadn't looked her way once.

Elijah had his arms crossed too, glaring at Eva who was standing on the opposite side of the coffee table in front of the sofa. He jerked his head in Temple's direction. "If you want proof Jericho's telling the truth, there she is."

The moment Temple had walked into the café to meet Elijah, she'd been desperately hoping he wouldn't give away the fact that they knew one another. But apart from that initial look of surprise, Elijah had gone along with her being "Ginger."

It was another thing she hadn't told Theo.

Theo again?

Yeah, she was going with Theo. He'd saved her sister. He wasn't going to be Jericho to her, not now.

Relief and a choking kind of grief threatened to rise up inside her at the memory of seeing Thalia's face, but she fought it down. Now wasn't the time. Especially not when four people were looking at her with varying degrees of hostility.

"Ah, yes," Zac said, a thin sarcasm edging the words. "The assassin who has yet to do her job."

On the way back here with Elijah, she'd given him a brief run-down of what was going on and what, exactly, she'd been doing. As it turned out, he'd known that Zac and the rest of his friends, the club known as the Nine Circles, had hired someone to take out Theo, but he hadn't managed to discover who it was, though he'd been trying.

Oddly enough, he'd looked almost relieved when she'd told him that she was the hired assassin, which was weird. He hadn't explained and that had puzzled her. At least until

Zac and Eva had turned up. And then it had become abundantly clear.

Zac and his friends were trying to take down Jericho, while Elijah, even though he hated Jericho himself, was trying to help Violet protect her brother

As Elijah had explained the situation to Zac and Eva, Violet had sat there quietly, the tension around her gathering tighter and tighter, obviously working herself up into a towering rage.

It hadn't exploded yet, but it was only a matter of time.

"I had my own agenda," Temple said levelly. There wasn't any point trying to hide it now, not when she actively wanted these guys to help Theo. In fact, if she told them about Thalia and about how Theo had saved her, then that was only going to help, surely? "My sister was taken by traffickers seven years ago. I've been trying to find her. The trail led to Fitzgerald, and from there it went on to Jericho. That's why I approached Zac for the contract. I wanted to find my sister."

Violet had shifted on the couch, turning to face Temple, her brilliant turquoise eyes cold. "So is that the only reason he's alive now? Because you don't have the information yet?"

It's not quite the only reason.

No, it wasn't. But they didn't need to know that.

Temple met Violet's gaze unflinchingly. "He gave me the information just before we met with Elijah. He showed me a picture of Thalia, and he told me he'd rescued her."

Something shifted in Violet's gaze. "Rescued her? What are you talking about?"

Briefly Temple explained how she'd managed to get close to Theo, about the girls he chose every Saturday night. About how, far from keeping them for the night as sex toys, he helped them escape.

"Why the hell would he do that?" Elijah demanded. "Surely that's risky?"

Of course it was. But she thought she knew why he risked it. She met the big ex-bodyguard's gaze. "He didn't explain, but I can guess. He's spent years working toward this one goal, years playing a part. Not being able to do anything for those women . . ." She stopped, remembering that bleakness in his eyes, the terrible weariness. "I think it must have done something to him. I think actively helping at least a few prevented him from going insane."

Violet made a sound, and instantly Elijah was going over to the arm of the sofa where she sat, reaching out to her. But she put out a hand, stopping him. Her face was pale, her eyes blazing. "I knew it," she said fiercely. "I fucking *knew* it." She turned her attention to Zac, her expression furious. "You were going to kill an innocent man."

Zac betrayed nothing. "We were going to take out the man behind the destruction of a good many innocent lives. He's still responsible for that, Violet, make no mistake."

"He's trying to bring it down!" Violet pushed herself off the arm of the sofa in a sudden, sharp movement. "He's trying to end it!"

"Princess." Elijah had come to stand behind her, slipping an arm around her waist. "It's okay. He's still alive."

But Violet ignored him, turning back to Temple, fury stamped across her delicate features. "You were going to kill him."

She understood the other woman's rage, God how she understood. "I was. That was the contract I undertook for Zac. And I was going to take his death for myself too, payback for my sister."

"He rescued your sister, so your revenge plan is fucked," Violet said. "And if it's money you're after then I'll double whatever payment Zac's offered. Just leave Theo alone."

Temple had no idea what her next move would be, she'd had no time to think it through. But she knew, with all the certainty of gut instinct, that she wouldn't be able to go through with killing Theo, not now. Violet was right. Her revenge plan would be an empty one.

Which means everything you've done has been pointless.

Ruthlessly she shoved the thought away. "I'm not going to kill him, especially not when he's the only one who can destroy that trafficking ring."

"So you believe him?" Eva's voice was sharp. "You believe he was telling the truth?"

Violet was still staring at her, and this time there wasn't only fury in her eyes but a kind of desperation too. Theo's sister wanted to believe.

"Yes," Temple said flatly. "He is."

"And where's the proof?" Zac asked.

Temple looked at him. "The proof is my sister, not that I needed any. Theo wasn't lying."

"Theo," the big mercenary echoed. "Not Jericho."

A stillness fell over the room. They were all gazing at her, and she knew what they were thinking.

"I assumed he didn't know that you and I knew each other," Elijah said slowly.

"No, he didn't."

"And I also assumed, that when he said you meant something to him, it was an act." His dark eyes narrowed. "But that kiss he gave you wasn't an act."

"Kiss?" Violet scowled. "What kiss?"

"Yeah," Eva murmured. "Good question."

A strange surge of possessiveness went through her. What had gone on between her and Theo was private. It didn't concern them. "That's none of your damn business."

Elijah ignored her. "He seemed comfortable being around a woman who's there to kill him. Does he know what you are?"

"Yes."

Eva muttered a curse. "Please don't say you told him who hired you."

Temple stared at her erstwhile boss. "What do you think?"

"I dunno. You had no problems at all with delivering me to that prick over there." She inclined her head toward Elijah.

The reminder was an uncomfortable one, though why, Temple didn't quite understand. Betraying Eva to Elijah had been part of the job and Elijah had promised that no harm would come to the other woman. And he'd been right. "That was as a favor to that prick over there. In return for information about my sister. I'm sorry, but Thalia trumps everyone."

Eva snorted, clearly not agreeing with that pronouncement. Well, she didn't have to. The past was the past, and nothing could change it now.

"Look," Temple said, trying for patience. "Instead of arguing about a stupid kiss, why not focus on what's really important? Like his plan for taking down the network."

"Yes," Violet agreed unexpectedly. "She's right. Who cares who kissed who? We need to decide whether or not we make an ostensible alliance with him, help him." She still looked furious, and Temple couldn't blame her.

Zac's expression was granite hard. "I'm sorry, is there a decision to make here? The man has destroyed countless lives, and I'm not getting involved with anyone who could be a potential threat to Eva."

Eva rolled her eyes. "You gotta chill out, Zac. I'm fine."

"I don't care how fine you are. It's not happening."

A cold shred of doubt gathered in Temple's gut. "Okay, I understand you don't trust him, and that's reasonable. But I'm here as a demonstration of that trust, and I'm pretty certain he wouldn't have handed me over to Elijah if he hadn't meant what he said."

"It's a meaningless gesture." Zac's precise British accent was clipped. "If he knows you're an assassin, he also knows you can handle yourself. Plus, I bet you anything he's also bloody aware that Elijah wouldn't harm you."

All true. All fucking true. She didn't look away from Zac's penetrating amber gaze. "I have information on him. I know his identity as Theodore Fitzgerald. I know where he lives. I'm a risk to his anonymity." She paused. "All of those things can be used against him, so it's not just violence directed to me he was concerned about, it's what that information could do to him if it got out."

Eva let out a breath. "She's got a point, Zac."

The big mercenary's attention flicked over to her. "You can't seriously want to do this. You, of all people."

Eva scowled and thrust her hands in the pockets of her black jeans. "Yeah, okay, so no, I don't. But . . . I'm torn. If Temple's right and Jericho really is planning on a big takedown, then I want to be part of that. I want to help. Fuck, that's what I've been trying to do for the past seven years."

"I'm with Eva." Violet's voice was flat with certainty. "I know you don't want to trust him, but at least give him a chance to prove himself. You don't have anything to lose after all."

That Zac didn't like this was obvious. His jaw was tight, tension radiating from him, making the cold in Temple's gut get even colder. "We have a USB memory stick with a lot of incriminating information on it. Which means we can do this without his help."

"Can you?" Temple asked quietly, feeling she had to say something. Anything. "Sure you might have some information, manpower and resources, but he's the one who's built all the alliances. Who has *all* the information the authorities need. He's at the center of all of it. If you attempt it and only manage to smash a couple of those rings, what's going to happen to the rest? The Triads, the Russian mafia, they're gun-shy. If they hear of shit going down, they'll pull out. They'll start protecting themselves and those networks will be lost."

"Fuck," Elijah muttered. "We're going to need him, Rutherford. No way around it."

"If what she's saying is true," Zac replied coldly.

"Why the hell would I lie?" Temple tried to make her voice sound completely level. "I have no horse in this race."

But the intensity in Zac's gaze didn't lessen. "Unless you're trying to save him."

"All right, all right," Eva murmured. "Enough. We need Alex and Gabe, and Honor and Katya in on this too." She moved over to the tall Brit and put a hand on his arm. "Why don't you go call them?"

There was something about the two of them that caught at Temple, in the same way watching Violet and Elijah together caught at her. A kind of understanding flowed between them, a wordless connection that had a part of her yearning in a way she hadn't experienced before. She'd never felt lonely in all the years since she'd left home, or at least, she didn't miss not having someone around who knew her and understood her.

The only yearning she'd felt for someone else was for her sister.

Yet now she could feel an . . . emptiness inside her. A hunger. She wanted someone to touch her like Eva was touching Zac. Wanted someone to hold her the way Elijah had put his arm around Violet. Someone who was there for her. Someone who made her feel safe on a level that went beyond merely physical. Someone who made her feel less alone.

Theo. You want that with Theo.

No. What she wanted was to find Thalia. Until that happened, she couldn't think of anything else, still less what was going on with Theo.

Zac had moved over to the windows, his cell phone in his hand, while Eva turned around, glancing over at Violet. She pulled a face. "We had to do it, Violet," she said quietly. "After everything that's happened, we had to."

Temple said nothing. She'd heard what had happened to the small, silver-haired woman. Eva had been kept for two years as a sex-slave by Fitzgerald himself.

Theo's father.

Imagine having to live with the knowledge that your father was a murderer. A rapist. A slaver. And then try to imagine being slowly turned into that very same monster by the person who was supposed to protect you . . .

Temple's throat constricted. And she'd thought her old man had been the biggest shit to walk the face of the earth. What had Theo's father done to him to make him think that faking his own death was the only option?

"He's still my brother," Violet replied.

Elijah had moved close to her again, sliding his arm around her and drawing her in close. She leaned her head against his shoulder, her gaze finding Temple's. "You said you believed him. Why?"

Carefully Temple considered her words. "Because we talked. And the things he told me . . . There was something in his eyes. He looked—"

"Tired," the other woman interrupted softly. "He looked tired. Yeah, I saw it too." She closed her eyes all of a sudden. "I can't imagine his life. I just can't imagine it. All the dreams he had, all those plans."

That awful ache had taken hold of Temple again, sinking its claws in deep. And even though some part of her didn't want to know, a greater part of her did. "What plans?"

Violet sighed and opened her eyes again, grief glittering in the depths. "He was going to get married. And once he'd finished his law degree, he had a job in a firm all lined up. He and his fiancée were even scouting out apartments. They were going to move in together . . ." Violet stopped. "Her name was Rose. She was lovely."

Oh God. He'd had a fiancée. He'd had a career. He'd had a life. And he'd sacrificed all of it.

The ache deepened into a dull pain, one that went right through her.

She hadn't had any plans. When she'd been smaller, before she knew how the world worked, she'd wanted to be a movie star or be on TV, because the lives of those people seemed far nicer than her own by comparison. Then she'd gotten older and realized that unlike those people on TV, there was no escape for her. Her family was on the poverty line, the local school was where the dealers hung out, and there were no jobs to be had unless you liked earning money on your back. No hope for a better life. The best she could have hoped for if she'd stayed was marrying some guy in the area who at least had a job and could look after her.

She didn't know what was worse: that Theo had had all of that or the fact that he'd had to give it up. At least she'd had nothing to lose.

"That's . . . awful," Temple said, conscious of the fact that her voice sounded thick.

Violet's blue eyes sharpened on her all of a sudden. "Why didn't he tell me about all of this? Why didn't he at least give me some hint of what he was doing?"

"He wanted to protect you." Temple held the other woman's gaze, willing her to believe it, because it was true. "He didn't want to drag you into it."

"He still should have told me. I've spent a whole month thinking he's this monster—"

"Don't make the mistake of thinking he's innocent," Eva cut her off shortly. "Sure, his intentions may have been good, but while he's been setting himself up as King Trafficker, people have been killed. Raped. Their lives utterly destroyed. And after sixteen years of that shit? No one stays unchanged." Her gray eyes flicked to Temple's, sharp, perceptive. "Do they, Temple?"

She didn't have sixteen years of "that shit." She only had seven. But there was no mistaking the look in Eva's gaze. *You've taken lives. You know there's no coming back from that.*

Anger moved inside her, slow and heavy. An instinctive, defensive reaction. She opened her mouth to deny it, but Elijah forestalled her.

"I'm not innocent." His voice was level. "And neither is Rutherford. Does that make us monsters, Eva?"

Eva's gaze flickered at that, looking over to where Zac stood talking on his cell phone. "No, I guess not."

Temple found herself gazing at the man standing at Violet's back with his arm around her. The man who'd helped her once years ago, who'd given her the tip with regard to Fitzgerald. He'd been the guy's right-hand man, his lieutenant, and she knew what that would have entailed. Elijah Hunt was as far from innocent as it was possible to get.

And yet there he stood, a lovely woman in his arms, and despite the coldness in his tone and the air of suppressed violence around him, there was something in the way he looked at Violet. In how that coldness vanished from his voice when he spoke to her. At his posture, protective and yet relaxed, his thumb stroking absently over the skin of her wrist.

Was that happiness? Had he found it with her? Was it possible for a man with blood on his hands to have that? To find some redemption?

Maybe for him. Not for you.

Zac must have finished his conversation because right then his voice fell silent and he put his phone away. Eva crossed over to him, going to stand right in front of him. He straightened, and, moving with extreme deliberation, he raised a gloved hand, took a handful of Eva's hair and pulled her head back. Then, obviously not giving a crap about all the people in the room, he covered her mouth in a hard, possessive kiss.

Shock pulsed through Temple. She kept expecting Eva to pull away, to say something sharp, sarcastic, and cutting, but the other woman didn't do anything of the kind. She merely stood there, letting Zac kiss her in that possessive way, her small hands spread on his chest.

Temple heard Violet murmur something to Elijah, but she didn't take it in, too busy staring at Zac and Eva. She shouldn't look, she knew that. Not at such an intensely private and vulnerable moment. But she simply couldn't drag her gaze away from the two of them.

Eventually, after what seemed like a very long moment, Zac's hold on Eva's hair loosened and he released her, trailing his fingers in a caressing movement through the long, white strands. He looked down into her face and again, something wordless passed between them. Then he lifted his gaze to where Elijah stood with Violet. "Alex and Gabe are in agreement." His voice was as calm and as level as it always was, as if he hadn't just kissed Eva passionately in front of everyone. "They think you should accept Jericho's offer, Hunt. Stop taking down operations here and ally with him. Then we wait to see if he does what he says he's going to do."

Elijah's expression was granite. "That's a fuck load of trust we're giving him."

"Then it's lucky we have an insider." And his gaze shifted to Temple.

She ignored the cold lump inside her that hadn't gone away, that felt like it was stuck there, a piece of grit inside an oyster that wasn't going to turn into a pearl any time soon. That was only going to hurt. "What are you thinking?"

"Yes," Violet said, her voice sharp. "What *are* you thinking, Zac?"

"All I'm thinking is that Temple here can make sure Jericho does what he promised," Zac replied mildly. "Make sure that whatever information he said he was going to release is actually released."

"What makes you think I can do that?" She had no doubt she could, even if she believed Theo wasn't going to make good on his promise. But she wanted to hear what the rest of them thought.

Zac raised one dark brow. "I'm sure you know already, Temple. Do I really need to say it out loud? Jericho's your lover. You're closer to him than anyone else."

There wasn't any point in denying it, not when she supposed it must be obvious. "Okay," she said carefully. "I can make sure he does what he promised."

"What makes you so sure we can trust her?" Elijah glanced at Temple, suspicion in his eyes. "If she's his lover, that doesn't mean she'll do anything for us."

It was a fair enough question. She didn't say anything, watching Zac to see what he'd say.

Zac's amber gaze settled on her. "She might if I told her that I'd find her sister for her."

Everything in her went tight, and she had to not show it. "Jericho told me she was alive."

"But did he tell you where she was? Does he even know? I can find her, Temple. And after all this is over, I'll tell you where she is."

It wasn't an issue, of course. Not when she was sure Theo meant what he said, that he *would* destroy his trafficking networks when the time came. But still, she wasn't going to refuse if it meant she'd be seeing Thalia sooner.

"In that case," she said. "I have no problem with making sure the information Jericho has gets into the right hands."

"And Theo stays alive." Violet was insistent. "No matter what happens, he comes out of this in one piece. Okay?"

Temple turned to look at the other woman, catching a glimpse of the barely hidden desperation in her blue eyes. God, she knew that desperation. She knew what it was like to hope. "Yes," she said, the only answer she could give. "I'll make sure he comes out of it in one piece. No matter what."

The others didn't say anything to that, and soon the conversation moved on.

But later, as she was coming out of the bathroom, she found Zac waiting for her in the little hallway just outside the door.

She paused, her heart sinking, a part of her somehow knowing what he was going to say. "This is about the contract, isn't it?"

Zac was leaning against the wall, his arms folded. "Yes."

"What about it?"

"It stands," he said flatly. "After Jericho has sent the information to the authorities, I want you to take him out."

Her heart squeezed suddenly tight. "Why?"

Zac's expression was hard. "Because it doesn't matter how good his intentions are, he's still a threat. An unknown quantity. He's a loose end, and I don't like loose ends. Especially not where Eva is concerned."

"He wouldn't hurt Eva," she said and believed it. He wouldn't, especially if he knew she was one of the women his father had hurt personally.

"How do you know that?" Zac's piercing golden stare was almost impossible to meet. "He's been the head of a global trafficking network for sixteen years. You don't get to be that powerful without a few bodies in the closet. And in this instance, a few of those bodies are going to be female."

The pressure in her chest increased and she had to fight to breathe. "I'm not saying he's innocent."

"No, but your instinct is to defend him, I can see it." He tilted his head, his focus on her sharpening. "Why? Is the sex that good?"

Anger rose, adding to the pressure. "It's got nothing to do with the sex," she snapped, not quite able to keep it out of her voice. "Jesus, you of all people should know that nothing is ever quite as black and white as it looks."

Something moved in his gaze at that, though she couldn't tell what it was. "Quite frankly I don't care how complicated or otherwise it is. My primary focus is keeping Eva safe, and if that includes taking down the son of the man who hurt her, then that's what I'll do."

She wanted to argue, wanted to tell Zac that no, Theo wasn't innocent, but he wasn't as guilty as he seemed either. Did that mean he deserved to die? Was there no hope for him? No hope of redemption?

Because if there's no hope for him, there's no hope for you.

She almost shook her head to get rid of the thought. It was different with her. She'd only been defending herself.

You weren't defending yourself from all those other people. You killed them for money.

The breath caught in her throat, the pressure in her chest intense, painful. "You find my sister, and I'll do whatever you want," she said, forcing the words out, forcing herself to say something so she wouldn't have to listen to the voice in her head. "And if that includes putting a bullet through Jericho then I will."

Zac didn't smile, only gave a sharp nod of his head. "Give me her name and anything else you can think that might be useful. I'll start putting out feelers to see what I can find."

She swallowed. "And Violet? What about her?"

Zac's jaw hardened. "I'm sorry for Violet, but my concern is for Eva. And for all the women that have been hurt by him and his father." He paused, searching her face. "Don't you want to take a little justice for your sister, Temple? For all those women who were hurt?"

This could be your shot at redemption. Your chance to right the balance.

Temple stared at him, feeling the weight of something terrible settling down over her. Something she'd thought she'd escaped. An inevitability. Maybe there was no hope of redemption for Theo. But maybe, if she did this, there'd be a chance for her.

"Yes," she said thickly. "Yes I do."

"Good." He pushed himself away from the wall. "This conversation is just between the two of us, understand? No one else needs to know."

"I understand."

It was just a contract, and she'd taken lots of contracts before. Killing a man was easy after all.

But as Zac walked away, Temple felt as though she'd just signed her soul away to the devil.

Jericho leaned on the rough stone rim of Bethesda Fountain in Central Park, his hands in the pockets of his leather jacket, watching tourists taking photos of each other. Not far away, Dmitri sat on a bench, ostensibly reading the paper. There were a few of his other guards dotted around the area, all of them blending in with the crowds the way they were supposed to.

Hunt had texted him that morning that he had an

answer for him and would deliver it, along with Temple, at eleven a.m. at the fountain.

Nervousness wasn't something he felt these days, and he didn't feel it now—at least he didn't think the strange unsettled feeling in the pit of his gut was nervousness. But maybe it was. Though, he had no reason to feel nervous. If Hunt wasn't on board, then Jericho would just have to forget his newly found scruples and take over his father's erstwhile empire by force.

He didn't want to do it, and he'd try not to hurt Hunt in the process, but if that's how it was going to go down, then that's what he'd have to do.

Most options, in his experience, tended to be limited ones.

And then, right on eleven, as a couple appeared at the top of the stairs leading down to the fountain, he suddenly realized what that unsettled feeling in his gut was.

It wasn't nervousness. It was excitement.

Because he couldn't take his eyes off the couple descending the stairs. Not Hunt, immediately recognizable in a black overcoat, but the woman beside him. Small and slender, red hair cascading down her back. Temple.

And it was her he was excited about seeing. Her, he realized suddenly, that he'd missed the night before.

He'd tried not to think about her at all, sitting in his office all night, drinking tumbler after tumbler of Scotch and none of it touching the sides. He'd been going over the information his men had given him about his father's empire, while at the same time dealing with issues in Europe. The Lychenkos were getting impatient, which was irritating, and he was debating the wisdom of arranging a happy accident for the pair of them. Probably not the best tactic when the rest of the family were getting cold feet, but at least it would get them out of his hair.

Certainly thinking about the Lychenkos was better than

thinking about the woman he'd given to Elijah. The woman he couldn't get out of his head, but should.

It wasn't because he was worried about her. Elijah wouldn't hurt her and even if he did, she was more than able to protect herself. No, he was far more selfish than that. It was because he was hard for her and wanted her under him. Wanted her fire between his hands, heating him up, because sometimes he just got so fucking cold.

He was cold now, too. Christ, he couldn't wait to touch her.

However, it wouldn't do to appear desperate so he stayed exactly where he was as Temple and Hunt approached. Hunt's expression gave nothing away, but Temple's . . .

He frowned. She looked pale, and there was a certain tightness to her jaw. Her gaze when it met his was opaque, but he didn't miss the flicker of wariness that moved in the gold depths. As if she was . . . afraid.

Jesus. What the fuck had happened? Had Hunt done something to her, after all? By God, if he had, he was a dead man.

Slowly, Jericho pushed himself away from the rough stone of the fountain, straightening up as Hunt came to a stop in front of him.

"Here she is," the other man said shortly. "Safe and sound."

Jericho ignored him, staring at Temple, trying to resist the urge to grab her and pull her to him. "Are you okay?" he asked. "You're not hurt?"

She shook her head. "I'm fine."

No, she . . . wasn't. Something had happened, he could feel it in his bones. Still, as much as that made him want to pull his gun and stick it straight up against Hunt's forehead, he restrained the urge. The alliance. That's what this was all about. That was the important thing.

So instead, he held out his hand to her in wordless

command. She didn't hesitate, stepping away from Hunt and coming to stand beside him, taking his hand and letting him interlace his fingers with hers. They felt cold. Then again, it wasn't the warmest day, and she was only wearing a coat.

He held her hand tightly, the unsettled feeling inside him calming. Fuck, it was good to touch her again. To have her skin against his, feel her warmth. He tightened his fingers even more, fighting down the almost overwhelming urge to pull her away to the car he had parked not far off. Push her inside and take her right there in the backseat, not giving a fuck about who was watching.

But Hunt was right in front of him, staring at him, the asshole's black eyes way too sharp for his own good.

"What's the decision?" he asked, trying to make it sound like less of an order.

"You have a deal," Hunt said flatly. "I'll put on hold my plans to dismantle the operations here and put it around that we're forming an alliance to take advantage of the European trade routes."

Adrenaline surged in his bloodstream, a great wave of it.

This was the last piece of the jigsaw and now he had it, the end was in sight. Fucking finally.

He kept the triumph and the relief locked down, betraying nothing. "Excellent. In that case, I'll require access to all the records you have on the various networks operating here. I'll also be sending in some people who'll be doing a little road trip for me."

Hunt's gaze narrowed suspiciously. "Why?"

"Because I can't take down all the networks and the people involved unless I have incriminating information. Which means I'll have to send people in to get it for me." He paused and raised a brow. "Unless you have some already?"

The other man was silent a moment, then he nodded slowly. "I'll take a look. See what I can find. Fitzgerald was careful with his records, but Eva managed to download a whole lot of crap from his computer. There might be something there that could be useful."

Jericho didn't flinch at the sound of his father's name. He'd long gotten past that stage. "There better be. The faster I get that information, the faster I can take down this shit once and for all."

Hunt's expression didn't change. "Just because I agreed to this doesn't mean I trust you."

"I'm not asking for your trust." He found he was stroking Temple's fingers over and over, an absent, comforting movement. Really, he should stop doing that. Yet he didn't. "Just remember that I could have come in and taken everything you have by force. At any time. And I didn't."

Hunt didn't like that, his dark eyes glittering with menace. "You could certainly have fucking tried," he said coldly. "Whether you would have succeeded is another story."

"Well, we can agree to disagree about that." He paused. No, he shouldn't ask. But then if he didn't, he'd probably never know.

Maybe it would make things easier if you didn't?

It *would* make things easier. And that was as good a reason as any to ask the question, since making things easier for himself was the last thing he wanted to do.

"Did you tell Violet?"

Temple's hand in his tensed.

He didn't look at her, keeping his gaze firmly on Hunt's. He would bear this no matter what the guy's answer was, he just fucking would.

"Yes," Hunt said. "She believes you."

His chest hurt all of a sudden, the adrenaline rush of before turning into something else, all of it gathering into a hard, painful knot right behind his breastbone.

She knew. She believed him. He wouldn't end this with her thinking he was the bad guy, the ultimate villain. That he was stained with the same kind of darkness their father carried around inside him.

"Oh, Peanut," he whispered softly, very, very softly, so that no one would hear him.

He wasn't going to see her after this was all over, that much he knew. He wasn't going to see her ever again. But that was for the best. For both of them probably.

There was so much he wanted to say, reasons, justifications, explanations. But he didn't say any of them. They were, after all, only one thing: excuses. And he couldn't give Violet, of all people, excuses. Couldn't give them to himself either.

So all he said was, "Tell her I love her." It would be the only chance he had to say the words to her.

An expression he couldn't name flickered through Hunt's black eyes. "I'll tell her."

Jericho held the other man's gaze for a moment longer, then without a word, he turned and walked away, his hand firmly gripping Temple's, heading in the direction of the lake.

She walked beside him silently.

"What did he do to you?" Jericho asked after a moment, keeping his gaze on the path ahead. "And don't tell me nothing, don't tell me you're fine. I can see you're not."

She didn't answer immediately, but her hand remained relaxed inside his.

They avoided another group of tourists and dodged a small knot of mothers pushing strollers.

"I met Violet," Temple said at last.

His jaw felt tight, tension across his shoulders. "Was Hunt telling the truth? Did she really believe me?"

"Yes. She did. And she—"

"No," he cut her off, not wanting to hear anymore. He'd

told Hunt to pass on his message, that's as much as he could do. It was better not to think about Violet now. "I don't want to talk about Violet. That's not what I asked anyway."

Temple sighed. "He didn't touch me, Theo. I'm damn well telling the truth too."

"What did I tell you about that name?" He shot her a warning glance.

Her mouth tightened. "Fine. Nothing happened to me. I was treated well. It's all good."

But it wasn't all good. Then again, it probably wasn't the best time to talk to her about it now. He'd get it out of her one way or another later.

He turned his attention away from her, staring straight ahead once more. "We'll be flying back to Paris tonight. I have a few issues I need to deal with personally."

"Oh." She was silent a minute. "My sister. You said you rescued her, that she was alive. Do . . . do you know where she is?"

Her sister . . . Ah, yes. That was the last thing he'd given her the day before. The picture of Thalia he'd managed to find.

"No," he replied. "I got Dmitri to put her on the first flight out of Paris. I know she arrived in the States and that she got help from the person I'd organized to set her up a new identity. Beyond that, I don't know what happened to her or where she went."

"Right." Another pause. "Is it possible to maybe find out?"

He could. He could get someone to investigate what had happened to Thalia, find out the information for her.

And you know what'll happen once she has it. She'll kill you and leave.

"I could," he answered. "But once you have the information, what's to stop you from killing me right now?"

Her face was pale, her expression with that hint of wariness to it. "Well, your plan to take down the trafficking rings for a start. I definitely don't want to kill you before that happens."

"No, you probably don't. Perhaps I'll investigate then, see what I can find out. And once this is all over, I'll give you the info if I find any."

This time she glanced at him, a bright flicker of gold, her expression unreadable. "Not before?"

A group of joggers enveloped them for a second and he waited until they'd gone.

"No," he said, the word was quiet.

She was quiet as they continued to walk on a little farther, then she said, "I gave you my surrender, and you still don't trust me?"

"Not when you won't tell me the truth."

"The truth about what?"

Shit, maybe now was the time.

He stopped, forcing her to stop too, tugging on her hand so she had no choice but to turn to face him. "The truth about what happened to you at Hunt's. Because something happened, Temple. You think I can't see it in your eyes? You're wary, you're distant. Something's changed, and I want to know what it is."

There was no flickering this time in her amber eyes. They met his without hesitation. "Nothing happened, Jericho. Nothing's changed. So whatever it is you think you're seeing, it isn't there."

But she was lying, and he knew it.

Hurt twisted inside him, unexpected yet somehow familiar. A pain like grief. Because he'd thought he'd had it, he'd thought he'd gotten her trust. Yet clearly he hadn't, so what could he do? He could use sex like he had before, force her to tell him everything using pleasure. Or he could withhold the information about Thalia.

Or you could trust her to tell you eventually. Because she'll never trust you if you don't trust her.

Well, he could wait for that moment if he had the time. But he didn't. And it wasn't likely she'd ever trust him anyway. He'd lost the right to win that from anyone a long time ago, just as he'd lost the ability to trust himself.

No, he only had the very little information about her sister that he could use. So he would.

Jericho smiled. "In that case you're going to have to wait until all this is over, won't you?" And he lifted her hand, brushing his lips over the backs of her fingers.

Temple shivered, watching him for a second.

Then she looked away.

CHAPTER FIFTEEN

Temple sat on the black velvet sofa in the office of Le Papillon Bleu, Jericho's Parisian club. Ahead of her were the big glass walls that looked out over the whole place, allowing him a view of everything that went on there. The office was set up high, a cube that projected out from the walls and looked as if it was only accessible via a set of steel stairs that led from one of the gantries that crisscrossed above the dance floor of the club. In reality, the office had another entrance through a doorway that led into the rabbit warren of the club's back rooms.

The office had a slightly vertiginous feeling since the floor was also transparent and made of thick glass and, allowing a view straight down into the dance floor itself.

She didn't look down. Instead she looked at Jericho, standing there in front of the massive glass walls, talking with a group of men with Triad tattoos peeking out from underneath their custom-made suits. She had no idea what they were talking about since they were speaking in Chinese, though that didn't seem to be a problem for Jericho. Whichever dialect they were speaking, he sounded as if he was fluent.

They'd gotten back to Paris early that morning after a tense flight where she'd avoided him by locking herself in her cabin and pretending to sleep. Half of her had expected him to bust down the door anyway, yet he hadn't, and she didn't know whether to be pleased about that or not.

As soon as they'd arrived back at his Parisian house, he'd left again with Dmitri, obviously going off to deal with the "issues" he'd mentioned back in New York.

Alone in the house but for the guards, she'd wandered around, trying to figure out what to do with herself. Wondering why he hadn't touched her since Elijah had given her back to him by the fountain in Central Park. Wondering why he'd been so distant.

But of course she knew why. She'd thought she'd hidden the strange distress that had gripped her the moment she'd seen him again, tall and muscular and lethal, leaning against the fountain's edge. He'd been in jeans and a dark casual shirt, wearing a leather bike jacket, a cap on his head hiding his gilt and tawny hair. Innocuous clothing for a man who was anything but innocuous.

As he'd pushed away from the fountain with that dangerous grace that characterized all his movements, his green-gold eyes immediately coming to hers, her heart had seized up in her chest, grief getting a stranglehold on her throat.

She'd agreed with Elijah not to mention that Zac and Eva were in on what was going to happen in case he decided to make a move against them. Just like she couldn't tell him about Zac's private conversation with her. She didn't think he'd take action against them, but she wasn't sure he wouldn't either so staying silent seemed prudent.

Except then he'd picked up on her distress and wanted to know what was wrong. And so she'd had to lie to him. A lie that had hurt him. Why else had he been so distant?

She hadn't thought that his distance would hurt her too. Hadn't expected that what she'd agreed on with Zac would be so very painful.

Music from the club reverberated through the office

walls like a giant heartbeat. The soundproofing in the office muffled it, but Temple could still feel the vibrations pumping up through her feet. On the dance floor beneath her, people danced, their bodies illuminated by flashing lights.

She didn't look. The people down there were the rich and famous of Paris, drawn to the club's exclusivity and the promise of decadence. They didn't know what went on in the VIP rooms of this club. They thought it was just a high-end nightclub with a few naughty strippers. They didn't know there were girls kept here, girls funneled through to brothels throughout Europe. Girls sold to men with too much money and hearts made of stone.

She'd only come here to find her sister, that's all she'd cared about. That and killing the man responsible for Thalia's disappearance. But that man was already dead, and Thalia was alive. She'd gotten out thanks to the man standing over by the wall and no doubt discussing more "shipments."

All you've done was for nothing.

Jericho's voice was low and deep and decadent, and one of the men he was talking to laughed in response to something he said. None of them looked in her direction. She may as well have been part of the furniture.

She had to do something. She had to. Seven years of training, of learning how to kill, of taking lives to practice her skills, to earn money to keep up the search. And her sister had gotten out that first year. So yeah, all those deaths and for nothing.

She had to make them mean something.

The lights in the office were very dim, barely there. They were hardly needed anyway given the lighting from the club outside spilling through the glass. Silver flashes chased over Jericho's face, illuminating the perfect line of one high cheekbone, the angle of his straight nose, the curve of his exquisitely carved mouth. He was beautiful, so beautiful.

But no matter what his intentions, he was responsible for so much misery. He'd saved Thalia, it was true, yet he'd let so many others drown.

There had to be some justice somewhere and maybe she was the one to deliver it. For all the girls that had been lost. For herself.

And perhaps for him too.

Her heart squeezed hard again, her throat tight and sore. But that was getting to be her usual state these days, so she ignored it.

Another ten minutes or so passed, and eventually the conversation Jericho was having with the Triad members finished up, Dmitri coming to show them out of the office and lead them back into the club.

The door shut behind them, cutting off the deafening flood of music abruptly, leaving a deep, heavy silence.

Jericho stood in front of the massive glass walls, his hands in the pockets of his black suit pants, his attention on his club. He had his back to her, the powerful width of his shoulders outlined as the lights flashed again. Like a king on the battlements of his castle, surveying his kingdom.

Or Lucifer looking out over hell.

"What kind of man spends sixteen years making himself into the devil himself?" It wasn't until the words came out that she realized she'd spoken them aloud.

The silence deepened, the throb of the bass beneath her feet. But she let the words sit there because she had to know all of a sudden. Whether she'd been wrong to give him what she had. Whether she'd been wrong to believe he'd do what he'd promised.

Finally, he swung round, glancing at her. His eyes were shadowed, his expression opaque.

She didn't look away. "You faked your own death. You turned yourself into a monster. You destroyed the lives of hundreds of women . . . Why didn't you go to the authorities sooner? Immediately? Why did it take all this time?"

Slowly, he turned around, leaning against the wall at his back. She couldn't tell what was going on behind his eyes. "You want to know whether I'm as bad as I seem to be, don't you?"

"Yes." She couldn't answer any other way.

"You know the truth, Temple. You've always known."

"Tell me."

"Why?" The flashing lights behind him cast his features in shadow, gilding his hair like moonlight. "You don't trust that I'm going to end it all, do you?"

"I . . ." She had her hands clasped in her lap, her palms damp. "I want to." And she did, she really did. "But men like power and you've been doing this long enough . . ."

"To what? Develop a taste for it?"

"Well, have you?"

He stared at her, his expression unreadable. "I'm going to bring this down," he said after a moment. "I'm going to end it. You can choose to believe it or not, that's up to you, but I will. I couldn't go to the authorities any earlier because if I did, some people would escape. Some of them would find ways to protect themselves and I didn't want anyone—*anyone*—to get away. This fucking business is a hydra. You cut off one head, and two more grow in its place. Which means if you want to get rid of it, you have to stab it right through the heart."

She swallowed again, her throat dry. "Sixteen years is a long time to work at something."

"Yeah, it is. But someone had to do it." His voice was still flat.

"And those girls you rescued? Thalia?"

"What about them?"

"Why did you do that? Surely that was a risk?"

He lifted a shoulder. "It was. But I was sick of not being able to do anything, not being able to lift a finger to help. I always kept having to keep my eye on the big picture and sometimes . . . it was nice to be able to do something about the small details."

The "small details."

"They weren't details, Jericho," she said softly. "They were women."

A muscle leaped in his jaw, and for the first time since they'd gotten back to Paris, she caught a glimpse of the man she knew behind the crime lord. The man he insisted he wasn't anymore. Theo. "I know they were women." There was something in his voice that was different now, an edge. "You think I don't fucking know that? Every fucking day they came into the club, and every fucking day I had to look at them, pretend I didn't see the bruises, pretend I didn't see the tears—" He broke off and turned sharply back to face the glass walls and the club beyond.

There had been pain in those words and anger. No, not just anger, but *rage*.

Oh, you know about rage, don't you?

"And if you pretend long enough," he went on, the words curiously toneless. "Eventually you don't see them anymore."

Grief caught at her. Because she knew how it could happen. Hadn't she been doing that herself all this time? Pretending that the contracts she took were only about money for services rendered. Pretending that the men she killed were all evil assholes that the world was better off without. Pretending so she didn't have to see the truth.

"For years I made myself listen to them." His voice was quiet now, almost inaudible. "To their tears and their screams. Because I needed to hear them, to remember what I was doing and why I was doing it. But that was the same. If you listen to the same thing over and over again, eventually it becomes meaningless."

There was a long silence, and she wanted to get up and leave the room, escape from the grief that pulled at her, from the pain that seemed to wind deeper and deeper into her heart with every word he spoke. But she sat without moving, her hands locked tight together, listening.

"I have to do it, Temple," he said softly. "Because it's the only way I'm ever going to escape."

He didn't know why he'd said all that, but even that night she'd been away, he'd missed having someone to talk to. And now she was here, he couldn't seem to shut himself up.

Stupid. He should never have brought her to the club, but he hadn't been able to bring himself to leave her behind. Having her presence near him soothed something inside him, at the same time as it made that same part ache.

Through the glass walls of his office, he watched the crowds writhing on the dance floor, their hands lifted, bodies moving in time with the beat of the music.

Christ, he hated this place. Hated the noise. Hated the people. And yet this office was the one private space where it felt like he could relax his guard for a moment. Where no one could see in, and he didn't have bodyguards tailing him.

Not that he ever did anything in here except business. And then, when that business was over, he would watch the crowds mindlessly. It was as close to peace as he ever truly got.

Behind him, he could feel Temple's presence like a fire at his back, warm and vital and bright. Yet she'd been quiet since they'd returned to Paris. No prizes for guessing why that was. Had to be whatever had happened at Hunt's. Sure, he probably hadn't helped by keeping his distance, but what the hell did she expect? They both knew she was lying when she said there was nothing wrong.

A subtle perfume wound around him, expensive and warm, a feminine sweetness with hints of musk. Temple.

He didn't move, keeping his gaze on the dance floor while concentrating all his awareness behind him. He could feel desire begin to shift in his bloodstream, flowing hot in his veins and gathering tight in his gut.

He hadn't touched her since New York, and his dick was really unhappy about that. But that was too bad. The last time he'd had her was too sharp and fresh in his memory, up against the window in the lounge in his townhouse, her golden eyes wide, looking up into his, showing him everything. And then the night following, how she didn't hold back. There had been nothing but honesty between them that night, and he didn't want to go back to the lies that lay between them now. Not when lies had been the entirety of his whole fucking life until now.

God, he was tired of it. So goddamn tired.

There was a silence behind him, but he knew she was close because he could feel the warmth radiating from her. It pulled at him like the promise of spring after a lifetime of winter, and he had to clench his hands into fists in the pockets of his suit pants to stop himself from reaching for her.

"Violet told me you had a fiancée," she said quietly, which was pretty much the last thing he expected her to say. "That you were going to move in together. That you had a career all mapped out."

Ah yes, the life he was supposed to have had. What a fucking joke that had been.

"Rose." Her name sounded strange and out of place here. "The daughter of a friend of Dad's."

"That . . . must have been hard to leave her." A pause.

"What happened, Jericho? Why did you give that up? Why did you destroy your whole life for . . . this?"

He'd never told anyone, never wanted to tell anyone. Because it said a lot about the man he'd once been and none of it good.

His father's son. His father's heir. His father's plaything.

Maybe he should. Maybe a little fucking honesty was what he needed right now.

He kept his gaze on the crowds dancing beneath him. "Will you tell me what happened at Hunt's?"

A pause. "Why do you think anything happened at Hunt's?"

Below him, a woman in the crowd lifted her hands in the air, turning around and around, her expression blissful. "Because something changed. I get the feeling you don't trust me the way you did before," he said, then he let out a short laugh at his own wishful thinking. "Not that you ever did."

There was another pause behind him.

"I can't tell you." Her voice was close. As if all he needed to do was turn around and she'd be right there in front of him, inches away. "I just . . . can't."

He didn't turn around. "Because you don't trust me."

"No." There was no hesitation this time. "I don't."

It hurt, no denying it didn't. "Good," he said anyway. "You shouldn't."

"Jericho—"

"My father taught me what I was from an early age," he interrupted, because if he didn't say this now, he never would. "I was ten when I was first brought to the Lucky Seven casino and brothel he used to own. He caught me following him because I wanted to know where he went on his 'trips,' so . . . he showed me. After that, he used to bring me in during the day, when no one was around, showing me around the place and telling me it was his kingdom, and that one day I'd inherit it. I loved it. It looked magical, like something out of a story, and the thought of being a prince was . . . exciting." The woman on the dance floor swayed to the music, ecstatic. She was high in all probability, and briefly he was jealous of the escape he'd never allowed himself. "I was fourteen when he first brought me to the club at night and told me I could pick any woman I wanted to lose my virginity to. After that I used to go there regularly, because Dad insisted I learn the ropes, that I needed to know all the ins and outs of his business if I was going to be his heir. At first it was just the casino side, and I loved the money aspect of it, the games of chance. It was exciting." His hands were clenched into fists, so with an effort, he unclenched him. "I was seventeen when he showed me how he ran the brothel side, and by then I was thoroughly his pawn. It was a business to me, and I was interested in how it worked. I didn't care where he got his girls from. I didn't care that some of them had bruises, that some of them came to work with red eyes. I didn't see their fear. I only saw what Dad wanted me to see."

The only sound was the slight exhalation of her breath and the sound of shock in it.

"At the same time as Dad was showing me all this stuff, he was also creating for me a facade of normality. Teaching me how to maintain it. He taught me from an early age that men like us were special, were out of the ordinary, and so we had to hide it because it scared people. I didn't question it. I believed everything he told me. He was God in my world, and everything he said was gospel."

"You were brainwashed." The sound of her voice was almost a shock.

"Maybe you could call it that. Or maybe it was just that I didn't want to see what was right in front of my face.

Whatever, I had a head for business, and I was good at it, I enjoyed it, so I helped Dad grow his business. That empire of his? We built it together, him and I."

More shocked silence from behind and just as well, she should be shocked. No one knew that the empire he wanted to take down and been partly created by him in the first place. Out of ignorance. Out of a desire to please the man who'd raised him. The monster who'd created him.

"Then one night, for my twenty-second birthday," he went on because he had to go on. "Dad brought me a girl. I don't know how old she was, but she must have been very, very young. And he told me that I deserved something special. A virgin, just for me. All the women I'd been with before had been . . . willing, or at least that's what I thought. But this girl . . . She was crying and she had bruises around her throat. She flinched whenever I moved and . . . for the first time I really saw her. I really looked. And I couldn't do it. I couldn't touch her. So I left. Dad ranted at me the next day, told me I was chicken-shit. That I needed to get over myself, that real men were stronger than that. Stronger than guilt or scruples. That real men relished the freedom of not having to obey society's rules and did whatever the hell they liked. I'd always believe him before, but that night . . ." No, he wouldn't close his eyes, blindness was inexcusable. "I got home, and Violet was waiting up for me. And I realized then that girl couldn't have been much older than my own god-damn sister. It felt like someone had ripped a mask off my face. I went to the Lucky Seven the next day, and all I could see was the bruises on the faces of all the whores I'd been with. The pain in their eyes. All the things I'd never seen before were suddenly right there. I told Dad that day I wanted out, that I couldn't be what he wanted me to be." Jericho felt his mouth begin to curl in a bitter smile, and he let it. "You know what Dad said? He said that I was a pussy. And that if I ran, he'd make Violet his heir instead."

A hand settled on his back, a slight pressure, a warmth he couldn't bring himself to shrug away no matter how much he knew he should. A comfort.

You don't deserve comfort.

He didn't. But surely, now he was so close to the end, he could take this.

"I knew there was no escape," he said hoarsely. "But I also knew that if I stayed, he'd turn me into what he was, and I couldn't allow that to happen. I'd spent so many years being a blind, self-entitled little fuck, letting all this terrible *shit* happen all around me, and I couldn't, I just couldn't . . ." The hand on his back pressed harder, and he realized his voice was shaking, rage cracking it apart. "I knew what I had to do. I knew I had to fix what I'd helped create, what I'd let fucking happen. And there was only one way to do it. I briefly considered killing Dad, but I knew how the system worked by then. Someone else would have taken his place, and the whole thing would keep on going. If I wanted to take it down, I'd have to be the one in charge. So that's what I did. I faked my own death because Dad would never have stopped searching for me if I hadn't, and I hoped that would mean he'd also leave Violet alone." There was an ache somewhere inside him, part of the guilt he'd long since ceased to feel because if he did, he would have gone mad. "I had to leave her. I had to take a calculated risk that she'd be okay. Out of all the things I've done, that's up there as being one of the hardest. Leaving Violet to that monster with no one to protect her."

Warm arms slipped around his waist, a lithe body up against his back. He could feel her head resting between his shoulder blades.

The ache became a raw wound deep inside. One that would never heal.

"Don't," he whispered. "Don't touch me."

But she stayed right where she was, her arms like iron bands around him, holding him together.

Then she said, quietly, "I killed my father."

CHAPTER SIXTEEN

She'd forgotten why she'd put her arms around him. To give him the only comfort she could offer or to stop herself from breaking into pieces, she didn't know. But maybe it didn't matter. Maybe all that mattered was the feel of all that hot, hard muscle, the ridged plane of his stomach rising and falling under her palm in time with his breathing, the tension that ebbed as she tightened her arms around him. The things he'd told her. The darkest parts of himself he'd revealed.

And regardless of trust or anything else, she knew she didn't want him to be the only one to lay bare his soul.

No one knew her dark secret. Not one person.

He didn't speak for a long moment and neither did she. Instead she pressed her forehead against his back, inhaling the warm spice of his scent. The cotton of his black shirt was smooth against her skin, and she just wanted to stand there, surrounded by the smell and the heat of him, holding on to him, taking some of his strength.

Because whatever else he was, he was strong. And determined. He had a powerful will and a bravery to match. A deep sense of responsibility too. All of those had been twisted by his father, molded into something they were never meant to be, and yet somehow he'd broken away.

And made a decision no one should ever have to make at twenty-two.

Her age. That still killed her.

"What did he do to you?" he asked, his deep, beautiful voice rolling over her.

And she could have cried at the assumption. Not "What did *you* do?" but "What did *he* do to you?"

"After Thalia disappeared, there wasn't anyone around to protect me any longer. And I knew what that meant. I knew he was going to go after me instead." She closed her eyes tightly, the blackness comforting. She tried not to think about this, tried not to ever remember, but if he'd had the courage to tell her what he'd done, then she could do no less. "So that night, when I went to bed, I took one of the kitchen knives and hid it under my pillow. I tried hard to stay awake, really, really hard, but I was so tired. Thalia was gone, and I'd spent a lot of that day crying and I just didn't have the energy to stay awake. The next thing I knew there was a hand over my mouth and Dad was. . . . trying to get my nightgown up." Nausea rose inside her, thick and hot, but she swallowed it down. She needed to say this. Had to. "I was groggy with sleep and I tried to shove him off, tried to scream, but he was so heavy. He just held me down. He . . . had his hand over my nose too, and I couldn't breathe . . . And that's when I remembered the knife. I think it was just instinct that had me reaching for it. I don't even remember much about what happened, I just remember grabbing it and putting it . . . somewhere. Anywhere to get him off me." There had been nothing but blackness, nothing but panic. "And then I shoved him and he just slipped off the bed, and when I turned on the light . . ." Her voice had gotten hoarse now, thick with the horror of it. "There was blood everywhere, and he wasn't moving."

Jericho's hands were suddenly over hers where they

rested on his stomach, large and warm and comforting. But he didn't say anything.

"I killed him," she whispered, the words muffled against his back. "I killed Dad."

"He would have suffocated you. He would have abused you." His voice was a deep vibration rumbling through her, full of certainty and anger. "You did what you had to do. Just like I did."

But it wasn't the same, she knew that deep in her heart. "No, not like you. You were trying to fix things. I didn't fix anything. I went off and killed people for money, because it was easy, just so easy—"

He turned suddenly, so quickly she had no time to move or step away. One moment she had her forehead pressed to his strong back, the next he was cupping her face between his hands, the lights of the club outlining the exquisite planes and angles of his forehead, nose, and cheekbones. Intensity burned in his eyes, a deep, gold flame.

"You survived," he said softly, fiercely. "You survived to find Thalia. And you did what you had to do to find her. No, those things you did can't be erased, and, no, you can't change them. But you didn't do them because you took pleasure in them or because they turned you on. And no matter what you think, you didn't do them for money either. You did them because you wanted to find your sister. Because she protected you. Because you loved her." His thumbs swept over her skin in a gentle caress. "That's all there is, Temple. That's all the reason there needs to be."

Her eyes were full of tears, and she didn't know why. "But I must have done something. I must have said something or . . . I don't know what. There had to have been something about me that made him do it. That made him want me. And afterwards . . . I didn't have to take those contracts, there were other things I could have done. I was just so . . ."

"Angry," he finished gently, the understanding in his voice nearly breaking her apart. "You were just so god-damn angry."

Despite her best efforts to stop them, a tear escaped and slid down her cheek. "Yes." The word was as cracked and brittle as old plastic. "Yes, I was."

His thumb brushed the tear away. "And you still are."

Of course he knew. Because the same bitter, frustrated anger gleamed in his eyes too. She turned her cheek into his palm. "There's nothing I can do about it. Nothing that can make it better. Sure, I did it to find Thalia, but that doesn't excuse murder. I keep thinking that perhaps . . . Perhaps there's something wrong with me. Perhaps I'm just a cold-blooded killer at heart. Perhaps that's why—"

"No." The word was flat and sure. "There's nothing wrong with you, kitten. Nothing at all. You had a shitty childhood that left you scarred at a young age, that left you having to protect yourself. What you did was survival, nothing more." He believed it. He believed every word, she could see it in his eyes. "You're beautiful and you're brave. You're so fucking strong and you're so fucking loyal. You're not a killer, Temple."

"But I—"

"I've seen evil, kitten. And I know what a killer looks like, believe me. Christ, I've seen so much of that kind of shit, I barely even notice it anymore. But you're not one of those people. You're not evil and you're not cold-blooded. There's a light in you, a brightness . . . God, you can't know what it felt like to see that in someone. After years of being around people who are dead inside."

She tried to blink the tears away, but they refused to stop. And this time, they weren't for her memories or for the sense of wrongness she'd always felt inside herself, but for him. For the shadows in his eyes as he looked at her. For the life he must have led if he'd seen brightness in someone like her.

"If I'm not a killer then you're not a monster, Theo." And she said his name fiercely, claiming it for herself.

He shook his head slowly, that terrible sadness in his gaze again. "You did what you had to do for love. For self-defense. For survival. I didn't. I built that fucking empire because I liked business. Because it was fascinating. Because I refused to see what was happening all around me—"

"Because you were brainwashed," she cut him off harshly, her hands coming up to grip his wrists, holding onto him. "That's what happens in cults."

"But I'm not brainwashed now. I know what I'm doing." His mouth curved in a bitter smile. "I've done it before after all."

"No." She gripped his wrists tighter, digging in, as if pressure alone would make him understand. "Your father did what he did for power. For greed. But you're not. You're doing it to fix things. To help people."

"But the end is still the same." His voice was gentle, so horribly, terribly gentle. Explaining things as if she was a child. "Don't you see? I've become exactly who my father raised me to be."

She could feel the beat of his pulse beneath her fingers. It was steady as a rock. He wasn't angry or upset about this. He was . . . resigned. And for some reason, that frightened her. "You're not," she said insistently. "You're *not*."

"People died. People were abused. It doesn't matter what my intentions were, I let it happen. I *made* it happen."

She was crying and she couldn't stop. "But you can't excuse what I did, then pile all the blame on yourself. That doesn't make any sense."

He brushed her tears away, ignoring her fingers digging

into his wrists, a strange expression on his face that looked like tenderness and yet surely couldn't be. "It makes perfect sense. There's hope for you, Temple. But there's no hope for me. This is what I am. This is what I was born to be."

She didn't understand why she was protesting so vehemently, especially when it was exactly this kind of admission of guilt that would make everything so much easier. All she knew was that she hated the sound of acceptance in his voice, the resignation. As if he'd long known that was the truth and had made his peace with it.

"So why not just go with it?" she demanded, anger rising up against the grief. "If you're so goddamn accepting, why not say 'fuck it' and keep the whole operation going? You've got all the power you want, all the money you could ever need. If you're exactly like your father, why get rid of your empire at all?"

He smiled and this time there was no bitterness in it, only sadness. "Because I promised myself I'd do this for Violet. For that young girl I left behind in the Lucky Seven. And I always keep my promises. Always."

But that didn't make it any better. In fact, it just made her angrier. Because she had a horrible feeling that there was another promise he'd made to himself. "You want to know what happened at Elijah's?" Her voice was thick with anger and pain, but she didn't bother to hide it. "Zac Rutherford and Eva King were there. They were the ones who hired me to kill you."

He said nothing, his thumbs sweeping backward and forward over her tear-slick skin, his gaze unreadable.

Why the fuck are you telling him all this?

She had no idea. He just had to know, and she couldn't stand lying to him anymore.

"They're in it with Elijah too. They're giving you the alliance not because they trust you, but to see what you'll do. And they want me to finish it if you don't." She took a breath. "Zac wants me to fulfill my contract, Theo. After all this is over, you're a loose end he wants me to tie up. And . . . I said yes. I said that I would do it. I said that I would kill you."

An expression shifted in his eyes, a ripple of something she couldn't interpret. "I know," he said quietly.

Then before she could reply, he bent his head and covered her mouth with his.

Jericho knew he should never have brought her here tonight. He should have done what he normally did and ignored his own needs, left her back at the house.

But he hadn't. And now he was desperate. To have her and to stop her from talking. Stop her from saying things that he didn't want to hear.

It didn't change things that Rutherford and his friends were involved. It didn't change things that she'd agreed to put a bullet through his brain. He'd suspected something along those lines anyway.

All he wanted to do, all he'd ever intended, was to survive long enough to destroy the web he'd created. And after that? Well, if that was death then he'd welcome it. Because he was tired, just so fucking tired. Of the isolation more than anything else. The sheer loneliness of it. Of not being able to confide in anyone, of not being able to even be himself, if he even knew who that was in the first place. Of not being able to hold anyone. Of not being held in return. Of not having anyone, not one single person, he could turn to.

He'd always thought he didn't want that. Always thought he didn't need it. Until Temple had come into his life and showed him just how badly he *did* need it. Did want it. How much he hated walking around every day not feeling a thing because if he did, he'd never survive. And when those feelings did manage to leak through somehow, how badly he wanted them to be something other than guilt or pain or regret.

She'd given him a taste of those other feelings. She'd shown him that he was still alive, deep down inside. But he knew it wasn't something he could ever keep hold of. He was too far gone, too far down the path. He wasn't the hero. He was the villain. And just as in any good story, there was only one ending for the villain.

But that was okay. He was tired. He wanted it to be over. He wanted to rest.

Yet first, before any of that, he just wanted her. Take what he could get without talk of hope or redemption or monsters. Live a little in the flame once more.

Her mouth was so warm, and there was salt against his lips from her tears, but it felt like years since he'd tasted her so he didn't stop. She made a little noise in the back of her throat, a soft groan. Her hands slipped from his wrists, her palms coming to rest on his chest, her head tilting back. And she began to kiss him back, and this time it wasn't tears he tasted, but desperation.

Christ, they always seemed to be desperate for each other, always seemed to be hungry. But then that made sense since the time they had with each other was so very limited. And soon it would be more limited still.

He let his hands trail down the smooth, silky skin of her throat, just letting his fingers rest across her collarbones. The apparent fragility of her astounded him. She was so small, so slender, and yet . . . There was so much strength in her, so much heat.

"I don't want to kill you, Theo," she whispered against his mouth. "I don't."

"It's okay, kitten," he murmured, because it was.

"Everything's going to be okay." And he pushed her back against the glass wall of his office, with the flashing lights of the club behind her, the dancers whirling beneath them.

He slid his hands down the fabric of the slinky black dress she'd put on that night. The cut was deceivingly modest, the neckline straight and high at the front, while dipping right down to the small of her back behind. And it had a slit right up nearly to her hip on one side. Librarian stripper, she'd called it when she'd come down the stairs that evening, shiny black platform Mary Janes on her feet.

He didn't care what it was. She looked like an ice cream on a blisteringly hot day, and he wanted to lick her right up.

She quivered as he trailed his hands over the curves of her breasts, his fingers brushing tantalizingly over her hardening nipples, then heading on down over her hips before sliding inside the slit in her dress. The skin at the top of her thigh felt like satin, smooth and warm, so he let his hand rest there a moment, stroking her with his thumb.

Her breathing was getting faster, he could hear it even under the beat of the music outside the office, and she trembled a little as he slid his fingers farther, pushing gently between her thighs, urging her to widen her stance.

She shifted, moving her own hands to the buttons of his shirt, pulling them open with trembling fingers. Then she was tugging the tail of his shirt out of his pants, opening it right up, her hands on his chest, touching him, stroking him. And for a moment he couldn't think, couldn't seem to form any coherent thoughts whatsoever.

It shocked him how badly he wanted her touch, how badly he needed it. And just how fucking good it felt to have her fingers sliding over his bare skin, to have her mouth burn in the hollow of his throat as she got rid of his shirt entirely.

He shouldn't let himself have this, but he couldn't seem

to bring himself to stop her. So he closed his eyes for a moment as her fingers roamed over his chest and shoulders, sliding down his back as she kissed his throat, her lips like sunlight moving over him.

"Turn around," she whispered as her fingers stroked the curve of his spine. "I want to see something."

He knew what she wanted to look at. The tiger. His own little bit of hubris. And part of him didn't really want to explain it, wanted to keep his hand right where it was in the soft heat between her thighs. But for some reason, he couldn't seem to deny her, so he did as she asked, easing himself back from her and turning around.

Her fingers on him, so light. Gentle. Tracing the lines of the tattoo as if it was a precious work of art. As if he was.

Something tight inside him clenched even tighter.

"It's beautiful," she whispered. "Does it mean anything?"

Pain. That's what it meant. The kind of pain that reminded him he was alive because sometimes he forgot how that felt. But of course, that wasn't all it meant. "The tiger represents strength and wealth and power." He paused then added, "It is also the protector of the dead."

Her fingers stopped a moment and he thought she might say something. But she didn't, and he was glad. He didn't want to talk about the tiger on his back or what it meant. It was too complicated, and there were too many meanings, meanings that had changed over the years.

And maybe she sensed it, because her hands slid to his hips, urging him back around again. She didn't look up at him, her fingers moving to his belt and unbuckling it. But he put his hands over hers, holding them still. "No."

Then she did look up, tipping her head back and meeting his gaze. He recognized that look in her eyes. They glowed bright gold with stubborn determination. "Yes," she said and she knocked his hands away, undoing his belt, flicking open the button on his fly. Taking hold of the tab of the zipper and tugging it down.

He was hard, and he ached so badly. And he knew what she wanted to do. But it didn't feel right. He didn't want her on her knees in front him, sucking him off in this place. In this office where there had been many women who'd done the same thing. Not to him, but to others, the men he'd formed alliances with. Men who didn't care that the women were bruised, that there were tears in their eyes and needle tracks on their arms. Women who'd been broken so many times they didn't even protest.

Women nobody saw because they'd ceased to exist as anything but property, part of the furniture.

But he saw them. He'd made himself see them. At least he thought he had . . .

They're not details, Jericho. They're women.

Oh fuck. He'd forgotten hadn't he? He'd forgotten what he was supposed to never forget.

"Temple," he said hoarsely, reaching for her again. "Not here. Please, not here."

But her hands were already sliding into his boxers, her cool fingers wrapping around his aching cock. And she was slipping down to kneel gracefully in front of him, avoiding his hands. "Yes, here." Her voice was so certain, so sure. "Look at me, Theo."

He didn't want to, but he made himself look down.

She was on her knees in front of him, her golden eyes bright despite the darkness of the office itself, full of golden flames. Full of that wild heat and energy he'd seen in her that first night as she'd danced for him in the VIP room. And just like the first night, he couldn't drag his gaze away from hers.

"You're allowed this," she said. "You're allowed to have this."

No, it wasn't about that. Was it? "Too many women have been on their knees in front of me," he said hoarsely. "Too many women who didn't want to be there."

"Did you make them then?" Holding his gaze, she circled his cock with her fingers and drew him out of his boxers. Then she held him in her fist, running her free hand up the back of his leg, her fingers spreading out on the back of his thigh, holding on tight. "Did you make them do this to you?"

"No. Not to me. But to others . . . They didn't have a choice."

"Well. I do."

"Kitten—"

"I want to do this, Theo. I want to give you something." *Like you deserve anything.*

"I . . . can't. You can't."

"I don't care whether *you* can't. This is *my* choice. Are you really going to deny me a choice?"

Christ, the beautiful little bitch. How could he protest that?

He stared down into her golden eyes, hard and wanting her, but she only stared back, daring and full of challenge as always.

She wasn't one of those women. She hadn't been broken by her background in the way some of them had been. She had survived. And more than survived, she'd come back from it fighting. There was so much strength in her and yet at the same time so much fragility. The combination was so intoxicating, mesmerizing.

How could he deny her anything?

He didn't say a word, and after a moment, watching him, she tightened her hand on his dick, put out her little pink tongue and licked him.

The feel of her tongue went through him like pain. The very best kind, woven through with raw pleasure and wet heat. His breath caught in his throat, and he couldn't take his eyes off her. So she licked him again, then swirled that tongue of hers around the head of his cock, and he had to put his hands on the glass wall in front of him to steady himself.

Jesus Christ. He couldn't remember the last time a woman had given him a blow job. Couldn't even remember the last time he'd wanted one. He'd lost his taste for them a long time ago, just like he'd lost his taste for sex.

Because you didn't deserve it. You didn't deserve anything that gave you pleasure.

And as far as he was concerned, he still didn't. Yet somehow he was letting her do this to him, making him feel so good, so *fucking* good. And he didn't have the strength to tell her to stop.

Those women. You should never forget . . .

But Temple was opening her mouth and swallowing him, and sensation shot like lightning down his spine, shattering both the thought and the memories into tiny, little pieces.

And there was only this moment and her mouth around him, the heat and the pressure. The pull as she sucked and the constriction of her fist around him. Only the pleasure that tore a groan from his throat, making him reach out with one hand to her hair, twisting those red curls through his fingers and holding on tight. Wanting to take control and yet at the same time wanting to let her take it, because she was fire and he wanted to burn.

One last time.

So he kept his gaze on hers, watching her suck him, harder, faster. Holding tight to her hair, urging her on. Accepting everything she wanted to give him, because this was her choice. Panting as the pleasure curled through every nerve ending, electrifying him. Scorching his blood, his bones. Scorching his soul.

"Temple," he whispered raggedly as he felt himself begin to come apart. "Oh, kitten . . ."

But then even her name was ripped away as the orgasm exploded through him, smashing through every barrier he had, taking his consciousness and shattering that too.

Leaving him with only one thing left to hold onto.

Her.

Temple rested her forehead against the hard plane of his stomach, feeling the muscles tense and shift in time with his ragged breathing. She was panting, his cry of release echoing around the small space of the office. His fingers were still in her hair, holding on tight as if he never wanted to let her go.

She didn't want him to either. She wanted to stay like this, with the taste of him in her mouth, the scent of him all around her. The feel of his hand holding her, all hard, possessive and strong. Yet somehow needy as well.

But this wasn't going to last, and she knew it.

All she'd wanted to do was show him that it didn't matter to her what he'd done. And it didn't matter whether he thought he deserved it or not. What mattered was that there were still pieces of him that hadn't been broken by the evil he'd been brought up in. Little pieces of Theo still alive in Jericho. And the fact that those pieces were even there was a miracle in itself. Only a man with a very strong will could have kept those alive. Only a man who was good at his core would have even wanted to.

It was clear he didn't believe in those pieces.

But she did.

Why? Why is that so important to you?

She didn't want to think about that question or the answer. Didn't want to think about anything at all. So when his fingers tugged, pulling her up on her feet again, she

went with it. And when he pushed her against the glass
once more, she let him.

Light flashed across his face, lighting up the brilliance
of his eyes, the gold flecks in them a match for her own.

Well, they'd always been similar in so many ways.

"You bitch," he said softly, stepping right up to her,
pinning her to the glass with his body. "You goddamn
beautiful bitch."

The look in those brilliant green-gold eyes of his was
complicated. Anger and desire and wonder all mixed together, burning so intensely she couldn't look away.

"What am I going to do with you?" His voice held that
rough velvet quality that she loved, the one she felt on
her skin like a touch, the vibration of it deep in her chest,
in her sex. "Tell me. What the fuck am I going to do?"

"I think you already know the answer to that." She was
breathless now and aching, the salty taste of him making
her almost light-headed with want. "Do I really need to
spell it out?"

But his hands were already moving to the hem of her
dress, sliding it up over her hips, his fingers trailing over
her bare skin and leaving shivers in their wake.

He smiled, that feral, hungry smile as he shifted his
hips. She could feel him hardening against her, his cock
pressing against the damp heat between her thighs. "No,"
he murmured. "But you might need to give me a minute.
I'm not quite as young as you are."

Temple tilted her hips, trying to find the right angle,
suddenly desperate for more friction. "I don't think you
need a minute," she whispered hoarsely and then gasped
as he shifted with her, his cock rubbing against her clit,
sending a bolt of white-hot pleasure through her. "God . . .
you're already there."

Light flashed, pulsing in time with the music, outlining

every perfect line of his face. His smile had vanished, leaving behind it so much hunger and raw need it made her breath catch.

"Arms up," he ordered.

And she obeyed, saying nothing as he peeled her dress up and off her. She hadn't worn a bra underneath it since the back wouldn't allow it, so now she was virtually naked but for the thong she wore and the stiletto Mary Janes that were part of the outfit.

The glass at her back felt cold against her heated skin, the contrast delicious. She shivered as Theo bent his head, as his mouth seared her throat, his hand cupping one breast as he kissed down over the other. Then she gasped aloud as he took her nipple into his mouth, sucking hard then biting her, sending curls of pleasure/pain through her.

Then he pinched her other nipple at the same time and she let her head fall back against the glass, a groan escaping her. She could feel the beat of the music outside, the only thing preventing them from being seen by the whole club the mirrored surface that reflected the dancers back at them. Protecting her. Protecting Theo.

Because it wasn't Jericho here with her, not now.

She lifted a hand and pushed it into the deep gold and bright gilt of his hair, all warm and silky against her palm. Her chest ached, tight with a big, heavy emotion she didn't want to name.

He lifted his head, his green-gold eyes meeting hers. Tiger's eyes. Protector of the dead.

Protector of the living too.

His hand slid down between them, over the front of her lace thong, his middle finger pressing insistently against her clit, making her shake. "Theo . . ." she said raggedly, not quite sure what she was going to say only that she couldn't keep it inside her. "I don't know . . . I don't know what this is."

His finger moved, circling around her clit, over and over, the pleasure crackling and burning like sparks falling over her skin. "You don't know what what is?"

"This . . ." Her breath hitched and she trembled, the movement of his finger making everything so much more intense, so much more everything. "I can't . . . I don't know . . . Oh Theo . . ." Her voice broke, though why she didn't understand. "I'm scared."

Something changed his face, and his other hand rose, sliding behind her to cup the back of her head. He smiled and this time his smile was warm, understanding. The sun rising on a long, dark night. It made the frightening feeling inside her worse and yet, weirdly, at the same time it made it better, though she had no idea how that worked.

"Didn't I tell you it was okay?" he murmured. "It will be. It will be."

Then he kissed her, exploring her mouth with such delicacy as he kept stroking her, kept winding the pleasure tighter and tighter, kept her trembling on the brink of a chasm so deep and wide she knew that if she fell, she'd never stop falling.

Yet she didn't want him to stop. Perhaps falling was what she'd been made for.

And then before she was ready he lifted his mouth, stopped the movement of his finger, ignoring her breathless protests. Reaching behind him to grab his wallet and extract a condom. He threw the wallet carelessly onto the ground, ripped open the packet, and protected himself.

Then he slid one hand beneath her thigh and pulled her leg up and around his waist.

Her mouth was dry, her throat tight. She couldn't seem to breathe. She felt desperate and needy and terrified of the feeling that sat in her chest like a heavy stone, a weight that pressed her down, held her pinned to the ground, helpless.

"Theo." God, her voice sounded so cracked and shaky, not like hers at all. "Help me."

His eyes were brilliant, like coins, and he didn't look away as he eased aside the lace of her thong. As he positioned himself. As he pushed inside her, so slow, so goddamn slow she nearly screamed.

Pleasure began to unwrap itself like a spring uncoiling, an inexorable tide of it, swamping her. She could feel herself coming to pieces, and there was nothing she could do to stop it, the heavy, scary sensation expanding, crushing her.

She did scream then, but he was kissing her, taking the sound of it into his mouth as he thrust deep inside her. And as he moved, pulling back and thrusting in, a slow rhythm like the pull of the moon on the tides, inescapable, inexorable, she understood that she wasn't in pieces. That she wasn't being crushed.

She was being put back together. She was being remade. Reborn.

Her arms came around him, holding him as he moved inside her, and she arched her hips, moving with him. Matching her rhythm to his.

And she stopped fighting it. Stopped being scared.

She opened her mouth beneath his and let the feeling in her heart bleed into her kiss, giving it to him, letting him taste it. Letting him know that even if he had no one else, he had her, and that he was right. It was okay. Everything would be okay.

Then the pleasure became even stronger, undeniable, and she didn't scream this time, she cried. She sobbed like she hadn't since she was a small child.

But he held her, gripped her tight in his arms, kissing her tears away.

So that when the edge of the chasm approached, she didn't flinch from it. Instead she hurled herself off the side of it.

And held onto him as she fell.

CHAPTER SEVENTEEN

As Violet approached the door of the private meeting room at Alex St. James's club, the Second Circle, fear squeezed hard in her chest, and she had to stop and take a breath.

"Princess?" Elijah's deep voice came from beside her.

"They're going to kill him, aren't they?" She didn't look at Elijah, staring hard at the ornate wooden door in front of them.

They were here to meet with Zac Rutherford and the rest of the Nine Circles club, mainly to see what Eva had managed to get from Fitzgerald's computer and whether or not it could be useful to send to Theo.

Elijah had put together a few things already, some video evidence, as well as a couple of incriminating emails and texts. But it wasn't enough. Theo needed information on the entirety of the whole network and to do that, they needed any files Fitzgerald may have had on his computer.

Unless of course, they didn't want to help Theo at all, and quite frankly, she wouldn't put it past them. Unfortunately, she could also see why they might not want to help, which didn't make her feel any better.

"You don't know that," Elijah said. "They want those networks down too."

"Yeah, but they don't trust him."

"Of course they don't trust him. If he wasn't your brother, would you?"

The fear twisted, because she knew the answer to that.

She turned, looked up at the man who'd kidnapped her, threatened to kill her, then had ultimately fallen in love with her, the way she'd fallen in love with him.

As usual the blunt features of his rough, scarred face were unreadable. Except for her, of course. She could read him, and she could see the concern in his dark eyes. He was worried for her. "Is it wrong of me, Eli? Is it wrong of me to want him to be okay?"

Something in his face softened a little. "No, of course not. He's your brother."

She let out a breath. "I mean, I can understand why the others don't trust him, not after what Dad put them all through. But . . . after what Temple told us. God. He's spent all this time working behind the scenes and actually trying to destroy the network. That doesn't make him anything like Dad."

"No, it doesn't." Elijah's voice was flat, the way it always was when he was delivering unpalatable truths. He was a hard man who didn't flinch from stuff like that, and that was part of what she loved about him. He never lied to her. "But sixteen years is a long time to pretend to be a villain, princess. Some of that sticks. You know that."

Of course she did. Elijah had spent seven years as her father's right-hand man, and he hadn't emerged from that unscathed. "Yeah, but you came back from it."

"And you remember what I was like," he said without hesitation. "I would have done anything to get what I wanted, and I didn't much care if that was right or wrong."

Violet lifted her chin. "You don't much care now."

One corner of his scarred mouth lifted in a rare smile, the one that never failed to make her feel like she'd somehow made it rain in the middle of the Sahara desert. "Well, I care about you."

"And Theo cares about me. I don't think he'd do anything that would hurt me."

"You don't 'think' . . ."

"I *know*, okay? He wouldn't." Even when she'd thought he was all bad, when after sixteen years of thinking he was dead, he'd suddenly turned up and taken her from Elijah by force a month earlier, he'd done it to get her out of the ruins of their father's empire, to keep her safe. And okay, so he hadn't let her in on his real reason for being Jericho, but she understood that was to keep her safe too. He'd always been her protective older brother and that hadn't changed, she could feel it in her heart.

Out of nowhere a memory came back to her, of the look in his eyes as he'd faced her in that dingy apartment in Alphabet City. The weariness in him. A bleakness that made her soul hurt. A man coming to the end of his strength.

Fear crept through her once again, and this time it wasn't so much about whether the others were going to kill him as it was about the fact that he might even welcome it.

No, that wasn't going to happen. Not if she could help it.

She turned and reached for the door handle. "Come on, let's do this."

The Second Circle was an exclusive private members' club owned by Alex St. James, one of the billionaire members of the Nine Circles Club, and was where the Nine held their meetings.

They had a private room that gave the impression of an old-fashioned English gentlemen's club, with tall library bookshelves, wingback armchairs, a long sofa, and a fireplace with a fire burning in the grate.

Honor St. James, her best friend, was standing next to

one of the armchairs by the fire, talking to a tall, broad-shouldered blond man. Gabriel Woolf, ex-biker turned billionaire construction magnate, Honor's lover and also Violet's half-brother. Which was still weird even after a month had passed since she'd found out about it. There had been some fairly awkward conversations with Gabriel over the past couple of weeks, but she thought the two of them were coming to terms with their unexpected sibling connection. Family was important to Gabriel, and Violet liked that since it hadn't been for her own family, the Fitzgeralds.

One thing was for sure; at least she knew she could count on both Honor and Gabriel backing her if she had to argue for Theo's life. And maybe she'd be able to get Alex, Honor's brother, on board too. He was sitting on the sofa with his arm around his lover and blonde Russian bodyguard, Katya, his head turned in Honor's direction. Alex had been estranged from his sister for a long time, but now they'd found each other, the two of them had gotten close. If Honor supported her, Alex would, Violet was sure.

Of course that just left the other two members of the club, Zac Rutherford and Eva King. And they were *not* friends of the Fitzgeralds, not at all.

Eva was sitting cross-legged in the armchair opposite Honor's, Zac, tall and massive, standing beside it like a knight guarding a princess. Eva had been her father's prisoner for two years, held as a sex slave, and not only that.

She'd also been the one to put a bullet through his head.

Violet still couldn't quite untangle her own feelings about her father's death, let alone the fact that this woman had killed him, which didn't exactly make her Eva's friend. But she couldn't deny the small, pale-haired woman had been through a lot, and it was understandable she didn't think much of the Fitzgerald family as a whole. What was more problematic was the fact that she would side with Zac.

Her gaze shifted to the man standing beside Eva's chair. The big ex-mercenary's expression was enigmatic, rather like Elijah's could sometimes be, which wasn't particularly encouraging. She knew Zac's primary motivation was protecting his lover and, after Eva's experience, she couldn't blame him. But that also made him extremely one-eyed. He was a strong-willed guy—hell, all these men were—yet there was something very black and white about Zac, and that really annoyed the crap out of her.

He was *not* going to be on board the "save Theo" train.

Elijah shut the door behind her and for a second there was silence as the six people already in the room turned to look at her and Elijah. Then Honor was coming forward, smiling, reaching out to give Violet a hug. Gabriel came after her, though he wasn't the hugging type, settling instead for a surprisingly warm smile, that she knew for a fact was pretty rare for him.

Alex grinned at her from his place on the sofa while Katya nodded a greeting.

Eva lifted her chin, while Zac merely inclined his head like a king accepting homage.

Arrogant bastard.

Gabriel had dragged over an armchair beside Honor's near the fire, indicating that Violet should sit. She didn't really want to, but Elijah's hand settled in the small of her back, gently urging her over to it so she went, sitting down and folding her arms, trepidation lying like a stone in her gut.

"So," she said after a second, deciding to get right to the point, "did you find anything in Dad's stuff we can give Theo?" She directed this to Eva, who was sitting there with a grim expression on her face.

"No," Eva said flatly, making Violet's stomach lurch.

"When I got into his computer a few weeks ago, I was looking for something we could take to the authorities. But as soon as I hacked in, a number of his files wiped themselves."

"Oh." Violet said, trying not to let her disappointment show. Great, she'd been hoping her father had had something there that could be useful, that could somehow incriminate his whole network. And then she'd send it to Theo, he'd do his thing with the rest of his operations, taking everything down, and then he'd come home.

You really think it's going to be that simple?

No, of course it wouldn't be. Nothing ever was.

"But." Eva held up a hand. "I *do* have a guy who's an expert on recovering deleted files. I gave the hard drive to him a week or so ago and he's been trying to see if he can get them back."

Violet stilled, staring at the other woman. "And?"

"And . . ." Eva grinned. "He managed to recover at least a couple. They weren't only deleted, but heavily corrupted as well, so it was a bit of a fucking mission to get them at least readable, but . . . They're good ones. Emails, financial records, lists of bad cops who were paid to turn a blind eye, plus a lot of other shit that could implicate people who definitely would *not* want to be implicated. All the good stuff in other words."

"That's fantastic," Honor said, glancing at Violet. "That's exactly what Theo needs, right?"

"Why don't we take this to the authorities ourselves?" Alex asked. "I mean, we were going to, weren't we?"

Violet's gut lurched again. Shit, she'd forgotten. Alex was no friend of the Fitzgeralds. either, not after what her father had done to Daniel St. James, Alex and Honor's father. Not after what had happened with a friend of her father's called Conrad South.

"We can't," Gabriel said, his voice a rough, deep rumble. He was sitting in the armchair, Honor perched on the arm next to him, his arm possessively around her waist. "Not if we want to take the rest of this shit down. You know what Zac told us."

Alex rolled his eyes. "Yeah, I know what Zac told us. So we're just going to rely on the fact that Temple—who, may I add, has already betrayed Eva once—will make sure Jericho does what he says he was going to? I mean, if that's even going to work."

Violet frowned and opened her mouth to reply.

But before she could say a word, Zac said, "I believe Temple."

"Only because she's under contract to you," Elijah pointed out coldly from his place behind Violet's chair.

There was a heavy, tense silence at that.

Elijah had told Violet a couple of weeks earlier that Zac had taken out a contract on Theo's life. She'd been upset, so much that Elijah had offered to send his own guy out to take down whichever assassin Zac had sent. But in the end, she'd decided that it wasn't worth the grief. If Theo truly had become exactly like their father, then death was the only option.

Until Temple had come along and the truth of Theo's intentions had come out.

There were so many reasons not to trust what Temple had said, and yet Violet had believed her instantly. Because she knew her brother. Sure, he must have changed at lot over the years, Elijah would be right about that. But she was sure that somewhere deep inside, he was still the big brother she'd loved. The protective big brother.

What he'd been doing all this time was exactly the kind of thing he *would* do, and it made total sense to her.

She wasn't just grasping at straws. She wasn't.

"A contract that should have expired by now." Violet tried to make her voice as cold and as hard as Elijah's. "We need him alive, Zac. You know that."

Zac's amber gaze was impenetrable. "And did I disagree?"

"Well, no." And he hadn't. But there was still something in his gaze, in his voice, that made her doubt. "You don't want him alive though, do you?"

"With all due respect, Violet, you don't know what I want."

"Enough." Elijah's hard tone cut through the tension like a sword, his hand coming to rest on Violet's shoulder, warm and heavy, calming her. "Let's deal with the facts as we have them now. We need Jericho alive, and we need to get him the information that's going to ensure the American networks go down at the same time as the rest of Europe's. And you know that getting that network down is a priority. I've spent seven fucking years getting it to this point and I'm not letting it loose now. Anything else we can deal with later."

"If that's what he's going to use the information for," Alex murmured. "He could want to use it to take over instead."

"If he was going to do that, he would have done it years ago," Honor pointed out calmly. "And he didn't."

Alex frowned at that, but didn't protest. Because really, what could he protest about? It was true, Theo could have come in at any time and wiped his father out. But he hadn't.

Violet didn't know why that was but maybe it had to do with the relationship between father and son. A relationship she knew nothing about.

"Why didn't he?" Eva's voice was soft, echoing the question that no doubt the rest of them were thinking. "I mean, he basically left the whole of the U.S. alone for years. Why was that?"

"Fitzgerald spent a couple of years negotiating with him," Elijah said. "Jericho kept stringing him along. But whatever the reason was, Honor's point was valid. I don't think he's after the operations here. Besides, even if he was, I have a few emergency backup plans in place. It wouldn't take much to take down all the shit here if worse came to the worst."

"Then I say we give this information to him." Katya's Russian accent was soft, decisive. "And the sooner the better."

"Hell, yeah," Alex murmured. "I don't trust Temple, but hell, what have we got to lose? If Jericho's lying through his fucking teeth, we'll soon find out, and we'll act accordingly. Right, Zac?"

"Yes," Zac said. "Yes, we most certainly will."

Despite Elijah's hand on her shoulder, Violet felt a chill steal through her. "What about afterwards?" she asked suddenly. "Once this is all over, once he's done what he's promised and he *will* do it, make no mistake, what about then?"

" 'Once this is all over,' " Zac echoed softly. "Yes, I want it to be over, Violet. I think all of us are ready for this to be over." He paused, and just for a moment, the barriers in his amber gaze disappeared, and she thought she saw something there, a glitter of some kind of emotion, she didn't know quite what. "And one way or another," he went on in the same tone, "it will be."

An hour later, the room was quiet, Zac shutting the door behind Alex and Katya, who were the last to leave.

Eva, standing by the fire, watched as he flicked the lock then turned back to her.

Her heartbeat sped up, because sometimes he liked to celebrate the end of a Nine Circles meeting by undressing her and then making love to her on a soft silk rug on the floor in front of the fire.

Well, he was shit out of luck tonight. Something was up with him and she wasn't going to be letting him touch anything until she found out what it was.

"Don't tell me," she said, meeting his amber gaze. "You're going to get Temple to kill him anyway."

He let out a breath then came over to her, his arms sliding around her and bringing her in close against the heat of his big, muscular body. He didn't often touch her in public, respecting the fact that she was still getting used to touch again after years of not being able to stand it. And some part of her quite liked that he didn't, because it made the way they came together in private so much more intense.

Like now, when every nerve ending she had woke up, trembling in anticipation of the moment when his bare skin would touch hers.

Except it was going to have to tremble in anticipation a little longer.

She put her hands against his broad chest, enjoying the feel of all that hard muscle beneath the cotton of his black business shirt, holding herself away so she could look up into his whiskey-colored eyes.

"Damn you," he said without heat. "Since when did I become so easy to read?"

"You're never easy to read. I just know you too well."

He sighed. "Angel . . ."

"You have, haven't you? You're going to get Temple to kill him."

"It doesn't matter what his intentions are, he's still a threat. And after this is all over, he'll still be a threat."

She spread her fingers out, feeling the strong, steady beat of his heart beneath her palm. "This isn't about me, though, is it? It's about you."

His gaze flickered. "What do you mean?"

"I'm talking about revenge, Zac." She searched his face.

"When I shot Fitzgerald, I took your revenge away from you. Don't think I don't know that."

His expression softened. "That was yours to take, angel. It wasn't mine."

"And yet you still want it. I can see that. It's why you're so set on getting rid of Jericho, isn't it?"

The strong line of his jaw hardened. "Fitzgerald hurt you. He hurt so many—"

"Yes, I know. But Fitzgerald is dead."

"His son isn't."

Eva slid a hand up Zac's chest, cupping his hard, stubbled jaw. "But his son may not be the same kind of guy. I mean, I don't know him, he could be. But he also might not. He might actually be trying to do the right thing."

"I realize that. It doesn't change what he's done, though. And it doesn't change all the lives he's ruined."

"Oh, bullshit." She let her fingers trail along his jaw, stroking. "You want your revenge. You want to take him out because you never got the chance to kill his father."

Zac stared at her, the fire reflected in his eyes, all gold and red and orange. "I never protected you, angel. And I should have."

God, this man. The past few weeks with him had been so rewarding, the happiest of her life, even with all the shit going down with Elijah, Violet, and her brother. She never thought she'd have this, never in a million years. Yet it wasn't all sunshine and roses. Zac had a will like iron, and his dominant nature absolutely refused to let him back down.

Luckily she was a determined bitch when she wanted to be, plus she had a secret weapon—the key to his heart. "Hey, you said it yourself, nothing can change what happened in the past and certainly not killing Theodore Fitzgerald." She dropped her hand from his jaw to the top button of his shirt, flicking it open. "And anyway, you *are* protecting me. And I'm safe."

"Why does keeping him alive matter to you?"

Eva went on to the next button, flicking that open too and spreading out the fabric, exposing a wedge of bronze skin. "I feel sorry for Violet. She's lost a lot, and I don't like the idea of her losing a brother, no matter what he's done." She looked up at him, willing him to understand. "You know how I feel about family."

"Yes, but—"

"And I don't want you to have yet another death on your conscience," she went on over the top of him, not giving a crap about the fact that he hated to be interrupted. "You have to know when to say enough, Zac. So that's what I'm saying. Enough."

Gold flames leaped in his gaze, and he reached suddenly for her hand, his fingers closing around her wrist like an iron manacle. "*I* say when it's enough, angel. Not you."

She didn't move, and she didn't look away. "You really want to fight me on this? You know I'll win."

He smiled, the edge of savagery to it that never failed to make her breathless. "Will you, angel? Will you really?" And gently, but very firmly, he brought her hand down and put it behind her, holding it down in the small of her back, forcing her against him.

She shivered. Fuck, she loved it when he got all Dom on her. But still, she meant what she said. There had been too much death in this whole situation as it was. Did there really need to be any more?

"Don't make me say the safe word."

"What? You're really going to safe out on me now?"

"I mean it, asshole. Too many people have died already and too many people have been hurt. People we know.

This won't help anything. It's just more fucking violence, and, quite frankly, I've had enough of that."

His smile faded and a tender look crossed his face, the look he only ever saved for her. "Angel, I'm sorry. But . . . I have no limits when it comes to protecting you."

Her heart tightened. "I know. But, my love, I think on this occasion, you need to have at least one." Slowly she raised herself on her toes, pressed her mouth to his, and whispered against his lips. "Safe word, Zac. *Void*."

CHAPTER EIGHTEEN

Jericho sat in the darkness and stared at the computer screen in front of him. He'd always been afraid that when the time came to finally pressing the button on everything he'd built over the past sixteen years, he wouldn't be able to do it. That he'd want to keep what he'd built. Or maybe even hesitate, have some sliver of regret at taking down the entire framework of his life.

What life?

Yeah, well, that was the fucking point, wasn't it? What he had wasn't a life. It had never been a life. And even before this, when he was his father's good little puppet, doing everything the old man said, what he'd had was a part. A role to play.

Nothing had ever been his. Nothing had ever been his choice. In fact, he could count on one hand the times in his life he'd ever had a choice about what he wanted to do.

Such as the moment he'd decided that there was only one way he could stop what his father was doing. And right now, the choice to send all the information he had to the authorities.

And Temple.

His heart clenched tight at the thought.

Yes, Temple had been a choice. Right from the moment he'd first seen her twisting around that pole. A choice he'd made for himself, not for any other reason. Because he'd wanted her, the first choice he'd made that wasn't about fixing his own fucking mistakes. The first choice that had been for himself. And so he'd made her his, the only thing he'd ever had that was his and his alone.

A choice that had brought both of them nothing but pain.

I'm scared . . .

He closed his eyes, the memory of her face burned forever in his brain. The look in her eyes as he'd pressed her up against the walls of his office. As he'd pushed inside her, felt her body grip him tight. As the pleasure began to overwhelm them both, her golden gaze going molten, burning with desire and need, and yes, fear.

He knew what she meant. He knew what she was talking about. Because he felt it too, and, yeah, it scared the shit out of him, as well.

Falling for her wasn't supposed to be part of the choice he'd made, and yet it had happened all the same. Fuck, if he'd had any choice about that, he'd have made a different one.

Opening his eyes, he stared at the screen once more. The time up in the corner read 2 A.M.

She'd be asleep in his bed, at least he hoped she'd be asleep. He hadn't seen her all day, closeting himself in his office the moment he'd gotten the text from Hunt to say some information had been sent through to him via an anonymous email address that had been re-routed several times.

The attached files had been heavily encrypted, but another email from another address had sent him a program he could use to decrypt them. And as soon as he had, he'd known that everything he'd been working toward, everything he'd been slowly building for so many years, was finally drawing to a close.

There were his father's records—not all of them it was true—but there was enough information in the ones he had, not to mention the intel that Hunt had already sent him, to bring down the entirety of the U.S. trafficking networks.

There was only one little problem with it, a problem so small it wasn't even worth worrying about.

In sending all that information to the authorities, he would also reveal his own involvement. Because he was the one who'd set those records up in the first place.

It didn't matter. It didn't make any difference.

All it would mean would be the revelation that Theodore Fitzgerald had been part of his father's empire. And that maybe that was the motivation behind his suicide.

You're forgetting Violet.

Yeah, that would hurt her. That would hurt her a lot. And there would be media interest once all this came out. She would be targeted by the press, no doubt, her father and brother both turning out to be part of a nationwide human trafficking ring.

It couldn't be helped. This was the only way to make sure the people involved were brought to justice and that the trafficking rings were smashed the fuck to hell, everyone caught in them freed.

Violet would cope, she would have to. At least this time she wouldn't have to do it alone. As much as he didn't like the prick, she did have Hunt at her side, and he was one bad motherfucker to cross. He would protect her, keep her safe.

Reaching for his phone, Jericho picked it up and typed out a quick message to Hunt. It would be early morning in New York, but he was sure the guy would see it pretty much immediately.

When this hits, Violet will become a press magnet. Take her away somewhere safe.

He waited a moment and sure enough, his phone vibrated a second later with a message from Hunt. *What aren't you telling me?*

Astute prick, wasn't he?

What makes you think that? Jericho texted back.

Because you know I've already got Violet covered, Hunt responded.

Jericho sat back in his chair, the only light in the room the glow from his computer screen and the screen in his hand. Had the guy not seen the records he'd just sent? Had anyone seen them? Maybe they had, maybe that was the real reason Rutherford was after his blood.

My name is in there, he texted. *Long story, but Theo will be implicated when this hits the media. Tell Violet that I'm making it right.*

There was a pause. Then the screen lit up again with Hunt's answer. *Tell her yourself.*

Jericho stared at the screen for a long moment. Then he turned the phone off and put it back on his desk.

No, he couldn't do that. He wouldn't be telling Violet anything.

He looked back at his computer screen.

Sixteen years he'd spent working to become the head of hell, making alliances, uniting various different networks, bringing all the devils together using the promise of money and power, and when that didn't work, violence. Years gathering the information he needed and secreting away where no one would find it. Information paid for in blood by people who'd died to get it to him.

He hadn't known it would take that long when he'd first begun. When he'd first walked into that strip club in Atlanta, just one part of his father's empire, and asked for a job as a bouncer. His very first step into the world that would bring him to this point.

He'd thought it would take him a couple of years at

most. But it hadn't been a couple of years. In fact, it hadn't been until he'd worked there a year that he realized the magnitude of what he'd taken on. And what he would have to do in order to finish it. What it would take from him in the end.

Too much. It had taken too much.

The email glowed on his screen, the first of many he would send over the course of the night and all with attachments, proof of his claims. It wasn't going to go just to the relevant authorities either, it would also go to the world's media as a safeguard. Especially because some of those relevant authorities would be implicated too. And he should know; he'd paid some of them himself to turn a blind eye.

By tomorrow, everyone would know.

By tomorrow, all of this would be over.

Who knew, that right at the end, it would be so fucking easy?

He didn't want to keep what he'd built, and he felt no regret. All he wanted was for this all to end.

Without any hesitation he reached out and pressed the button.

And sent the first email.

Temple woke with a start. The room was in darkness, completely silent, nevertheless she knew something had woken her. An intruder of some kind. Her body coiled into instant readiness, her senses already trying to make sense of the darkness around her.

A low, sensual laugh came from down the end of the bed. "I should have known I could never surprise you."

The shadows resolved themselves into the shape of a man. And there was only one man who had that kind of laugh.

Theo.

Slowly she sat up, a strange foreboding clutching deep inside her.

She'd gone to sleep in his arms after spending most of the previous day alone since he'd been secreted in his office all day doing God alone knew what. Except even though he hadn't told her, she could guess what he was doing: preparing to take down the empire he'd built.

Then much later he'd come to her that night, taking her hard and rough and desperate. As if he was trying to escape something. She hadn't asked him what was wrong, hadn't pushed him to share. Mostly because some part of her didn't want to know. Just like it didn't want to know now.

She swallowed. "What is it?"

"Come with me. I want to show you something."

The expression on his face was impossible to read in the shadows of the room, his voice not giving anything away. But she knew it wasn't going to be good. That nothing that happened from here on would be good.

He held out his hand, and the foreboding inside her deepened.

Don't go. Don't go with him.

"What are you doing, Theo?"

"You'll see. Come on, kitten."

Refusing would be cowardly, and she wasn't a coward, so she slid naked from the bed, reaching for the T-shirt of his he'd left on the floor and slipping it over her head. Then she took his hand, his warm fingers closing around hers.

She should have asked him what he'd been doing all day. She should have tried to find out. But . . . she was afraid.

Weren't you supposed to not be a coward?

The heavy thing in her chest, the feeling that had frightened her so much at the club, shifted like the earth subsiding after an earthquake. It was a horrible feeling.

God, she hated being afraid, hated feeling powerless, but the stone sitting just inside her ribs was making her feel both those things, and she really didn't know how to deal with it.

Her heart hammering for no good reason she could see, Temple followed him out of the bedroom and down the hallway to his office.

The lights were on, glaring in their brightness, hurting her eyes. She blinked as Theo dropped her hand and went around the big dark oak desk, sitting himself in the chair behind it.

He wore what she was coming to think of as his usual Jericho uniform, dark suit pants and a business shirt with the sleeves rolled up, no tie, and the top few buttons undone. Today his shirt was a pristine white. With his dark suit pants, it made him look ascetic as a monk.

Except no monk had a face like a fallen angel or green-gold eyes so sharp they could cut you in two. No monk had a mouth that could make you get down on your knees to beg for a taste or a voice that you'd sell your soul to hear.

Her throat was tight, the feeling something bad was going to happen getting stronger. "What's happening, Theo?"

He had that smile on his face, the terrible one that was regret and sadness and understanding all rolled into one. "I think you know."

Oh Christ. She struggled to keep her breathing even. "Elijah got you the information you wanted?"

"He did." Theo's gaze dropped briefly to the computer screen in front of him. "I'm just in the middle of sending as many emails as I can to various authorities, plus the world's media." He glanced back at her, and amusement entered that terrible smile. "Tomorrow's going to be one hell of a day for a great many people."

She swallowed. "So . . . you did it."

"I did," he said slowly. "I really did."

"This is the end?"

"Yes." A small hesitation, his smile turning bittersweet. "In more ways than one."

"Theo—"

"I estimate I have about an hour before people start realizing what's happening. And then probably my IP address will be traced since I'm not trying to hide it, which means people will be coming here."

Her heartbeat was accelerating, and she didn't know why. "Then . . . then we should go, we should get out—"

"Jericho will be found shot dead in his office."

The words fell across her, heavy and final, like skyscrapers collapsing.

She blinked at him, not understanding. "W-what?"

His smile was fading, the sun disappearing behind a cloud. The sun disappearing forever. "Jericho needs to die, kitten. He can't survive."

"You mean, you need someone to be Jericho so you can get away? That's what you're talking about, right?"

But of course it wasn't. And she knew that deep in her heart.

"I mean *I* need to die, Temple," he said with such hideous gentleness that she wanted to scream.

She was already shaking her head. "No. No, Theo. No, you don't."

Yet he only looked at her. "It was always the way it was going to end. It's the way it *has* to end." He shifted, pulling open a drawer in the desk and taking out a gun. A Glock. He put it on the desk and pushed it over toward her. "You have a contract to fulfill, Temple. A revenge to take. Now's your chance."

The heavy feeling in her chest began to seep down through her, spreading everywhere, turning her to stone. There was a roaring in her ears, and she couldn't seem to breathe.

His green eyes held hers, unflinching. "I think I can guess what Zac promised you. Not just money right?" Without taking his eyes off her, he reached for the manila folder that also was resting on the desk top and pushed that next to the gun. "I did some searching yesterday. Inside the folder is everything I could find about Thalia, including her address. She's living in Minnesota. Shouldn't be too hard to get there."

Her lungs felt like they were encased in concrete, her throat so tight it was like she was being strangled.

"I don't want you to give me anything, Temple," Theo went on softly. "You can take Thalia's address right now and leave. But . . . I'd like your face to be the last thing I see."

As if someone had punched her straight in the center of her chest, air suddenly filled her lungs, sharp as an electric shock, making her take a harsh, rushing breath.

I'd like your face to be the last thing I see . . .

"No." The word was explosive, echoing around the room. And she was walking, striding up to the desk, propelled by that terrible, infinite heaviness that was weighing her down, that filled her so she could barely speak. She slapped her hands down hard on the dark oak surface. "No. You're not . . . You're not fucking dying. Where the hell did you get that idea from?"

He didn't look away, and the expression on his face held all the fierce, determined will that she knew was part of him. The will that had kept him going for sixteen years. "Do you know what Hunt sent me? Records from my father's computer that somehow Eva managed to decrypt. Emails, spreadsheets, names. It's all there. Everything, including my name."

A sliver of ice slid down her spine. "What do you mean including your name?"

"My name is there in those files because I was the one who set up those records in the first place."

"But—"

"I told you I helped him," he went on remorselessly. "I told you I was part of turning his business into such a fucking success. I helped him build the fucking thing, make it better, more profitable, and those records were part of it."

Her voice seized. She couldn't speak.

"What I'm saying," he said, gentling his voice. "Is that even if I live through this, my options are limited. I could reveal my identity, turn myself in, go to jail. Or I could risk one of my former 'colleagues' hunting me down and taking their revenge." He paused again. "Or you could pick up that gun and . . . set me free."

She couldn't look at him, couldn't bear the expression in his eyes, so she looked down at the gun sitting on the desk between them, dull silver and lethally gleaming. The outlines of it were blurring slightly, and her cheeks felt wet.

Fuck, was she crying?

She blinked hard, but the blurriness didn't go away and neither did the tears.

Set me free.

"No," she said hoarsely. "No. That's not what . . . I can't . . . No."

"Yes." His voice was so soft, so terrible in its certainty. "I'm tired. I'm just . . . so fucking tired. It's been sixteen years, and I can't do it anymore. I want it to end, I want it to be over."

Tears streamed down her cheeks, and that was weird because she thought she'd cried all the tears she had after Thalia had gone. But no, apparently there were more. A lot more.

She didn't want to look at his face because she knew what she'd see there. The weariness that went deeper than merely physical. An exhaustion that went soul-deep.

You knew what it meant the first time you saw it. You just didn't want to think about it.

Because if she'd thought about it, she'd have to wonder why it bothered her so much. Why it made grief choke her. Why it scared her when nothing else did.

Why she was crying now and couldn't seem to stop.

She cared, that was the problem. She cared about him. *It's more than that. You love him.*

Temple lifted her gaze from the gun to Theo's face. Made herself look. Made herself see the lines around his mouth and eyes, the lines of an unbelievably difficult and harsh existence. Made herself study the shadows in the green depths of his gaze, the darkness of guilt and anger and pain. Because it didn't matter that she didn't want to see those things, they were there. They were part of him. They were part of what made him who he was.

And they were the things that would take him from her in the end.

"I don't want to do this," she said hoarsely. "I don't want to."

"I know. I know you don't. But I'd rather it be you. It's justice, don't you see? Justice for Thalia. For all those other women. For everyone I've destroyed." He reached out and picked up the gun then took her hand, placing the stock of the weapon in her palm and closing her fingers around it. "Take your revenge, kitten. Please. Fulfill your contract. Let me go."

The gun was cold and heavy, but his fingers were warm and steady. He wasn't scared, and she knew he must have come to the realization about how it would all end a long time ago. And had accepted it.

Tears were starting to drop into the desk top, little glittering spots on the oak. But she didn't look at them. All she could see was his face.

He's right. This is justice. This is your chance at redemption. Your chance to clean the slate.

It would give meaning to everything she'd done to get

to this point. All those deaths she'd doled out, the lies she'd told, the money she'd stolen, the people she'd betrayed, the father she'd killed. Avenge her sister. Achieve her goal.

It would not have been for nothing.

"Go on." The emerald glitter of his eyes was almost mesmerizing. "Don't be afraid. I know you won't miss."

Temple took a shuddering breath and raised her arm, the muzzle of the gun centered on his forehead. And clicked off the safety.

He didn't close his eyes, keeping them on hers, and the expression on his face was so unbelievably calm. Almost as if he was at peace.

Her arm began to shake, a tremor she couldn't still.

One bullet and all of this would be over. Her mission would be at an end, and she could go find her sister. Start another life somewhere else with a clean slate.

With the blood of the man you love on your hands.

The feeling in her chest was a wrecking ball, crushing all her insides, crushing her heart. Because she knew, she fucking *knew,* that if she did this, if she pulled that trigger, there would be no redemption. It would cripple her, stain her, for the rest of her life.

She could live with the fact that she'd killed people for money. She could live with the fact that she'd killed her father.

But she could not live with the guilt of killing the man she loved.

No matter how much he wanted her to.

"No," she said, hoarsely at first. Then stronger. "No. I'm not going to kill you, Theo. I'm not."

The look in his eyes changed, the peace draining from them. "You *have* to, Temple. I need you to."

"No." Slowly, she lowered her arm, her hand still shaking. "I can't do it. I won't."

He moved then, so fast she wasn't expecting it. Reaching

forward over the desk to grasp her wrist and pulling her
arm back up, then leaning forward and pressing his forehead right up against the muzzle of the gun. His eyes
were full of those sharp edges, like broken green glass.
"Pull the fucking trigger."

She tried to twist her wrist out of his grip but he was
too strong. "Fuck you."

His grip tightened. "Do it."

"No!"

Theo's mouth curved in a terrible simulacrum of a
smile, and this time there was no gentleness in it, no bittersweet amusement, no regret or understanding. There
was only a cold, burning rage. The flame that burned in
the heart of a man who called himself Jericho. "You know
what Dad used to tell me?" His beautiful, beautiful voice
was twisted and broken. "He used to say that his blood ran
through my veins. That I was a true Fitzgerald, his true
heir." The broken glass in his eyes glittered. "Every day he
used to tell me how fucking proud of me he was and how,
if I kept working hard, one day I'd have an empire even
bigger than his." He laughed and there was nothing warm
in it, only ice. "And hey, what do you know? He was right.
I do have an empire bigger than his."

Her breathing was coming hard and fast, her heart tearing itself apart in her chest. "So?" she demanded. "What
the fuck is that even supposed to mean?"

Theo stood up in a sudden surge, holding her wrist,
pressing the gun hard to his forehead. "What does it mean?
It means that every day—*every fucking day*—I have to
wake up to the fact that everything he said is true. Every.
Fucking. Thing. His blood *is* in my veins. I *am* his heir.
I *am* a true Fitzgerald." He was breathing hard, anguish
in his eyes. An anguish that broke her a little bit more.
"How do I live with that? How the fuck can I go on knowing he was right? How the fuck can I deal with the fact

that I'm not just Evelyn Fitzgerald's heir. I *am* Evelyn Fitzgerald!"

She didn't know where the anger came from, the anger that broke her paralysis and made her remember that she wasn't just a woman completely at the mercy of the clawed and sharp-toothed creature that was tearing great holes in her chest. Maybe it came from the pain and the guilt burning in his eyes. Pain and guilt that burned inside her too.

"I don't care," she said fiercely. "I don't care who the fuck you think you are. Do you think you're the only one who has to live with guilt?" She shoved the muzzle of the gun hard against his forehead, breaking the hold he had on her wrist, forcing his head back. "Do you think you're the only one who has to live with every fucking mistake they've ever made?" The rage surged inside her, hot and raw, like a forest fire burning out of control. "Boo hoo, little boy. I killed my goddamn father! I've killed so many other people I can't even remember who they were, but do you see me begging for death?" She was panting now, meeting his furious green gaze head-on. "Do you see me forcing a person I care about, a person I love, to kill me? To take my life because I'm too fucking scared to live with what I've done?"

His chest rose and fell, fast and hard. "Temple—"

"No," she said furiously. "No, you don't get to talk. You've had your goddamn turn! It's my turn now." She jabbed the gun against his forehead again, relishing the catch of his breath. "You're a coward, Theo. You're just a fucking coward. And you're taking the easy way out. Because if I can live with everything I've done, then you can too."

"You don't understand," he said and his voice was cold. "You can't possibly understand."

"No? Maybe I don't. Maybe I've got no damn idea." She heaved in a breath, the tears coming again, pouring down her face. "But then, you don't know either. You don't know what it's like to have someone I love asking me to kill them. Someone who matters. Someone who should fucking know better!"

He began to shake his head. "Temple, no."

"No, what? That you can't matter? That I can't love you? Well, too fucking bad. You *do* matter. And I love you. And I'm not going to kill you." She lowered her arm. "I told you once I didn't know where my line was. Well, I know now. You're my line, Theo. You're my fucking line in the sand, and I'm not crossing it."

His expression burned, full of fury. "Then I'll do it myself," he said in a voice she didn't recognize and made a grab for the weapon in her hand.

But he was too slow. She was already turning, drawing back her arm, hurling the gun at the window of the office. The glass shattered, the gun crashing through it and out into the garden outside.

She was shaking as she turned back to him, anger and grief raging inside her, the wrecking ball of that heavy feeling, the weight of all that love crushing every part of her.

"Go and do it then." Her voice was nearly as cracked and as broken as his. "Go and find your fucking gun. Take the easy way out. But don't kid yourself it's justice. Don't kid yourself it's some kind of noble gesture. Because it's not." She swallowed, her throat aching and sore, her cheeks wet with tears. "All it is, is selfishness."

Bright gold flared in his eyes. "And so? Don't you think after sixteen fucking years in hell, I've earned a little bit of selfishness?"

"No. If I haven't, then you goddamn well haven't either." Temple lifted her chin, ignoring her tears. "You need to find your line in the sand, Theo. You need to find the line you will not cross. Because until you do, all you'll ever be is your fucking father."

There was a terrible, terrible silence.

He just stood there and right before her eyes, his expression began to close up, the shutters coming down, the sharp emerald ice freezing out all the brilliant gold. "Get out," he said curtly. "Go while you have the chance."

She raised a hand, wiping futilely at the tears on her cheeks. "Come with me. If we go now we can—"

"No."

The denial was hard, flat, and what was left of her heart lurched. "You're going out into the garden aren't you?"

He put his head back, drawing himself up to his full height. Tall and strong and so vitally alive. "This is my reward, Temple. This is what I promised myself. This is *all* that kept me going all those fucking years, and I don't give a shit what you think about it. I am owed this, and I'm taking it."

And just like that all her rage seeped away, leaving her feeling small and cold. A shadow of herself. "You can't," she said in a thin, thready voice. "You can't. You have to . . . hold on."

"Hold on to what?" His tone was bitter, like arsenic. "To hope? There's no hope, not for me. There never was."

The tears refused to stop falling no matter how much she wiped them away. "There is hope. There's *always* hope, Theo." She didn't know why she was saying such shit, not when hope had always been in short supply for her. And yet the words kept coming anyway. "You . . . just have to believe in it, even if you can't see it. Even if you don't think it's there."

"That's the problem with you, Temple," he said coldly. "You have no idea what you're talking about. You're too fucking young."

Desperation rose inside her. "Promise me you won't do this, Theo. Promise me you won't use that gun."

But his gaze had shifted to someone behind her. "Get her out of here, Dmitri."

"Theo." She should be turning, preparing to fight off the man behind her, but she couldn't bring herself to turn away from the man in front of her. The man who'd finally be the one to break her. "Theo, promise me."

His green eyes were the last things she saw as something hit her hard over the back of her head.

Then there was nothing but darkness.

CHAPTER NINETEEN

Jericho stepped out into the darkness of the garden. He could hear sirens in the distance, but it wasn't likely they were coming for him. Not yet. He had a bit of time.

It was cold tonight, the sky clear, but the stars were lost in the glow of the City of Light.

His breath fogged in the air.

He walked carefully over to the patch of lawn beneath the window of his study, where broken glass glittered in the light, and after a minute of careful searching he found the Glock in the shadow of a rosebush at the edge of the lawn.

Truth was, he didn't need this particular gun, not when his house had an armory down in the basement. But something inside him wanted the Glock, and right now, he couldn't bring himself to deny the urge.

Bending, he picked it up from the dirt and brushed it off. The stock fitted perfectly in his palm, the light gleaming along the short, stubby barrel. And he was sure, if he concentrated, that he could feel the warmth of Temple's hand lingering in the metal.

Is that why you wanted this gun? Because she was the last one who'd touched it? Fuck, you're an idiot.

He stared down at it, rage simmering inside him.

Yeah, he was an idiot. A fucking fool to think she'd

grant him any kind of mercy. She didn't think he deserved it, not even after sixteen fucking years. Well, shit, he didn't need her approval. He knew what he'd earned and what he hadn't.

His life hadn't ever been his, but couldn't he have his death? Wasn't that allowed?

"Do you think you're the only one who has to live with guilt?"

Christ, what did she know? Sure, she'd done some bad shit, but not like he had. Her father's death had been taken in self-defense and the contracts she'd taken on had all been for assholes who'd deserved it, or at least that's what she said.

She was a child. She knew nothing.

"Do you think you're the only one who has to live with every fucking mistake they've ever made?"

His hadn't been mistakes. He'd known, even back when his father had introduced him to the Lucky Seven, deep down he'd known what kind of place it was. What kind of people operated it. What kind of people forced others into slavery.

He'd known because he'd been one of those people. Purposefully he'd allied himself with his father, and purposefully he'd closed his eyes to what was going on around him. He'd helped his father's business become more efficient, more profitable, and those were not mistakes in any way.

He turned the gun over in his hand, running his fingers along the barrel. The muzzle against his forehead had felt . . . right. Pity she hadn't had the guts to pull the trigger.

"Do you see me forcing a person I care about, a person I love, to kill me? To take my life because I'm too fucking scared to live with what I've done?"

Jericho took a breath and for a moment all he could see

was the anguish and rage in her golden eyes. *A person I love*. Him. She was talking about him.

He tightened his fingers on the gun. No, she was wrong. It wasn't love, it was a combination of sex, physical chemistry, and a common experience, nothing more. She was so young she probably wouldn't know love if she fell over it anyway.

Would you?

Love. He knew love. Oh, not the twisted form his father's took, but the look in Violet's eyes every day he came home from school. Every day she was there to greet him, reaching her little arms up for a hug, the lisp in her voice as she'd said his name. She'd been the only bright spot in his life. The only good thing.

But it hadn't saved him. It had only made him endure sixteen years of living in hell. Sixteen years of being the Devil himself. Love was the whole reason he was here in the first place, and right now, it was just another thing he didn't want to feel.

He glanced up at the window of his office. He'd always envisaged the police finding his body in front of the computer, having committed suicide after the break down of his empire, but what did it matter if it was out here? In the garden, out in the night air? Hell, if he turned a little bit to the left, he'd see the Eiffel Tower, and that wouldn't be a bad last thing to see. He'd always loved Paris after all.

It's not her.

No, it wasn't. But maybe she was right. Maybe that had been an unfair thing for him to insist on. He just hadn't expected her to care so deeply.

"You're my line, Theo. You're my fucking line in the sand, and I'm not crossing it."

His chest felt tight, and it was difficult to breathe. The sirens were coming closer. Perhaps they were coming for him after all, in which case he needed to end this and quickly. Especially because Dmitri would be coming back soon, having seen Temple safely stowed on the jet back to the States. And he hadn't told Dmitri of his final plans for himself. A shitty way to treat a friend, but that couldn't be helped.

Lifting the gun, he placed the muzzle against the side of his head. It felt cold.

He looked at the lights on the iconic tower, shining in the night. Christ, why weren't there any stars? There should be stars, there really should be.

Of course, Temple had a line. He always knew she would. She was at heart a good person.

"You need to find the line you will not cross. Because until you do, all you'll ever be is your fucking father."

He closed his eyes. He had no lines. He'd systematically destroyed every one in pursuit of his goal, because even having one would have given away his intentions.

No. You do have a line.

Violet. Yes, he had Violet. But that was all. That was the only one.

It's not all. You have one other.

His breath rushed into his lungs, then out again. A desperate sound, like someone drowning.

You have her.

The sirens were close now, shattering the night, and he could see lights flashing. If he waited any longer, the garden would be full of police, and this final choice would be taken from him like every other fucking choice in his life.

Because he didn't have her. She was gone, and he'd been the one to send her away.

"I killed my goddamn father . . . I've killed so many other people I can't even remember who they were, but do you see me begging for death?"

No, but then she was stronger than he was. She was stronger than anyone he had ever known.

"There's always hope, Theo . . . You just have to believe in it, even if you can't see it. Even if you don't think it's there."

Why was he thinking this? Why could he not stop thinking about her? He had to pull this fucking trigger and end it, take the reward he'd promised himself. Because she was wrong, there was no hope for him. He was damned, and he had been from the moment he'd been born.

"Promise me, Theo."

So much desperation in her voice. So much pain. Why did she care so very much about him? What had he ever done to deserve it?

"You just have to believe . . ."

Jericho opened his eyes. His hand was shaking, and he could feel the muzzle of the gun moving icily on his skin in time with the movement. All it would take was a single muscle impulse sent from his brain to his finger, and that bullet would fire, and all of this would be over. His pain would end.

But hers won't. And neither will Violet's.

There were shouts from the front of the house. the sounds of breaking glass, shots being fired. The police had finally come and here he was, standing in the darkness of his garden. Still alive.

He didn't believe in hope. He didn't believe love would save him. He didn't believe there was any way for him to be redeemed. He had become his father, no two ways about that.

But Temple believed. Violet believed. And he believed in them.

And life was a choice as well as death.

The shouts and gunfire were getting close, the sound of helicopters in the sky. A window smashed nearby and someone screamed.

There would be no rest. There would be no reward. But

maybe his kitten was right. Maybe this was justice after all. He *should* live with what he'd done. He *should* live to bear the guilt of every sin. It was no less than he deserved.

Slowly he let the gun drop from his hand, and it landed on the ground with a heavy thump. Then he sank to his knees on the grass beside it. The soil was muddy and wet from recent rain, which made it easy to carve out two distinct lines in the earth with his finger.

And once he'd finished, he didn't look at the Eiffel Tower shining in the distance, or up at the black sky, searching for the stars somewhere beyond the city lights.

He looked at the ground and the two lines he'd drawn. His two lines in the sand.

And he was still there looking at them when, minutes later, the police came for him.

CHAPTER TWENTY

Pillar of New York Society in Human Trafficking Scandal!

Violet made a disgusted sound and abruptly pushed shut the laptop, shoving it across the coffee table. She'd been glued to media websites all morning, watching as the news broke of the discovery of a major human trafficking ring that spanned the globe. Already the media had revealed that her father had been a major player, news crews converging on the Upper East Side townhouse where her mother now lived.

And it wasn't only her father who'd been outed. The names of others were all over the papers, wealthy CEOs, a couple of generals, movie stars, and at least three senators. And that was only in the U.S. The shocking details of the rings and the men involved had severely shaken Britain and Europe as well.

Everything Theo had promised, he'd done.

She should have felt good about that, but she didn't. Because in all the screaming, hysterical articles flooding the web about it, there was not one mention of him. Not one. No mention of a man named Jericho either. It was like he'd vanished into the ether.

It made her feel sick with worry, and God knew she was already feeling sick enough as it was.

She looked over to where Elijah stood by the windows,

checking the street outside to see if the media had found out where they were yet. No one knew she'd virtually moved in with Elijah. He'd kept a very low profile himself out of necessity.

As she stared at his tall, broad figure, another thought struck her. He'd worked for her father and now he was ostensibly filling the power vacuum her father's death had left, his name was likely to come up. And not in a good way either.

Shit.

As if sensing her sudden fear, he turned, his black eyes meeting hers for a second before dropping to the laptop. "Don't look at them anymore," he said flatly. "It only upsets you."

"I know, but I just want to see if Theo's okay."

"There's been no mention of him?"

"No. Nothing."

Elijah's dark brows pulled down. "He'll be okay, princess."

"No, he won't. You saw him last month, when you came for me in Alphabet City. You saw that look on his face."

"What look?"

"You know which one I mean. He was over it, Eli. He was over everything."

Elijah was silent a moment, frowning at her. Then he said, "We'll get Eva to look into it. She should be able to find out what happened to him."

Violet shook her head, suddenly feeling exhausted and overwhelmed. "What if he's gone? What if something happened to him?"

Elijah crossed the distance between them, coming around the coffee table and sinking down onto his haunches in front of her where she sat on the couch. He put his hands on her knees, resting them there, the warmth of his palms a comfort she couldn't do without. "We'll find out, princess," he said quietly. "We'll find out what happened to him, I promise you."

She sighed. There were no empty assurances from Elijah, just the facts. But that was how life was, wasn't it? Sometimes you got exactly what you wanted, and sometimes you didn't.

"Rutherford has offered the use of his island," Elijah went on. "To escape the media attention. I suggest we take him up on it."

"What? You mean run away?" As nice as the thought of escaping to a Caribbean island was, she didn't want to run and hide. She wanted to be here, where it was all happening and where she might get news of Theo.

"No, I don't mean run away." Elijah's frown became fierce. "When I emailed those records to your brother, he asked me to protect you. Not that the prick needed to. I would have done that already. But just so you know. I think he would have wanted you out of the public eye."

Yeah, he would have. That was very Theo. "But it's not just me, though, Eli. Your name is going to be in those records somewhere."

Elijah's expression didn't change. "I realize that."

"But what about you? What about—"

"We'll cross that bridge when we come to it, princess. Now, my primary focus is taking care of you."

Damn him. When he got that look in his eye, there was no moving him. Then again, he had a point. After all, perhaps it wasn't just Elijah and herself she had to think about anymore.

Almost unconsciously, Violet put her hand on her stomach.

And Elijah, always observant, saw it.

He went very, very still. "Princess?" There was a hoarse edge to the name he called her, his black eyes focusing on her, concentrated as laser beams.

It had been nearly six weeks since that moment in the alleyway, the moment she'd lost both her virginity and her heart to the man crouching in front of her, staring at her as if she was the sun and the moon and the stars all rolled into one.

The moment when they'd had unprotected sex.

After everything that had happened afterward, she'd kind of forgotten about it. Her life had changed so much, and there had been so many emotional upheavals. Too many to worry about the implications of one instance of unprotected sex.

Except maybe not worrying about it had been premature.

Jesus, she had no idea what to say to him. "I . . . I'm late."

"How late?" Clearly he'd come to exactly the same conclusion she had.

"Um, two weeks I think. And . . . Eli, I'm never late."

He said nothing. His grip on her knees was almost painful, the look on his scarred face fierce with emotion, black flames in his eyes. Then suddenly he rose to his feet, pulling his phone from his pocket and pressing a button.

"Eli?"

He didn't answer, only stared down at her. "Rutherford," he said into the phone. "We'll be taking you up on that offer. How soon can we leave? Yes . . . I can have us ready by tonight. Oh and one other thing . . ." He turned and walked quickly through the hall doorway, closing the door behind him, the sounds of his conversation cutting off.

Violet let out a breath, feeling shaky and raw. She didn't have the energy to fight with him about leaving, and if she was right in her suspicions, then perhaps it was better they left anyway. Being hounded by the media while newly pregnant wasn't high on her to-do list.

Five minutes later, Elijah came back out of the hallway, pocketing his phone, heading straight for the apartment's front door.

Violet pushed herself up off the couch. "Where are you going now?"

He didn't pause. "A drugstore. We need a pregnancy test kit."

Oh fuck. She clasped her hands together hard. "Eli."

He put his hand on the door, ready to head out.

"Eli, stop."

He stopped. "What?"

"Look at me."

Slowly, as if he was very reluctant, he turned around, his dark gaze meeting hers. He was a difficult man to read at the best of times, and even though she knew him better than anyone, she had no idea at all what he was thinking now.

"I'm scared," she said simply. "If I'm pregnant . . . I don't know what to do."

For a moment he was silent, staring at her. Then he walked over to where she stood and slid his fingers into her hair, pulling her head back. And he kissed her, hard and possessive and full of all the passion he kept locked away inside him.

When he lifted his head, the look in his eyes was blazing. "*You* don't have to do anything," he said fiercely. "*We* are going to do this together, okay?"

She leaned against him, the hungry part of her soaking up the strength of his body and the certainty in his eyes. "I mean . . . Do you want this, Eli? We don't have to—"

"I want this." He cupped her face between his hands, staring at her with so much intensity she felt like she was going to catch fire. "I fucking *want* this, princess."

The tight, sick feeling inside her lessened just a little bit.

"Oh . . . good. Because I think that I want this too, I just . . . All this stuff with Theo is making everything so difficult."

"I know." He continued to stare fiercely at her. "We're going to Rutherford's island, and we're going tonight, okay? No arguments. Even if you weren't potentially pregnant, I think I'd insist."

"Yes, okay." She allowed herself to relax a little bit more, turning her face against his palm, relishing the warmth of it. "But I don't want to be out of touch. I want to know what's going on, and I want to find out what happened to Theo." She glanced up at him. "What did you ask Zac? And don't deny it. You left the room so I wouldn't hear what you said."

Elijah traced her lower lip with his thumb, a gentle touch. "I asked him point blank about the contract he'd taken out on Jericho and whether it still stood."

Violet went very still. "And?"

"And he said he'd thought about it and decided to cancel it. He's trying to get in contact with Temple right now."

She swallowed. "And did you ask—"

"Yes, I did. Once he's spoken to Temple, he'll let us know if there's any new information on Jericho. He just can't get hold of her at the moment."

Anxiety twisted inside her again, making her stomach feel unsettled. "Oh."

"Don't worry, princess," Elijah said with unaccustomed gentleness, his touch soothing. "Rutherford can find anyone, and he'll find Temple. It won't be an issue."

She nodded, letting out a shaky breath. "Yeah, you're right." But her stomach churned again as if in protest. "Oh God . . ."

Elijah frowned. "Are you okay? You've gone very white."

"Uh no. I don't think I am." She pulled away from him,

nausea roiling inside her. "Why don't you go get that kit? While I . . . get to the bathroom."

Temple's phone rang, making her breath catch and nearly causing her to swerve off the highway. Cursing, she found a place to pull over and turned off the engine, reaching for the phone, her heart thudding hard inside her chest.

Please let it be him.

But when she looked down at the screen to see who was calling, it wasn't. It was Zac Rutherford.

Bitter disappointment gathered in her gut, her throat tight, her eyes scratchy and hot.

She had no idea what had happened to Theo. None. After Dmitri had smashed her over the back of her head, she'd woken up on the jet already heading down the runway.

That flight to New York had been the longest, most agonizing, most frustrating seven hours of her life. She'd demanded answers from the staff on the jet, but they either wouldn't, or couldn't, give her any information.

She didn't know if he was alive or dead, and the last she'd seen of him was that cold, sharp look in his eyes as he'd stared at her. As she demanded his promise.

But he hadn't given it to her. He hadn't. And now there was a big hole in her chest where her heart should be, the remains of it crushed beyond recognition.

The only thing she had left to hold onto was the address he'd left her, Thalia's address. The last thing he'd given her.

When the jet had landed in New York at last, she'd found herself being ushered onto yet another plane, this time heading to Minneapolis, the ticket already paid for. So she'd gone because she didn't have anywhere else to go and nothing else to do.

And when she'd arrived, she'd half expected yet another

of Theo's minions to be there waiting for her, but this time there wasn't anyone. By then she'd realized that of course there wouldn't be anyone, not when the news was full of the international trafficking-ring scandal. Any employees of Jericho's would now be long gone.

She'd avoided the media, afraid of what she might see. Afraid that the last she'd hear about Theo was the news of his death splashed across some national paper or some website. And if that made her a coward, then so be it. Another reason why love was so shitty. It made cowards of everyone.

Instead, she'd headed straight out of the airport for the nearest rental-car company.

Now she was halfway into a three-hour drive north to the tiny town where Thalia supposedly lived, and Zac was calling her, and she had no idea how he'd gotten her number, especially since the phone was brand new, one she'd found stuffed into the bag full of clothes that had also been on the plane. Included in the bag had also been a wallet full of cash. She'd wanted to leave that, but since she had no time to collect her credit cards from the storage locker where she kept most of her personal stuff, common sense had made her put it in her pocket instead.

Outside, it had started to rain, an icy downpour that had her shivering despite the hot air she had blasting from the car's heater.

The phone rang insistently and she didn't want to answer it. She didn't care about his stupid contract. Theo was in all likelihood dead already, and so was that part of her life.

So was that part of her heart.

She swallowed, but some part of her couldn't leave it alone and so she reached out and picked the damn thing up, pressing the button. "How did you find me?" she asked without preamble.

"Eva's very good with security camera footage," Zac said, his British accent precise as it usually was. "We were searching car-hire firms near the airport in Minneapolis, looking for you. Once we'd found out which one you visited, it was relatively easy to pick up your cell phone signal."

"How did you know I'd be in Minnesota?"

"Because that's where your sister lives."

"You couldn't possibly know that."

"I don't. It was a lucky guess. Though I can't think of too many other reasons why you'd visit Minnesota."

Temple closed her eyes, the rain on the roof of the car almost deafening. "What do you want?"

"You and I have a contract, Ms. Cross. I want to know what happened with it."

"If you're asking whether I killed him then no, I didn't. So you can keep your money, I don't want it. I've already got what I wanted which is the location of my sister."

There was a silence down the other end of the phone.

"What happened to him?" No mistaking the authority in his tone. It wasn't a request.

Temple found her throat tightening up again. "I don't know."

Zac muttered something she didn't catch, then he said, "Tell me what happened, Temple."

She swallowed past the lump in her throat. Why should she tell him? What had passed between her and Theo in that office was nothing to do with anyone else. Nothing at all. Still, Theo deserved credit for what he'd done, and Zac Rutherford needed a goddamn lesson in trust.

Tears filled her eyes, but she blinked them back. Hard. "Theo sent the emails. I didn't have to make him. And you probably know this already, but his name was in those records of his father's. Because he'd set them all up himself years ago."

"Yes." Clearly this had not come as a surprise to Zac. "I was aware of his involvement."

"He was brainwashed." She wasn't going to let Zac believe the worst of Theo. She just wasn't. "His father basically brainwashed him from birth. That's why he was 'involved.' That's why he set up those records. He was just a kid who'd been manipulated by one of the best."

"You're excusing him?"

"No, I'm telling you the facts. If anything it's a goddamn miracle he realized what his father was doing before it was too late."

There was another silence.

"You know what Fitzgerald was like," she went on, because she couldn't just leave it. "You know what a manipulative bastard he was. What chance did a kid have against that?"

"Violet seemed to have had a chance."

"Violet wasn't his designated heir," she snapped, anger and grief crowding for space in her chest. "Violet wasn't taken to the Lucky Seven at fourteen and told she could have her pick of the whores."

Again, silence.

"He means something to you, doesn't he?" Zac asked.

"That is none of your fucking business," she croaked, hardly able to speak

There was a soft exhalation of breath. "So he sent the emails. What then?"

Then he wanted me to kill him. He wanted me to take his life.

"Then nothing. His bodyguard hit me over the head and when I woke up, I was on a plane on my way to New York."

"So you have no idea what happened to him?"

I hope he's not dead. I hope he's not lying on a slab somewhere in a morgue with no one to claim him. No one to bury him.

A tear leaked out despite her best efforts, sliding slowly down her cheek. "No. I don't. I haven't heard from him since I arrived back in the States."

"He could be in custody then."

"He could be."

"You don't believe that?"

What could she say? No, she didn't believe it. There's always hope, she'd told him, because hope had been the thing that had kept her going through the last seven years. Rage had propelled her, but hope had given her direction. Hope that somewhere, somehow, her sister was still alive.

And Thalia *was* alive. That hope had been realized. Which should have made her hold onto the one remaining shred that Theo was okay. That he'd listened to her.

But it didn't. She felt as if everything was slipping through her fingers. Like water, no matter how hard she tried to hold onto it, it drained away. Leaving her with nothing.

Maybe he'd been right all along. There was no hope for him and never had been.

"I believe I will find my sister," she said thickly. "Any more fucking questions?"

Another small pause. "Only that I'm canceling our contract. If Jericho proves to be alive and has eluded the law, you are under no obligation to take action."

She said nothing. If Theo was alive she wouldn't be taking action anyway. There was no action to take.

"Oh and Ms. Cross?"

"What?"

"If you need anything, let me know."

Like she needed anything. The only thing she needed was Theo, and she wasn't going to be getting that. Not ever.

Don't you want to know if he's even alive?

She looked out into the driving rain though the window,

the outside world looking like it was underwater. And she was drowning.

You have to know.

Oh fuck. Looked like her stupid heart couldn't let go that last shred, that last spark of hope. She'd been living with it too long, hoping for too many years.

"I do need something." Her voice was a mere scrape. "I need to know if he's alive."

He never thought he'd end up here, in a featureless basement in some featureless building. He thought he'd be long gone, long dead.

At least that what he'd always planned.

Seemed like nothing went to plan these days.

Jericho took another look around the room he'd ended up in. Walls painted in a kind of dingy white. A fluorescent light on the ceiling with one of the bulbs flickering. A worn wooden table in the middle with a chair on either side of it.

The kind of room straight out of a police procedural or some thriller.

The kind of room people were taken to before they disappeared.

It was a vaguely disturbing thought, which was strange because being disappeared was exactly what he wanted. Or it had been since they'd taken him from his Parisian garden. He wasn't sure how long ago that had been since he'd lost track of the time.

The police hadn't been gentle when they'd pushed him facedown into the mud, right on top of the lines he'd drawn and stuck a gun into his back. They hadn't been gentle when they'd cuffed him and thrown him into the back of a police van either. There were bruises where they wouldn't be seen and it was likely that one of his ribs was broken.

He didn't care. Pain was something he'd long accepted was his due. Yet, as the police had taken out their displeasure on him—not a few of them probably worried for their own hides since the names of police who'd looked the other way had been in those emails he'd sent too—he'd found he had to make himself lie there and take it, had to quell the urge to defend himself, to fight back.

Apparently now that he'd made the choice to live, dying wasn't something he wanted to do.

Shitty timing, especially now he was looking down the barrel of a life sentence.

He shifted on the chair he'd been cuffed to. The metal around his wrists had left welts, and his cheekbone hurt like hell, courtesy of a toe of a size eleven boot to the face. Fuck, maybe they'd broken that too.

He hadn't been charged with anything, but it was only a matter of time before they found out his real identity. Before they realized that Theodore Fitzgerald hadn't died after all. Before they realized who Jericho was. What he was.

There was a door in front of him, and he thought he heard footsteps outside it. Then again, he'd thought he'd heard footsteps before, and nothing had happened. The door had remained closed.

Jesus, how long had he been here? He didn't know. Felt like days. Felt like forever.

Without warning, the door opened suddenly, and a man came in. He looked to be in his late fifties, early sixties, and was dressed beautifully in a formal black suit. Under one arm was a thick folder, which he threw down on the table, before turning to shut the door very firmly behind him.

"Mr. Fitzgerald," the man said in English, his accent American. "Or is it Jericho? Which would you prefer?"

Jericho leaned back in his chair, studying the other man. He had a sharp face, a narrow mouth, and sharp, assessing blue eyes. A man not to be fucked with in other words.

"You can call me whatever you like," he said, "Mr. . . . ?"

The man's narrow mouth quirked. "MacDonald."

"Mr. MacDonald."

"MacDonald is fine." He pulled out the chair opposite and sat down. "You've been a busy boy, haven't you?"

Jericho sighed. His cheekbone hurt. His ribs hurt. He was exhausted. And for some reason all he kept thinking about was the look in Temple's eyes just before Dmitri had taken her away. The desperation in them.

"Promise me, Theo."

"If you're expecting me to deny my involvement in any of this, I'm not going to," he said wearily. "Ask me anything. I'll tell you. Names, dates . . . You name it, I've got it."

MacDonald, who had to be CIA surely, narrowed his blue eyes, studying him for a long moment. Then he glanced down at the folder on the table and pushed it in Theo's direction. "I've been chasing you a long time, did you know that? In fact, that's just one of the folders we have on all the disappearances, the murders, the drug deals, and all kinds of other evidence we've managed to compile on your little trafficking ring. You've led us on quite a dance."

Jericho didn't look at the folder. Instead he kept his gaze on the man opposite him. "I'm sorry, but your file is now redundant. Those emails I sent should have all the evidence needed to bring those involved in the ring to justice."

"Including you?"

"Yeah." He didn't hesitate. "Including me."

MacDonald didn't say anything for a long moment. Then he murmured, "There's lots of dangerous information in those files, Mr. Fitzgerald. Lots of important people named."

Jericho didn't look away. "That was the general idea."

"The general idea of what?"

"The general idea of taking the whole fucking thing down."

MacDonald's gaze narrowed further. "Yes, tell me about that. Tell me about taking the whole fucking thing down."

So Jericho did. And he didn't leave anything out. He told MacDonald the whole story, about his father, about faking his own death, about his descent into the crime world. Every single thing he'd done, every crime he'd committed. He even told him about the women he'd saved, not because he thought that would make any difference to the final outcome, but because he didn't want to hide anything.

MacDonald didn't say a word, only looked at him with those impenetrable blue eyes, a slight frown on his face, not giving anything away. And when Jericho had finally finished and silence had settled in the room, MacDonald remained quiet, letting the silence deepen.

Perhaps MacDonald didn't believe him. That was fine. If so, it wasn't as if belief was something Jericho needed. All the files, all the names—including the names of all the girls that had passed through the ring—were now with the authorities, with the media. And someone was doing something about them. That was all he needed.

"So, let me get this straight," MacDonald said after a while. "You spent sixteen years gathering alliances, gathering information, and all so you could take as many of these guys down with you as you could."

"Yes."

"And you perpetrated some of these crimes. Deliberately."

"Yes." He didn't add anything, didn't try to make it sound better, didn't allow himself any more justifications.

"All in the name of smashing the global ring eventually."

"Yes."

MacDonald leaned back in his chair and folded his arms. "That's one hell of an undercover operation, son."

Jericho lifted a shoulder, trying not to wince as the movement caused his ribs to shift and pain to lance through him. "It's the truth. Not that I care whether you believe me or not. The evidence should speak for itself."

"Yeah, the evidence is pretty compelling, I'll give you that," MacDonald allowed.

"So?" He shifted his chair surreptitiously, trying to find a position that wasn't agonizing and failing. "Are you going to charge me or are we going to continue with this pointless conversation?"

"Pretty impatient to get to that jail cell, aren't you?"

"No, it's just that my bullshit threshold is getting progressively lower the longer this goes on."

McDonald stared at him for a long silent moment. "I got to say," he said finally, "you sure have a lot of tenacity. Not many men would spend sixteen years carefully building up an empire of this magnitude only to bring it crashing down."

His side ached. His face ached. And he was so goddamn tired. He wanted this fucking conversation to be over. "I already told you my reasons."

"Because of your dad, huh? Because you wanted to take revenge on him?"

If only it was that simple. But it wasn't. "It wasn't only to do with my father. I made some mistakes. And I wanted to fix them."

But the look in MacDonald's eyes was shrewd. "You after redemption, son?"

For some reason the words caught at him unexpectedly, a pain sharper than the others. Redemption. What a crock of shit. As if there was any redemption for a man like him.

"I'm not your son," he said coldly, letting the other man

see who he actually was. Jericho not Theo. "And this fucking conversation is over. Charge me and be done with it."

MacDonald tilted his head. "No, you're not my son at all, are you?" He let out a long breath and abruptly leaned forward, putting his hands flat on the table. "What you are, Jericho, is a man with a singular experience and very specific talents. You're useful, in other words. Too useful, in fact, to waste."

Jericho went still. Something was going on, and he knew it. "You need to be clearer, Mr. MacDonald, because I don't know what the fuck you're talking about."

"We spend years on your tail, trying to track you down, but you managed to avoid every goddamn trap we laid for you. Now that takes brains. That takes guts. That takes tenacity. And we want those things, Jericho. We want your experience, your contacts. We want your ability to be someone else so seamlessly no one ever suspects who you are. In other words, we want you."

He stared at the other man. "What do you mean you want me?"

"It's very simple. I want you and you want a shot at redemption and don't give me that denial shit. I know you're lying. So here's my offer. You can either spend the rest of your life in jail, wasting all those talents of yours. Or you work for us. Me specifically. We need a clean-up crew on this trafficking ring of yours. We need someone to make sure all that shit is actually mopped up, that no one's filling the vacuum. And more important than anything else, we need to make sure the girls on the lists you sent us are freed."

For the first time in years, genuine shock held him completely still. This could not be what it seemed to be. An out. It just . . . couldn't. "You're not serious."

"Oh, believe me, I'm deadly serious. You're a valuable commodity. The CIA wants you on our side."

Anger was slowly bubbling up inside him. Because he'd chosen his path. Back there in the garden he'd found his lines in the sand, and he'd accepted them. He wasn't going to cross them. Life not death. Jail not freedom. It was his penance, his atonement, and he'd made peace with that.

And apart from anything else, he didn't want to be a tool for anyone else. He didn't want to be used the way his father had used him.

"Why me?" he demanded, suddenly furious. "Why the fuck do you want me to do this?"

If MacDonald found his tone offensive, he didn't show it. "Like I said, no one else has your connections. No one else knows the lay of the land like you do. And no one else knows how these assholes think. You've been one of them, which means you can see things we might miss. You can get people to talk who won't want to talk to us. You can go places we can't."

But he was already shaking his head. "No. I'm not your goddamn tool to use however you see fit. And besides, I have debts to pay. I've accepted that prison is where I'm going to pay them."

"Uh huh. So, you'd rather sit in jail and rot, not lifting a fucking finger, instead of going out and actually freeing all those women you sold into slavery." MacDonald's words were level and flat and cold.

Jericho hated every one of them. Because here he was again, having the choice he'd made taken from him.

And like MacDonald knew exactly what Jericho was thinking, he went on, "I'm not forcing you to do anything. I'm not making you do this. All I'm giving you is a choice. It's a shitty choice, but then that's life isn't it?" MacDonald's blue eyes were hard. "You can play the noble criminal card, paying your debt to society for the next forty or so years, wasting all those God-given talents of yours in a prison cell. Or you can take action. Free those women yourself and make sure no other asshole starts setting themselves up to be the new king of the heap. Help us get the rest of those bastards. Because that's your atonement right there."

All I'm giving you is a choice.

Jericho stared at the other man. Yeah, it *was* a choice wasn't it? In the same way life had been a choice. Sure, the guy wasn't wrong, it was a shitty choice, but nevertheless, it *was* one he could make himself. One that he could make his own.

"It wasn't supposed to be this way," he heard himself say, like a goddamn fool.

"Nothing ever is," MacDonald said. "So what's it to be? This is a one-time offer. You take the prison option, you're there for life, no coming back."

Perhaps it wasn't right he'd been offered this chance. Perhaps it went against every idea of justice there was. And what he should be doing is accepting that and choosing jail. Paying his dues to society locked away.

Or . . . he could make the life he'd led mean something. Use the experiences that had been forced on him, that had broken him, to help other people. Fix things in a real, practical way, not the big-picture, abstract goal that had ruled him for so long.

Because MacDonald was right. No matter how he denied it, he *did* want redemption. He *did* want to make up for all the things he'd done.

There's always *hope, Theo . . .*

His heart seized inside his chest. He hadn't wanted to believe her. He hadn't. Because he'd thought there was no hope for him. Had been certain right down to his bones. And yet right here, right now, MacDonald was offering him something more. A little sliver of hope.

If he had the guts to take it.

Because when it came down to it, that was the real choice, wasn't it?

To believe he was beyond redemption and accept his fate. Or to believe that he still had a chance. That there was still something good in him. Something worth saving.

Temple had believed that. And she'd seen something in him worth loving. So could he really throw *her* choice away just because he was too afraid to hang onto that last shred of hope?

He couldn't. He had to be equal to her. He had to make her choice mean something too.

"If I do this, I'll need a new identity." His voice sounded rusty, not like himself. "I can't be Theodore Fitzgerald anymore. He'll have to stay dead."

MacDonald didn't show any surprise whatsoever. As if it were already a done deal. "Already got that covered. We managed to keep your name and your involvement in your father's empire out of the media too—don't want them digging up old photos of you and plastering them all over the Internet."

A dizzying relief opened up inside him. So that was one less thing for Violet to contend with at least. "Good." Less rust now, thank Christ. "I'm going to need help also."

"Help?"

"There are a couple of people who helped me take down this ring, who know who I am. And who will go down with it because of me." A certainty was running through him now, building slowly but surely. A new kind of determination. "They're good men, with skills you'd find useful, I think. Plus they know this world like I do." He looked the other man in the eye. "I want them exempt from any charges."

MacDonald's brows rose. "You're in no position to make demands."

Of course he wasn't, but he would anyway. MacDonald

needed to know exactly what type of guy he was taking on. "You want me doing this, then I need those men with me."

There was a pause.

"Names," MacDonald snapped.

"Elijah Hunt and Dmitri Vodyanov."

"I'll see what I can do." The other man's gaze narrowed. "Any other demands?"

There was a strange kind of strength filling him, not one that was physical because he still felt fucking exhausted, but another sort. A strength that came from hope, from belief. A strength that he knew in that moment had always been missing from him before.

The kind of strength that he'd always seen in Temple, yet never understood where it came from. Well, he knew now.

All this time, she'd been right. There *was* hope.

He suddenly wanted her, longed for her more powerfully than he could remember wanting anything in his entire life. She loved him, God knew why, but she did. And he'd let her go. He'd made her hold a gun to his head for his own selfish reasons. She'd given him a gift and he'd flung it back in her face.

Promise me, Theo.

"Yes," Jericho said. "One more thing. I have to get to New York."

MacDonald frowned. "Why?"

"Because I have a promise I need to keep."

CHAPTER TWENTY-ONE

Temple pulled over to the curb and killed the engine. Across the street stood a small white house with a big yard. A boy of what looked to be around five was in the yard along with a dark-haired man. The kid wore a fielder's glove and was dancing around and leaping as the man threw him a baseball, which he missed, laughing and running after it, the man calling encouragement after him.

Nervousness churned in Temple's gut and she checked the address again. This was the number Theo had given as being Thalia's house. Except what the hell the man and the kid were doing here, God only knew.

Perhaps she shouldn't head in straight a way. Waiting a bit longer might be better.

Coward.

Yeah, Jesus. Hadn't this moment been the one she'd been dreaming of for seven years? The moment that had driven everything she'd done. The moment when she'd see Thalia again.

She swallowed, staring out the window at the man and the boy in the yard. It might not be Thalia's house, though. Maybe she'd moved on and someone else had moved in. There was a chance Theo's information might be wrong, after all.

Her fingers curled on the steering wheel. Fuck, okay,

so sitting here and going over all the likely scenarios was stupid. She should get up and say hi to the man in the yard. Ask him if someone called Thalia lived here. Easy.

She'd almost got herself to the point of loosening her grip on the steering wheel and opening the door, when suddenly a figure stepped through the front door of the house. A woman. She held a couple of beer bottles in her hands, going down the front steps and over to where the man stood, holding a bottle out to him.

The rain had cleared an hour or so back, the setting sun throwing red and orange rays over the house and the yard. Picking up the bright copper gleam in the woman's dark hair.

Temple's heart went still.

Thalia.

The man called something to the kid, turning to take the beer and smiling. Then he slid an arm around Thalia's waist and brought her up close for a kiss.

And the scene reset itself.

The kid had red hair, virtually blazing like a bonfire. The same color as Temple's. And she caught a glimpse of his face as he raced triumphantly over to Thalia, clutching the baseball. He looked like her. He looked like her sister.

Thalia laughed and gave the boy a big hug.

And Temple's heart began to beat again, heavy and slow.

Thalia had a son. And a husband. Thalia had a life.

The scene through the window blurred. Fucking tears. Seven years and she hadn't cried, not once. Now she couldn't seem to turn the tears off.

Thalia put down her son and leaned her head on the man's shoulder, and they both watched as the little boy tossed the ball in the air, his hand outstretched to catch it.

You can't do this.

Temple raised a hand, wiped at the tears on her cheeks, her plans shattering into a million tiny little jagged pieces. Because of course in all her imaginings of this moment, Thalia had been alone. Yet now she wasn't, and that changed everything.

Her sister had found something after the hell she'd been through with their father, after all the years of protecting Temple. She'd found a family of her own. She'd found some happiness. How could Temple disturb that? And she *would* disturb it. Coming back and bringing back with her all those memories, bringing back all that darkness.

And what would she even say if Thalia asked her what she'd been doing? That she'd killed people for money? That she'd spent years in the world of sex trafficking trying to find out where Thalia had gone? That she'd spent the past couple of weeks with the man who'd bought her?

Temple closed her eyes, a thick bubble of grief expanding in her chest.

Thalia had been freed not long after she'd gone missing and yet she'd stayed missing. She hadn't returned to her old neighborhood, and Temple knew because she'd hung around it even after she'd killed their father. Just in case. Just in case Thalia came back. Just in case Thalia tried to find her. But she hadn't. And that only meant one thing.

Thalia didn't want to be found.

And who could blame her?

Tears dripped down Temple's face and onto her hands that were clasped hard in her lap. Well, she sure as shit couldn't. If she was Thalia, she'd have run and never looked back. Leaving the past behind her. Leaving all the horror.

And who was Temple to bring it all back?

She opened her eyes, staring at the figures of the family out in the yard.

All she'd ever wanted to know was that her sister was

alive and now she had that confirmation. And more than that, not only was her sister alive, but she was happy. She had a family. People who loved her. She had a place.

And there was no room there for Temple. A hit woman who could kill a man with her bare hands. Who had blood on those same hands, so much blood. No, she couldn't bring that blood into her sister's house. There was no place for her there.

She'd always had hope, that was all she'd ever had to hold onto. But now it felt like the last little piece of it was slipping inexorably out of her hands.

Because it's not only your sister you've been looking for. You've been looking for forgiveness too.

Temple didn't bother to wipe the tears away this time. Because she knew deep down it was true. She'd wanted to tell Thalia she was sorry. That she wasn't worth the sacrifice Thalia had made to protect her. She never had been. How could she? How could anyone?

But there would be no chance to apologize. And no chance of forgiveness. Not now.

So she just sat in the car and watched Thalia and her family play in their yard. And when they went inside as the sun went down, she continued to sit there, watching until the moon rose and the stars came out.

Only when the last light in the house went off, did she slowly start the car's engine.

And drove away.

"I have an update." Zac stood in front of the fire in the meeting room of the Second Circle, his hands behind his back. "And I thought we needed to all be here for it."

"What kind of update?" Gabriel asked, dark eyes narrowing. He was sitting in his usual chair, Honor gathered on his lap. "This week's been a fucking nightmare because of the Jericho bombshell, and I've got a shit load to do."

Well, Gabriel wasn't the only one. The effects of the downfall of the trafficking ring and the discovery of previously respected members of the New York business community being a part of it were still resounding even a week later.

Luckily, despite everyone in this room having close personal ties to Fitzgerald and the other perpetrators of the ring, none of their names had surfaced in the media. Mostly thanks to Eva and her expert doctoring of Fitzgerald's files. Which was good since the last thing they all needed was their own experiences dragged through the world's media.

"I heard from a source that Jericho was taken into custody last week," Zac said carefully. He was conscious of Eva sitting in her chair just to his right, her legs drawn up beneath her, sipping ginger tea out of a bone china cup, the little philistine. He'd been trying to get her to like actual tea but she kept refusing to even try it, which meant that one of these days he might have to use it as a punishment.

Eva was silent at this news, mostly because she already knew it. Just like she knew what he was going to do about it. Which was precisely nothing.

But it wasn't only Eva's use of the safe word that had changed his mind about Jericho, it was also the fact that she was right. This had to come to an end somewhere. All the violence and the revenge and the hurt. It had to stop. And so he was doing his part and letting it go. He didn't like it, but he was doing it.

"And you're sure about this source?" Alex murmured from his place on the couch.

Zac lifted an eyebrow. "Do you really need to ask me that question?"

"Okay, sure. So he was taken into custody." Alex gave

him a look. "You still want to kill him? Because I guess that's going to be a bit more difficult."

"But not impossible. I have contacts behind bars too."

"Of course you do," Alex muttered.

"Zac." Eva's voice was soft. A warning.

He glanced at her, meeting her calm gray eyes. "A promise is a promise, angel. I'm not going to hurt him."

"Good." She took another sip of her tea and glared at the rest of them over the rim of her cup. "And no one else is going to either, okay?"

"Hey, I was on Violet's side," Gabriel said. "I never thought that was a good idea."

"Especially not seeing as he's your half-brother," Honor murmured.

Gabriel blinked. "What the fuck?"

"If Violet is your half-sister then logically Jericho is your half-brother," Zac clarified, amused by the other man's look of shock. "You both have the same father after all."

"Christ, did you never think of that?" Alex was obviously finding this amusing as well. "You've got a bigger family than you thought, brother."

"Holy shit," Gabriel muttered.

Honor patted his hands where they rested on her stomach. "Good job you didn't kill him then, Gabe."

"What does this mean then?" Katya asked slowly. "If he's in custody, then perhaps this whole . . . thing is over?"

A silence fell in the room as the implications began to sink in.

For two months, untangling the secrets and lies Fitzgerald had woven around their entire group had dominated every moment. But now that was coming to an end.

Where did that leave them all?

Zac didn't need to look at Eva to know, but he did

anyway, and found her looking back, a smile playing around her mouth.

Oh, he knew all right. Yes, he knew.

"I think it probably does, Katya mine." Alex slid an arm around her waist, drawing her in close. "Now what the hell are we going to do with our lives? I don't know about you guys, but I'm planning on going to Vegas. Maybe get smashed and lose a few hundred K on the tables. Then perhaps a quickie wedding at the Elvis chapel."

Katya scowled. "And who are you planning on getting married to?"

He grinned. "A cocktail waitress maybe?"

"Oh dear," Honor sighed. "Don't kill my brother, Katya. I've only just got him back."

Katya sniffed. "He is just lucky I like Elvis."

"Do we know what's happening to Jericho?" Gabriel asked, staring at Zac and ignoring the banter. "I assume he's being extradited back to the States?"

Zac shifted on his feet. Although he'd found out that Jericho was alive, he hadn't been able to get any other info, a failure that always annoyed him. "My source wasn't able to pass on any further information, so no, I have no bloody idea."

Gabriel's expression was impossible to read, though Zac knew him well enough by now to know what the other man was thinking. Jericho had been pointed out as being family, and now Gabriel would want to keep tabs on the guy.

"Violet needs to know," Honor said. "Especially now that—" She stopped suddenly.

"Now that she's what?" Zac stared at her.

Violet and Elijah were making use of his island, though he hadn't heard from either of them since they'd arrived there a week ago. He assumed they were okay, but . . . Had something happened to them?

"Damn." Honor looked rueful. "She didn't want me to say anything."

"Anything about what?" Gabriel's voice was a growl. "I'm her fucking brother."

"Half-brother," Honor amended. "She's pregnant."

"Oh," Gabriel said. "And the father is—"

"That prick Elijah, yes." Honor finished, a smile playing around her mouth.

There were smiles and a few exclamations, the atmosphere in the room lighter than it had been in months.

It was good to see it. Made Zac realize just how far he had come, how far they *all* had come.

"Then I think Violet should know as soon as possible, shouldn't she?" Zac reached for his phone and headed toward the doorway, leaving the others to talk while he made the call.

It wasn't until he'd stepped into the hallway that his phone began to ring. He frowned, staring at the screen. The call was coming from a number he didn't recognize, which was always a bad sign.

"Rutherford," he answered curtly.

There was a slight pause and then someone said, "I don't think I need to tell you who this is."

The voice was deep, rich. Male. He'd never heard it before. Nevertheless, he knew who it was. "Jericho."

"That name doesn't belong to me anymore," the man said. "Jericho is dead."

"What do you want?"

"Straight to the point. I like it."

Zac leaned against the wall. "I was just about to call your sister. Tell her you were alive."

"Ah. And how did you know that?"

"I have my sources."

"Naturally. Will you also tell her you'd kept the contract out on my life?"

He almost smiled. Damn. He would have enjoyed matching wits with this bastard. Pity he was behind bars. "Isn't this a terrible waste of your phone call?"

"You're assuming I only have one."

Zac stilled, staring at the wall opposite. "I heard you were in custody."

"Oh yes, about that. I'm not. At least, not anymore."

Shock coursed through him, which was a novelty since nothing much shocked him these days. "You're free?"

"Not entirely. As free as I'll ever be, I suppose. But you don't need to worry. I won't be bothering your little group of friends anymore."

"I suppose you're not going to tell me how you worked that?"

"No. That's on a need-to-know basis and all that shit."

"Ah. Okay, then. So there was a reason for this call, I assume?"

There was a brief silence. Then Jericho said, "I just need you to tell Violet I'm okay. That she doesn't need to worry about Hunt. I've taken care of it. No one's coming for him."

Curiosity and a certain amount of respect turned over inside Zac. "You cut a deal didn't you?"

"That's between me and Hunt. Will you tell Violet what I said?"

"Yes. Okay."

"There's one more thing." Another pause, longer this time. "I need to know where Temple is."

Zac concentrated on the other man's voice. There was something in it, something that sounded like . . . yearning. And he recognized it because he'd felt exactly that same thing for so many years. "I've cancelled the contract, if that's what you're worried about."

"I don't care about the fucking contract." A thread of emotion wound through that dark, rich voice. "I just want . . . I just need . . ." He stopped. "She probably thinks

I'm dead, and I need her to know that I'm not. I need her to know I want to see her." Emotion soaked through the words, and this time there was no mistaking it. It *was* yearning.

"Okay," Zac said, because he couldn't, after all this, refuse. "I'll tell her."

"Give her this number. Tell her she can call if she wants. And if she doesn't . . . I understand."

"You don't want her number?" Zac asked, curious.

"No." Another pause. "This choice has to be hers."

Approval shifted inside him, because a man who respected choice was a man who deserved respect in return. Still, the man was also a fucking criminal. "I'm not ever going to approve of your methods, Jericho," Zac said. "And if you hurt Temple, I'll—"

"Temple doesn't need your protection, Rutherford," Jericho interrupted, and the thread of emotion was gone, his voice cold. "She can look after herself. Besides, since when did you ever care about whether she was hurt or not?"

Zac grimaced. That was a fair point. But he remembered the note of grief in Temple's voice when he'd called her to cancel the contract. She'd felt something for this man. And Zac had suddenly been gripped by protectiveness because he knew what it was like to feel something for someone. And to lose them.

"She was an employee of mine once," he said, not prepared to confess anything beyond that. "And I look after what's mine."

"Yeah, well, so do I." Another pause. "Temple *is* mine. Understand?"

Zac recognized that note too. Possession. Again, he approved. "Understood."

Jericho didn't speak again, and there was a click as he ended the call abruptly.

Zac lowered the phone slowly, debating. His gut told

him that Jericho wouldn't hurt Temple, at least not physically. But that wasn't what Zac was concerned about. He knew about strong women who hid fragile souls, and Temple was one of those women.

Yet, she'd asked him to find out if Jericho was still alive. So he would tell her. And not because that bastard had asked for it, but because Temple had.

However, when he called her, there was no response so he had to leave a message. She could call him back if she wanted to know more. Like Jericho said, that was her choice.

The next on his list was Violet, but he got no response from her, either. Leaving another message, he then put his phone back in the pocket of his jacket.

Enough of this shit. He wanted to get back to Eva. He had something important to ask her.

Temple stood on the sidewalk and stared at the entrance to Eva's building on the opposite side of the street. It was cold, and she was shivering a little, her hands stuffed into the pockets of the black leather jacket she wore.

She still hadn't recovered from the message Zac had left on her phone three days earlier. Every time she thought about it, her throat would go tight, and she couldn't breathe, pain and joy in equal measure making everything inside her clench hard.

Theo was alive. And not only that, he was somehow free. And wanted to see her.

She didn't know what had happened to her. Where the strong, fuck-off attitude that had gotten her through the past seven years had disappeared to. Perhaps she'd left it behind in Minnesota, along with Thalia. Because she certainly didn't feel strong anymore. She felt like she'd been hollowed out, as if all that strength had been drained right out of her, leaving her nothing but a fragile shell. As if anything, even the slightest vibration would shatter her.

A vibration such as actually seeing him again.

Which was why she hadn't immediately contacted Zac. Because she didn't know if she wanted to see Theo. She didn't know if she could bear it. She had no idea what he wanted from her, not when her last memory of him was of cold, sharp green eyes and denial.

Whatever it was, he was somehow free, which made no sense. In fact, the only thing that did make sense was the knowledge that seeing him again would break something inside her. Something that couldn't ever be repaired.

If you're not going to see him again then why are you here?

It was a pretty good point. Standing outside Eva's apartment building trying to gather up the courage to knock was probably one of the more stupid things she'd done in her life. Then again, despite the gut-deep knowledge that seeing Theo again would be a bad thing, she was desperate to talk to someone else about it.

Except she had no one else. She had no friends, and the only other person she could have contacted was her sister, and she'd already walked away from her.

That only left Eva. Her erstwhile employer. And the woman Temple had delivered into the hands of her worst enemy.

When Temple had been held in Elijah's apartment, Eva had seemed to be pretty chilled about it admittedly. But she guessed turning up out of the blue to Eva's home wanting to chat was another thing entirely.

Temple swallowed, her hands clenching inside her jacket.

Maybe this really was a stupid idea. Maybe she should just turn around and walk away. Catch the train to JFK and take the first plane out of here, the way she'd been planning.

Yet for some reason she stayed where she was, staring at the building.

Until suddenly the door opened and a small figure came out, pausing on the steps, staring in Temple's direction.

Oh, fuck. It was Eva.

Hot embarrassment flooded through Temple. To be caught hanging around staring at her building like a stupid teenager . . . God, could this whole situation get any worse? Blindly, she turned to go.

"Temple." Eva's voice came from behind her.

She started to walk, ignoring the other woman, her face burning.

"Temple." There was a certain authority in Eva's tone. "What the hell are you doing here?"

Despite everything in her telling her to keep going, Temple stopped. She didn't turn. "How did you know I was here?"

"I have cameras on the street. You've been standing there for an hour."

Temple closed her eyes. Jesus. She was a fucking basket case. "I'm sorry. I just . . ."

"Just what?"

There was no help for it. She was going to have to tell her the truth. "I . . . wanted to talk to you." Taking a deep, silent breath, she turned around. "I need some advice."

Eva was standing not far away. A familiar sight in her black skinny jeans, black Docs, and black Iron Maiden T-shirt, a black leather jacket over the top of everything. Eva had worn pretty much that same outfit every day Temple had worked for her as her driver.

Today though Eva wasn't wearing her beanie, her white-blond hair in a loose ponytail down her back. She was also wearing a necklace, another difference since Temple couldn't remember Eva wearing jewelry before. It was a small silver padlock on a short chain around her pale throat.

"Advice?" Eva folded her arms, the look on her face suspicious. "You've been hanging around out here for an hour just for advice?"

This was dumb. She should be walking away, not revealing how vulnerable she was to this woman. How barren and isolated her life was that the only person she could talk to was a former employer she didn't know very well.

Eva's gaze narrowed all of a sudden. "Is this to do with Jericho?"

Temple blinked. "How did you—?"

"I'm with Zac. And he tells me everything."

"Oh. Right."

"So you know he's alive then?"

The words made something heavy collect in her chest, and she couldn't speak. So she only nodded.

"So this advice . . ." Eva paused. "Yeah, I still don't get why you're here, talking to me."

"Because I haven't got anyone else to talk to, that's why." She hadn't meant to say it, but the words burst from her all the same, and she had to look away, painfully aware of what a pathetic figure they made her.

"But don't you have a sister to—"

"No." The denial was flat. She wasn't going to explain to anyone what had happened with her sister. That was one vulnerability too far.

Eva didn't press, but her gray eyes were assessing. "Okay then," she said. "I guess coming here to ask for my advice takes balls. Especially after what you did."

Temple shifted on her feet, uncomfortable. "Yeah, well. I'm sorry about that. I was . . . doing a favor for Elijah and he promised me information about my sister."

"I would say no harm done, but of course, there was harm done."

Temple didn't know what to say. She'd done it for Thalia, and maybe a few weeks ago that would have been all the explanation she would have given. Not now, though. "I'm not sure what else I can do," she said quietly. "I'm sorry. That's all I've got for you."

Eva was silent a long minute. "I'd ask you in, but I still don't like having strangers in my house. It's nothing personal."

"Okay." Temple shifted again, the rubber soles of her Chucks scraping over the concrete. "No problem."

There was an uncomfortable silence, one that Temple couldn't seem to break. She didn't know where her courage had gone. She felt like a fool.

Eva's steady gray gaze was needle sharp. "What is it then? Come on. I don't want to stand here in the fucking cold all day."

Temple swallowed past the lump in her throat. "Zac said that . . . Jericho wanted to see me."

"Uh huh. So what's the problem? You don't want to see him?"

"It's not quite that simple."

The other woman grimaced. "It never is. I guess you two have a thing happening?"

A thing. How strange to reduce all that feeling, all that desperate pain, that sadness, into two words. A thing. "I suppose you could call it that."

"Right. So he wants to see you, and you . . . ?" She trailed off, raising a brow.

"I don't know," Temple forced out. "I've been kind of existing on hope for a long time. Hope that my sister was alive and that I could save her. But now I know she's alive and happy, I don't have anything else to hope for. Does that make sense?"

Something that looked like it might have been sympathy flickered over Eva's face. "Yeah, I think so. But how does that relate to seeing Jericho?"

Her eyes were prickling again, fuck it. She blinked fiercely. "If I see him and things . . . don't turn out, I'm afraid that all hope will be gone. And if all hope is gone, I don't know how I'm going to keep going." She took a little breath. "I need hope, Eva. I need something. And while I know he's alive out there somewhere, I still have it. But if we meet I'll know for certain one way or another if he wants me. And if he doesn't—" She broke off, unable to say it.

"I get it," Eva said quietly. "You want the not knowing so then you can hope."

Temple nodded. "I guess that makes me a coward, doesn't it?"

"No." Eva's voice was flat with certainty. "That makes you a survivor."

Temple's throat felt thick and sore. God, she was tired of all this emotion. Tired of feeling like all her skin had been stripped off her, leaving raw nerve endings exposed to any breath of wind, every change of temperature. Making her hurt.

Yeah, she was a survivor. Which meant she needed to protect herself if she wanted to keep being one.

"But," Eva went on unexpectedly, "sometimes you have to decide what's more important. Just surviving isn't enough, Temple. Believe me, I know. Sometimes you have to reach for more than mere survival."

Temple's breath caught. More. What was more? She hadn't ever had it.

You did. With him.

Eva was staring at her, a strange look on her face. "Do you love him?"

Instantly the tears Temple had been fighting threatened

to overflow, and her voice had vanished yet again. But this was an important question and one she knew she had to answer, no matter how much that revealed, no matter how vulnerable it made her. "Yes," she croaked. "Yes, I do."

There was a curious intensity in Eva's silver eyes. "Then that's all the answer you need."

CHAPTER TWENTY-TWO

After moving restlessly around the room Rutherford had taken him to, Theo, unable to keep still, eventually had to make himself sit down in one of the wingback armchairs near the fireplace.

Christ, it had only been fifteen minutes and already he felt like a nervous schoolboy.

Rutherford had called him back that morning to say that Temple was willing to meet and offering the use of the study in his Upper East Side historic brownstone as a meeting place.

Theo hadn't wanted to see her again in public, not when what he wanted to say to her was so very private, and since he was stuck in a shitty hotel in Hell's Kitchen, which wasn't suitable either, he decided to accept Rutherford's offer.

He didn't particularly want to be beholden to the asshole, not when Rutherford had been so keen to kill him, but Temple was one of his lines. And given that nearly a week had passed since he'd had any response to his question, he'd been thinking she'd given up on him and didn't want to see him again.

Another surge of restlessness went through him, and he pushed himself out of the chair, moving over to the tall bank of bookshelves against one wall, staring sightlessly at the titles.

He didn't know what he was going to say, other than to give her the promise she'd wanted. And to tell her that yes, he'd found his line in the sand. That he'd been prepared to go to prison for his crimes. That he'd been offered a chance in a million, and he was going to take it. Because of her.

He didn't have long. MacDonald had allowed him a week in New York to sort out whatever affairs he had to sort out, but then he had to be back on a plane to Paris to begin the next part of his life.

Having to accept other people's orders wasn't something he particularly enjoyed, but at least MacDonald had promised him autonomy in how he went about this clean-up mission. It would be the leaving that would be the hardest. Leaving Temple . . .

His chest felt hollow at the thought. It was for the best, though. Because it wasn't as if he had anything to offer her but his absence. He had no idea how long this mission would take, and anyway, it was clear the CIA had other plans for him afterward. He wouldn't be coming back to New York anytime soon.

There was a noise behind him. The door shutting quietly.

The hollow feeling in his chest yawned wide.

He turned.

She was standing by the door, her hands stuck in the pockets of the black leather jacket he'd given her, her chin lifted, big golden eyes guarded. Her hair was loose, the red, roaring bonfire of her curls falling down her back.

She looked different. The delicate architecture of her face seemed sharper, her skin pale and drawn. And she was holding herself stiffly, as if something inside her had broken.

So small. So fragile. Vulnerable.

Had he been the one to break her? Had what he'd nearly forced her to do shattered that indomitable strength of hers? She'd always had it, right from the moment he'd seen her dancing around that pole in the VIP room. A bright, vital energy. But something had happened, and that energy was gone as if a fire had been doused or a light switched off.

It made something inside of him break too.

"Temple," he said hoarsely, halfway across the room before he'd even realized he'd moved.

But she held up her hand sharply in a "stop" gesture, and he halted as if he'd been shot. "Don't." Her voice was thick. "Don't come any closer."

His heart was beating fast. Too fast. "What happened, kitten?"

"Don't . . ." She shook her head. "Don't call me that either."

He ignored that. "What happened?"

Temple stared at him, her expression rigid, but he could sense the pain seeping out of her anyway.

"Kitten." It was a plea this time, because he found he couldn't stand seeing her like this.

But she ignored him the way he'd ignored her. "Why are you here, Theo?" The question was so quiet, almost lost under the sounds of the city beyond the windows. "What do you want?"

He tried to calm the raging thing inside him, that wanted to go to her, scoop her up in his arms, and demand that she tell him what was hurting her. So he could fix it. So he could heal it. But it was difficult.

Lifting a hand, he ran it restlessly through his hair. "Well, obviously I wanted you to know I was alive."

"You didn't need to see me for me to know that."

His hand dropped as he met her gaze. She was looking at him as if he was a loaded gun pointed straight at her, fear a dark shadow in her eyes.

She'd looked at him with fear before, but never like this. Never as if she was afraid he'd hurt her.

It devastated him.

He took a step toward her and she went rigid. "Temple. Tell me what's wrong."

"Nothing's wrong. Just . . . stay where you are." Her shoulders had hunched. "Answer the fucking question. Why are you here? Why do you want to see me?"

But he couldn't stay where he was. Something was wrong. She was hurting, she was looking at him like she was afraid, and he couldn't stand it. The thing inside him was like a black hole, hungry and desperate for her, and he didn't think he could hold himself back any longer.

He didn't know what the feeling was. He only knew he couldn't live another second if he wasn't touching her.

So he ignored her outstretched hand, ignored her desperate protest, ignored the fact that she was backing away without any of her usual grace. He closed the distance between them, reaching out to grab her, gathering the soft warmth of her up in his arms.

"No," she gasped and struggled, pushing at him.

He ignored that too, tightening his arms around her, inhaling the sweet, musky scent that was all Temple, a wave of some intense, raw emotion smashing through him. A deep sense of possession, of satisfaction. Of truth.

Finally. *Fucking finally.*

She twisted, her physical combat skills kicking in. But he just held on as she kicked and struggled, turning his face into her neck. "It's okay," he whispered softly. "It's okay, kitten. I'm here."

Abruptly she went limp, breathing fast and hard, the material of his T-shirt in her fists. She didn't look up, her gaze steadfastly on his chest. Then slowly her forehead tipped forward until it was resting against the cotton of his T-shirt. She made a soft, ragged sound.

And his heart clenched hard because the sound was a sob and it ripped him in two.

He lifted her off her feet, scooping her up like a child and carried her over to the armchair he hadn't been able to keep still in before, sitting down with her in his lap. And she didn't protest this time, she only held onto his T-shirt and sobbed against his chest like her heart was breaking.

He didn't say anything because there was nothing to say. No more words of comfort he could offer. All he could do was hold her, give her back the strength she had lost, let her know that she wasn't alone. That she had him.

None of this was going the way he'd intended, but he didn't give a shit. Right now nothing else in the world existed but her.

She had her face buried in his chest, her hands gripping his T-shirt, her shoulders shaking as she wept. So he stroked her hair, then the graceful arch of her spine. Up and down, soothing her. The way he'd done once, long ago, for his little sister.

Time passed, and he didn't know how much, but eventually her sobs quieted and she was silent. She didn't move, keeping her head pressed against him.

Nothing else mattered but this moment. Nothing else was as important to him.

Nothing else would *ever* be this important to him.

It was time to stop denying that hungry thing inside him. It was time to stop pretending he didn't know what it was.

He knew.

"After I had Dmitri take you away," he said into the silence, "I went out into the garden. And I found that fucking gun. And I lifted it to my head. I wanted to pull that trigger so much, you have got no idea. I wanted out. I wanted to escape. I just . . . didn't want to do this shit anymore." He paused. "But all I could hear was your voice telling me I was a coward. Telling me if I pulled the trigger, I'd be just like my Dad. Telling me that if you lived with your guilt then I could live with mine. And telling me that there was hope. That there's always hope, even when you think you can't see it."

She shuddered, her fists clenching in his shirt. But she didn't speak.

"But most of all," he went on, giving her all he could, "I remembered you telling me you loved me. And I realized I couldn't pull that trigger after all. Because you believed there was something in me worth loving, and if you believed that, then maybe I should too."

She was silent, her face turned against his chest.

He let his hands stroke over her hair, relishing the silky softness of it. "That was my hope, Temple. You gave that to me. You made me aware that there was a choice, and life was one of those choices." A red curl glowed against his skin as he wound it around his finger, stroking it with his thumb. "I've never had much in the way of choices in my life, but you gave that one to me. You made me aware I could take it if I wanted. So I did. I chose life. Because I also figured out where my line in the sand was. And it's you, kitten. My line in the sand is you."

She had gone very still, and he could feel that hungry, raging thing in his heart go still with her.

And the truth unfurled inside him like a bolt of bright silk, revealing an intricate, beautiful, fascinating pattern. A pattern he could spend the rest of his life studying and never get bored.

"I had all these reasons to give you about why I came back," he said hoarsely, not wanting to move in case the feeling that gripped him would disappear. The sheer fucking wonder of it. The immensity of it, so powerful that if he moved, it would shake them both into pieces. "I wanted you to know that I was sorry I didn't give you my promise.

Sorry I made you hold a gun to my goddamn head. Sorry for pretty much everything. But those were all fucking excuses." He took a breath. "I came back, Temple, because I love you. And I couldn't go another day without seeing your face."

She kept her head right where it was, pressed against the hard warmth of his chest. Not daring to breathe. She felt exhausted, all the meager store of courage she'd gathered together before she'd stepped into the room, utterly gone.

She hadn't been able to believe how badly she'd fallen apart.

But the moment she'd seen him standing by the bookshelves, so heartbreakingly familiar, it was as if she'd encased herself in armor only to find that the enemy had rocket launchers.

Then he'd turned and the rocket had fired straight through her chest, tearing her apart as if her armor was made out of tissue.

He was wearing those nondescript clothes again. Jeans and a T-shirt, and she couldn't have even said what color they were. Because the only thing she could see was his face. There were fading bruises on one cheekbone and eye socket, yet the beauty of him struck her again like a blow to the head, making her feel dazed. And his eyes, a deep green lake with a golden sunrise flaring slowly, brilliantly over it.

And she knew she'd been stupid to come. That she should never have listened to Eva. She should have gotten on that train and gone straight to the airport, never to come back to New York again.

But she hadn't, and now she was in this room with him, and the hope she'd been gently nursing all this time had gone. Because she wouldn't be walking out of here whole. He had broken her, and she would stay broken.

It was pathetic to realize. It made her ashamed of her-self.

And then he'd somehow managed to pick on her dis-tress, coming for her, and she'd had to hold out her hand to stop him to somehow limit the damage. But he'd ignored that too, taking her in his arms instead.

She'd tried to struggle. Tried so hard to be strong, to fight him off. But being close to him, feeling all that hard, strong muscle around her and the heat of his body against her. Feeling the desperate hunger in her soul wake to life, the hunger she'd been keeping at bay all this time, that wouldn't be denied.

Then he'd whispered those words in her ear. "It's okay, I'm here." And she'd fallen apart completely.

It was too much, too strong. This want inside her, this need for him. She had no experience of it and no defenses, and it decimated her.

She'd sobbed in his arms like she was being torn to shreds. The pain of walking away from her sister. The loneliness that now lay ahead of her. The knowledge that there would be no forgiveness for anything. The terrible ache of lost hope . . .

She didn't want to believe that there was something to hold onto now. Almost couldn't bear to do it. But he'd said those words and she didn't quite know what to do with them.

Temple didn't want to look at him, didn't want to raise her head, tear herself away from the warm darkness and familiar cinnamon and sandalwood scent of him.

But she made herself do it, lifting her head and meet-ing his gaze, not caring that she probably looked awful with her hair everywhere and tears staining her cheeks.

His eyes were the color of the sun rising. Brilliant gold. And she saw the truth in them, along with uncertainty too, and a tenderness that made her breath catch.

"You what?" she said, her voice a frayed, ragged, shred.

He pushed a curl back behind her ear and smiled, more tenderness making the tattered remains of her heart ache. "I love you," he said simply. "And I wanted to see you again. But I wanted you to have the choice, because I know I have no right at all to ask for anything from you." His hand drifted to her cheek, one finger tracing the line of her cheekbone and she shivered helplessly. "Make no mistake though, I may not have the right to ask for it, but I want it all the same." His finger dropped to her mouth. "Tell me what happened. Please. I don't like to see you so upset."

She was trembling. "I . . . went to see Thalia. I always thought she'd be alone, but she wasn't. She had a kid and a husband and . . ." Her throat closed up. "I couldn't . . ."

His hand stroked along her jaw, down the side of her neck, a deep, terrible sympathy in his eyes. "I understand. You didn't want to upset her and her family. You didn't want to bring it all back to her."

Of course he would understand. How could she forget? They were the same. He had his darkness, just as she did, and they'd carry that for the rest of their lives.

"No, I didn't." She shook her head. "There must be a reason she hasn't tried to find me—" She stopped again, the pain still raw.

His stroking fingers gently gripped her chin, holding her tight. "What? You think it's because she didn't want you?"

She couldn't give him anything but the truth. "She gave up so much for me, Theo. So much. The things she had to do to protect me . . . I can't ever repay that. I'm not ever going to be worth that sacrifice. And I just wanted to tell her how sorry I was. I just wanted her to . . ." She couldn't go on. Couldn't say it.

"Oh, kitten," he said softly, his beautiful voice like a warm blanket all around her. "You don't have to tell her you're sorry. And you don't need her forgiveness. Because there's nothing to forgive."

"But what Dad did. What she had to do to protect me—"

"She did it because she was your big sister. Because her job was to protect you." He let go of her chin, took her face between his big, warm palms, the intensity of his expression making everything inside her quiet. "Because she loved you, Temple."

His face blurred, and she could barely speak. "How can you possibly know that?"

"Because I have a little sister too." That beautiful voice of his had grown almost as ragged as hers was. "And it was my job to protect her. And I did."

Violet. Of course.

She blinked away the tears, trembling and unable to stop. It didn't seem that simple. To just accept that someone would have done something for her, purely because they loved her. "But I never did anything for her. I didn't even know what was going on. And then after she'd gone, what I did to Dad—"

"Temple." His hands were so strong, and yet they held her so very gently, cupping her face as if she was infinitely precious. "Did you mean what you said?"

She looked up into his green-gold eyes, the intensity in them making her shiver. "About what?"

"You told me you loved me. Did you mean it?"

"Yes." The word was more a croak than anything else.

"You knew what I was and yet you loved me anyway. Despite everything I'd done."

"I . . . did. I mean, I do."

"Well, I know you, Temple Cross. And I know what you are and what you've done. And I love you anyway. And I know your sister will feel the same."

She didn't know what to say to that, because she had no words left.

But that was okay, because then Theo leaned forward and kissed her, and there was tenderness in the kiss and sweetness and an acceptance she never thought she'd find.

She opened her mouth beneath his, not caring suddenly about what would happen after this, what they would do or where they would go. It didn't matter.

Because she had everything she needed most in the world right here in front of her.

After a very long while, his fingers twined in her hair and he pulled her away gently. "There are some things you need to know," he murmured. "The CIA cut me a deal after I was taken into custody in Paris. They want me to help them clean up the mess now the trafficking ring has been broken. Make sure there's no one deciding to make a grab for power and that the women who've been captured are freed."

She stared at him. "I wondered how you got out. Are they forcing you into it?"

Another of those beautiful smiles. "Well, it was either a lifetime in jail or I help them. I decided to help them." The smile faded a little. "They kept my name and my involvement out of the media, and they've given me a new identity. It's my penance, kitten, and I need to do it."

Of course he would. She understood that. "So what are you saying?"

"That I haven't got long here. I have to be back in Paris in another couple of days."

Pain tightened its claws in her. "Oh, Theo . . ."

He cupped her jaw, the pain echoing in his eyes too. "I know. But I have to do this. It's the choice I made."

She put her hand over his, holding the warmth of him against her skin. "How long will you be? I mean, you'll be coming back, won't you?"

But there was only brutal truth in his expression. "I don't know. They have plans for me and I suspect they may want me for other underground crime operations."

She wanted to cry. "You wanted this to end. You wanted to be free. I can't believe—"

He put his thumb across her mouth, silencing her. "No. Don't say that. I want to do this. I need to. Jericho's dead and so is Theodore Fitzgerald. I'm someone new. This is what I've been trained for. And if I can help more people, then that's what I'll do."

It made sense. It all made sense. And yet it seemed so unfair, to finally have him within reach, only for him to be taken from her again.

Unless . . .

She swallowed as an idea came to her. A plan. And why not? It wasn't as if she had anything better to do. And shit, she'd been trained for it too.

"I won't let you do it alone," she said suddenly fiercely. "I'll come with you."

Surprise flickered in his eyes. "What do you mean?"

"I almost didn't come here to see you, Theo, because hope was all I'd been surviving on. The hope that you might feel the same way about me that I feel about you. And I didn't want to come because I couldn't bear to if you took that hope away from me. I'd rather not see you than lose that. But I came and now . . . you do feel the same." She swallowed. "Theo, you said I was your hope. Well, you're mine, and I can't lose it again. I can't."

He was frowning. "I can't ask you to join me. I can't ask you to involve yourself in more violence."

"You're not asking me. And I'm not asking you either. I'm telling you. I need you. And I'm coming with you whether you like it or not."

He said nothing for a long time, staring at her as if he was memorizing everything about her.

"God," she said half desperately. "I mean someone's got to protect your pretty ass, don't they?"

He didn't smile, his jaw tight. "You really would?" he asked finally. "You'd really come with me?"

She didn't answer him. Instead she reached out and buried her fingers in his hair, pulling his mouth down on hers, giving him her answer in a kiss that was love and desperation and determination and need all in one.

"I don't know if they'll go for me having a partner," he murmured against her mouth. "But I'll convince them. If you're sure."

"I'm sure." She shifted in his lap, straddling him, kissing him harder, deeper. "Promise me you will, Theo."

Strong hands in her hair, pulling her head back. The look in his eyes burned her, ignited her, set her blazing. "I promise, kitten."

And he kept his promise.

Because he always did.

EPILOGUE

FIVE YEARS LATER . . .

Theo sat on the bench in Central Park and watched a man and a woman play catch with a little girl. The summer sun gilded the woman's blond hair and turned the man's a glossy black. The kid's was a deep gold.

Kind of like his own.

"I wonder how long it'll take them to spot us?" Temple murmured quietly from beside him.

"If they haven't already then Hunt's lost his edge," he murmured back, stroking her fingers where they interlaced with his. The touch of her skin was warm, grounding him and settling the unease in his gut. "Were you this nervous when you met Thalia?"

Temple laughed softly. "Seriously? You didn't hear me telling you I needed to throw up about ten million times?"

Ah, yes. He did remember now. So many dangerous situations they'd both been in over the past five years, and yet it was meeting their respective siblings again that had put the fear of God into both of them.

Temple's had had a happy ending. Thalia had promptly burst into tears and welcomed her sister with a hug that threatened to squeeze the life out of her. Then, unexpectedly, she'd given Theo the same hug. Because even after all this time, she still remembered what he'd done for her, how he'd saved her. And it turned out that Thalia *had* tried looking for Temple after she'd gotten back to the States. But, traumatized by her ordeal, it had taken her a while to feel mentally ready to find her younger sister, and by the time she had, Temple had gone. And Thalia hadn't been able to find her.

He and Temple had ended up staying a week with Thalia in Minnesota. And he'd thought, after spending so long working for the CIA, that finally being released from his contract with them and then spending a week in small-town American would be suffocating.

But it wasn't. It had been . . . like a weight had been lifted off him.

It had been a long five years. A hard five years. He wasn't as young as he'd once been, and he had a bullet wound in his shoulder that still gave him trouble.

But now he was free. Finally.

He and Temple hadn't decided what they'd do with the rest of their lives—the CIA had made it clear that they might require his services in the future and he hadn't been averse to that and neither had Temple. But for now, the world was their collective oyster.

Except first, there was someone he wanted to see.

Violet threw the ball to Hunt, laughing as their daughter leaped and caught it before he had a chance to grab it. All carefully orchestrated naturally, but the kid was ecstatic, teasing her father with the ball then squealing in delight as he tried to grab it off her.

A perfect family picture.

"I want that," he said. "One day, I want that."

Temple's fingers squeezed hard around his. "Then you should have it. You're not getting any younger after all."

"You didn't seem to think that last night," he commented lazily, giving her a sidelong glance. "In fact, if I recall, you were the one who wanted to go to sleep."

Her mouth curved, her golden eyes brilliant. "Hey, you try being coherent after four orgasms."

Out in the summer sun, Violet called something to Hunt. Then she turned to where Theo and Temple sat on the bench.

And Theo's heart went still.

Violet began to walk toward him. Then she began to run.

Temple let go of his hand. "I think someone wants to say hi, Theo."

He stood and his heart began to beat again, fast and hard.

And then Violet was there and he opened his arms and she flung herself into them.

"Hi, Peanut," he whispered in her ear. "Long time, no see."

Looking for more hot billionaires?

Don't miss the first novel in the brand-new
Tate Brothers series

THE DANGEROUS BILLIONAIRE

Coming soon from St. Martin's Paperbacks